THE
DEVIL
THREE TIMES

THE DEVIL THREE TIMES

RICKEY FAYNE

FLEET

FLEET

First published in the United States in 2025 by Little Brown
First published in Great Britain in 2025 by Fleet

1 3 5 7 9 10 8 6 4 2

Copyright © 2025 by Rickey Fayne

The moral right of the author has been asserted.

A CIP catalogue record for this book
is available from the British Library.

Hardback ISBN 978-0-349-12721-7
Trade paperback ISBN 978-0-349-12722-4

Book interior design by Marie Mundaca
Printed and bound in Great Britain by Clays Ltd, Elcograf S.p.A

Papers used by Fleet are from well-managed forests
and other responsible sources.

Fleet
An imprint of
Little, Brown Book Group
Carmelite House
50 Victoria Embankment
London EC4Y 0DZ

The authorised representative
in the EEA is
Hachette Ireland
8 Castlecourt Centre
Dublin 15, D15 XTP3, Ireland
(email: info@hbgi.ie)

An Hachette UK Company
www.hachette.co.uk

www.littlebrown.co.uk

After Zora.

In memory of Rickey Sr., Margaret, Walter, Norah, William, Larry, and Linda.

For Norma, Kenetha, Vickie, Miya, and Xander.

THE
DEVIL
THREE TIMES

Laurent Family Tree

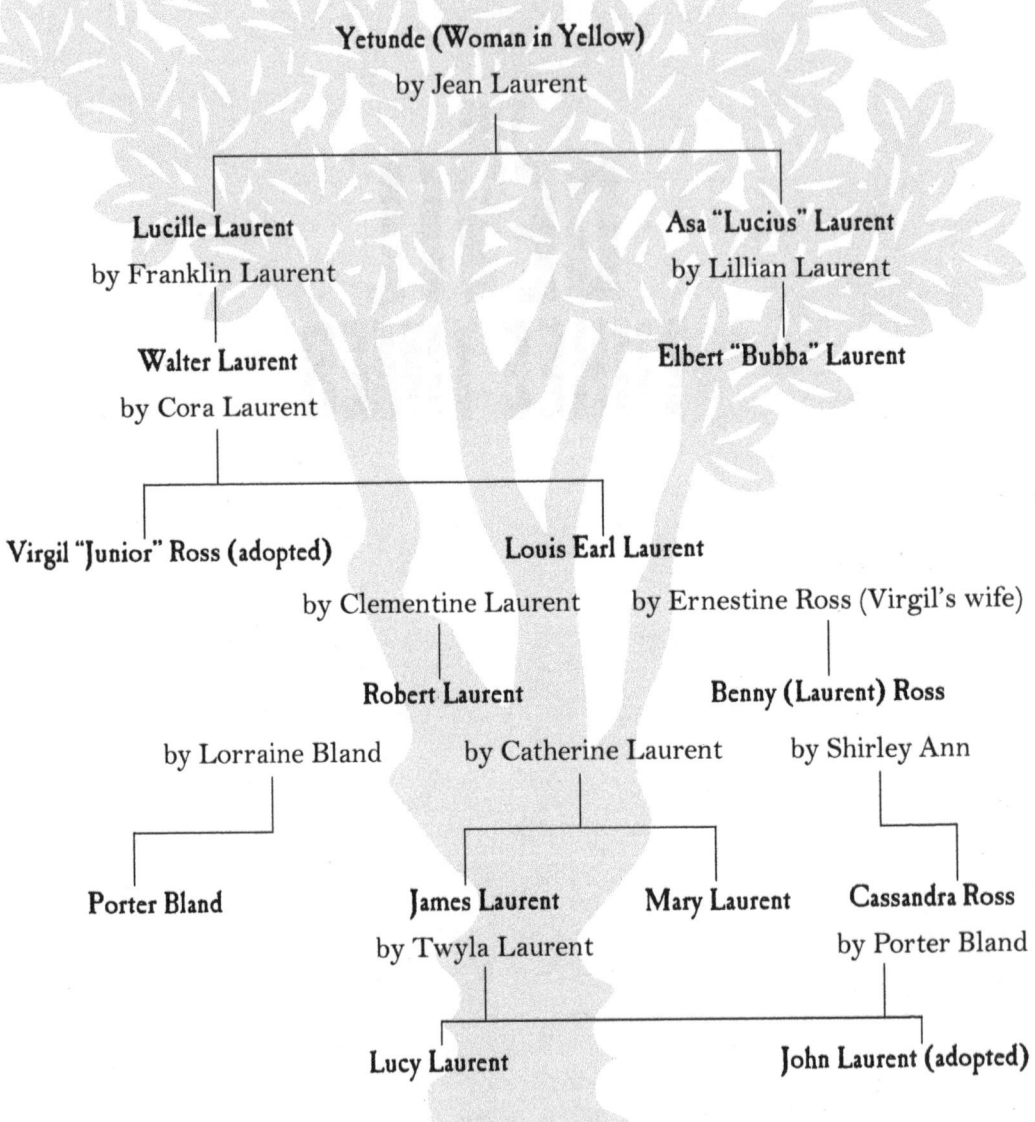

Yetunde (Woman in Yellow)
by Jean Laurent

Lucille Laurent
by Franklin Laurent

Asa "Lucius" Laurent
by Lillian Laurent

Walter Laurent
by Cora Laurent

Elbert "Bubba" Laurent

Virgil "Junior" Ross (adopted)

Louis Earl Laurent

by Clementine Laurent

by Ernestine Ross (Virgil's wife)

Robert Laurent

Benny (Laurent) Ross

by Lorraine Bland

by Catherine Laurent

by Shirley Ann

Porter Bland

James Laurent

Mary Laurent

Cassandra Ross

by Twyla Laurent

by Porter Bland

Lucy Laurent

John Laurent (adopted)

IN THE BEGINNING was the Word, but before the Word spoke there was the Devil, and he was hell-bent on sowing unrest and upheaval among the angels in heaven. You see, the Devil loved nothing so much as stirring shit up, inciting seraphim to fisticuffs—Jophiel and Michael all but threw hands when the Devil doused the former's flaming sword and blamed the latter—and, worst of all, confounding that tall, not terribly bright archangel Gabriel's mind with questions like: How does God expect us to reconcile free will with Providence Divine?

When God heard that, he said: Now, Devil, I done put up with your foolishness long enough. And before the Devil could plead his case, God stomped His right foot, parted the clouds, and, like a storm from paradise, the Devil rained down.

The Devil sat there on the cold, dark earth with his head hung low, powerful lonesome, and when God said: Let there be light, he hid in the shadows. From there, he tempted Eve with his serpent, loosed Cain on Abel, and taught Noah how to drink and get naked.

Now, Noah's folks liked the Devil, and the Devil liked Noah's folks. Anybody who can hold their liquor and keep their lies straight is never long in wanting friends. But he couldn't joke with Noah's folks like he could angels. They didn't banter, trade tall tales, kid, or have woof tickets for sale. I mean, it was sad. Those poor folks couldn't cut the monkey if it held the knife for them. Case in point: One day, the Devil greeted Ham by asking him how he got to be so high on the hog, live so large. But Noah's son couldn't pick up what the Devil put down. Just stood there as blank-faced and bewildered as the day he caught

3

an eyeful of his daddy's manhood. And so, though it pained his conscience, the Devil had no choice but to trick Nimrod, Ham's grandson, into getting him home.

You see, Nimrod claimed his might rivaled God's. Ruled according to a merciless code. Nimrod's people couldn't do nothing without Nimrod's say-so. All the Devil had to do to trick Nimrod was testify to all the ways God flouted his laws.

God's crimes were as numerous as they were inimical: being everywhere and nowhere all at once, working in ways mysterious, and bringing the world into being without Nimrod's input. Who gave God leave to make the Earth and the heavens? Nimrod certainly hadn't sanctioned it. What was more, the Devil said, pacing back and forth in front of the court, the Great Maker added insult to injury by failing to present Himself to Nimrod, stand trial, and account for His many offenses. How could Nimrod abide such impertinence? Unless — and here the Devil paused for dramatic effect — could it be, Nimrod was not as powerful as he'd led folks to believe? Was the only power Nimrod had over the people the power the people conceded?

All at once, the people turned to Nimrod, considering. How bad was this man, really? Already they were plotting, already they were scheming; Nimrod could feel it. His iron grip was slipping. Nimrod's only hope was to string his bow to back his boasts, fire arrows into heaven, and hit something, anything, celestial.

I'm no expert on the science of it, the Devil said as a high-arcing arrow clattered to the ground mere feet from him. But you might have a better shot at God if you aimed from higher up. What if you built a tower?

That just might be the best idea anyone has ever had, Nimrod said, seeing at once the project's potential to unite the populace and divert attention from his gross incompetence.

The Devil could hardly believe folks had let someone so self-interested lead them. No matter, once he climbed the Tower of Babel and spread his wings, he would be home, free of these terrible people.

Just as the Devil was in spitting distance of the pearly gates, though, God wrinkled His nose, confounded all the bricklayers, reached out from the clouds, and flicked the tower down.

The Devil kicked around for a while, propping up empires and watching them fall, making waves wherever he found calm. Before long, he heard tell of God sending down His *only* son, which hurt the Devil's feelings because, even though they butted heads now and then, the Devil always thought of himself as God's own. But he didn't harp on God counting him out and was ready to forgive his father's every trespass if he could just get back home.

And so the Devil set out to find Jesus, God's favorite son, and caught up to him in the wilderness, hunting up four-leaf clovers, worrying the manes off dandelions, and watching the wind blow clouds about. The Devil spent forty days and forty nights trying to reason with Jesus, brother to brother.

Jesus, the Devil said. I'm not evil, not really. How could I be? Ain't nothing in me God ain't put there. Ain't a thang in my heart God didn't smile upon. All I want is to get back home.

When Jesus heard the Devil's words, he wept, 'cause you know Jesus real softhearted, especially when it comes to fathers not doing right by their sons. Jesus himself didn't hear from his real daddy until he was damn near thirty-one.

Jesus said: Devil, you really have touched me. My wings ain't strong enough to fly us both up to heaven. But if you can hold out just a little bit longer, I'll bend God's ear and see if we can't work something out.

And so the Devil bided his time for a few more eons, making bargains here, turning a soul or two away from God there, but his heart wasn't never really in it. When he'd just about lost all faith in Jesus, Jesus came to the Devil in a dream.

I been working overtime on God, Jesus said, and He still ain't budged. I'll keep after it, but in the meantime, I need you to help me. You heard about what's happening in Africa?

5

The Devil said he hadn't.

Jesus said: They're robbing up Black folks from there and working them to death in America.

Huh, the Devil said. Ain't that something. But he was only half listening. No human suffering could rival his own. All the Devil took from Jesus's words was that Jesus had yet to find him a way home.

Jesus hauled off and backhanded the poor Devil. *Plap*.

Listen to me, Jesus said. It is something, and you the somebody who needs to fix it.

Ain't that God's problem? the Devil asked, trying to rub some feeling back into his cheek, wondering what on earth had turned his sweet baby brother so evil-mean.

You'd think, Jesus huffed, but He's up in heaven twiddling His thumbs. Says all humans are one race, acting like He can't see color from His gold throne.

The Devil was struck dumb. He ain't never once in his life imagined Jesus would fix his mouth to talk wet about God. And if you was struck too, then the joke's on you, 'cause if ain't but one thing in this world true it's that Jesus loves him some Black folks and Black folks love them some Jesus. It's like they're the hand and he's the thumb, and he gets powerful angry when he sees them done wrong.

Go south, Jesus told the Devil. Free my people and watch out for them until I return. You do this for me, and I promise that one day I'll find a way to get you home.

And when the Devil woke, that's just what he did—and is, even now, still trying to do. That's why Black people have to go through hell to get free and how come to this day, the Devil won't leave them be.

BOOK I
Paradise Lost

The Woman

YETUNDE
(Unmarked)

I ASKED THE woman next to me if she knew my name.

She told me she did but had grown tired of repeating it to me long ago. Perhaps your name does not want you anymore, she said. Perhaps it is time to find another.

This angered me. If a woman knows a thing, I told her, and another woman asks it of her in earnest, she must tell it. I tried to turn away from her, only there was no turning. In turning's stead I found agony: A pulsing pain beat the back of my head like a small drum. I tried to raise my hand to my head but found I could not. I was flat on my back, shackled to the floor.

Where am I?

Ach, the woman said, the most tiresome question of all. You are in the belly of a large boat. I will not tell you again.

Laughter pealed out of the darkness. Startled, I raised my head. Across from me, the outline of a man, also lying flat, barely visible, took shape. Chuckling, he reared his head. Had I been able to extend my legs, my feet would have kissed his feet. The boat lurched. I felt as if I were standing at the edge of a deep chasm, staring down into its fathomless depths. Above the laughing man, a break in the black of the hold allowed a sliver of light to cut across his face.

If I were you, the man said, I would start by asking *what* I am.

I told him that I was not a what but a who.

Perhaps, he said, laying his head back down so that the light shone red on his chest now, but what is a who?

No, I said, attempting to stretch limbs I could feel but not move, I'm not a who, I'm a *we*.

He laughed his laugh again. What kind of *we* does not know their name?

With a *we*, I said, wherever one thing stands, another stands beside it. And as I said this, I knew it to be a true thing. That a true thing had made use of my tongue to speak.

Now there is a start, the woman said, but she still would not tell me my name. So I asked her if she had known me before this, and she said yes. Yes, she had known me for quite some time. I peered into the darkness.

Sister? I asked.

Yes, my sister replied.

We were a *we*, weren't we?

Yes, she said.

And then you died.

Yes.

When my sister died, she came to live again in me.

I may not be alive, my sister said, but for as long as you stand, I will stand beside you.

I am not now standing, I told her.

Ach, she said. You know what I mean.

I sighed. Relief, my sister was here with me. But this relief was not to last, for as soon as it washed over me a door opened, and the light of day robbed me of my vision.

Before my eyes could adjust to the sun, we were unchained, marched topside, given water, and instructed to throw overboard the dead. There, afloat on a wide river, as my countrymen hefted the dead up over the side of the boat, I raised my hand to the pained part of my head where, on the right side, I felt a scar and, underneath the scar, a knot.

As the dead were lapped up by the waves, a man, one whose child numbered among the dead, flung himself overboard. During the ensuing tussle, an ofay watched me. Wherever I went, the green of his eyes followed. The sun was hot and high and bright. Nowhere was there shade.

I marveled at the wideness of the water. The river I had grown up drawing from was lined with umbrella trees, fringed with sweetgrass, emerald when looked upon from the hills rising above it, and clear when cupped in hand. The dead-swallowing river was a deep, borderless blue.

When I turned away from the water, the laughing man from the hold was at my side. Where does this river bank? I asked him.

He said this was no river, but rather a bigger water called the sea.

I wanted to ask the laughing man more, but he bowed his head and left my side when the staring ofay approached us.

I knew nothing of the ofay's kind, save what I had seen transpire when my countrymen ran afoul of his. For this reason, I cast my eyes downward at this one's advance. The ofay grasped my chin and lifted my head. Once my eyes were level with his, he reached into his coat pocket and produced a small red fruit.

Apple, he said, placing it in my hand.

I held it up to my face. It didn't smell like anything and so I gave it back to him.

He took a bite and chewed, his eager eyes fixing mine all the while. Once he had swallowed, he held the fruit out to me. I raised it to my mouth. It was tart but sweet. My sister, however, peering out from my eyes, did not like the taste and induced me to spit it out onto the ofay's crisp white shirt.

My sister and I had been born to different mothers. I was born, and then the next day, a stranger appeared at our father's doorstep, carrying her. Or was it me who was carried by the stranger and my sister's mother who took me in? Sometimes it is not clear to me out of whose memory I speak.

You speak from your own memory, my sister said. Do not attribute the muddle of your mind to me.

Okay then, which of us did the stranger bring?

Ach, she said. I do not concern myself with such trivial distinctions.

When my sister used me to spit on the staring ofay, the same one who would later call himself my master, a Dahomean man next to him, whom my countrymen belowdecks called the Traitor, raised his hand to strike me. I winced but felt nothing. The staring ofay had stayed the Traitor's hand, gripping his wrist firm in the air, and despite myself I admired the ofay's strength. After this, everyone else was shackled and forced back belowdecks, but I was allowed to stay above and, with the staring ofay standing beside me, watch the sun sink into the depths of the sea and the crescent of the moon, flanked by stars, rise high above the night's horizon.

From then on, I was with the ofay always. Unshackled, I slept on the floor of his quarters, ate food from his table, and sat between his legs with my back against his cot, the light of the setting sun upon my face as he rebandaged my head wound each evening. I wish I could tell you I hated the clumsy ministrations of the ofay's callused hands, say I shrank away from his saccharine breath and lavender shaving soap, refused his preserved fruits, salted meats, and crusty bread, and stalwartly rebuffed his every kindness, but it is not in my nature to bear false witness. As a consequence of the ofay's familiarity, my countrymen wanted nothing to do with me and ignored me as they did the Traitor. Save the laughing man, who never failed to seek my gaze whenever he was brought above deck.

In the time it took for one moon to wane and another to wax, my head wound healed and we docked in the port of a city of hard gray ground, tall buildings, many ofays, and countrymen dressed in the ofay fashion, speaking the ofay language. The others were marched to a large house in the middle of the city to be auctioned off. Pitying them their fate, for I had not yet realized the staring ofay had purchased me, I sought the laughing man to whom I had been shackled as my countrymen were marched by, but his face did not number among them. Often, I have wondered what fate befell him; if one day, while I was alone with the ofay, he was thrown overboard, or if he had slipped his chains and flown away.

The staring ofay and I stayed together in a room with a window overlooking the town square. It had a bed, a bureau, a dining table, chairs, and a water closet with two basins: one for eliminating waste and the other for filling with water with which one could wash. Using the latter, I bathed myself in private for the first time since I had left home. When I finished and came out, the staring ofay held out a yellow dress and gestured for me to put it on over my head. On the table was a tray with leavened bread; cheese, which I later came to understand was curdled milk from a cow; and an array of what were then, to me, strange fruits.

Sit, the ofay said.

Sit? I said, running my hand over the bed.

The man shook his head and gestured to the chair beside him. I complied.

Bed, he said, pointing to the bed.

Bed, I repeated.

Chair, he said, reaching across the table and grabbing the chairback. Yes?

Yes, I said.

He smiled, released the chair, and took up my hand.

Apple, he said, holding the red-and-white orb with a leaf and stem out to me. It was nearly identical to the one on the ship.

Apple, I repeated.

He picked up the orange ball and said, Orange.

Orange, I repeated.

He picked up one of the small purple ovals and said, Grape.

Grape, I repeated, and when I finished speaking, he held it up to my mouth. When I ate it from his fingers, he smiled.

The only foods familiar to me, aside from the apples, were the bananas and the bread, a version of which had been served to us on the ship, and so these were the only foods I dared eat. The ofay's eyes were on me while I chewed.

Back home, my sister said, staring could get a man killed.

What home? I asked.

Then the ofay posed the question he was to repeat countless times over the course of my internment to him: To whom do you speak? This question was among the first sentences I learned of the ofay's language.

This one is strange, my sister said. She stood us up, walked us over to the bed, and sat us down. Yes, of all the strange ofays, she said, this is the strangest one I have seen.

And just how many ofays have you seen?

Enough to know I do not like this one. Better off for you to have been sold like the others. Better yet for you to have drowned and joined me.

You are just jealous.

When my sister married the second son of the chief, she sulked and cried until one day, finally, her husband returned to our father and said: All right, I will marry the scrawny one, too. Our father had warned him prior to the wedding that we would not be easily cleaved.

No, my sister said, you have it the wrong way around again. You were the one who cried and sulked when I was gone and begged Father to marry you to my husband. There was nothing you would let me have for myself.

You cried, too.

Not nearly as much as you. Besides, what in your situation is there to envy? Him? she said, gesturing to the ofay. If I were alive, I would never suffer his touch.

The ofay, who had been watching me closely, pulled his chair up beside the bed and took hold of my hand.

To whom do you speak? he asked again.

My sister recoiled from me and lay down upon the bed with her hand over her forehead in exasperation. I tried to pull my hand away, but the ofay held fast to it, just as he held my gaze. Perhaps, I remember thinking, this is some sort of courtship ritual common to his people. In Whydah, the coastal city of the Dahomean king, we saw from the windows of the barracoon a number of our countrywomen in ofay dress. Through whispers, we learned that these were the wives of the ofays who had settled the coast to trade with the king.

Perhaps he intends to make me his wife, I said to my sister, remembering the women married to ofays back in Dahomey.

Then my sister rose from the bed, entered into me, and used my mouth to spit on the ofay. It landed on his cheek and dribbled down his shirt.

He raised his hand, and I closed my eyes, waiting for the blow. But to my great surprise, he laughed and did not strike me. He was only raising his hand to wipe the spit away.

My sister stood up out of me and leaned close to his face. This man, she said, peering into the green of his eyes. This man is not sane.

Whole days we passed alone in the room this way: the ofay staring at me, feeding me, finding reasons to place his hands upon me, patiently tolerating my sister's violent rebuff of his advances. The only times his eyes and hands were not upon me were when they were on his texts. The ofay had a traveler's trunk filled with a number of bound volumes he consulted throughout the day, flipping first here, then there, comparing the text in one book to a diagram in another.

One day he showed me an illustration of a woman lying in the middle of a circle. Around her were various symbols scrawled in chalk.

After pushing the bed and bureau to the far corner of the room, he knelt and, with great care, copied the symbols onto the floor. Then he had me lie down and cross my arms while he drew the shades and lit a number of candles. He stood over me and read aloud from the volume, but to what end? I did not know. After repeating this exercise twice more, he grew frustrated, threw the book across the room, and, slamming the door behind him, left me alone for the first time since I had been captured.

Run, my sister exhorted.

Run where?

Anywhere. Go. Now.

I knew nothing of the place to which I had been removed aside from how much water stood between it and what was left of home. For a long while I sat staring out the window, imagining what route I might take were I to leave. Along the thoroughfare walked a number of my countrymen. Some of them were free, but most were in chains. Aside from his straying hand, the ofay had yet to perpetrate any of the cruelties I had seen others of his kind visit upon mine. I had not been made to work. I had not been subjected to any sort of overt sexual advance, and since I had left the ship had not been beaten or shackled. Instead, I had been clothed, fed, stared at, and made to lie on the floor. I could not yet picture how my situation might be improved, but I saw clearly all the ways in which it might worsen.

Later, the ofay brought back with him the Traitor from the ship. Seeing me there, sitting on the bed, wearing my new yellow dress, the Traitor balked and made a snide comment, the meaning of which I did not have to know the language to understand.

The ofay was stern with him once again. I relished the sight of the pale man dealing roughly with one of the swine who had stolen into my village under the cover of night to kill and capture and enslave.

Then you remember, my sister said.

Yes, I told her. I remember.

The day they came for us, my sister and I had arisen early to fetch water from the river. By the time we returned, the huts nearest the western gate blazed bright and smoke rose in stacks high over the village, blotting out the early sky. It was not until we reached the planting fields that we saw the Dahomean warriors, and now, each night, after the sun sets, I see them again.

I lay my head down to sleep, and on the ceiling above me, a one-eyed Dahomean man smirks, raises his bow, and shoots an arrow through the neck of a fleeing elder whose head, arms, and legs are on fire. I turn my head, and, cast on the wall beside the bed, a tall cowrie-crowned warrior woman in red catches a man by his dreadlocks and slashes his throat. Once his body falls, she stands over him and hacks into his neck with her sword until, seeming to tire of this, she throws the knife aside, turns the man over, kneels on his chest, and, with both hands, grips and twists his head free of his body. Every time I close my eyelids, the thatched roofs of my kinsmen's homes burn bright behind them.

My sister drops her basket and races toward what is left of our home. The water splashes my legs as my feet follow hers. We reach our hut and are met by another sword-wielding, cowrie-crowned woman. This one holds by the hair our husband's head. My sister screams, lowers her head, and drives it into the warrior's belly, taking her to the ground before she can raise her weapon against us, and beating her with balled fists. I run past them into the burning hut, smoke and blaze all I see.

Hands in front of me, feeling my way to the pallet on the floor where we left them, I find our babies, my sister's and mine, hidden, not crying, not cooing. My hands wrap them in a blanket, and before I can stand, before I can think, my legs are running. Outside, my sister beats the body of the cowrie-crowned warrior, even though it is stilled, even though her fists are raw and bloodied. My sister, my beautiful sister, she does not stop until my lips form the shape of her name. There are more warriors, but, strangely, they do not give chase, and we do not rest until we reach the river.

My people were river people, and after my sister and I came of age, our mother brought us to its banks and told us how we were born of the water and how, upon our deaths, it was to the water we would return. Wherever one thing stands, another stands beside it. But that morning, when we brought our daughters to the river, there was not time enough to explain how they were a whole they, that they would stand together in the next life, even though they had yet to stand in this one. It was while I stared into the flow of the water and all it did not yet conceal that I was struck on the back of the head. The world went blurry, then black. By the time I regained consciousness, my sister, having felled one warrior before catching the sword of another, was on the ground, bleeding. She could hardly draw breath, let alone stand. If I wanted her to live, they said, I would have to carry her, so I carried her. I carry her still.

The Traitor, admonished, sat down in the chair across from me and began to ask questions in one of the dialects of my native tongue. The ofay, he said, wants to know who you talk to. Who the other person you address is.

My sister, I told him.

And she is deceased?

Yes.

He translated. The ofay smiled.

This man, the Traitor said, he wants for you to speak to the dead on his behalf.

My sister is the only one who talks to me.

Then lie, the Traitor said. Your life with him will be easier if you tell him what he wishes to hear.

The Traitor turned away from me to converse with the ofay, seeking to extract some form of payment, as the ofay later informed me. He'd lost favor with his king and had bartered with the ship's captain for safe passage in hopes of making a life in New Orleans, where he'd heard Africans could live free. But the free Africans were particular and would not accept him into their society. When the Traitor made ready to leave, I asked him what I was to call the ofay, if this was where we were to live, and whether I was to be his first, second, or third wife.

You may call him Laurent. You will remain here for a time but are to later be removed to his estate north of here in a place called Tennessee. As for the wife order, the ofays, at least the ofays here in this land, they do not make wives of our countrywomen as they do in Whydah.

Then what is to be my relation to him?

At this, the Traitor shook his head and laughed.

That night, I dreamed of my sister. We were by a river. She was teaching me how to weave a basket tight enough to hold water. I listened carefully and wove it just the way she instructed me, only when I dipped my basket into the flow of the river, it would not hold the water. Determined to make a basket without the aid of my sister, I went downstream, where she would not follow. There, I found the laughing man from the ship. He was standing at the base of an umbrella tree, fishing. I approached him. At his feet lay a basket identical in every way to the one I held.

He smiled and asked me if I wanted to see his catch.

I did.

He lifted the lid of his basket. Within, there was a green, wild-eyed serpent, coiled around two sleeping children, one black, one white. I tried to wrest the children away, but before I could, the serpent struck me.

The Runaway

FRANKLIN LAURENT
(1826–1890)
Father of Walter Laurent
Husband of Lucille Laurent

BY THE TIME the Devil made it over the ocean, down the Mississippi, and into the backwoods of West Tennessee, Franklin had run and been caught by Robert Reeves twice. The first time Franklin ran, Robert trailed him to where the creek marries the river and dragged him back by what was left of his right ear. "I'd have let you go," Robert told the boy, "if you hadn't have been fool enough to run south." The second time Franklin ran, he feigned sleep until he heard Robert snoring, sneaked out of the cabin they shared, and saddled up Reaper, the fastest mare in the Laurent stable. But before Franklin could clear the line of poplars Jean Laurent planted to secret his land from covetous neighbors—neighbors who still couldn't fathom why Captain Jack Talbert, the man whom their fathers had followed first into battle against the Indians and then, later, in a caravan of covered wagons, to the eastern banks of the Mississippi, had all but gifted his plantation to a queer Creole sailor whom nobody had even so much as laid eyes on when the county was rife with Protestant planters of marriageable age while others, those who'd heard the rumor about him and his daughter, wondered how he'd ever found anyone willing to marry her at all—Robert whistled. Reaper reared, turned tail, and unsaddled Franklin. "I don't much mind what you get up to," Robert said as he helped the boy to his feet, "but leave my horses be." Later, Franklin heard from Ms. May, the only other person who'd been on the place as long as Robert Reeves, that back in Kentucky, back before Robert was sold downriver, Luke, the only child Robert and his late wife had been allowed to keep, was shot by a patroller as he crossed the frozen Ohio on their master's stallion. Twenty years later, after he'd abandoned his own wife and son for the Oklahoma territories, Franklin rose out of sleep half hearing Robert call out to him the same way the old man had called for Luke in his dreams.

Franklin wasn't born a slave, and if it wasn't for Ashford, the man who killed Opa, the only mother the boy had ever known, he might have spent his whole life free. Opa found Franklin in a burlap sack by the river when he was a baby. Back before Captain Talbert forced what was left of her people west, Opa slit her husband's throat with the same knife she used to teach Franklin to field dress deer. Besides her late husband, Ashford was the only white man Opa had ever allowed to get within shooting distance of her, and so it was this, not the murder of her husband, whom she'd found lying with her younger sister, that Opa closed her eyes to life regretting as Franklin met the butt of Ashford's rifle.

Jean Laurent, having a penchant for unbroken slaves, purchased the dark brown knock-kneed boy no one at the Memphis market would buy at a discount. After breaking the boy off a piece of his sandwich— he was half-starved—Jean had Maurice, the saddle-colored manservant he'd inherited from his father-in-law and whom his father-in-law had clearly sired, take him to Robert Reeves to look after. That night, Franklin promised himself he'd kill Ashford, Jean, Maurice, and anybody else on the place who stood between him and his freedom, and in the morning, before he could wake up good, he was handed a hoe and put to work chopping cotton.

Young Franklin had never seen a cotton plant before and, as he was shown how to use the hoe to scratch the earth beneath it, couldn't fathom why anyone would want so much of it. Slowly, and with more effort than Ms. May, who watched the boy from the next row over, felt was necessary, Franklin hefted the hoe parallel to his hip and brought it down just short of the ground, scraping over the stalks of the dandelion and pigweed—both of which had made better use of the late summer showers than the okra she'd planted the week prior—and missing their roots entirely. By the time the sun was high, he'd messed over two whole rows. Ms. May, knowing the cleanup would fall to her, made Franklin return the hoe to the barn, gather up what all everyone else had chopped, and use the wheelbarrow down by the woodshed to drive it over to the refuse heap. He'd made three trips before it was time to break for water and corn cake, and would make five more before hearing Rufus's dinner bell ring.

Laying the wheelbarrow on its side, Franklin turned to watch Rufus, who, owing to the ghost his mother saw in the last days of her pregnancy, wasn't fit for hard labor, raise and lower the cowbell like he was whitewashing an invisible fence that ran from the outdoor kitchen up near the big house, down past the fields, and on over to the low-slung row of slave cabins. There, in the lane between the cabins, Franklin got in line to receive a bowl of salt pork and corn mush. After being refused seconds, he returned to his cabin, lay down on his pallet, and passed out.

"Don't you know no better than to wash up before you lay your head down to sleep," Robert said, shaking the boy awake.

"I'm tired," Franklin said, turning over.

"Little boy," Robert said. "You ain't yet begun to know what tired means."

As Franklin got off the pallet, thinking, knowing, just which way he was going to slit Robert's throat, Robert cut the boy an inch of tallow soap off a block he kept under his cot. Later, once they got along better, Franklin would be the one out in the smokehouse helping

Robert make that soap, stoking the fire, washing and rendering the fat, straining out the gristle, waiting for it to cool, and stirring in the lye before letting it harden.

"Here," Robert told Franklin. "This should be enough to get you clean."

There was a path down to the creek, but Franklin cut through the woods and, because he liked the feel of fresh ground underfoot, strode far afield of the twin sycamores linking arms over the creek where everyone else drew water, walked until he could no longer hear the carousing children whom he longed to join, and kept walking until he heard only the rushing of water. It was owing to this that he happened upon the woman. She was standing on the bank, attempting to lift a carrying pole with a water bucket attached at each end. The only woman Franklin had ever known was Opa, and Opa, who had undergone the change of life long before she freed him from that burlap sack, had never been pregnant. And so, when the woman turned to face him head-on, he stared in slack-jawed wonder at the way her belly pulled her dress taunt.

"You going to help me or just stand there, staring?" she asked.

Franklin sidestepped down the hill, crossed the creek, and took up one of the buckets. The woman leaned down and took up the other. They left the carrying pole where it lay.

"Back up toward the row?" Franklin asked, wondering why she'd drawn water from the far side of the creek.

"No," the woman said. "Down a little ways."

They walked deeper into the woods, following a meandering deer path until there was nobody but him, the woman, and the evening birds flitting in and out of the trees. When they reached the woman's cabin, they set the buckets down on a newly hewn wood table beside a wicker basket of apples.

"Whose little boy are you?" the woman asked, sitting down to the table.

"Nobody's," Franklin said, eyeing an apple. Out in the clearing near where he and Opa lived, there had been an apple tree. Each fall, Franklin would gather up armfuls of the fruit and carry it in for Opa to slice, slather in pine syrup, and bake in the woodstove.

"You got to be somebody's."

"Well, I ain't."

The woman sat up in her chair and grasped the boy's chin to better see him.

"You favor my people," she said, lifting his chin. "You could be my boy."

"Your people ain't from here?"

"No," she said, seeing in her mind's eye the village by the river that had once been but now was not, "and neither are yours."

"I don't have no people. All I got is me."

As the woman eyed Franklin, seeing in the cast of the boy's shadow the generations that had passed before him and sensing, vaguely, those that would follow, which were to be hers also, Franklin noticed the platformed feathered mattress with the soft red wool rug poking out from under it and wondered why her cabin was so far from the others and would have asked had not his gaze alighted again upon the basket of apples.

"You like these," the woman said, picking up an apple.

"I do when they're sweet."

"You can have as many as you want," the woman said, holding out the apple. "I can't stand the taste of them anymore."

Whenever Robert Reeves sent Franklin to wash, Franklin visited the woman who, for as long as he was allowed to see her, was never without some kind of treat she'd lost the taste for. As Franklin ate, the woman told him of her home and her people. How her mother made a stew of cassava and fish every Sunday. The way her father laughed in his sleep. How the dead spoke to the living in waking dreams. Once, while she was walking in the grove abutting the river, she saw a beautiful man sitting cross-legged at the base of an umbrella tree. He called to her by name, but she did not answer. The man sat, half in shadow, facing away from the water, which meant he was not a man but a spirit. If she answered his call, the spirit would follow her all her days and enter her dreams at night. The woman's people were river people, and it was known among them that water bridged the worlds of the living and the dead.

"What did you do?" Franklin asked.

"I drew water and pretended I did not hear him."

"And that worked?"

"No," the woman said. "It did not."

Robert Reeves, wanting to know where Franklin disappeared to each evening, followed the boy to the woman's cabin one day and, later that night, told him about the time he'd seen the woman gather dirt from graves and how, at night, she flew all about the place dropping in on folks' dreams. All this had led Robert to believe that the woman was the Devil's wife.

"The Devil's wife?" Franklin asked, scratching his head.

"Yeah," Robert said. "Ain't you know the Devil's got a wife?"

"So what if she is?" Franklin asked Robert. "What's so bad about that?"

Up until the moment Robert warned him of the woman, Franklin had never heard the Devil's name. Opa, though her father had owned Christian slaves, wasn't what was then called a "praying Indian" and didn't hold truck with white folks' God. Franklin knew there was more to the world than what he could put his hands to, but he understood also that it—whatever it was—was beyond reckoning. And so he lived and acted according to his intuition, knowing what was in him must also be of it. Religion then, its Commandments, its restrictions on who he could and could not love and where and why and how, was nothing more to Franklin than slavery of another order. He couldn't fathom why any slave, having already one master, romanticized an afterlife in which they served another. And so once Franklin learned of the outcast who wanted nothing so much as to confound God's order, he decided, even before meeting the Devil at the crossroads the third time he ran, to cast his lot with the fallen.

"I'll tell you what's so bad about it," Robert said. "Back in the before time, there was a rich man, and one day a crow came to his window and told him the date Death would come for him. So he called his two sons to his bedside and divided up between them what all on this side of life he had to give. To Jack, his son by way of a good wife and a long marriage, he give all his money, and to John, his son by way of love, he give all his power.

"Now, Jack went down the road to a gambling house and doubled the money his father give him shooting dice with the sawmill men. That night he went to sleep with a belly full of meat. The next evening, he took his money, went a little bit farther down the road to where the riverboat men gambled, and doubled it again. After that, wouldn't nobody he knew play him. Said he was too lucky. He turned to go back home, but then this fellow standing outside, puffing away on a fat cigar, told him that if he wanted a real high-stakes game, all he had to do was keep walking down that same road, so he did. Jack walked and walked, and all while he walked, the path narrowed and widened, went straight and turned crooked, but he didn't see no gambling houses.

"When he was 'bout ready to turn around and go home, he spotted a man leaned up against a tree where two roads crossed. The man wore a wide-brimmed hat and was dressed down in black. Jack called out to him, thinking maybe he could ask him how much farther down the road the next gambling house was.

"'You a gambling man, are you?' the man in black asked Jack.

"'Yeah,' Jack said, rubbing the spot in his pocket where he kept his blade, 'I reckon I am.'

"The man reached into his back pocket and pulled out a fat wad a cash.

"'I'll play you.'

"Then the man reached into his side pocket and pulled out a pair of dice.

"'Just so you know,' Jack said, taking the dice in hand. 'I'm on a lucky streak.'

"'Oh yeah?' The man laughed. 'Let's see just how far that luck'll get you.'

"Jack put down half his money. They rolled, and the man in black bested him.

"'Again,' Jack said, and this time he put down the other half of his money. They rolled, and the man in black's number came up again.

"'You must be the Devil,' Jack said. "Cause cain't no natural-born man run up them kind of numbers on me.'

"'Yeah,' the man said, grinning. 'I been known by that name.'

"Jack hung his head low; he just couldn't believe he'd been fool enough to part with his father's money so fast.

"'Tell you what,' the Devil said. 'We'll shoot one last time. If you win, you get all your money, plus mine. If I win, I get your life.'

"Jack wiped the sweat from his forehead, scooped those dice up and blew them, and shook them, and turned his head to the sky like he was calling on the Lord to save him. Then he took a deep breath and shot them dice sideways. They hit the road spinning and turning and turning and spinning like they wasn't never gone stop. The Devil, seeing this, stomped his foot down once, and I'll be damned if them dice didn't fall flat on his numbers.

"Jack stood up and said: 'Well, Devil, which way you want it?'

"'That's it?' the Devil said. 'You giving up already?'

"Jack turned out his pockets.

"'I got nothing left to bet,' he said.

"The Devil grinned and said: 'Jack, I'm feeling right generous this evening, so I'll make you a deal. I'll let you have your life, but only if you bring me your brother's power.'

"Now all the while Jack was shooting dice, his brother John was building him a house high up on a hill to hide his power, because he knew to his soul Jack would come asking after it. And sure enough, before he could finish laying the foundation, here Jack come, hectoring him over it.

"'I need it,' Jack said to John's turned back. 'I need that power something awful.'

"'Well, you can't have it,' John said, raking cement. 'I done already put it in the ground up under what's about to be my house.'

"Jack eyed the cement, already thinking of how he might be able to dig it out.

"'The Devil told me he'd spare my life if I could just get him that power.'

"'Is that all?' John said, turning to face his wayward half brother. 'You can fix that easy.'

"'How?' Jack asked.

"'All you have to do is go to the Devil's house back in Africa and make a deal with his wife. Everybody knows that,' John said, taking up his rake again.

"'How the hell am I supposed to get back to Africa?'

"'The same way the crow does. Fly.'

"Now, Jack huffed when John said this, because flying was the thing he hated most. But he decided he loved his life more than he hated flying, and so he walked a piece-a-ways from his brother, studied the sky long enough for his shoulder blades to ache, and dove up into it, the same way anybody else would a river or a lake.

"Jack crossed the ocean on his own wings, and when he got to Africa, he saw a house that was half-black and half-red, and knew from that that it belonged to the Devil. He landed, tucked his wings in, and started to walking. When he got to the house, he spied a pretty young woman watering a garden. She had beautiful black skin, bright white teeth, red shoes, and a yellow dress cut to tease the mind with what the eye couldn't see. That must be the Devil's daughter, Jack thought, because he couldn't fathom someone so young and beautiful being married to the ugly man he met at the crossroads. What Jack didn't know was this: Her yellow dress was keeping her young. She'd won it from the Devil a thousand years before and was the only person, dead or alive, who could best him at a game of chance. He walked over to the woman, introduced himself, and asked where he might find her mother.

"'She's around here somewhere,' the woman said. 'Why you asking after her?'

"'I lost my life to the Devil, and now I come to ask his wife to give it back.'

"'Well,' the woman said, considering Jack. 'She might be willing to help you, but then again, she might not. But you know,' and here the woman paused and tilted her head to the side like a thought was just coming to her, 'she'd be much more likely to help if the man asking made her daughter his wife.'

"'I guess that makes sense,' Jack said, figuring it would be better to marry than to burn. 'I'll hunt up a reverend.'

"Jack turned to go, but before he could take a step, the woman, who was awfully strong, grabbed his arm.

"'This the Devil's house. We don't need no reverend to know one another as man and wife.'

"Before they got started good, the Devil came home and put a stop to it. He wasn't sore or nothing. Even the Devil knows not to let marriage get in the way of good lovemaking.

"'Well,' the Devil said, 'if that's what y'all want, I won't fight you. Jack,' he said, turning to Jack. 'You'll be needing your money if you aim to keep this woman. And woman,' he said, turning to the woman. 'Do you and I still have an understanding?'

"'We do,' the woman said.

"'All right,' the Devil said. 'Now off with the two of you before I change my mind.'

"And so Jack and the woman went outside.

"'Where do you live?' the woman asked Jack.

"'Over in America, on the other side of the wide water.'

"'Buckra still running things over there?'

"'Yeah, but don't worry. I can handle him.'

"'All right.'

29

"'What's your name, anyway?' Jack asked.

"'My name is too long for any man born of a woman to pronounce.'

"'Then what am I supposed to call you, woman?'

"'Woman is fine.'

"'All right, then, woman,' Jack said. 'Hop on my back and I'll fly us both across the water.' She did, and before she knew it, Jack was aloft.

"After they'd gone, the Devil started to work on a hex, but no matter how hard he worked it, it wouldn't come off. The woman had stolen his power. That's the reason the Devil kicks up so much trouble over here. He's searching for his wife, hunting her up to get back his power."

"What kind of power did she take from him?" Franklin asked Robert. "What can she do that the Devil can't?"

"I don't know," Robert said. "And I pray to God you never find out. What I do know, though, is that if you don't let her alone, you'll come to regret it."

Franklin didn't know if he believed Robert about the woman being the Devil's wife, but he could see for himself that she wasn't like anybody else on the plantation. Once, when he'd slipped away from the fields in search of food, he'd found the door to the woman's cabin barred. Hearing her voice, he peeped through the window and saw Ms. May laid out on the woman's pallet while the woman stood over her, making loops in the air with a smoking bundle of herbs. The woman turned her head and spoke as if there were a person on each side of her. Franklin searched the cabin but only saw Ms. May, who, as the roundness of the woman's belly loomed over her like a dark cloud, appeared to be asleep. He called out to her, but the woman would not answer and acted as if she didn't see him standing there with his face pressed against the window. It was then that the thing happened. The thing that, if Franklin had heard secondhand instead of seen, he wouldn't have believed. A cloud parted overhead, and a sudden ray of afternoon light shone through, and the cabin's interior was covered, floor to rafter, in the iridescent tendrils of a spider's web. Later, when Franklin asked about Ms. May, the smoke, and the thin bright bands of color, the woman smiled and offered Franklin another apple.

Another time, after he'd awoken from a dream in which Opa had stuffed him in a sack and tried to drown him, he rose, sweat-drenched, and went walking in the woods, hoping to calm his spirit. A candle had been lit in the woman's window. He approached, peeked in, and was surprised to find Jean Laurent, his so-called master, seated at the woman's table with his head in his hands, sobbing, while the woman sat back in her chair with her hands clasped over her belly and stared past him. Franklin stood there at the window watching, and all while he watched, the woman's lips never stopped moving. The woman was hurting the slave owner, but Franklin couldn't for the life of him figure out how.

Every now and then, Jean Laurent's wife, Lillian, got it into her head that the slaves she'd inherited from her father, Captain Talbert, who was also a deacon, needed churching, and so when Jean Laurent went to New Orleans a few weeks after Franklin arrived on the plantation, Lillian sent for Reverend Cranston to go down to the cabins to preach at them. Cranston, the grandson of Scottish indentured servants, believed God put white men over Negroes and Indians to civilize them and teach them obedience, so that they might learn the truth, the light, and the way. "For Jesus said that no one," Cranston preached from the soapbox he kept in the seat of his wagon for just such occasions, "no one, comes to the Father except through me."

It was these sermons that first got Franklin on the side of the Devil. Anybody who aggravated Cranston so good couldn't be half as bad as folks made out. And so, unlike Walter, the son he would have by way of the woman's daughter, Lucille, Franklin did not rebuke the Devil when, the third time he ran, after following the North Star until it was absorbed into the light of dawn, the Devil, who was leaning against a tree by the side of the road, tipped his hat to him. "What you doing out here all by your lonesome?" the Devil had asked the boy. "Ain't you got nobody to ask after you? A mother to love you? A father to feed you?" But what Franklin couldn't shake of slave religion, even after he'd made his way to Oklahoma, was the way shouting moved him.

It happened the first Sunday Franklin heard Cranston preach. After the sermon, Ms. May, worried for the boy's soul, pulled Franklin aside and told him that listening to Cranston mess over Scripture wasn't church, not really. And so later that evening, she took him to the clearing on the other side of the creek and showed him what happens when God works in you.

It was dark out, but there was enough light from the stars for Franklin to make out people dancing and shouting. "That," Ms. May said, pointing to Elijah, who, to Franklin, seemed to have lost all control of his body, "is what it means to go to church." As Franklin watched Elijah dance, he caught a funny sort of fluttering in his stomach he didn't rightly know what to do with. It wasn't until years later, after he'd lived among and began to worship with Opa's people, that Franklin would come to understand how the shouting had called the man he would become forth from the boy he was. He heard his freedom in the music. Glimpsed a flash of his coming happiness in the way Elijah, who would later become Franklin's lover, articulated his limbs. Stole away a bit of the by-and-by to tide him over in the here and now.

It was as Franklin tried and failed to hunt up that churched feeling later that week that he learned why the woman's belly stuck out so far. The question of why the woman's belly was so full while the rest of her was so skinny didn't keep Franklin up at night, but it did cross his mind from time to time. Eventually, he satisfied his curiosity with the revelation that the woman must have stuffed herself with sweets she hadn't lost the taste for whenever he wasn't around, which was why, in the few weeks since he'd arrived at the plantation, her belly had grown bigger. She must be holding the good stuff back for herself, Franklin thought one day as he watched her waddle a blackberry pie from the cookstove to the table. Even Opa had kept the best cuts of venison for herself because who in their right mind would ever think to share the best of what they had with a thrown-away child? And so that day, as Franklin walked among the poplars hoping to recover a piece of what he'd felt Sunday night to help him cope with the backbreaking, foot-splitting, knee-aching day in, day out of cotton-picking season, he did not expect to hear the woman cry out. Recognizing the voice and forgetting the pain in his feet, Franklin crossed the creek running.

When he reached the woman's cabin, he threw the door open and found the woman laid out on the floor, belly up. She held her stomach and writhed on the wet floor, just like Opa did after she'd been shot. Franklin had to get help. He turned and ran back toward the creek before the woman could tell him what it was she needed.

"The woman," Franklin stammered out when he found Robert Reeves at the stable, "the Devil's wife. She's dying."

"Dying?" Robert said, turning away from the bay colt he was grooming.

"She's laid out on the floor holding her stomach. I think I might have seen blood. I think she might have been shot."

"She ain't been shot," Robert said, leading the colt back into the stall with its mother. "Go find Ms. May and tell her it's time. Then run over to the big house and tell whoever answers the door the same."

Franklin turned and glanced back toward the direction of the creek.

"You can't do nothing for her," Robert said. "What she need from you is to do what I say."

After finding Ms. May, Franklin darted up the path through the fields, ran around the kitchen, and came to the back of the Laurent house to knock. No one answered, so he scrambled around to the front and bounded up the steps. There was a bell, but he was too short to reach the string, so he knocked on the whitewashed door and kept knocking until Maurice answered. Maurice, who held a particular disdain for all the slaves on what he still thought of as his father's plantation, especially the blue-black ones, reared back and smacked the boy. By then, Franklin was so out of breath that he could barely stand up straight, let alone get his words out, but he didn't wince or back away. He stayed standing until he found his air.

"The woman down by the creek," Franklin said as he held Maurice's eyes. "It's her time."

Maurice went red-faced and backed away into the house, leaving the door open wide enough for Franklin to see inside. The entryway floor was polished dark wood, like the stairs Maurice had disappeared up, but had a red rug with gold trim that reminded him of the one in the woman's cabin. Franklin would not see inside the house again for twenty years, when, covering his mouth with the crook of his elbow, he'd kick down the smoldering door in order to save Asa, one of the twins to which the woman was now giving birth, from burning alive. Franklin would have stepped inside and had a look around, but before he could, Jean Laurent shot through the door with Maurice in tow.

By the time the three of them made it to the woman's cabin, Ms. May had already helped the woman into the bed and was crouched beside her.

"It won't be long now," Ms. May told the woman.

Jean Laurent walked over to the bed. Ms. May stepped aside to allow Laurent room enough to bend down and press his forehead to the woman's. The woman cried out and Franklin tried to go to her, to comfort her the way he hadn't be able to comfort Opa, but Maurice caught him by the elbow, flung him out, and closed the door behind him.

Near the creek, Franklin saw through the trees a shock of red hair, doe eyes, and the squinched fox face that could only belong to Lillian, Laurent's lawful wife. To avoid meeting her, Franklin doubled back and hid behind a live oak tree. From there, he watched as Lillian peered into the window of the woman's cabin, her face reddening, her fists shaking. She let out an animal cry pitched somewhere between a squeal and a scream that trailed off into heaving sobs. After Maurice opened the door, hugged Lillian to him, and half walked, half carried her back to the main house, Franklin took her place at the window.

Later, when Franklin told Robert Reeves what all he'd seen before Ms. May shooed him away, Robert joked that the boy had learned the birds and the bees the wrong way around.

"If I was you," Robert said, "I wouldn't go fooling around with that woman no more."

"Why not?"

"I done already said why not, which is more than I should have to."

That evening, after overhearing Ms. May tell Robert Reeves that the woman had given birth to twins, Franklin cut through the woods and returned to the cabin to see the woman's children for himself. The lit window of her cabin could be seen from the trees along the creek, and so Franklin was not surprised to find her sitting up at her kitchen table, nursing her newborns. Opa had walked around naked in the summer to stay cool and so there was nothing novel to Franklin about the sight of the woman's breast.

"The boy won't be sated," she told Franklin as he pulled a chair out for himself. "And the girl won't take my nipple."

She gave the girl to Franklin to hold while she continued to nurse the boy. The girl's eyes were shut tight when the woman placed her in Franklin's cradled arms, but when she felt the boy's warmth they opened. Franklin peered down at the girl, and the girl, wide-eyed, gazed up at him. The newborn's gaze unnerved him. It was almost as if he could feel her looking down the length of his life, past their marriage, and deep into the Oklahoma earth under which he would one day be buried. The strangeness of this sensation repeated itself when he woke from a dream about Opa to find the girl, woman enough now to fill out her mother's dress, standing over him.

"Do all babies stare like that?" Franklin asked the woman, glancing over at the boy, who, milk-drunk, had fallen asleep at his mother's breast, and then back to the girl, whose gaze, even as he handed her back to her mother, hadn't wavered.

"No," the woman said, thinking of her daughter in Africa, the one whose eyes flitted at every novel sight and sound. "Not all babies."

By the time Franklin made it out of the woods and up the lane, he was trying, already, to forget the eerie sensation the newborn baby girl inspired in him. As he walked, he wondered, not for the first time, if he could convince the woman to run away with him. Franklin's plan was to follow the river south and get back to the shack in the clearing he'd shared with Opa. The shack was no bigger than a woodshed, but if they all slept on the same pallet there was room enough for the four of them. They could be a family of sorts. It was owing to this line of thought that he did not notice Elijah's slender-hipped figure leaning against the wall of the cabin he shared with Robert until it reached out and tapped his shoulder.

"You want to see something funny?" Elijah asked.

Franklin followed Elijah up the lane and on past the cotton fields until he heard what he at first believed to be a vixen howling in distress. Elijah stopped walking, squatted down behind a young birch tree, and gestured for Franklin to do the same.

"What is that?"

In response, Elijah raised his finger to Franklin's lips and used the other hand to point toward the direction of the keening. Franklin squinted into the dark and saw two people, one man and one woman, a few yards off. The man was on top of the woman, rocking himself back and forth between her parted knees as she moaned. The man was Robert. The woman was Ms. May.

"What are they doing?" Franklin asked.

"Being nasty," Elijah told him. "They come out here because they don't think nobody can hear them. But I seen them when they sneaked off."

Franklin turned away.

"Why would you want to show me that?"

36

"I don't know," Elijah said, tilting his head down. "I thought you might like it."

"Don't show me nothing else," Franklin said, standing up and feeling as if he were out on a river in a canoe he couldn't help but rock.

Elijah followed.

"I was just trying to make friends," he said, shoving Franklin to the ground and straddling him. "You think you're so much better than everybody else. Like you free or something."

Franklin had once tried to heft the carcass of a buck Opa had felled up onto his shoulders. The deer had brought him to his knees before laying him flat, but he'd never before felt a live human body on top of his. The sensation thrilled him.

"Get off me."

"Make me."

They tussled, and though Elijah was three years Franklin's senior and had been fighting his older brothers, Isaac and Jacob, since he could crawl, he found that he wasn't able to pin Franklin for more than a few seconds. No sooner had Elijah gotten Franklin under him than he found himself flat on his back with Franklin on top of him again. Neither was able to best the other, and by the time Robert and Ms. May had made their way back down to their respective cabins, all their anger had given way. Elijah, feeling he'd made his point, relented, rolled over, and lay down in the grass beside Franklin, panting.

"I saw the way you was watching me the other night," Elijah said, after they'd both caught their breath.

"I wasn't watching you no kind of way," Franklin said.

"Yes, you were," Elijah said, turning to face him. "I saw you."

On their way back, they crossed paths with Maurice as he carried a newly carpentered oak rocking cradle in each hand. Maurice averted his eyes and pretended not to see the miscreant who'd deigned to knock at the front door of his father's house in broad daylight, where any white man coming to visit might have seen, and by the time he'd set the cradles down on the woman's doorstep—he certainly couldn't have been expected to arrange them for her — he'd already devised a fitting punishment for the ragamuffin.

That night, as Robert Reeves snored in the pallet across from him, Franklin stared into the dark and let everything that had happened that day bloom big in him. It was him who'd answered the woman's cry and fetched Ms. May. Him who'd gone to the big house and stood toe to toe with that sourpuss, Maurice. Him who'd wrestled and almost bested Elijah. He'd been happy with Opa, but he'd also been bored. Incredibly bored. Aside from the few times a year Ashford came to trade, every day was the same and nothing ever happened in the clearing he and Opa called home. But here — with Robert, and the woman, and Elijah — things happened.

The next day, while Franklin was out in the fields picking cotton, one of the overseers called him to the barn. It was a bright fall day. The sun was slanting in through the wooden slats that comprised the barn's roof so that Maurice, who was sitting on a hay bale with a straight razor in his hand, was half in the dark, half in the light. In the corner, near the back wall, a cast-iron pot hung over a fire Robert Reeves stoked with a rusted poker. Franklin tried to catch Robert's eye, to see in the man's face what this was all about, but Robert wouldn't so much as glance at him, wouldn't turn his gaze away from the fire. Franklin began to run, but before he could, the overseer gripped his shoulders.

"You can hold still," Maurice said, "or you can lose an eye."

Maurice pinched the top of Franklin's ear between his forefinger and thumb and stood for a full minute studying it before bringing down the cool of the blade and slicing a hot corner of the lobe away.

"Do as you're told," Maurice said, holding Franklin's ear lobe in front of his face, "or I'll take the other one, too."

While Franklin stood there, not yet able to connect in his mind the bloody flesh between Maurice's fingers with the searing pain on the side of his head, Robert Reeves put a hot iron to the side of Franklin's head to cauterize the wound. He'd have cried out in pain if he thought anyone in hearing distance would care, but he knew they wouldn't and so he didn't.

"Go back to the cabin and lie down," Robert said. "You got the rest of the day off."

After the lunch bell rang, Ms. May came to visit Franklin. He raised his head to her but said nothing as she dabbed his ear with a wet cloth and bandaged him. When she was finished, she sat down on the pallet and put the boy's head in her lap.

"When I was a girl, I had a baby sister Captain Talbert named April. Now, I loved April something fierce. Our mother passed birthing her, so she didn't have nobody to take care of her but me. She might as well have been my baby. When April got to be about seven, Captain Talbert came to tell me he'd sold her to Mr. Ripley, who lived up on the north end of the county. It wasn't even a week before she slipped off and followed the river back here. Said she didn't like it up at Mr. Ripley's. Said she wanted to stay with me. I took her back, but it wasn't long before she slipped off again and Mr. Ripley started to missing her. When he came to fetch her, he told Captain Talbert that if he couldn't keep her on the place he might as well sell her downriver. So the next time she slipped off, I took a switch to her, made her bleed, and told her not to come back. Said it was her that killed my mother, and that I was glad to be rid of her. That beating hurt her something awful, but as bad as she felt then, it'd be worse if she was sold downriver."

"You saying that woman had them do this to me?" Franklin asked Ms. May.

"I'm saying a little hurt now is better than a lot of hurt later."

After Franklin refused his bowl of evening corn mush, Robert Reeves came in carrying a wrapped napkin bundle. Franklin shut his eyes tight and feigned sleep. Robert set the bundle down on the floor and told the boy that what happened to him was bad but if he didn't learn to mind, he'd have worse. Franklin opened his eyes and glared at Robert.

"Now, I'm not saying it was right or fair, but there's a lesson in it. They got your body. Ain't no choice in that. But it's up to you whether or not they get at what's up here," he said, putting his finger to the boy's forehead. "You can't let them get at what's up here."

Franklin turned over and faced the wall. An ant was crawling down the side of it, so he knew that somewhere around him there were at least a hundred more.

"I know you hate me," Robert said. "You should. You can't trust and do and think for nobody else round here but yourself. Not if you want to be free."

"What you know about freedom?" Franklin asked.

"I know enough. Running and papers ain't the only way to get at it. Watch me. See if I don't do just what I want. Get just what I need. You do as I do, and you'll be all right."

When Robert left, Franklin unwrapped the bundle, saw it was cake, and knew immediately that the woman had sent it. He threw it to the floor. He didn't want anything that she or Robert had to give him. But then, later that night, he picked the cake up and began to eat it, hoping the sweetness would soothe his aching. He'd never felt so much pain before and didn't yet know how to turn his mind away from it, how to leave that part of his body behind and turn toward sleep, to hold in dreams all that waking life would not allow him to touch, and so, after eating as much of the cake as the dark would allow him to put his hands to, he eased the cabin door open, failing in his attempt to not wake Robert, and walked until he reached the woman's cabin.

There was enough light from the moon for him to see the woman and her babies. The cradles were stacked in the corner and the children were in bed with their mother, one under each arm. Watching them sleep, he wondered if his own mother, the one who left him by the river for Opa to find, had ever slept holding him like that. He'd never been able to picture her, never been able to imagine anything more than a shadow.

He thought of waking the woman, of seeing the babies one last time, of saying goodbye, but then he remembered his ear and thought better of it. He turned away from the window and walked back toward the creek, wondering if the thing in him that caused him to care for the woman and her children was the thing that kept people enslaved. Franklin had only been on the plantation for a little over a month, but already he knew that if he was to escape he'd spend the rest of his life wondering and worrying about the people he'd left behind. The woman wasn't his mother, and her too-hungry boy and wide-eyed girl were not his brother and sister, but he knew that if anything were to happen to either of them he would never recover.

Once Franklin reached the water, he knelt, cupped his hands to take a drink, and squinted up at the stars who, one by one, had begun to people the sky. He stood and, even though he knew it would hurt, removed the bandage from his ear so the white of it would not make him more visible to patrollers. He knew also that if he followed the flow of the water south, it would lead him to the river and that the river would, eventually, lead him to Opa.

Robert was right, he thought as he made his way along the water's edge, oblivious to the fact that Robert was no more than a few paces behind him. It wasn't only whips and chains and the threat of death that kept people from running. If he was going to be free, truly free, he thought as he made his way back to the river, he couldn't allow himself to feel anything for the woman or anyone else, ever.

The Last Daughter

LUCILLE LAURENT
(1838–1915)
Sister of Asa Laurent
Wife of Franklin Laurent
Mother of Walter Laurent

EVERY BODY'S GOT a beginning and every body's got an end. My beginning was my blood, which come to me so late that Momma and I both got to believing it'd never come at all. When my blood finally did come, Momma showed me how to wash myself, and when I washed myself, I felt good. But then one day, Momma sent me to the stable to peep in on Robert Reeves, and when I peeped in on Robert Reeves, I saw Franklin working his shovel, and seeing Franklin work his shovel made me want to wash up real good. Most folks don't know how to read a man's shadow and take the measure of him from it, but I could look to where the light wouldn't touch Franklin and know he'd never been held the right way as a child. His head had been turned, first one way and then the other, so that he didn't know whether he was coming or going. Seeing how dizzy his spirit was made me want to wrap my arms around him and hold him still. I seen the same thing once in a blind man trying to feel his way to freedom by rubbing the moss on one tree, walking a spell, and then rubbing the moss on another the day after Buckra claimed his last living son. I seen it again in my brother after he got renamed Lucius. Most everybody I know got they heads turned the wrong way. I don't have arms enough to hold them all.

For months, I washed and washed and thought of Franklin and washed again, but then one night the washing didn't cool what burned in me. I needed him. There was no moon, but I've never needed light to see. I crossed the water, strode the lane, eased the door to his cabin open, stepped in, and eased the door shut again. I tiptoed over to his pallet and leaned over the stillness of his lips — the pink blush of them peeking out of his blue-black skin — and breathed in his scent, knowing that part of me had already left my body to find a new home in him. He let out a breath, and I breathed it in. His dreams were purple, bruised in some places, bright in others. I whispered his name, and his name in my mouth was tangy and sweet. I touched myself, slowly, and then touched his lips so that my scent would find him in his dreams.

The next day, I rose early, washed in the creek, put on Momma's dress, the yellow one Daddy gifted her back when he was still kissing her feet, and made my way over to the kitchen.

Raina, I said to Sara, the cook — because that's the name her mother wanted her to have but not the one Captain Talbert was willing to give — I'm taking these here biscuits, so you better see about fixing some more.

All right, she said, getting up on her feet and retying her apron. But you bring back that pan.

I cut across the yard and on over to the stables. I knocked, even though the door was open.

Robert's still asleep, Franklin said, looking at the horse and not at me. I wanted him to look at me. He'll be on a little bit later.

I'm not looking for Robert, I told him. I'm looking for you. I brought you some breakfast.

Breakfast? he asked, glancing up from the horse and over at me

43

like he didn't know the meaning of the word. He smelled like how fresh-cut wood does after it's been left out in the rain.

Yeah, I said, holding the pan of biscuits out to him. Breakfast.

He took a biscuit for himself, sniffed it, and then eyed me as he took a bite. Watching him eat made all the places I wanted him to put his mouth tingle. He wanted me to leave him alone but he also wanted them biscuits. I told him I had to take Raina her pan back and so we stood there in silence. Him eating and me watching him.

Does your momma know you're over here?

Don't worry 'bout her. Worry 'bout me.

I reached out to take his hand and he let me, and because he let me, I brought the rough warmth of it to my cheek. Both of my hands could fit in the palm of one of his. He peered down at me. I saw myself in his eyes and knew that he would refuse me now, but if I kept at him, he wouldn't be able to refuse me later.

I held you when you were just a baby, he said. You know that?

Yeah, I told him. I remember.

That wasn't a dream last night, was it? he asked, backing away from me.

It was and it wasn't.

When I brought Raina back her pan, I caught my brother peeking out of one of the second-story windows. I waved, but he acted like he didn't see me. Sometimes when I see him up there in that window or out riding around or sitting up on the porch talking to his not-momma, I want to scream. Used to be he'd sneak out and come visit, but then the momma that was not his momma cried over it, and so Daddy took the whip to both of us. For a long while, I couldn't fathom why they took him and not me. Folks tried to tell me it was because he was light and I was dark, but I couldn't understand it. When I looked at my brother, all I saw was myself. Now, I didn't like being whipped, but the pain of the lash never out-ached the agony of losing my other me, and so I stood in the front yard and called to him. I called out to him and waited for the him that used to be. He wouldn't come. I beat on the front door so loud that Daddy came out and threatened to whip me again, but still he wouldn't come see me. Momma said that my brother wasn't my brother no more, but in my dreams I would see him seeing me, and it was the same as when we were two bodies with one shadow between us.

When we were little, Momma took us to the river and taught us the way of things. She pulled up some dirt and said: This here dirt is your body. And then she lifted her hand up to the sky and let the wind carry the dirt away. Then she cupped her hands and took up some river water and said: This here water is everything in you that ain't body, and the river is where everything that ain't body begins and ends. She opened her fingers. The water flowed out of her hands and into itself again.

It's written that God made man from dirt, but that ain't the way of it. The way of it was that the river made herself a woman and walked on the land. And the river woman was one, but she was also many. Just like you. You're yourself, but you're also everybody that came before and everybody that will be here after you leave. Taking a cup of water from the river don't stop it from being a river, and taking a cup of water away from the river don't keep what's in the cup from being river water.

Momma said it was the river woman who scooped up the water, mixed it with the dirt, and in doing that she made all the trees and the flowers and the people. She took one drop of life water and made a seed, and that seed became a tree, and that tree became the mother of all trees. She took a handful of water, sprinkled in some dirt, and threw it back in the river, and that dirt became a fish, and that fish became the mother of all fishes. And then she took the dirt into herself and gave birth to children after her own image.

Momma took up some dirt, mixed it with water, and worked it over in her hands until she made a ball of mud and said: But you ain't the one or the other alone. You the two coming together to make themselves one. You two were one thing that was two things. Then she broke the ball of mud in half and put one clump in each of our hands, because wherever one thing stands, another stands beside it.

You, she said to me, are one thing. And you, she said to my brother, are another.

After my brother's new name found him, Momma said she was sorry for letting us be born, but then, after she found out about me and Franklin's might-be baby, she said that she was sorry for just me. I was sitting at the table with the tea. Momma was over by the woodstove, then she was by the bed, and when I laid my head down on the table and closed my eyes, she was in my ear, worrying up them pretty girl-babies in the river and the man whose head was lopped off before his spirit could slip his skin. All this happened back in Africa, before she crossed the wide river with the white-eyeing shadow, my daddy, and the day the moon blocked the sun out of spite and she—seeing the two in the one, the light in the shadow—knew that she was, once again, carrying two babies and not one: my brother, the one who was taken, and me, her last daughter, the only child she'd ever keep. She got Ms. May to show her how to make the tea but didn't drink it, which she said was a mistake. But then, when my blood stopped, she said there were no mistakes but showed me how to make the tea anyway, because every woman ought to decide for herself whether what's ailing her is a beginning or an end.

When I found Franklin at the stable and told him that I didn't drink the tea, I saw myself in his eyes again, only this time I was standing alone. Whichever road I walked, like as not, I'd walk it alone.

My brother being taken was one beginning, and me coming up pregnant was another. Both times I had to learn to walk knowing that my feet were the only ones making tracks. Learning to walk with nobody beside you when walking beside somebody is all you've ever known is harder than learning how to walk in the first place. I know because I remember. When I was little, I would walk along the creek just to see my own reflection walking beside me. Sometimes my brother was walking in the water under me, but most times all that was in the water was another me. I knew for sure what was in me was not a mistake when I went out by the water and saw my brother looking up at me. I would have the baby, and when I had the baby, my brother would come back, because what was mine was his and what was his was mine, even if he was soul-sick, and had his head turned, and didn't know he wasn't free.

The Lost Son

ASA LAURENT
(1838–1917)
Son of Yetunde
Brother of Lucille Laurent
Father of Bubba Laurent

I'LL NOT APOLOGIZE for my actions. All I'll say in their defense is that Hobbes was right. It is passion, rather than reason, that drives man's behavior. A dictum that, though starkly at odds with my rationalist education, is the only compass by which I might faithfully chart my life's course. From the time I came to live with my father and up until his untimely death, he pressed me to put my faith in logic, maintained that all life's mysteries could and would one day be solved by critically inclined men such as himself. He went to great pains to make me reason's master, going so far as to make me copy *An Essay Concerning Human Understanding* over by hand as an adolescent. Though French was my father's first tongue, he lionized Locke and eschewed Rousseau — the philosopher with whom my sensibilities most readily align. Needless to say, my replication of Locke's fabled text failed to produce the desired effects. I am passion's slave.

I was much alone as a child. A result of both my father's isolationist tendencies and Lillian's fear that my complexion might out my true parentage. I knew little of life outside of my father's estate, save what I read in books secreted from Lillian's library. Much to my father's dismay, my moral and intellectual development owes more to his wife's novels—Magua's villainous pursuit of Cora Munro, the improbable rise and fall of David Copperfield's fortunes, Anne Elliot's heart-rending refusal of Wentworth—than to Locke's treatises or Kant's critiques. I blame especially a juvenile misreading of *The Sorrows of Young Werther* for the shameful period after the fire in which I was wholly given over to mawkish sentiment.

My father was not an affectionate man—I'd never seen him so much as kiss Lillian's brow—and, aside from him and his wife, the only person with whom I had regular contact was Maurice, a servant who was disdainful of my presence. Before I came to live in my father's house, my natural mother was forever hugging me to her, and until the night Lillian cleaved me to her, I'd not realized how much I missed it. Now and then my mother—who was my father's slave—would, from afar, bestow upon me a knowing glance, confirmation that my time with her was not some sweet dream from which I'd been waked but rather a different, better life out of which I'd been cruelly wrenched. Though welcome, such fleeting acknowledgment was—to a child in want of love—a meager portion. Such was my lot.

Years passed, and by the time temptation parted Lillian's lips, loosened her stays, and let fall her petticoat, I'd been so long in suffering the absence of loving touch that I falsely believed its deprivation the mark of a man's mettle. In the end, however, I was easily seduced— the too-willing Clarissa to Lillian's lavender Lovelace. Ought I to be faulted? Labeled a deviant? Shamed for choosing to bask in the light of Lillian's love rather than dwell one moment longer in the dark cave of my loneliness? I should think not. I would sooner take the pin from Lillian's gold serpent brooch—now clutched within my hand—and claw out my own eyes than part with the memory of her touch. No human being should ever go in want of loving touch.

*   *   *

The first night Lillian came to me, I was alerted to her presence by the creaking hinge of my bedroom door, accompanied by the glow of hand-mottled candlelight. I was awake, but kept my eyes closed, hoping she would go away. With a thud, she set the candleholder on the corner of my nightstand, and bent over me, allowing her stringy hair—which, when I first came to live in the house was a dark coppery red but was now a light auburn—to fringe my ear.

"I know you're awake," she said, sitting down on the edge of my bed. I opened my eyes. Between the moon and the candle, there was just enough light for me to make out her delicate frame. Though she'd managed to put on some weight in the years intervening my removal, she was still slight. Her eyes shone pale and, in the moonlight, did not appear wholly unkind.

"Do you ever think of your brother?" she asked, still facing the window.

She was speaking of Lucius. The boy I was meant to replace. I sat up but made no reply. I had only ever glimpsed my half brother from afar. Then, he was nothing more to me than the spindly silhouette of a boy in the second-story window of my father's house. He never came outside, and before he died, I was never allowed in. Occasionally, I would see him in the study, sitting in my father's lap, poring over the books that would one day be mine. My mother named me Asa, but after my half brother Lucius's death, I was given his name. An affectation that, every now and then, and only when my father was absent, Lillian dropped in order to tell me how fortunate I was to bear his name.

"He would have been six and twenty as of tomorrow. Sometimes I try to imagine what he would look like now. How tall he would have grown, whether or not he would have resembled my father, but all I can picture is you. Why is that?"

Again, I said nothing.

"You should be grateful you know," she said. "Do you know what your life would be if you had not come to live with us here?"

"What do you want, Lillian?" I asked. We'd long dispensed with any pretense of civility.

"To talk is all," she said, acting as if she'd been struck. "Can't a mother talk to her son?"

"A mother can, yes."

She stood then and, taking up her candle, made to leave but, before she did, turned to me.

"I don't imagine you'll ever believe me, but I care for you a great deal. You must understand that I was out of my mind with grief the night you were brought to live here. I begged your father to send you back, but he refused. So then I thought that, perhaps, I could transfer what I felt for Lucius to you. Put my energies toward giving you a better life, the one Lucius might have had. To be a mother to you," she said, turning back to the window. By then, the overgrowth of the intervening woods had all but blocked my view of my mother's cabin, but my mother's cabin was what her eyes sought out. "But I suppose you've too much of her in you for that to have ever been possible. That you, like your father, will always have more love for her than for me."

I'd not known a woman such as Lillian could envy a slave. I had not yet learned of what drew my father to my mother, if the attraction was mutual or coercive, if he took liberties with her, or if she coveted the advantages of exciting his appetites. All I knew was that, as a result of their special relationship, my twin sister and I were spared field work and allowed to roam as we saw fit.

After my half brother passed, my father and Lillian came each night to my mother's cabin to imbibe a decoction containing a fungus that, once ingested, allowed one to inhabit briefly the world of the spirits. My sister and I were gathering waterworn rocks by the creek when we spotted my father and Lillian through the trees, plodding toward us. My sister went to fetch herbs for the decoction while I ran ahead to my mother's cabin to warn her of their approach. Our mother, fearing that the recently departed child would find in my sister and me ready hosts, usually sent us away, but when my father and Lillian arrived at the cabin, he prevailed upon her to allow us to stay. My mother went to work brewing the tea while my father and Lillian seated themselves at her table. My sister and I sat on the floor sorting the rocks we'd gathered, daring not to look at either the table or our mother. We were then much afraid of the woman our mother became when she consorted with spirits. A shadow passed over her, and though she spoke with our mother's voice, we knew she was the stranger.

As steam from the brewing decoction began to cloud the air, the strangest sensation came over me. I felt as if I were rising up out of my body, looking at myself from above. It was then that the ghostly figure of my sickly, bespectacled half brother materialized from the steam, and as my mother strained the decoction, I sat there staring at him. My mother, who was by then the other woman, the one my sister and I feared, poured the tea, and as my father and Lillian imbibed it, the figure of my half brother evaporated, and I found myself rising to my feet. The next morning, I awoke in Lucius's bed with no memory of the intervening hours.

"I'd have been a mother to you if you'd have let me," she said now, openly weeping, "but you're a stranger to me. A stranger who answers to my son's name."

I stood, took the candle from Lillian's hand, replaced it on the nightstand, and hugged her to my breast. I disliked Lillian, but I could not countenance her tears. Her sobs moved me to pity. She was not given to histrionics. I considered then, for the first time in my life, my removal from her perspective. How blind a child is to the emotional life of adults! How effortlessly such blindness subsists beyond puberty! I could not, cannot, fathom the grievous agony of watching your husband's bastard, a bastard who, at his father's direction, rebuffed your every attempt at maternal intimacy, replace your lately deceased son.

She returned my embrace with some exuberance, and as her arms tightened around me, I began to see her late-night intrusion for what it was, a rather desperate ploy for attention. How terribly alone in her marriage she must have felt to have sought me out in my father's stead. It had never occurred to me before then that Lillian was as subject to my father's callousness as I was. I had, in an as yet fruitless attempt to ingratiate myself with my father, shunned Lillian, the only other person in the world who might understand and sympathize with the precariousness of my position. Our sufferings had at their root the same cardinal wound. In that instant, my father's wife—a woman whom I'd always considered my enemy—became not only an ally but, potentially, a friend, a development that, for me, was as astonishing as Emma's discovery of the depth of feeling she carried in her heart for Knightley.

Lillian raised her head from my chest. I wiped away her tears, and she, relishing the gesture, rested her cheek in my hand. As the candle-light flickered in her eyes, I glimpsed in their ecstatic expression the rushing waters of the Rubicon I was on the verge of crossing. I removed my hand. Lillian, with some celerity, caught and replaced it, holding firm to my wrist and, in the same instant, bringing her lips to mine, altering, indelibly, my life's course.

Before Lillian's lips aroused it, I had no concept of sexual desire. Even as an adolescent, I never understood the carnal interest in women obliquely alluded to in books. I occasionally awoke with an engorged member, but I could hardly attribute its appearance to any external stimuli, let alone know what to do with or about it. I could look upon the naked body of an attractive woman—as my father had once, in a New Orleans brothel, induced me to do—and feel nothing. But when Lillian kissed me, it was as if the sun, having been obscured by heavy cloud cover for nearly the whole of my life, suddenly broke through, blanketing the landscape with its rays. Where before there had only been shades of gray, now there were vivid greens, rich blues, tempestu-ous purples, and fiery reds. It is only by image that I can approach the feel of Lillian's lips, the warmth of her breath, the intoxication of her scent, the thrill of her body against mine. Though I had virtually no knowledge of the mechanics of sexual intercourse, I ached—even as her tongue probed my mouth—to bring my body into further contact with hers. The whole of me yearned toward her. When she broke our kiss, wiped her mouth, took up her candle, and left, I knew not what I should do with myself.

Lightheaded, I felt my way back to the bed, which was now cold. In darkness I lay down, listening to her departing steps, sensing with the whole of my being where she was at each juncture, smelling lavender, and feeling, after the door to her bedroom closed, as if a part of me—a part that I had heretofore been unaware of—had gone with her.

Before that fateful kiss, I had resolved on a plan of escape. Leaving the estate was my only chance at happiness. There was no prospect of marriage. Even if I were interested, no woman in town worthy of the name Laurent would have me. My father's reputation as a heretic—not to mention the suspicion my bronze complexion aroused among the townsfolk—all but guaranteed that. There was no hope of reestablishing relations with my mother and sister for, as much as I had longed to return to them as a child, the man I'd become, the man my father raised me to be, was another animal entirely from the boy they'd known and loved. Though sometimes, when I looked through the window in which I used to observe my half brother and see, through the tops of the trees, the cabin where my mother and sister lay, I imagined that I'd never left, that I was there with them. Yet and still, any reunion would only serve to breed disappointment on all sides. To remain on my father's estate was to condemn myself to a life of loneliness.

But any hope of leaving I harbored was safe only if my father's eyes did not alight on it. As I was oft reminded, my privilege was provisional. I was only allowed to avail myself of the entitlements afforded a young master-in-waiting if my behavior accorded with my father's conception of who his son should be. His wish was for me to assume control of the estate, and acting in concert with it was a condition not only of his good graces but of my existence. To survive, I secreted myself from my father and wore the face of my deceased brother, acting as a master-in-waiting would have, while maintaining the standard of living to which I'd grown accustomed. I had by then been given access to the estate's accounts and had, over the course of the last few years, laid by enough to purchase a modest tract of land in Virginia, just far enough from West Tennessee to outrun my father's reach.

My only impediment to striking out on my own was the fact that I was still my father's slave in name. If I were to leave, he would have more than enough documentation to prove his ownership of me, and if he gave himself over to vengeance, as he was wont to do, he might even go so far as to sell me downriver. But if, out of paternal love, he turned any incriminating documents over to me as he once, while drinking, promised to do, I would be free to do as I liked. Until such time, I resolved to hold myself at a distance, appear to fulfill my filial obligations, and harbor in secret ambitions of flight.

But, as I lay there in bed, turning over within my skin the memory of Lillian's touch, I feared that leaving was no longer possible. There was now the awful power her body exerted over mine to account for. (Even now, the memory of love's first kiss compels me. I cannot lie still and think of Lillian. The feeling is too great. I must write. I must walk. I must stand.) I knew, almost from the moment her lips touched mine, that I could not free myself from my father without considering that freedom's effect on his temper, for, in my absence, Lillian would surely bear the brunt of it. One kiss had dulcified years of bitterness, dismantled months of planning, and replaced cold apathy with searing compassion. How nimbly passion's arrow pierces reason's armaments! How swiftly feeling reverses fortune! Even if I could manage to drag my body elsewhere, my mind would be always upon her—a state of affairs that would have seemed incredible only hours prior. In order to proceed with my plan, I would have to either bury my nascent affections for Lillian—an undertaking that,

as I lay in bed feeling still her lips' imprint, seemed impossible—
or relinquish any ambition of flight.

Whether it was owing to his mother's visit, the anniversary of his birth,
or my peculiar state of mind, I know not, but around dawn, when sleep,
fitful as it was, finally came, the specter of my half brother appeared
to me in a dream. Unlike the ghosts you may have read of in Dickens,
my brother carried no clanging chains and came not to teach but to
take; to consume and spend through me the life he'd not been allowed
to live. Relentlessly, and with an alacrity his frail body could hardly
have mustered in life, my brother pursued me through the corridors
of an otherworldly dreamscape of my father's house. I ran, trying first
one door and then another, but each of them led invariably unto more
corridors, until, finally, the door to my father's study appeared. I stopped
running, opened the door, and shut it behind me, only to turn and see
Lucius standing there.

I tried to go back out into the hallway, but the door would not
open, and so I had no choice but to turn and face him. He raised his
hand as if to strike me. I cowered, shielding my face with my arms. He
laughed, and when he laughed, the room began to quake. I closed my
eyes and braced myself for the blow. When it didn't come, I lowered my
hands. I could see myself reflected in the green of his eyes, our father's
eyes, only now he was the cowering figure. Our positions had reversed.
I was standing over him, and he was crouched down, bracing for a
blow from me. I had become him; he had become me.

If, after the night Lillian and I kissed, my father noticed any change
in me or in his wife, his countenance did not betray it. He spoke and
acted as if Earth's polarity had not reversed itself. For my part, I did

not know how I was to comport myself in the presence of either. The ground was shifting beneath my feet, and I counted each unfaltering step as a minor victory over the heady and malicious forces at work within me. At breakfast, when my father asked for the bread, I passed the bread, but all the while my mind was on Lillian and in what ways I would be made to pay for what had transpired between us.

In the meantime, I managed as best I could to go about the work of the day. My father had long ago turned over to me the management of his estate. At one and twenty, I was put in charge of the overseers. I found most of the men compliant, but I did have to fire or otherwise reprimand the occasional drunkard. It was hard work, but I found I had a talent for it. I enjoyed mitigating expenditures, projecting crop yields, and, in general, keeping the plantation in productive working order. As my responsibilities increased, my father, believing himself to be on the brink of some discovery, devoted more and more time to the reading and writing of Spiritualist texts. Each week I briefed him on the condition of the estate, and each week he grew less interested. The further my father removed himself from the day-to-day operations of the estate, the more time he spent perusing esoteric texts.

My father belonged to a sect of Spiritualists, an American off-shoot of Swedenborg's New Church, which sought to exploit the "natural enlightenment" the famed theologian ascribed to Africans. In my father's only journal to survive the fire, I found a half-penned treatise:

> Our bodies inhibit us, we beings of flesh and bone, imposing always upon us their limits, though our psyches sense, yearn toward, and in passing shadows glimpse presences within and around us that are comprised, seemingly, of no substance at all. But there are Negroes among us who, through innate ability, are able to move within and among the world of the spirits. If we are ever to, while living, learn what lies beyond the veil, we must harness their power and seek the truth from those who have ventured out into eternity before us, the dead.

His writings fail to mention, of course, that my mother was his sole means of communicating with the dead, and that these so-called truths were often limited to what his deceased relatives thought about him and what ways he and his friends might increase their fortunes.

My father was much revered by his acquaintances back in New Orleans, but as of late he'd withdrawn himself even from them, leaving their letters unanswered and choosing to spend his time at home alone instead of making trips downriver to visit them. Which is why, during a respite, as I read alone in my room, I was much surprised when he rapped on my door.

"You've been avoiding me," he said.

"I haven't," I said, still reading. The book was *Adam Bede*, a new work by one Mr. George Eliot.

"Take Athena out. I haven't felt much like riding, and she needs the exercise. And while you're out, see if there's anyone you might fancy."

My father oft entreated me to take sexual advantage of the slaves, but remembering my mother and sister, I could never bring myself to follow through on this directive. Besides, there was only one woman I fancied.

"I'll take Athena out," I said, closing the book.

"When you get back, I would like for you to read this and tell me what you think," he said, handing me Andrew Jackson Davis's *The Principles of Nature, Her Divine Revelations, and a Voice to Mankind*. An utterly ridiculous volume seeking to apply natural laws to spiritual phenomena, raising more questions than it half-heartedly attempts to answer. Whenever my father happened upon me reading anything other than philosophy, he pressed upon me one of his texts.

"Of course," I said, accepting from him the volume.

Though he rarely left the estate, my father maintained a good stable, devoting two slaves especially to horse grooming. One, Uncle Reeves, had been on the plantation for longer than anyone could remember and was, once upon a time, loaned out at quite an expense to train other slaves. Now he could barely manage the walk from his cabin to the stable. The other was Franklin. Often, when I happened upon them, Uncle Reeves had put Franklin to work mucking the stalls while he, with considerable effort, brushed, hand-fed, and conversed with the horses as if they were people.

That afternoon, I found Franklin napping on a bed of straw. I called to him, and when he failed to rouse, I endeavored to wake him with the toe of my boot. But before I could, he caught my foot, surprising me. I was shocked, not by his insolence but by the abruptness with which he transitioned from sleep to wakefulness; there was no intermediating state. One moment he was snoring, and the next I was caught firmly in his grasp. Once he opened his eyes and beheld me, he let go and righted himself.

"Where's Uncle Reeves?"

"His joints acting up. You want Athena?"

I nodded.

He got up, walked over to Athena, and attempted to lead her out. It was clear from Athena's reticence that she was leery of Franklin, and I feared she would be skittish the whole ride. To my relief, Franklin saddled her gently, petting and smoothing her neck, whispering softly into her ear. He was no Uncle Reeves, but he certainly had a way with horses. Once Athena was out, he proceeded to brush her down, and as he did so, I could not help but notice the wax and wane of his black, sinuous skin with each stroke. The sun was still high, and as it filtered in through the gaps in the roof above the rafters, patchworked rays of light illumined his arms, his back, and the contrast, the play of shadow and light, the blackness of his skin working close up against the chestnut mare, had a curious effect upon me.

"She's ready for you," he said, tightening the saddle straps.

I drove Athena at a trot through the woods and down to the creek, following it a few miles before it merged with the river. I had nowhere in particular to go and couldn't bring myself to ride into town, so I ended up circling the grounds, spotting here and there a deer, here and there a fowl, and after a short while, I rode back to the stable, whereupon I found Franklin asleep again.

A bit of drool hung from the corner of his mouth and, as I watched it slide down the black of his cheek, I considered having him tied to a post and making an example of him. Sloth, if not snuffed out quickly, could spread like a wildfire, slowing production and leading, inexorably, to financial ruin. Though Franklin's behavior irked me, I ultimately decided against having him whipped. Pain only worked as a deterrent if it was applied judiciously, to discourage specific tangible actions within an intelligible framework. Furthermore, if I were to have him tied to the post now, he would know that his insolence had an effect on me. To allow a slave to feel that they have any power over you was a dangerous thing. The first lesson my father taught me was that the psychology of when and how you beat a slave was more important than the physical pain the lashing inflicted.

A few months after my removal, I grew bold enough to sneak out of my father's house and meet my sister in the woods. We moved among the trees, walking hand in hand, and, lying in the grass, using the lines in the sky our fingers drew, made thought pictures of the stars. It was strange, seeing her clandestinely after moving and acting as one for so long. It was as if, by some cruel misordering of fate, we had been born as Plato envisaged the first humans. Like them, we had four legs, four arms, and a Janus head, and were, after being pulled apart by a petty deity, separated and forced to live singly. In the early days of my removal, meetings such as this were my only succor. But I was forced to give them up after Maurice, who followed us into the clearing one night, told my father that I'd sneaked out to participate in some sort of incestuous pagan ritual.

Maurice had intimated, on more than one occasion, that I had risen preternaturally above my station, and he was determined to make me suffer for it. Everywhere I went, his eyes were upon me, searching out insufficiencies, desiring to see me punished. If I neglected my fork and ate with my hands, he drew my father's attention to it. If I uttered a word of pidgin — my mother oft spoke to us in an admixture of English and her native language — he took note, and I was made to repeat the corrected parlance until my tongue ached. Later, I learned that Maurice was Lillian's half brother. That he, Ana, the maid, and Sara, the cook, were all her father's issue. I have no doubt that Maurice paid me such scrutinous attention out of envy. Had Captain Talbert granted Maurice, his only son, the same privileges that were foisted upon me, the whole of the estate would have been his.

The next morning, my father had my sister beaten. After a breakfast of eggs and beignets from which Lillian was uncharacteristically absent, my father invited me to take a walk with him. Though the night before had been warm enough for my sister and me to sleep outside under the stars, there was now a chill in the air.

It wasn't until we made our way to the barn that my sister, who was tied to the whipping post, came into view. Maurice was standing beside her. His expression, a horrific smirk, induced more fear in me than his brandishing of the whip. I turned away the first time it was brought down upon her, and when I did, my father secured my head in his hands and, as the lash struck her, pried my eyes open with his fingers.

At first, I felt each blow as if the whip were being brought down upon me. But then, as the lashes continued, I began to disassociate myself from her. I found then that I was much interested in the finer workings of the whip upon her skin. I had never before seen the air so excited with blood, which, with each lash, rose in vivid red arcs, ran in scarlet rivulets down her bare back, and splattered and plopped rust brown upon the packed dirt beneath the post. It was only once the back of her dress was in tatters that I took her place.

My hands were brought around the post — by then slick with blood and sweat — and tied with the same rope used on my sister. After I was secured, my father placed his hand on my shoulder, brought his eyes level to mine, and asked me whether I wanted to be his son or his slave—his progeny or his property. He told me that whichever I chose was of little consequence to him, but that he would not allow me to live with one foot in each world. I opened my mouth but could not find words enough to answer.

Maurice, after handing the whip to my father, rent the back of my shirt with his bare hands, tearing violently at the collar, ripping the fabric down to my trousers, and then, delicately, pulling the frayed edges away so that my bare back was wholly exposed to the air. I turned my head to face my father, and instead of meeting my gaze, he raised the whip high, reared his arm back, and threw the lash forward in the same manner in which a fisherman casts out his line. I never met my sister in the woods again.

When I returned to my room, I found a note from Lillian on my bed. I paced about the room, apprehensive of the potential burdens it bore. For as much as the thought of her proximity thrilled me, I could not help but fear the morass of an emotional entanglement with my father's wife. I sat down on the bed and then, after a moment, stood. I went to the window, then made as if to walk out the door, before sitting down and opening her note. It was merely an invitation to tea, an invitation that smelled rather strongly of her scent.

I had seen little of Lillian in the hours following our kiss. She took her meals alone in her quarters the whole of the day. Her avoidance of me was a relief, for I did not know how I should go about breathing the same air as her. The formality of the note—for it was writ upon a calling card—hinted that she sought to reestablish our relations at a remove. But I could not help but wonder why she sent a note at all. She could, more easily, have sent Ana. Or, as she had the night prior, come herself. And why go to the trouble of scenting it? Was the note an extension, rather than a foreclosure, of her intimacy? I closed the door to my room, returned to my bed, lifted the card to my nose, lay back, and drank in her scent.

Lillian took her tea in the anteroom to her boudoir. The room, a space in which she received only her most intimate visitors, had western-facing French windows that overlooked the house garden, the stables, and, at teatime, the setting sun. As a child, I'd rather have suffered inanition than take tea in this room, a weekly ritual initiated by Lillian to which my father begrudgingly assented. In the early days of my removal, my father, skeptical of his wife's overtures, fearing she would coddle me as he believed she had Lucius, sought to poison me against her by intimating in private crude innuendo regarding her father and her virtue. For this reason, I could not disentangle Lillian's quarters from the dread of what in my father's imagination time spent alone with her might elicit.

That afternoon, I found Lillian so deeply engrossed in a book that she did not stir at my approach. Beauty such as hers is most evident in moments of thoughtful repose. Lillian was small in stature, pale, and somewhat shapely, with light green eyes and a vulpine face brought into relief by the pinning back of her hair. Her lips were slightly parted, and as she bent forward to better see the book nestled in the bunched scarlet muslin of her tea gown, her expression was pensive, yet mirthful. The human soul is such that no onlooker can ever fully penetrate its depths. Even the most intimate of relations can, in the right light, appear foreign to us. I took a step back and rapped gently on the door, and though she did not yet see me, her face tightened into the severe expression I had formerly loathed.

"Come in," she said, placing a ribbon in the book and turning to set it down on the side table. I was so focused on Lillian that I had neglected to read the book's title, though I should have known from the cover that it was *Jane Eyre*.

"I think it's done steeping," she said, once I'd taken the chair across from her. Long accustomed to being served, she made no move to pour the tea.

"Allow me," I said, reaching for the white porcelain teapot and pouring a very weak brew into first her cup and then mine. Setting the pot down, I held out the sugar. "One cube or two?"

"Oh," she said, looking down her nose at the sugar bowl. "I prefer to take it plain."

"I didn't know," I said, setting the sugar down, feeling chastened.

"There's no reason you should," she explained. "I take it both ways, though I prefer it plain. It's just that...your father likes to have his sweetened, and he, well, he can't bring himself to imagine that anyone might enjoy having it in a manner he finds unsuitable to himself. So, when I'm with him, I take sugar."

"I understand," I said, remembering how, when I first came to live in the house, my father induced me to drink milk at every meal because it was what he had done as a child, even though the thick, cloying liquid upset my stomach. "I understand perfectly. How are you liking your book?"

"I like it fine."

"Really? When I first read it, I found it rather too intimate."

"I imagine you would."

"What is that supposed to mean?"

"You're an Austen lover, through and through. I like Austen, but I find she paints her portraits at a remove. The people are but pinpricks upon a broad canvas. In reading her, I feel as if I'm peering down from too great a height."

"There's a lot to be said for propriety. When I read *Jane Eyre*, I feel at each turn as if I am on the verge of accompanying her to the toilet."

Lillian laughed, and in that laugh I perceived, fleetingly, the shadow of the woman whose gentle repose I'd interrupted. It was this that prompted me to ask how she came to know of my preference for Austen.

"Do you think every book in this house was purchased by your father? I've lost track of how many times I've gone looking for *Pride and Prejudice,* only to find it in your room."

"And all this time I thought it was Ana searching it out and return-ing it."

"I've always been curious as to why you prefer Austen. I'd have thought Scott or Cooper more in line with your tastes."

"Austen has a way of making you believe you know who someone is and then, in an instant, reversing your perception of them."

"Yes, but there's no nuance. They're all saviors or villains or bores. Here," she said, brandishing *Jane Eyre,* "there's depth. Even the villains have depth."

"You think Mrs. Reed has depth?" In my first reading of the novel, it was Lillian's face I pictured as I read of Mrs. Reed.

"More so than any of the Bennet sisters. Mrs. Reed is a woman whose mind has been arrested by grief and loss. A terrible loss, which Jane, unfortunately, embodies," Lillian said, glancing out the window. The light of the sun, which had been obscured by cloud cover, gilded the room. "I don't condone her ill-treatment of Jane, but given the cir-cumstances, I understand it. Each time I reread the scene of her death, I half hope she'll see her grievous error and repent."

"It would have been a poorer book for it," I put in.

"Perhaps, but a happier one. Ana!" she broke out suddenly. "Is there something you need?"

I turned around. Ana was standing in the doorway behind me.

"No, ma'am," Ana said.

"Then why are you skulking about?"

"I only came to see if anything was wanting."

"It isn't."

"Yes, ma'am," she said, turning away, stomping quite loudly down the corridor.

"Now," Lillian said. "You must tell me how your instruction in Latin is progressing."

I was not studying Latin. My father had deemed it a useless exercise, an indulgence in line with the sort of extravagance that led to his own father's financial ruin. But before I could remind her of this, she leaned forward and whispered: "Give it a moment."

I waited and, after a moment, discerned the sound of muted footsteps making their way toward the servants' stairs.

"She thinks I haven't caught on to her tricks," she said, taking up her teacup, "that I can't best her at her little games, but she is gravely mistaken."

Not knowing how to respond, I took another draft of tea.

"Grief," she said, meeting my eyes once again, "such as that can make one act in irrefutably shameful ways. We cannot take the full measure of Mrs. Reed by the yardstick of her lowest moments."

"Her lowest years."

"Her lowest years, yes. But enough talk of books. Our tea is getting cold."

We drank. I'd never taken tea without sugar before. The flavor was vaguely reminiscent of the herbs my mother used to forage and hang to dry in twined bundles from the ceiling. That Lillian could delight in this flavor endeared her to me in a way I could not then articulate. That afternoon, Lillian, the woman whom I had for years begrudged for wresting me from my family, became my first true friend. At tea, we reveled in our common interest in literature and, at night, shared with one another confidences too personal to disclose in the light of day.

After her mother died, Captain Talbert, Lillian's father, gave up society. As a result, her only childhood friends were her father's slaves. She never forgave them for growing up and going to work in the fields. After a rather protracted period of grief, Captain Talbert took up with Eunice, his cook, and she bore him Maurice, Ana, Sara, and an unnamed boy who, shortly after Eunice passed in childbirth, died in the midwife's arms. It was around this time that Lillian's father, drunk and lonely, began sleeping in her quarters, giving rise to the rumors that ruined almost every viable prospect of marriage save my father, who, owing to his lack of property and religious beliefs, could not afford to be too discerning.

We did not speak of the kiss that passed between us and, by tacit agreement, did not touch. When she visited me, I sat up at the head of the bed and she alighted on the chair at my writing desk. I had not, and have not since, known any greater intimacy with another living person, aside, of course, from my sister, in my entire life. She talked to me as no one else ever had, and as she talked, I felt as the sailors of old must have upon hearing the siren's song. I did not care that my ship—now dashed, shattered, and spinning within the watery vortex of a whirlpool—was destroyed and that I was adrift on a splintered quarter of mast, so long as I could still hear her voice, still learn more, so long as she kept talking to me of her books, her studied opinions— for though she well hid it, Lillian was, in most respects, better read than my father—and her life. I could not then fathom how far out to sea my love for Lillian would carry me. I only knew that land was nowhere in sight.

The more I came to appreciate Lillian, the more I began to resent my father. I came to see him as a Shakespearean villain of sorts, an exiled usurper who, like Prospero, and through lies and flattery, tricked Lillian's father into marrying her to him and then stole her inheritance after losing his own. If in the intervening years Lillian's light had grown dull, it was only because he had cast his shadow upon it. Ever since I had come to live in his house, he had attempted to mold me after his own fashion, but the more I learned of his ill-treatment of Lillian, the more I strengthened my resolve to become another order of man from him entirely, to use all that he had taught me against him and, like Caliban, curse him with it.

I was out beyond the slave cabins near the creek when I perchance witnessed Franklin ford it and head deeper into the woods. Minding my father's fears of rebellion and remembering the insolence with which Franklin met me in the stable a few days ago, I decided to follow him. It was dark out. Leaf-mottled moonlight was light's only source but by then, if needed, I could have navigated the grounds blindfolded. I had only to follow the sound of Franklin's footfalls to keep track of him.

My father spoke of Negro rebellion as if it were the white mare on which the first horseman of the apocalypse would ride. "You must take heed," he'd said, holding a snifter of brandy aloft in one hand and the newspaper in the other. "When the master class falls, all of Western civilization will follow." Like Jefferson, he believed black revolt an inevitability and took every precaution he could to defend against it, concealing within each room a loaded gun, stocking enough spirits to ensure no idle slave, or master, on his plantation was ever in want of alcohol. His fear of slave uprisings began with the revolt in Saint-Domingue. When he was a child, echoes of what had transpired there reverberated all about the country, especially in and around Louisiana, where he was born and then lived. After overhearing the atrocities visited upon his countrymen by the Negroes, my father dreamed, nightly, of Lucretia, the nursemaid who was the closest thing he'd ever had to a mother, slitting his throat in his sleep.

Around that time, news reached us of the raid on Harpers Ferry, sending my father into a panic, deepening my frustrations with him. After hearing of John Brown's exploits, my father wanted me much at his side. Whether my father's confidences were lavished out of love or out of fear that I might align myself with the rebels, I knew not. Only that such confidences led, inexorably, to my having to complete random tasks ranging from the painstakingly tedious to the ludicrously obscure. One day, he even sent me out into the woods to search for overturned pots, convinced this was the surest sign of an impending rebellion. As ridiculous as my father's apprehensions were, paranoia of this sort is often contagious, and one evening, while I was out taking my constitutional and saw Franklin, I found I had contracted it.

I did not realize Franklin was on the path to my mother's cabin until a candlelit window came into view — my mother's home was the only slave cabin with glazed windows. I hid myself behind a tree and watched as he approached and, without knocking, opened the door. I knew nothing of my mother's social life save that, until called upon for her expertise, she held herself apart from the other slaves. I was much surprised to see, especially at that late hour, Franklin visiting her.

Curious, I walked toward the cabin and approached the window, confident that the light within would obscure my benighted form. The cabin had not changed since I last saw it some twenty years before. There was a large straw-and-feather pallet on a wooden platform in the corner, a woodstove, and a crude wooden table. My mother, who, to my eyes, appeared not to have aged, bent over the stove to feed the fire while my sister, standing up on a chair with her back to the window, affixed a bundle of herbs to one of the rafters. Franklin sat comfortably at the table, eating a cobbler of sorts, while I stood outside of my first home, smelling the wood and the herbs and the dirt and the musk as I had not had occasion to since I was a small boy.

Satisfied with the fire, my mother took a seat at the table beside Franklin while my sister continued to fuss with the hanging herbs. They spoke in low voices. I know not what of. I could hear nothing save the sound of my sister's humming. My mother's face was uncharacteristically stern, and I could tell from this that she was then inhabited by the other woman, whom, as children, my sister and I greatly feared. After my removal, I saw this woman more often than my mother, as it was she that my father would call upon to commune with the dead. On those evenings, my father would don a red cloak and wave a silver watch before my mother's face. The timepiece was merely a prop, part of a play my father authored so that he might feign percipience for members of his Swedenborg sect. Although the surrounding landowners thought my father and his beliefs queer, the effect that these table-turning exhibitions had upon the society my father invited up from New Orleans — though he'd lived in Tennessee for forty-odd years, he only associated with the caste of Louisiana Creoles to which he was born—was wholly successful, despite the fact that this other woman spoke to my father contemptuously and with much scorn.

It was to this other woman that Franklin now sat listening as she, using my mother's mouth as her vessel, spoke. She appeared to be giving Franklin some sort of directive, the purpose of which I could not construe, and that, after a bit of back-and-forth, he reluctantly accepted. She then stood and retrieved from underneath the bed a root, raised it to her mouth, kissed it, and then pressed it into Franklin's hands. Realizing that Franklin was to take his leave, I turned from the window, tripping as I went over an upended cast-iron cook pot. The pain in my foot was so great that I nearly cried out. It took everything in me to hobble alongside the house and take cover in silence.

I did not fear Franklin's discovery of me so much as I feared losing the opportunity to learn what business he had with my mother. After seeing them together, I did not believe, as my father did, that my mother was in the midst of hatching a plot against him. Her position on the plantation was enviable. She had never been made to perform hard labor and, to my memory, had never been whipped. She and my sister were allowed to come and go as they pleased. There were poor whites who had not so much privilege. I could not imagine freedom bettering their circumstances. I was, however, curious as to what errand she, or rather the other woman, had sent Franklin on. Why, of all the other slaves on the plantation, she took him into her confidence. However, encumbered by the injury to my foot as I was, I found that it was now much harder to match Franklin's pace. I quickly lost him.

But then, just as I was fording the creek, an animal bayed. Thinking it a calf in distress, I followed the sound through the woods to its source. We had recently secured a flink of Holstein cattle, at quite an expense. Two had already succumbed to wasting disease. One had milk fever. And another had escaped into the woods after knocking over a loose fence post and had yet to be recovered. Needless to say, I was fearful of losing another, and so, despite the pain in my foot, I followed the sound to its source.

I noticed first the rhythmic rustle of leaves, moving in concert with the moans, and discovered at the base of a young beech tree two black men writhing: one bent over, bracing himself against the tree, his face contorted in what was either agony or ecstasy; the other, legs slightly bent, feet shoulder-width apart, stood thrusting intently. So singular was this man's aim, so set was he on achieving it, that, though he faced me — though I was very nearly upon them — he did not see me.

Moonlight fell in rays of blue and white upon their skin. I approached and, squinting, discerned that the upright man was Franklin. The other was Elijah, a field hand. As I watched Franklin, I thought of that day at the stable when I happened upon him asleep. If his grabbing of my foot had resulted in a tussle, there would have been no question of his overpowering me. If he'd wished it, I'd have been penned beneath him, subject to his whim, slave to his every desire. I gasped, and in the same instant, Franklin's gaze fixed me. He did not stop or try to right himself but instead leveled his eyes and stared as if I were the slave and he were the master. If I were ever to be at ease in my own home, I must devise some means of selling Franklin.

Upon returning to the house, I went straightaway to my father's study. In keeping with his habits as of late, he was behind his desk, hunched over a piece of parchment, with no less than three volumes open before him, writing furiously. I had to rap on the door three times before he deigned to nod his head in acknowledgment. Seeking to turn him against Franklin, I gave my father a full report of what I had witnessed transpire between him and Mother, making sure to reference the overturned pot. It was only then that he laid his quill aside.

"It's just as I feared," he said, lifting a bottle of brandy up from his lower desk drawer and refreshing his drink. "It's all her doing. The rash of uprisings. The discord in Congress. All of it."

"Indeed," I said, thinking it best to humor him. "I know you value

Franklin's expertise, but he's a bad influence on her. We should sell him."

"Are you daft? That boy is the least of my concerns. Has it escaped your notice that I have not left this house for the better part of a year?"

"I just assumed that you were too deep within the throes of your interesting research to bother."

"All of my *interesting* research, as you so condescendingly put it, is in service of one aim," my father said, taking a drink. "To break whatever spell it is that your mother, yes, *your mother*, has put on me."

He was quite unstable, and, not for the first time, I began to worry for his mental health.

"I can't set foot outside this house without breaking into hives, and it's all her doing. I should never have taken her on. But her visage, the way she stood apart from the other Negroes, how greatly the sea moved her, despite her circumstances, endeared her to me. I had to have her," he said, rather wistfully.

I'd never heard my father speak with so much emotion before. I doubt I'll ever understand the true nature of his and my mother's relationship.

"I desired nothing so much as to understand her. Every night I dreamed of her, and each passing day I was drawn, irresistibly, toward her. I moved her to my quarters, for I could not stand the thought of her languishing belowdecks. Captain Stevens, seeing the curious effect she had upon me, advised me to throw your mother overboard, but I could not bring myself to. In the end, he was right to worry. It was for your mother that I gave up sailing and consented to Talbert's desperate proposal of marriage. I'd hoped this backwater would afford me enough time and privacy to teach her English, delectate in her gifts at my leisure, but her power is not of the sort to be harnessed. Your mother is in league with forces neither of us can comprehend. My only chance at staying alive is to try and see if freeing her will appease her enough to relinquish me from her grasp."

"What about Franklin?"

"Have you heard a single word I've said?" my father shouted, slamming his fist down on the desk, overturning his snifter of brandy. "Forget Franklin! He's of no importance. Your mother is the only problem worth solving. Appeasing her, by whatever means, is the only way in which I might save myself."

That night, I dreamed again of my half brother. Only in this dream, he was alive, and I had never come to live in the great house. As he peered at me out of the window of his room, I wandered the grounds, darting between the trees much in the way I had as a boy, except this time, when I crossed the creek, a light emanated from my mother's cabin. Through the window, I saw myself prone upon her table, surrounded by herbs. She was moving her hands about the air, murmuring in the language of her people, as my sister held the hand of the me that was upon the table. The light emanated not from the candle but from my mother, and as I looked on, it overtook my vision, obscuring all else. Half-blinded, I blinked and saw clearly that the light I perceived in my dream came from Lillian, who, candle in hand, had entered my room while I slept.

When I sat up, she placed the candleholder on my nightstand and sat down beside me. She was trembling. The night was black, but in the flickering candlelight, I was able to discern what about her face disturbed me. Around her eye, there was a purple bruise, which I'd first mistaken for a shadow. I put my hand to her cheek. She held it to her face and unleashed a torrent of tears.

That evening, while I was out following Franklin, she'd had an argument with my father, regarding what he termed her ill-treatment of Ana. Ana, her half sister, had, for some time, been my father's lover. Earlier in the afternoon, Lillian explained, she'd happened upon Ana in her dressing room, trying on one of her new silk gowns, an offense for which any other slave might have been beaten. Of the two sisters, Ana was, objectively at least, the more striking. She possessed the aquiline features of their father, Captain Talbert, whose portrait hung in the main hall. The resemblance, once noticed, was quite unimpeachable, and the attributes were much improved by both the honeyed tone of Ana's skin, framed by deep bronze curls, and the oval, more feminine structure of Ana's face. I have no doubt that Lillian's dress did much to complement Ana's form, so, alongside the breach in decorum, there was, I'm certain, a fair amount of sororal envy. Lillian, with what she perceived to be tremendous restraint, slapped Ana and considered the matter put to rest. But then, as she was dressing for bed, my father confronted her, his face contorted in anger. She told him that Ana was hers to do with as she wanted, and for this he struck her. I could not help but wonder then how many blows from my father she'd sustained over the years and borne in silence.

Pushing the bedclothes bunched between us aside and scooting closer to her, I wrapped my arms around Lillian and pulled her to me. She crumpled into my arms, weeping, and despite her tears, my blood stirred. Seated as we were, with my front facing her and her nearly in my lap, Lillian could not help but notice my arousal. It was then that, as if reentering the dream from which I'd just been awoken, I felt as if Lucius were in the room with us, looking down on me. I know not whether he approved of or was repulsed by my proximity to Lillian, only that our intimacy drew him out.

In an instant, the distance between her lips and mine closed. One moment I was gazing into Lillian's parted lips, and then, as if propelled by some unseen force, just as the wind asserts itself upon an open sail, I was upon her, hungrily pressing my mouth to hers, and wanting, needing, to take full possession of her. Having no knowledge of sexual intercourse, save what I had lately seen in the woods, I stood up and attempted to bend Lillian over, desiring desperately to see on her face the same ecstatic expression Elijah had borne, to feel in myself Franklin's prowess.

But Lillian would not allow herself to be bent over. With a dexterity I had heretofore never witnessed, she pushed me back down onto the bed, turned me over, lifted up my nightgown, and straddled me. However, as her hand endeavored to guide my engorged member into the warmth of her sex, I ejaculated. Lillian, once she realized what had happened, laughed, cupped my face in her hands, and kissed my forehead before dismounting me and using the hem of my nightgown to wipe the semen from her thigh.

"Have you ever been with anyone before?"

"No."

"Not even a—"

"No, not even."

"How refreshingly unlike your father you are. May I ask why?"

"I don't know. I just never wanted to."

"But you wanted to with me?"

"Yes."

We lay there for a long time, gazing into each other's eyes. But then, just as I was falling asleep, she took me in her hands and, with gentle strokes, coaxed the blood back into my member. Once I was fully erect, she climbed on top of me and, balancing herself by placing one hand on the headboard and the other on my bare chest, she took from me her pleasure. Once she finished, she lay down beside me and closed her eyes. As I lay there watching her sleep, a deep—and thoroughly satisfying—sense of relief washed over me. She let out a sigh and then turned and wrapped her arms around me. Whatever impediments there might be to our union, I would do all within my power to sustain it.

The next morning, I arose alone and naked as Adam to the faint early morning light that precedes the rising of the sun. Had I not still smelled Lillian on me, I would have attributed the whole of what had transpired between us to a fever dream. As I lay there relishing her scent, a terrible shame rose within me, coating the back of my throat with a most bitter bile. My shame arose not from the memory of the act but rather from that most cruel and unrelenting of human emotion's conspicuous absence. Given half a chance, I would do it all over again. I sat up, seeing as I did a dark figure crouched by the window, but when I turned, it disappeared. "Let us descend," I whispered to the now invisible figure, reckoning it to be the first in the envoy of hell's host that needs must ensue so great a sin. "Let us descend." Remembering then my father's directive regarding my mother's freedom and wanting, for as long as possible, to remain in his good graces, I dressed and set out for her cabin.

As a child, my exile from my mother had been strictly enforced. But now, as an adult, I purposefully avoided her. Whether this avoidance was out of embarrassment or fear of rejection, I knew not, but even though my father's logic was muddled, his instructions were clear. I was to offer my mother her freedom in exchange for her mercy.

Dripping with sweat and naked to the waist, Franklin ascended the bank as I neared the creek. He endeavored to change directions. I altered my steps so that our paths could not but cross.

"What business do you have with my mother?" I asked outright.

"No business at all, sir," Franklin said. "Only visiting, is all. Don't mean nothing by it."

"See to it that your visiting doesn't keep you from minding the stable."

"Headed there directly, sir," he said.

"Is that so?"

"It is, sir."

"And mind that you keep to your cabin at night," I said, taking a step forward and closing the distance between us. We stood nose to nose. "I don't want to find out about you traipsing those woods anymore."

"You won't catch me out there in them woods, Master Laurent,"

Franklin said. His face as unassuming as a simpleton's. "It's a sight too many haunts round down that way for my comfort. One caught hold of Robert Reeves a while back, and he ain't been right since. Might be it was one of them you saw out traipsing, as you say, and you just thought it was me."

"You mean to stand there and tell me it wasn't you I saw last night with Elijah?" I asked, hoping to strike through his mask of black servility.

"I do, sir. Me and Elijah was over to Bible study at Ms. May's last night. She knows some verses, and sometimes she has a mind to kind of gather folks around and recite them for us to puzzle over. I'd steer clear of them haunted woods if I was you. Ain't no telling what's out there waiting to catch hold of you."

I'd watched Uncle Reeves use this same sort of affected superstition and ignorance on my father for years. It was the rhetorical equivalent of Brother Rabbit's tar baby. The more you tried to parse the logic of the ignorance, to strike out against it, the deeper in it pulled you. But my desire to meet the man behind the mask — the man I'd glimpsed in the moonlight — was so great that I could not help but strike out at it anyway.

"Do you like it here, Franklin?" I said. "At times I get from you the impression that you might prefer to live downriver."

"I ain't never thought on that," he said, and though he narrowed his eyes, his face remained placid. "I don't know 'bout too many places. But I imagine that if you think I'd be happier elsewhere, like as not I'd be inclined to agree."

I shook my head in frustration. The mask would not break, only bend.

When I dismissed Franklin, he brushed past me, staining as he went the shoulder of my shirt with his sweat. I watched as he plodded through the trees and regained the trail leading from the slave cabins to the creek, but even though he knew my eyes were upon him, he did not go back to the stable but rather returned to the cabin he shared with Uncle Reeves. When he was out of sight, I lifted the soiled portion of my shirt to my nose and sniffed. It smelled, disgustingly, of his musky sweat. But—as one is wont to do with spoiled milk and other noisome scents—after I crossed the creek, I could not help but raise it to my nose again.

After knocking on the door to my mother's cabin, I found myself, for the first time in over a decade, standing face-to-face with my twin sister, who was, quite to my astonishment, pregnant. If she was surprised to see me, her face did nothing to betray it. She stepped aside and, with a wave of her hand, invited me in as if she'd been expecting me.

I knew not in what manner I should greet my mother, and so I merely nodded and took a seat in the chair across from her. She stood and, without a word, walked around the table and wrapped her arms around me. My sister stayed standing by the door, but once my mother returned to her seat, she walked around the table and, with considerable effort, for as I said, she was very pregnant, lay down upon the bed.

Once my mother resettled herself, I put the case before her as plainly as I could. Omitting my father's suppositions regarding her goophering of him, I told her of his desire to have papers of manumission drawn up for her. In lieu of reply, she stood up from the table and walked around it to the woodstove.

"Have you eaten?" she asked.

"Did you understand what I just said? Father would like to give you and Lucille your freedom and the means to make a fresh start."

Using a wet burlap rag, she removed from the stove's interior a steaming cast-iron pan, the contents of which filled the room with the scent of baked nuts and blackberries.

"You used to eat this by the handful when you were a boy," my mother said, setting the crudely baked pie on the table in front of me. It was not a proper pie but rather a savory-sweet compote of whatever fruit was in season, with a ground-nut crust, which my mother cooked directly over the fire until the contents bubbled up and trickled over the sides of the pan into the flames.

"That was a long time ago."

"Not so long," my sister said from where she lay on the bed.

"If you like," I said, staring down at the still bubbling pie, "I could make some inquiries for you. Find a place where you both could be comfortable."

"We're comfortable here," my sister said, sitting up.

"And where would you go?" my mother said, cutting into the pie and dumping a slice onto a wooden plate. "What would you do while your sister and I are starting fresh, hmm?"

"I would stay here."

"With your father and that nasty woman?"

"I could find a good place for you," I said, averting my gaze. "You wouldn't worry for anything."

"So you are telling me," my mother said, pushing the plate in front of me, "that you, though you are free to do as you like, though you are my son, my blood, will, while I and your sister establish ourselves elsewhere, as you say, remain here, trading flesh with your father?"

I chanced a glance at my sister. She was staring up at the ceiling.

"When I was brought here to this place in chains, I thought that was the worst thing. I thought this is the worst thing that could ever happen to me. And then you were taken from me, and I thought, this is terrible, but at least he will be cared for, at least he will not be made to work in the fields, but, I tell you, if I had known my son, my flesh and blood whom I nursed with my own bosom, would one day grow up to live like a vampire off the blood and sweat of others, I would have, myself, killed him."

"Momma," my sister said, still looking up at the ceiling. "Don't say that to him."

"What?" she said, turning to my sister. "Your brother is man

79

enough to own slaves, man enough to come here and talk of giving me my freedom, but you do not think he is man enough for me to speak truth to him?"

"I'll have the papers drawn up and delivered," I said, standing up. "Do with them what you will."

"You know," my mother said, looking through me, past me, "when my village burned, I thought I had lost everything, everything. But then, when I did not die, when, despite everything, I lived, I came to see that what was most important I carried in me. I carry her still. It is a gift. I have not been able to raise you in the way that you should go; that, among other things, the man you call father stole from me, but I promise you, my son—for no matter how pale you are, you are my son, and your children, and your children's children, no matter how pale they are, will be born of my blood—I promise to do everything within my power to show you what in life is most important."

"As I said, I'm having papers of manumission for you and Lucille drawn up. Do with them what you will."

Later that evening, I found Lillian knitting in the drawing room. I had not seen her since she'd left my bed, and so I did not know on what ground our relations stood. For her, I was ready to forsake all, but considering that she was still my father's wife in God's eyes and given her piety—for my Lillian was a Christian woman—I was uncertain of her feelings toward me. She could have, at any point in the intervening hours, and in order to save her immortal soul, repented. But, to my immense gratification, and seeing I was in a state of distress, she called me to her side. Sitting at what I deemed a chaste distance from her, I relayed to her my father's as yet unfounded fears and the disturbing interview with my mother resulting thereof.

"I'll never understand his obsession with her," she said, peering down at the not-yet scarf snaking her legs. "I told him to get rid of her years ago, but he wouldn't hear of it then. Now he wants to grant her manumission, as if she doesn't already come and go as she likes."

"What would you have him do?"

"Sell her. Make her someone else's problem."

All while Lillian spoke, her hands never ceased their work upon the scarf. Each winter, she and her aunt Jessup exchanged hand-knit scarves.

"I'll not pretend to understand any of your father's Spiritualist claptrap, though I have seen things since she was brought here that I can in no other way explain," she said, putting aside her needles and concentrating fully upon me. "But, aside from that, I find her presence deeply unsettling, and I have no doubt being rid of her could not help but improve everyone's health."

"She's still my mother," I said, contemplating the green-and-black yarn between us. "I still feel some filial obligation toward her."

"Look at me," she said, taking my chin in her hand. "You don't need her anymore. You have me. We have each other."

I kissed her, lustily, rapturously, imbuing into the embrace a lifetime's worth of unspent passion. Lillian, remembering the hour, pulled away from me. As we sat there, inches apart, gazing hungrily into each other's eyes, a shadow passed over us, briefly obscuring the sunlight that shone through the window across the hall. I rose and ran to the threshold of the drawing room, hoping, fearing, to catch sight of who had chanced upon us. It had to have been one of the servants, for my father would certainly have stopped. Sara or Ana might be reasoned with, but if it was Maurice, all hope was lost. However, once I gained the hall, the figure, whoever it was, had, like the shade I'd seen in my room upon waking, disappeared.

* * *

For three days, I lived in fear of my father's discovery of my and Lillian's relationship before Maurice, not daring to meet my eye, came out to the storehouse, interrupted my weighing of the cotton, and summoned me to my father's study, as he had not done since I was a child. Leaving Goodwin, the overseer I distrusted the least, to finish, I trod slowly across the lawn, savoring what were, potentially, my last moments of freedom. For, though I had settled affably into my role as my father's son, I never forgot that I was his property. A year ago, I would have scarcely conceived of his selling me, but given his instability as of late, and my newly consummated relationship with his wife, I could not rule out the possibility.

Though the door was open, I knocked upon entering the study. In the time since my last visit, he'd taken all of his books off the shelves and placed them in stacks of indiscernible logic. Loose paper carpeted the floor, the couch — where he slept — and the desk behind which he presently sat. Open before him was the leather-bound ledger of slave births, deaths, purchases, and sales, a sight that could not but confirm my worst fears.

"I know my wife seeks to poison you against me," he said, averting his gaze as he opened the lower desk drawer and removed from it a bottle of brandy and filled two snifters. "There is no boundary she will not cross in her campaign to sour everything I hold dear."

He invited me to sit in the chair across from his desk and handed me a snifter. In lieu of drinking from it, I set it down on what I did not then realize were my papers.

"Lillian was sixteen when her father all but begged me to marry her. I thought she'd outgrown these childish games, but age has made her more dangerous. First, she sought to wrest from me my legitimate heir, coddling him into weakness, undercutting my every effort to instruct and strengthen him, not satisfied until he passed away from a sickness that, had she not shut him up in the house, he would easily have overcome. And then she set her sights on you, pretending not to know the difference between you and him, begging me to bring you home with us. A charade I would have dismissed outright had I not seen myself in you."

And here, my father winked at me.

"I may have given you his name, but rest assured, I have never once in my mind confused the boy we buried with you. I should have known Lillian would devise some means of turning you against me, an aim I could not then have fathomed she would so thoroughly debase herself to achieve," he said, shaking his head. "As it stands, Asa, I do not believe I am long for this world, and so I wanted to give you these in hopes of clearing up any reservations you might have about my affections for you when I'm gone."

"Should I call for a doctor?" I asked.

"I'm afraid it would be of no use," he said, raising the snifter I'd set down and pushing the stack of papers toward me. The papers that determined whether I was a man or a slave.

"It's a hard thing to be a father to a son," he said, staring into his snifter and swirling the amber liquid around it. "One feels all the love a mother does and yet knows, despite this love, despite the desire to lavish affection enough to match one's inner feelings, it is incumbent upon the father, as it was incumbent upon his father before him, to make of the son a man. I'd hoped that my giving you a place here was enough to inoculate you against Lillian's poisons, but I see now that, in order to make my affection known to you, I must support my actions with words. You are, and forever have been, nothing less than a son to me."

When he said these words, I closed my eyes, remembering how once upon a time, when I lived with my mother, I longed for him to acknowledge me. I thought then also of the conditions under which I had been offered the privilege of his paternal recognition, the day he whipped my sister and put before me his choice. No matter which decision I took, I would be beholden to him, his slave in thought, if not in action, as his acknowledgment of me was contingent upon my willingness to play the part of Lucius. But now, if his words were to be believed, he loved me not for taking his other son's place, but for being me myself. Could it be that the filial piety endemic to my captivity was, though it rang false within me, true to him? Were the expectations he placed on me—his desire for me to manage his estate and revive his family name—natural, common to a father's wishes for his son? At what point, to him, did I cease to be a slave? When did I become my father's son?

"All the work you've put into maintaining this estate has not escaped my notice, nor have your extracurricular bank transactions. Don't worry," he said, seeing how I'd started. "I admire the initiative, and, since I'd made plans already to leave all to you, you've done nothing more than split your own money into separate accounts."

"Is there anything I can do for you?"

"No," he said. "Save one thing. This business with you and Lillian. I have no objection to your keeping her as a consort if that is your desire. But please marry respectably, and with your new wife bear children worthy of our name. Lillian is ill-suited to childbearing."

Not knowing how to respond, I said nothing.

"I don't have much time left," my father said. "Promise that my efforts with you have not been in vain."

That evening, I sat for a long while staring at my papers. Among them were my mother's bill of sale and a ledger page recording the birth of myself and my sister. With these, I could go wherever I wanted. Do whatever I wanted. As I held them, my mind turned to Franklin, who, when I roused him that day in the stable, let drop his mask of servility and acted as a man in full possession of his self might act. When I resolved on my plan to steal these papers and free myself from my father, I believed my thinking to be quite apart from the everyday slave. Was it possible that I was not exceptional? Did the inner lives of all slaves belie the self they presented to their masters? Franklin was a man of his own mind, whereas I, for the whole of my existence, was no more or less than what my father desired me to be. Could it be that what made one a slave was not one's race but rather one's inability to, in any circumstance, by any means, meet their own needs and satisfy their own desires irrespective of their status or station? Both Franklin and my mother did as they pleased while I was beholden to my father's will.

Though my daily routines were unaltered, my life had been upended. I felt as if, after harvesting wheat, separating the grain from the chaff, and driving my wagonload to the miller, I had returned home to find my kitchen overflowing with loaves of bread. The quickest way to kill a man's will to live is to present him with his heart's desire. With no proverbial yoke to strain against, I knew not who or what I was. Besides, my interview with my father, his fear of his impending death, sounded out my latent filial affection toward him. No matter what had transpired between us over the years, he was still my father. I could not abandon him on his deathbed.

And so—though my worst fears had been abated, and my greatest hopes realized—my life continued just as it had before. I saw to the affairs of the estate, read in the afternoons, and, in the evenings, with my father's consent, shared my bed with Lillian. But the whole arrangement felt untoward, and I paled at the thought of anyone else learning of it. In those days, an uncanny sense of dread pervaded the air. The life I led was not a real life but a shadow life, a purgatory I— by dint of sin—was forced to inhabit until judgment was rendered and the light of my true nature illumined the path to either heaven or hell.

In this state of ambivalence, and with a profound sense of foreboding, I drafted my mother's papers. I delivered them myself, hoping to talk my mother into accepting my father's terms. But when I arrived at the cabin, my mother was gone.

"Gone where?" I asked.

"Out to get some herbs. Come in," my sister said, stepping back from the door and waddling, for she was still very pregnant, over to the woodstove, above which was a shelf with a number of smoke-sooted jars. She took one down and, after setting a teapot atop the stove to boil, muddled the contents into a fine paste. "You want some tea?"

Not knowing what was in this so-called tea and remembering all too well the potency of my mother's herbal remedies, I declined.

"That's too bad," she said, shaking her head. "Well, if you're not going to have any, the least you can do is sit with me while I drink it."

I sat down at the table in front of the blackberry pie, which had gone untouched. I thought that she'd have given it to Franklin, seeing as how my mother so enjoyed his company.

"Momma baked that special for you, you know. She dreamed you was gone come visit. I tried to tell her you wouldn't want it, but she didn't listen," she said, scooping some out of the cast-iron skillet and ladling it onto a wooden plate.

"How is it still warm?" I asked, watching the steam rise from the oozing berry compote.

"She threw the other pie out and baked another for you before she left," Lucille said, pushing the plate toward me.

While Lucille readied her tea, which, from the smell, was likely chamomile, I took up a wooden spoon, the sort of which I had not for a very long time held, and ate the pie. It wasn't as sweet as the confections to which, in my father's house, I had grown accustomed, but it was well spiced. Upon eating it, I was transported to a time in which the whole of my world was confined to my sister, my mother, and this cabin. I ate, abandoning myself to the pie, forgetting even my sister until, tea in hand, she sat down in the chair across from me.

"Would you like some more?"

"No," I said, pushing the empty plate aside. "I wanted to talk to you again about getting you and your mother settled somewhere safe, where you can be more comfortable. I have your papers here. Have you given any thought to where you would like to go?"

"Our mother."

"Yes, our mother. Where is she, by the way?"

Lucille smiled, and as she smiled, her shadow, which had hereto-fore been mimicking her movements rather expertly, grew weary of the task. Peeling itself from the wall, it paced the length of the cabin before abandoning its post altogether so that, behind my sister, where once there had been shadow, there was now only light.

"I told you already," she said. "She's gone out to get some herbs."

"What sort of herbs?" I asked, glaring at the bright blank wall behind Lucille. A candle burned on the table, but the light came from Lucille herself. Everything about her was luminous. Especially her eyes, which were bright hazel, edging toward green, contrasting starkly with the black of her skin. I was reminded then of a paint-ing in my father's study, a seascape of a ship caught in the midst of a storm. The ship, stripped of its sails by strong winds, blends into the background and is barely distinguishable from the sky. The true subject of the painting is the water itself, the cold, vibrant serenity of the tempestuous waves. The subtle intensity of the palette, which verged on the supernatural—reds, oranges, and tinges of yellow ema-nating from the sun refracted in the otherworldly blue and white of the water—increased the dramatic tension between the sky, the sea, and the helpless ship trapped betwixt them. The point of view is above the level of the water yet lower than a passing ship, so that the onlooker, like the lone sailor in the painting's lower right quadrant, feels as if they might, too, succumb to a cruel, watery fate. Sitting there, across from my estranged sister, I felt as if I were that ship, and that those eyes, her eyes, had always been upon me, lighting my path, panning out over the wind-worn waves, guiding me to safe harbor.

"I don't know," Lucille said. "You think she tells me anything?"

"Right," I said, mulling over the fundamental nature of human existence—how brief and fleeting and profoundly wondrous the enterprise was. "Of course."

There was a knock upon the door.

Lucille stood up from the table, walked over to the door, and opened it, filling the room with a dark effluvium that crystallized into the form of a handsome figure in a black wide-brimmed hat as Lucille closed the door. His blackness was such that I half believed the figure was my sister's recently absconded shadow made flesh. His comeliness called to mind the visions that overtook Hawthorne's Young Goodman Brown in the wilderness. "The fiend in his own shape is less hideous than when he rages in the breast of man." Be this the true visage of the fiend, it is no wonder the Devil finds such willing purchase in man's breast.

"Is she here? Robert Reeves is asking after her."

"He hurting that bad?"

The shade, for I could not then call him a man, nodded. Lucille turned from him, took a chair from the table, stood atop it, and plucked from one of the hanging bundles of herbs a few stalks of wild lettuce. She cut the stalks lengthwise and squeezed the milky white sap from them into a cup. I perceived then, as if through a glass, darkly, bands of yellow light besiege my sister, binding themselves to her body, making of it a bright, brilliant chrysalis. I had fallen through a rift in the veil and had ended up in the liminal space between the physical world and the spiritual realm. The realm through which, though my mother and sister in their waking hours oft trafficked, the rest of us only enter via death or in dreams.

"Come back if you need a stronger brew."

"I will," the shade said as he took the cup from Lucille's outstretched hand. "But I don't imagine he'll hold out too much longer."

"Was that the Devil?" I asked after he took his leave.

"May as well be, for all he keeps up."

"'Come, Devil; for to thee is this world given.'"

"I think you might should lie down," she said.

Assenting, I stood and, with faltering steps, made my way to the pallet I'd not chanced to lie upon since my removal. I fell asleep and dreamed that Lillian, wearing the yellow dress my father used to make my mother don when he called upon her to perform for his sect, was seated on the bed beside me in my sister's stead. Framing her was a billowing black effluvium that sought not to intrude upon the yellow of her dress but rather to accentuate its splendor. I blinked, and she was gone. I blinked again, and standing there in Lillian's stead was my mother. She shone her eyes upon me, and as she proceeded to stroke my hair, I began to feel a deep and profound peace, such as I had not known since leaving my mother's side as a boy.

"You are sick of an illness to which your father has already succumbed," she said, cupping my chin in her hand. "But do not worry, my son. I will cure you of it."

"What about Lillian?" I asked. I did not then think to question the nature of the illness or what means of curing it she had devised; such was my faith in my mother. "Will you cure her, too?"

"I can make no promises."

"But you will try."

"Yes," my mother said begrudgingly. "I will try."

Despite the news of my father's ill-health, I was very much grateful that I and Lillian would be cured, and said as much. My mother, radiant now, with what I then countenanced as her generosity, stood and, though her eyes were glassy with tears, grinned and kissed the top of my head. She glided, as if on skates, past my sister and, before taking her leave, entreated her to take care of me, for us to take care of each other. I closed my eyes, feeling then as if the great clock of my life had unwound, as if every wrong had been set right. A feeling that was not to last.

Upon waking, I sat up, momentarily disoriented by both the absence of my mother and Lillian. There was only my sister, who sat staring at me fixedly. I recalled then how, in my early years, I had no sense of myself apart from her. So tightly bound were we that neither of us could lay claim to self-consciousness apart from the other. We thought and acted in accord with one another, seldom needing more than a glance to know each other's minds. When we played, it was never in games of competition, such as I have witnessed in other children. We ran through the woods and down to the creek alongside one another, but never raced. And though there were other children around, we never felt the need to seek their company. We were a society unto ourselves. Owing to this, my mother never bothered to distinguish us from one another, dressing us alike and referring to us by one name. Even now, memories flash before me which could only have belonged to her. Now, though she sat mere feet from me, the distance between us was unfathomable. The warm press of a tear rolled down my cheek. I had allowed my father to taint the memory of my sister, who never desisted in her fraternal feeling for me. I was much ashamed.

"Where has your shadow gone?" I asked, crying openly, for I was much affected by its absence.

Lucille stood up from the table and, as if she'd merely been waiting for a reason to do so, rushed to my side, and embraced me.

"It should have come back," I cried. "It needn't have left without you."

She said nothing but, in reply, cleaved to me so firmly that I could not breathe. The black effluviant substance that surrounded my mother in the dream had crossed into reality.

"Where is the smoke coming from?" I asked, standing.

"What smoke?" she said, coughing and, as it were, wiping away her own tears.

I stood, went over to the door, opened it, and saw smoke rolling over the tops of the trees.

"Stay here with me," she pleaded, grabbing my arm. "Please."

The heat of the flames was palpable from as far back as the last row of the slave quarters. So large and luminous was the blaze upon the horizon that it seemed as if the sun, while setting, had ignited the sky. As I stood in rapt astonishment, the visage transmuted itself, and for a moment, the flaming house looked as if it were on the verge of rising up into the night sky. Had I been a mystic, I would have taken the image for a sign occasioning the dawn of a new era. I could not have known then how right I was. As I drew nearer to the house, I observed a number of slaves engaged in using wooden buckets to draw water, but by then the fire was well past containment.

The red of Lillian's hair bobbed up and down as if she were the fire itself in miniature. She was held in place on the front steps by Maurice, and upon first glance, he appeared to shove her toward the flames. I quickened my pace, but as I approached, I saw that he was holding her back, preventing her from running in.

"Ana!" she cried. "Where's Ana?"

I cast my eyes again upon the fire. The house was well-nigh consumed. I couldn't imagine anyone making it out who hadn't already.

"Let me go!"

I know not whether it was the sight of Lillian's desperation, or the effects of the pie Lucille served me (I'm certain it was not on Ana's behalf, who at worst went out of her way to directly impede my aims and at best barely acknowledged me), but I, with no thought as to where exactly in the house she might be, ran into the fire.

I searched the kitchen first, wrongly presuming it the point of origin. Strangely, it had not yet burned. I ran up the servants' staircase and found the hallway completely black, but as I walked, the smoke and flames, with seeming purpose, made way for me, moving around me as I came upon Lillian's quarters. There was no sign of Ana and so I turned to leave. As I made my way back down the hall, exhaustion overtook me and I decided to lie down, just for a moment, on Lillian's chaise longue. Once I settled there, though, I did not have the strength to stand again. I searched for something to occupy my mind and found Lillian's journal on an end table. I tried to read it, tried once more, but the smoke from the fire and the brightness of the flames proved too much for my eyes and so, in the end, I held it to my chest and waited for the fire to consume me.

My mother traversed the immolating hallway. Her hair, which was always braided, had been let out. The wiry kinks framed her head in a black halo, and though her dress was aflame, she was unburned. I called out to her, but she, pretending not to hear me, continued down the hall. I called out again, but she did not answer. On the ceiling above me, the form of my half brother hovered just below the burgeoning flames, his likeness, the Sword of Damocles incarnate. Laughing, he descended, straddled me, fixing me in place. Some faraway part of me knew that this was only a hallucination, that I should marshal my forces and escape, but, though the desire for self-preservation was renewed, I could not raise my head or move any muscle my brother's ghost touched. I heard then a clatter of hooves, smelled jasmine, and saw, passing by at a canter, a hooded figure astride a pale horse. It was Death.

As I lay there cursing my brother and awaiting Death's return, I found on Lillian's side table the gold serpent brooch that once belonged to her mother. Desiring a token of hers to accompany me into the next life, I took up the brooch, pinned it to my shirt, and shoved the leather-bound journal into my waistband. After hearing footfalls, I turned to the door, expecting Death.

There, in the pale rider's stead, was a black shadow made substance. My brother, fearing the black man's approach, relented. I squinted up at the dark figure but could not perceive his face. The black of his hands reached down and attempted to heft me up. I resisted, thinking the fiend had come to drag me to hell. Though I now know that it was Franklin who rescued me from the fire, I could not then disentangle his visage from the Devilish specter my mind superimposed onto him. It was as if each physical entity and act carried with it a supernatural twin to which my eyes were more finely attuned. Even now, when I recollect the events of that fateful night, I see—as if cast in phantasmagoric shadows upon the wall of Plato's cave—a black-winged angel, wrestling me to the floor of Lillian's room, subduing me, dragging me into the hallway, out of what, in fantasy, seemed the kingdom of heaven, and into the hell of reality as such. Sometimes, when I sit by the water and consider my life as it was—my all too brief time with

Lillian, the relative luxury of my father's house—I hold up the memory of what was then against what it now is—the two-room hovel I share with Lucille—and cannot but see the truth of delirium's fiction. But I suppose it is better to reign in hell than to serve in heaven.

Once we were out on the lawn, my brother's form appeared again. He peeked out of the window in our room just before receding into the flame that burned its way down the whitewashed walls. I searched out Lillian. Neither she, nor Maurice, nor Ana was anywhere to be seen. I asked Franklin if he knew of what happened to Lillian. He said that the last he saw of her, Maurice was helping her and Ana into the buckboard. I asked where they were headed. He knew not. Though it must have been to her aunt Jessup's at the north end of the county. I began to lie back, for I was very tired, but, before I could, Franklin extended his hand and helped me to my feet.

"Why?" I asked as he pulled me upright. "Why save me?"

"On account of your momma."

We walked down to the shallowest part of the creek bed, crossed, and came to rest at a great sycamore tree, the likes of which I had not before seen. The light of the fire ignited the white underbelly of the leaves, and so bright was this visage that, at a glance, the tree seemed also to burn.

"We should leave. These trees might could catch," Lucille said upon approaching us at the creek's bank. She had in hand a tin bucket of cool, clean water from which she induced me to drink. The glow of the fire played strangely upon her face so that she was half in shadow, half in light. After I had my fill of the water, I handed the bucket to Franklin. He drank deeply before taking the bucket in his left hand and pouring the remainder of the water out onto his right arm. It had been singed. Black skin flaked off as he washed the wound. He'd burned himself rescuing me.

"You and Asa go on," Franklin said. "I'm going to go make sure everybody is squared away."

I tried to stand, but faltered. Lucille came to my side, propped me up by putting my arm around her shoulders, and helped me to stand. She held fast to me and did not let go until we reached the clearing south of my mother's cabin where the slaves buried their dead. There sat a congregation of women, children, and men who had tired of watching what later became known among them as "Freedom's Fire." It was only much later that the full weight of the losses I sustained that night—my home, my love, my mother, my father—bore down upon me. In some respects, my mother and father represented the two poles of my being, and, after losing them both, I was forever torn between them.

Often, I've lain awake wondering about that final interview. If my mother stormed into his office as he tossed his journals out of the window—for he, I learned later, though Maurice and Ana both had entreated him again and again to leave, decided his writings were of more import than his life—and recounted the litany of offenses he perpetrated against her as he, ignoring her words, ordered her to help him save his volumes from the flames. Or if they, knowing that there was nothing left on this side of life for either of them, forgave each other all, for—though the order of the world placed him above her—they had, for a brief while at least, loved one another as equals, embraced their fate, and met the fire together.

By then the wind had changed, and it was almost as if there had never been any smoke at all. The night air was chilly, but the graves were warm, as if heat were radiating up from the bodies buried below. As Lucille and I sat, I ran my hand over the ground and, in looking about, perceived a variegation of color—blues, reds, greens, and yellows—that seemed to emanate from the graves. I lay back and let the warmth pervade me, breathed in the wild jasmine, a scent I still associate with death, and gazed upon the stars. I couldn't remember the last time I'd lain in the grass and contemplated the night sky.

Lucille rested on her elbows in a pensive pose that would have been childlike were it not for the protrusion of her belly. Her hair was wrestled into two tightly woven braids that began just above her forehead and rolled over her small and delicate ears like a wave before joining at the base of her neck. Her eyes seemed to conceal some deeper truth, some secret of the universe far beyond my comprehension. Lucille jostled my shoulder and pointed up toward the night sky. I followed her finger first to Orion and then to Gemini. Using them, and drawing in more stars as needed, she sketched for me the image of a woman. As she worked, the image began to take on a life of its own, leaving the initial constellations upon which she drew to flit among others. The woman was running; no, she had taken flight. I touched my hand to my sister's distended belly. My sister placed her hand upon mine.

BOOK II

Sins of the Father

AFTER JESUS CAME to him, the Devil left the cave on top of Mount Sinai, where he was holed up, and went down to see what had become of the world in his absence. Once upon a time, he knew every living person by name; now there was just too many, and hardly any of them spoke the old languages. It didn't take long for him to see what all had gotten his brother so bent out of shape. Europe had turned her tribal conflicts global. Ain't nothing in this world been new since Cain killed Abel, the Devil thought as he watched the British, French, and Spanish, who were — and the Devil could tell this by looking — all cousins, war over land in America, Asia, and Africa.

He had a sense of how to put an end to what Europe was doing, but it wasn't until he happened upon a white boy by the name of John Newton, who was enslaved to a Sherbro woman in what would later become Sierra Leone, that he knew just which way he wanted to go about it.

"I been watching you," the Devil called to John as he was digging up some sweet potatoes. "That woman don't give you no kind of rest, do she."

"Yeah," John said, "she works me pretty hard."

"I bet you hate her."

"That's about the size of it, yeah."

"Seems to me these Africans is evil," the Devil said. "Kidnapping a poor English boy, making him work all day and night."

"Well," the boy said. "It was my own folks what took me. I got pressed into the naval service."

"And so the Africans stole you once your ship reached the shore?"

"Well, no. I tried to run away from the navy and they flogged me for it. After that, they sold me to the Africans."

"Still, though, seems like that woman could free you if she wanted. That's what you would do if you had slaves, ain't it? Christian boy like you."

"I would?"

"Yeah, you would. You got a good heart, John Newton, and God sees it. God sees it all. And He'd be ashamed to find one of His own carrying on that way. Owning slaves and such."

Each night, the Devil worked on John, trying as best he could to impart to him the evils of this slave trade. But by the time he got him to where he could almost see right, an agent of the boy's father had sent for him, and before the Devil knew it, John was on a ship bound for home.

"Must be nice," the Devil told John Newton once he'd caught up to him on a ship just off the coast of Ireland, "to have a father that would go to such lengths for his son."

"It is," John Newton allowed, though in his heart he still begrudged his father for taking so long to rescue him. "It's real nice."

"Yeah, I imagine it feels pretty good, being free."

"It do," John Newton said. "It really do."

The Devil grinned.

"I reckon now you'll be wanting to spread that feeling, right?"

"Of course I do. But you know, I been thinking on it, and I don't know if this is quite the right time to speak out against slavery. I don't think folks is ready to hear it."

"You were ready to hear it when you were enslaved."

"I was," John Newton said, toeing a line of rope at his feet. "But everybody ain't like me, and slavery's so fixed into how things is running now. It'd have to take something pretty powerful for folks to bend their ears to it."

"Like a sign from God."

"Exactly," John Newton said, eager to kick the can of abolition far enough down the road from him to make his fortune. "A sign from God would move folks to it."

At this the Devil leapt up off the ship and into the air. Now, John Newton had seen a great many things in his time at sea, but never a man leaping up into the air and sprouting wings. It was then that the West Wind, seeing the Devil up in the air and John Newton down on the bow of the ship, decided to test his strength and started to blow, filling the sails with his air and pushing the ship toward England. Then the East Wind, not wanting to be outdone by his brother, sucked in all the air he could and emptied his lungs in the direction of America. The clouds, who loved nothing so much as when the winds tried to outbox each other, darkened and gathered in tight and low over the ship. The waves, not wanting the clouds to have a better view than them, rose, and boy, if that boat didn't rock. John barely had time to grab hold of the rope before the ship crested a wave and the deck was awash in salt water. John looked around him. Above him was gray sky, broken only by the still-spreading bright black wings of the avenging angel; below him was troubled water. John closed his eyes tight, held fast to that rope, prayed, and kept on praying until the waters calmed and the boat stilled.

"That sign enough for you?" John Newton heard the Devil say. He opened his eyes, looking first to his left and then to his right, but he didn't see the Devil anywhere. John vowed then and there to devote himself to God, and thirty years after he made his fortune buying and selling Africans, he helped make abolition in England possible.

The Devil left John feeling so-so about where he stood. He'd planted a seed, but it was in shallow ground, and he didn't know whether it would take root and flourish. And so he rode the West Wind back to Africa, where, unbeknownst to himself, he'd find love.

Good Ground

REVEREND WALTER LAURENT
(1862–1961)
Son of Franklin and Lucille Laurent
Father of Louis Laurent

WHEN THE DEVIL came for Walter Laurent, Lucille and Franklin's only son, he found him in a ditch down the road from the juke. Earlier that morning, Walter had stumbled out of the makeshift bar and into the light of dawn with a terrible aching in his chest. He could breathe but could hardly walk, and so he sat himself down at the base of a sycamore tree to catch his air, not knowing yet that what bore down upon his chest was the weight of his sin. Years later, as Walter preaches to his congregation of the blind man who saw trees walking as men, he will picture himself lying under that sycamore and pity the two-and-twenty-year-old boozehound he used to be.

It was Franklin who gave Walter his first taste of liquor. "Take a sip of this, son," he'd said the night after Elijah returned to Talbert County. "It'll put some salt in you." Walter, twelve then, tipped the cup of white dog to his lips. It burned the back of his throat, but then, after the burning subsided, it cooled, curled into his belly, spread all throughout his limbs, numbed his workaday pains, tingled the tips of his toes, and blurred the rough-wood walls of the cabin into a soft amber-and-russet mosaic. Franklin held the jug out for Walter to take another sip, but before he could, Lucille knocked it out of his hand. Franklin laughed, stood up, walked around the mess of liquor and glass, and, slamming the door behind him, left.

After Walter was born, Franklin felt the light of Lucille's love dim. It was as natural for a mother to dote on a newborn as it was ridiculous for a man to begrudge the attention his wife paid his son, Franklin knew this, but, yet and still, he could not help but feel a pang of envy whenever Lucille held Walter to her breast. He hoped his jealousy would fade with time, but it only deepened as the boy grew older, and so rather than give voice or action to what he knew was senselessness, Franklin slipped off to the juke while his wife and his son, who, more often than not, spent the night curled next to his mother, leaving little to no room for Franklin, were fast asleep. It was at the juke that Franklin found himself in a card game across from Elijah, whom Franklin had not seen since he and Lucille jumped the broom behind her mother's cabin.

"I thought you'd left," Franklin said, shuffling the deck and seeing in the riffling cards the way Elijah had turned his head after he and Lucille were pronounced man and wife. Franklin and Elijah had never put words to what they did alone at night out in the woods, and up until the moment Elijah sat down and Franklin felt his blood rush, he hadn't realized what all it meant to him.

"I came back," Elijah said, not daring to meet Franklin's eye. After months of walking the back roads in and around the Mississippi plantation where they were born, neither Elijah nor his brothers, Isaac and Jacob, heard tell of their mother or the daughter she'd given birth to shortly before the brothers were sold to Laurent. Elijah's brothers, who had fonder memories of Mississippi than Tennessee, took over a tenancy from the son of the man who had sold them to Laurent. Elijah worked with them until one morning, while he was harnessing a mule, he decided he couldn't.

"I can't shake it," Walter overheard Elijah tell Franklin one night after he, hearing his father leave and then, a little later, seeing the lantern light in the barn, went out into the night to learn what men got up to while boys slept. "The feel of you. I just can't shake it." He'd later use Elijah's words in a sermon, an allegory for the awesome power of Christ's love, how it takes hold of you. Though he wouldn't remember where it was he'd first heard them.

Now Walter stood up from the base of the tree and, owing to the liquor as much as to the pain, tripped and fell over into a ditch. He lay there for a while, thinking this moment was going to be his last, just knowing he'd never marry, never have his own piece of land or see the way the grassy plains stretched out under an Oklahoma sky, a sky his father had—in a letter dictated to his and Elijah's nearest neighbor's oldest daughter—invited him to come live and work under. "Here," the letter had said, "away from the eyes of white folks, a man may be a man and do just as he pleases."

Before Franklin and Elijah lit out for Indian Territory, Franklin and Lucille had made a home for Walter among the former slave quarters of the Laurent Plantation. All the land from their cabin to down past the burned-out foundation of the big house was owned by Walter's white-passing uncle, Asa. No one ever told Walter about slavery or how his uncle came to own land, but there were enough sideways comments from Franklin, who couldn't stand white people and barely tolerated Asa's company, for him to put the pieces together. After Franklin left, Walter began to sneak sips from the jug of moonshine Franklin had hidden in the woodshed behind their cabin.

Lucille tried everything she could to curb her son's thirst for liquor. Walter avoided her whenever she set her mind to fixing him, but on the day before the Devil found him, Walter was too liquor-sick to stop Lucille from boiling a bucket of river water with jimsonweed, pulling a stool up to his bed, and forcing him to drink until he sated whatever it was that made him so goddamned thirsty. The river water had worked well enough for Walter to go a whole twelve hours before slipping uptown and getting drunk again.

"It's a shame," the Devil said when he happened upon Walter in that ditch. "A crying shame to see a man so deep into a bottle that he can't stand up straight."

Walter reached his hand out to the Devil. The Devil looked down his nose at the outstretched hand.

"You sure you want my help?" the Devil said, leaning back on his heels. "You look to be mighty comfortable down there."

"I want to get up," Walter said, "but I got this here pain in my chest that just won't let me."

The Devil stepped down into the ditch, toed Walter's side with his boot, and ordered him to stand.

When the boot hit Walter's rib, the weight lifted and the pain went away. Later, while he preached of the woman who knew that if she could just touch the hem of his garment, she would be made whole, it was not Jesus's pearly white robe Walter pictured but the black sole of the Devil's boot.

"Follow me," the Devil said.

Walter rose.

And so Walter and the Devil walked, and as they walked, Walter saw other people, men and women, Black and white, walking, too, only nobody was going the same way as them, and the longer they walked, the fewer people there were. Walter watched the back of the Devil's head, the wide black brim of his hat, until the sun rose up into it, and they kept on walking until the heat of it licked at the back of Walter's sweat-drenched neck. By then, the soreness of his legs was as painful as the aching in his chest. But he did not flag and, for the whole of that day, matched the Devil's pace.

When they stopped, the Devil took his hat off his head and turned to Walter.

"I seen that weight bearing down on you from a mile off and knew I was the only one who could lift it. Would you allow me to lift it?"

Seeing that they'd come to the Big Hatchie, the long, wide river, Walter remembered how, when he was a boy, Lucille had almost drowned him. She'd taken him there intending to teach him her mother's ways, but before she could tell him the story of the woman and the river, the one in the many, she saw what she thought was a white man watching them from behind a stand of trees on the other bank, and so the part of Lucille that was her mother, who had been forced into slavery on the bank of a river, held Walter under the water to conceal him. Even though Walter was just a boy, he was old enough to know when his mother wasn't his mother anymore. He wasn't strong enough to get away from her. By then the sun was low, and in the instant it took for the ghost of Lucille's mother to grab hold of Walter's shoulders and force him under the water, its reflection blazed bright in her eyes.

Years later, when Walter preached to his congregation of the fire next time, he saw not the seven-headed serpent or the brimstone that, on the day of reckoning, would surely rain down, but the killing sun in his mother's eyes. By the time his uncle Asa, the man whom Lucille had glimpsed in the woods, waded out and wrestled Walter away from her, the sun had already ignited the line of treetops separating the earth from the sky, and his lungs had nearly filled with water.

"I would," Walter told the Devil. "I can't carry it no longer."

"Then kneel," the Devil commanded.

Walter knelt.

The Devil rolled up his sleeves, put one hand on Walter's forehead and the other behind his head at the base of his neck, sending warm chills down Walter's spine. The Devil's hands smelled sweeter than the fields of sorghum his father and Elijah planted after working as farmhands for a Creek freedman nicknamed Bolo, on account of his penchant for the tie, and saving enough money to buy the abutting hectare of land.

"What do you know of the Father and His begotten Son?" the Devil asked.

Franklin had warned Walter of religion, of how it took hold of the mind to enslave the body. "I just shook one master," Walter heard his father tell a traveling preacher. "I ain't in the market for another." Then, Walter had no reason to go against his father, but after Franklin left, and his uncle, Asa, taught him to read using the Bible, the only book he could find, Walter questioned his father's wisdom. If there was a man in a white robe somewhere up there, odds were he didn't give a damn about what happened to him and his, but at the same time, Walter knew there had to be more to the world than what you could put your hands to. Sometimes, when he was out alone in the woods or by the creek that separated their land from the land his uncle leased to sharecroppers, he would get this feeling, and this feeling would let him know there was a rightness to things. A rightness you didn't have to see to know, because it was working all in and through you. But he couldn't stay out in the woods forever. He'd have to go to Wilkins's store for Uncle Asa—who, after walking into the store, seeing the redheaded stock boy who was his son, and turning pale, walked back out and sent Walter to buy his sundries for him—and collect and dry herbs for his mother. He'd have to give way to white folks with a simpering hat tip. At some point, someone would hand him a bottle. And at some point, he'd see the sky through the lens of its bottom.

The Devil read what all was written on Walter's heart and said: "You got more in you than what can be drunk out of a bottle. I'm here to tell you that the begotten Son has called you to lead."

"I'm no leader," Walter told the Devil.

"You got three witnesses what can testify different. The first is the blood, what the Son gave of his own free will so the world might be saved; the second is the water what got laid out by the Father in the beginning; and the last is the fire the Holy Ghost let loose so that the spirit of the Lord would burn like a torch in man. Do you deny those witnesses?"

Walter did. He couldn't even stop himself from drinking, even after what happened with Cora. Cora's folks sharecropped for his uncle, and Walter had been sweet on her since before he knew how good it felt to crawl into a bottle. But when Cora told him her blood hadn't come and all but begged Walter to make her honest, he denied her. He wasn't fit to be a husband let alone a father.

"There's them that leads because they want power," the Devil said, "and them that leads because they're called to it. I'm calling you to it. Do you deny my call?"

Walter nodded, and when he nodded, the pain in his chest tightened.

The Devil took his hand off Walter's head and stepped back. Walter touched the spot on his head where the Devil's hand had been and felt blood. He lifted up his hands, and blood flowed out of them. He stood up. Blood was everywhere around him.

The Devil shook his head, turned his back, and started walking toward the water. Walter stood and tried to follow, but his feet wouldn't stay under him. He stumbled, then crawled, and ended up splashing around in the water, but to his amazement, the Devil was still walking. He tried to swim back to shore, but the current was too strong. It was like a hand had reached out from the water and was trying to pull him under. He swam and he swam, but no matter how hard he kicked, he couldn't get no closer to shore. The Devil was standing on the other side of the river with his hat cocked low, dry as a bone.

"Ain't no salvation for them that denies the Son's call."

"Please," Walter begged, barely treading water. "I ain't fit for it. It ain't for me to be called."

The Devil watched as the current pulled at Walter like it wanted to swallow him. It was all he could do to stay in one place and keep his head above it. Later, after his son Louis came home from the war renouncing the Word, telling Walter he didn't want no parts of his God, Walter would know his son had gotten his hard-heartedness from him. Walter knew just what the Devil wanted him to say, but he couldn't do it. He couldn't find it in himself to make that kind of promise. He turned away from the Devil, gathered all the strength he had left in him, and started swimming back toward the other shore. He kicked and he kicked, but try as he might, he couldn't make no progress. At the time, he felt as if he were a fly caught in a spider's web, but later, when he preached this story to his congregation, he told them the feeling was akin to being bound to a cross. He looked to the sky. All the color had gone out of it, and the brightness that was once above his head was now down in the water with him. The river was no longer flowing. All Creation had come to a standstill and Walter was wading waist-deep in a lake of fire.

Over on the shore, Walter saw the Devil sitting up on a throne, using Lucille's arched back as a footstool. It was then that Walter finally realized who and what he was reckoning with. He looked to his mother, but his mother had on her face the faraway look she wore when she was doing her "work" and wouldn't meet his eyes. Farther up the shore, he saw Franklin and Elijah, now old men, walking hand in hand. Walter called out to his father, but his father did not answer. He looked to the other shore. On it, Walter saw his generations, men with his mother's eyes, women with his father's face, children who looked upon darkness and saw light within it. Beside them was a man who looked identical to the Devil, wearing a white robe. The man nodded to Walter, reached up into the slate-gray sky, and pulled down a horn. The white-robed man was Gabriel, and if Walter didn't relent, didn't give himself over to right, Gabriel was going to put his lips to that horn and blow down all Creation. Walter knew then that arms were just too short to box with God.

"Jesus," Walter cried out. "Jesus!" And when he called the name of the Lord, the fire died down, the waters calmed, and he was able to swim to shore.

He was no longer on the Hatchie, but rather on the bank of the creek no more than an evening's stroll from his mother's cabin. Walter removed his boots, which had soaked through to his socks, set them down on the bank beside him to dry, rolled up his sleeves, raised his arms to the sky, and stood in the warmth of the evening sun. The pain in his chest returned and would continue to plague him until the Devil visited him on his deathbed seventy-odd years later, but in that moment he rejoiced, for his steps had been ordered and his feet set on solid ground.

What Fire Won't Burn

ELBERT "BUBBA" LAURENT
(1862–1945)
Son of Asa Laurent

I'M NOT ONE to whine and fuss over what the War between the States cost us. I don't harp on what's owed, what all was lost. What I do is come home from Mr. Wilkins's store, wash up for dinner with Momma, and eat whatever it is Ana has managed to scrape together, knowing there's many a man laying his head down at night hungry. But when I catch sight of that candlelight flickering out in the barn, my stomach gets tight. The food goes bland in my mouth. I want to get up from the table and throw open the back door, running. Instead, I muddle through dinner, pass on dessert, and wait for Momma to fall asleep before letting Myra Mullins wild me to where I can't tell dawn from dusk. It's an achy-sweet kind of burning, Myra's touch. I know it ain't right, but I just can't deny myself her loving.

Come morning, I watch the sunlight tease out everything the night hid away. Time was, Myra would be down the ladder and halfway home before my eyes could find what all my hands had felt. I brush a copper lock out of her face and know from the way her eyelids flutter that she's dreaming up church bells and the lie of a white dress. I shake

110

her awake, already feeling the twin barrels of the shotgun Buck Mullins will shove between my shoulder blades if Myra gets herself caught up here with me like she's been angling to.

"Get up," I tell her. Myra slits those unearthly green eyes at the bright fall sky peeking in through the rotted rafters. She blinks and then frowns at me like she don't know my face. I shake her again. When she sits up, the warm spot she made on my chest cools.

"Bubba Laurent," she says, real coy. "How long do I have to wait for you to make an honest woman out of me?"

Myra has her sights set on a shotgun wedding, and if it comes to that, Buck won't wait for me to say "I do" or "I don't" before he pulls the trigger. There's always been bad blood between the Mullinses and the Talberts—my mother's people. I'm a Laurent, but everyone has always lumped me in with the Talberts because they don't know my father's folks. Jean Laurent, the man whose name is on my birth certificate, died in a fire before I was born. But my having Laurent as a last name never stopped Buck from thumbing his nose at me when he comes into the store, no matter how cordial I try to be.

"You know your daddy would never have me," I tell Myra.

"What if it's not up to him?"

"There's not a judge that would marry us without his say-so," I remind her. "Besides, him and Jeff Morris already got the china picked out. I saw the order in with Jeff's violet water on Wilkins's books just the other day."

Myra scrunches her face in disgust. "I can't stand that violet water. It gets all over everything."

"I thought you liked it."

"Well, I don't. I want a man to smell like a man."

"What's a man smell like?"

"You."

The first time I brought Myra up here, she spent the whole night staring at the stars, dividing the constellations between us: Libra for her, Orion for me, Gemini we could split. Before she passed, Myra's mother taught her to map the stars. Said a woman should know exactly what all hangs over her head.

"What if one day you and me just up and left?" she asks, taking my right hand and holding it between both of hers. I try not to think of how nice it would be to have her do this in our own house, in our own bed.

"You know I can't."

"Why not?"

"I can't leave Momma."

Myra sighs, sits all the way up, and pats around the hay for her underclothes. I pull her dress down off the railing and hand it to her just for the pleasure of watching her slip into it. Once she has it on, she works her fingers over her hair, brushing all the hay and dust into the sunlight's mottled rays. As I watch her, I can't help but hope that, with my buying a stake in Wilkins's store, Buck will have a harder time denying me Myra's hand.

Myra started being sweet on me a few years after I finished school. The plan was for me to go to college up north, but once Momma finally let me take a look at our finances, it was clear that there wasn't money enough for me to go anywhere, so I stayed on with Mr. Wilkins instead.

It was there that I first saw Myra. She'd come by with her friends wanting nothing more than to peep in on me.

"She's cute," Mr. Wilkins had said.

"She's young," I countered.

Mr. Wilkins laughed. "I used to say the same thing about Sarah when her mother started asking me around to tea, and now she's older than I am."

I shook my head and went back to filling a bag of cornmeal for Mrs. Leeks.

"Listen, son. You're not half as old as you think you are. That girl likes you and looks good. Those few years y'all got between you don't mean nothing."

I put Wilkins's words out of my mind and didn't give them a second thought until that traveling show came to town. I'm not partic-
ularly fond of traveling shows, but that day Momma and Aunt Ana
were bickering over some old foolishness neither of them wanted to
give voice to, so I went to the show to get out of the house. In one of
the tents, there was a mulatta with a yellow scarf on her head playing
the part of the gypsy, charging a penny a fortune. I handed my money
over, not thinking much of it, and let her turn cards for me.

"Ten of Pentacles," she said, flipping the first one. "It means
wealth."

"That must be the past," I muttered.

"No," she said, meeting my eyes in a way that not even Aunt Ana
dares to. "This is a coming thing."

She flipped another card. "The Knight of Cups," she said. "You
should follow your heart wherever it leads you."

I nodded, wondering what on earth had compelled me to waste
my money. Behind the fortune teller, someone outside the tent walked
up and stopped. I could tell it was a woman from the silhouette, but I
didn't know it was Myra until I stepped outside.

The fortune teller turned over the last card. On it, there were two
wolves standing by a river, staring up at the moon. She narrowed her
eyes and glanced from me to the card and back again.

"What's that one mean?" I asked.

"That you're hiding from yourself."

Something in me shivered. "How do you hide from yourself?"

The woman shrugged, picked up the cards, and started reshuffling
the deck.

When I stepped outside, Myra and her friends were there, standing around. Myra had on a blue-black skirt, and her hair was curled
and pinned up. I reached into my pocket and pulled out a penny.

"On me," I said, holding out the coin, but she took my hand instead.

"You don't want to get your fortune told?" I asked. Myra's hands,
then and now, are hotter than they have any right to be.

"I'd rather share yours," she said.

Her friends laughed, but Myra was serious. Still is. I tried to pull my hand out of hers, but there wasn't any give. Behind her, at the center of the circle of tents, a long-haired man on stilts, who wore a top hat and red-and-black-striped coattails, spit fire out into the air. The blaze of it flew up behind Myra.

"How old are you?" I asked.

"Sixteen," she said.

"Sixteen when?"

"Next June."

I yanked my hand from hers. She laughed.

"Go on somewhere," I said. "Go on before somebody says something to your daddy that gets me shot."

She smirked, turned on a heel, and walked her pretty little self on away from me. Myra's walk, out of step with the skipping stride of her peers, was sure, long, and slow. Her hips rocked from side to side, allowing the pleated hem of her dress all the time it wanted to sweep away at her ankles. When she and her friends stopped at the concessions to buy fry bread, she looked back, grinning with the knowledge of all her walk awoke in me. The fire blower spit again, backlighting Myra's grin. I've known since then just which way my stars are ordered.

Used to be I'd sneak back into the house by climbing up the trellis, easing open the window, and crawling to my bedroom just to muss up the sheets before making my way to the kitchen for breakfast. But I gave that up the morning Ana told me she was tired of trying to wash the barnyard smell out of my clothes. "You grown now," she said. "Act like it." The smell couldn't have been half as bad as she made it out to be. The barn hasn't housed any animals since the Confederate Army commandeered every ungulate they could wrangle. The receipts, which lay preserved in the top drawer of Momma's bureau, attest to the fact that before the Talbert Rifles set off, there was at least a head of cattle out to pasture and a dozen horses in that barn.

Ana swears that the ghosts of those same horses whinny when the moon is full. But I can't see why any horse, dead or alive, would bother coming all the way back here from Shiloh. If Myra hadn't claimed to hear them, too, I'd have thought Ana was funning me about how I spent my nights out there. Now the pasture is overgrown, the fields have gone to seed, and me and Myra are the only living things giving the barn any kind of use.

The next day, as I make my way back, I see Ana in the yard, bent double, playing at the line of azaleas fronting the house. I hang my head a little when she stands to greet me. If the loan doesn't come through, I don't know how much longer we'll be able to keep her on. Momma said she wanted to be the one to tell her, but I know from the way Ana smiles that she's yet to broach it. It's only fair to let her know the situation far enough in advance for her to ask around and find a new position.

"Let me go," she says, laughing. "Let me go where, Bubba?"

"It's not for certain," I say. "But if things keep on the way they have been, we won't be able to afford you."

"Afford me?" she says, throwing her shears down into the fresh-dug flower bed. "You think your momma's paying me to stay here?"

"If it comes to it, we'll give you a good reference. In the meantime, do you have any people you want me to write to? Anybody you might want to visit with if we can't place you right away?"

"No," she says, bending down to pick up her shears. "I don't have no people outside of you."

I find Momma at the kitchen table, messing over a bowl of oatmeal. She's got on a faded blue dress, her favorite, and is holding the paper out at arm's length, away from her face. Momma's farsighted and can't see anything closer than her outstretched hand. She sets the paper down when I come into the kitchen.

"You look well rested," she says.

Momma hates Buck Mullins just as much as he hates me. She's delighted that I'm keeping his last daughter from marrying respectably, though she's hinted more than once that it's past time for me to find someone of our ilk to marry. What she thinks our ilk is, I don't know.

"Don't start with me today, Momma."

"Just making an observation is all."

At my place setting, Ana's set out rye toast, eggs, and a cup of coffee already sugared and creamed the way I like it. As I sit down to eat, she passes by the kitchen window.

"Momma, Ana says she's not being paid."

"Ana's a liar. Always has been. I give her money every other week."

"That's for groceries, Momma. She turns around and gives that money right back to me to bring back from Wilkins what all you and I need to eat."

"Oh. Well. She should budget better. You know her kind aren't known for being good with money. You can give her some money out of your loan if it'll make you feel better. Though I honestly can't imagine what she'd spend it on."

"I been meaning to talk to you about that. I spoke with Mr. Wilkins about how he got his loan, and he says the only way I can get a manageable rate is to put down collateral."

"Robin Wilkins isn't a Talbert. Without Talbert money, there would be no bank."

"You can't get a loan on just your name anymore."

"I'm not selling any land."

"It'll come out all right," I say. "We'll just put that branch out by the creek down. Nobody's ever done anything with it, anyway."

"If your grandfather hadn't have sold so much land, we'd still own this whole town."

"Momma, if he hadn't sold it, there wouldn't be no town. Besides, they just hold the deed until I can pay the money back. They can't develop it or anything like that."

"And what if you can't pay it back?"

I take a sip of my coffee. It burns my tongue, but I keep drinking. Momma knows Wilkins is barely turning a profit and isn't keeping pace with folks' needs. He has a catalogue people can order from, but it takes weeks to ship, and by then people could have gone to Memphis or Jackson to get what they needed. He's still running a country store, and, more and more, Talbert's becoming a town. With just a few changes, I could make it pay, but Wilkins won't let me implement any of them until I buy in.

"I promise I'll pay it all back before anybody at the bank thinks to look at that land."

"I'm sorry, Bubba. I just don't like it, I really don't."

"We've got to do something, Momma. We can't just sit here twiddling our thumbs."

"Then you can put on a tie, march down to that bank, and tell Nelson Roberts just how much money you want."

"Nelson Roberts is dead, Momma."

"What? Since when?"

"At least ten years."

"Well then, who are you meeting with?"

"Frank Hotchkins."

"Hotchkins?" she yells, clanging her spoon into the empty bowl. "I've never in my life heard of any Hotchkins. Where did they come from?"

"I don't know the man's history. I just know he runs the bank."

"Nothing in this town's been right since those filthy soldiers marched on us. Pulled up all my aunt Jessup's pretty flowers and paraded themselves down Main Street after burning my daddy's house down — with *your* father in it."

This is another one of her lies. The Talbert family used to have a plantation over in what's now called Laurent, but it burned down well before Union soldiers set foot in Talbert.

"Momma. None of that has anything to do with who's running the bank."

"Yes, it does," she hollers. "I know. *I* was there."

I stand up from the table, knowing better than to waste my morning trying to argue with her.

"And I'll tell you another thing," she calls after me. "Putting up land for money is common."

I reach the washroom managing, barely, to refrain from yelling back that, despite the fact that we're surrounded by acres and acres of arable land we can't afford to cultivate, we *are* common. Instead, I wash up, put on my good black tie, and head to my meeting.

"You're late," Mr. Wilkins calls out as soon as I walk through the door. "You're never late."

"I'm not late today, either, Mr. Wilkins." I take my tie off and put it on the shelf behind the counter. "I had my meeting over at the bank today, remember?"

"I remember," he says, although it's clear from the way he squinches his brow that he doesn't. "How'd it go?"

"They won't lend me anything without collateral."

"I was worried that might be the case. You can't talk her into putting up a parcel?"

I shake my head.

"I'm sorry to hear that, Bubba. I'll hold off on selling as long as I can."

"I'll figure something out, Mr. Wilkins."

"I know you will."

We're almost out of tobacco and coffee, which are just about the only two things we can count on selling every day, so I come out from behind the counter to restock them.

"Hold off awhile. We got a delivery needs to go out."

"Where to?"

"Address over in Laurent."

"We deliver out that way?"

"We deliver to them that pays us to."

"All right," I say, though I don't much feel like running all the way out to the edge of the county for a delivery.

"Ginny's watered and the wagon's loaded," Mr. Wilkins says, reading my face. "All you have to do is drive her."

I step out the back of the store and into the shade of the alley. Ginny glances off the side of the building, no doubt hoping that if she doesn't meet my eye, then I won't drive her out into the sun. She knows it's the wrong time of day to be making deliveries, especially as far out as Laurent. "Isn't that right, girl?" I say, scratching Ginny between the ears. She still won't acknowledge me. Instead, she hangs her head like she's just dropped something down a deep well.

I climb into the seat, take up the reins, and ease Ginny out of the alley and into the square. Skip Bragg tips his hat to me from out front of Milner's Hardware. I tip mine back.

Once we clear town, I work Ginny up into a nice, even clip. She keeps it up for as long as we're on the paved road but slows a bit once we turn off onto the packed dirt trail the Negroes have taken to calling Lucille's Lane. Only Negroes live out this way, and I pass more than a few of them heading into town on foot. They know to make way for Ginny and Mr. Wilkins's wagon.

The only white man on the side of the road is under the shade of a sycamore. He's modishly dressed: brown suit, good leather shoes, and a well-made straw hat. He waves his hand for me to stop, but I keep going. I let folks ride every once in a while. Today, I'm in no mood for company.

The directions are for the last house before the trail dead-ends. I pull over in front of a large white house with a wraparound porch and forest-green door. There's a large pecan tree to the right of the house and a smattering of peach trees out back just before the yard gives way to brush. To the left is a small garden full of what must be a late planting of sweet potatoes. Behind them are clotheslines where an older Negro woman hangs pure white sheets out to dry. She sees me and hollers something I can't hear to someone I can't see and walks around back. The front door swings open and out comes a man that, if I didn't know any better, I would have sworn was white. But as he approaches, it occurs to me that he could be Indian. They've been known to take up with Negroes now and again. He just stands there, shading his eyes from the sun and staring.

"You all wanting a delivery?" I call out.

For a moment, I think he might be hard of hearing. I fix my mouth to call out again but stop once he starts back to walking. He comes up alongside the wagon. He appears to be in his fifties but could be older. You never can tell with niggers and Indians.

"Are you Lillian's son?" he asks.

"I might be."

"You are. You and her got the same eyes."

I know from him asking about Momma that he must be white, though I can't imagine what association she might have with a man who lives all the way out here.

"Load's in back," I tell him. "You got anybody young around to help you carry it?"

"Got a nephew around here somewhere," the man says. "But Lord knows where he's gotten off to."

"All right," I say, climbing down and walking around back of the wagon. The man follows close behind me, and I'm surprised to find that he smells like lavender. As I hand him two sacks of feed, I look him over. He's taller than I thought he was, almost my height, broad-chested, with something golden and feral in his stare, lynxlike. He takes a sack in each hand and then, after eyeing my face past the point of discomfiture, worries the dry dust of the driveway by dragging the bags behind him up to the porch.

"If those bags bust," I say under my breath, "I'm not coming back to replace them."

Once he gets halfway to the house, I heft the crate full of sugar, cornmeal, salt, and flour up from the wagon. He sets it down beside the sacks of feed, out of breath. I guess this is what passes for a day's hard work for men who perfume themselves.

"How's your mother getting along?"

"She's all right, so long as her hands are occupied."

"That's good to hear. Real good," he says, grinning—I don't know what for. "Wilkins treating you right?"

"Is there anything more you need, mister? I got to get back to town."

"No," he says, studying my face. "Give me a minute and I'll get you your money."

He goes into the house. A few Negroes come from the direction of the brush with water buckets. They look over at Wilkins's wagon as they pass, no doubt wondering what it's doing all the way out here. In that thought, they're not alone. The man returns with the cash folded tight and an old leather-bound book.

"This here is for Mr. Wilkins," the man says, handing me two dollars. "And this last bit here is for your trouble." It's a crisp five-dollar bill.

"Thank you, mister."

"No," he says. "Thank you."

I turn to leave, knowing already how I want to spend it. A place down in Lakeland sells these chocolate bonbons Myra can't get enough of. I'm so distracted thinking on how grateful she'll be, I don't even notice the man following me back to the wagon until I climb in. I turn to him. He's clutching the leather-bound book in both hands.

He casts his eyes down at his feet the same way Negroes do when they want a favor from you. "I don't mean to trouble you any further," he says, "but I'd really appreciate it if this found its way to your mother."

121

"What is it?"

"A journal."

I take it from his outstretched hands. The leather is well-worn and smells faintly of woodsmoke. I fan the pages. The entries are in my mother's hand.

"How did you get this?"

There's something familiar about him, the way he holds his face.

"I can't say."

I close the journal, set it down beside me, and drive away. I don't want to give him the satisfaction of having me ask what all he might have been to my mother.

On the way back, I see the same man from earlier, the one with the straw hat, walking toward town. I make up my mind to stop and offer him a ride. My hope is that pleasant conversation with a stranger will keep my mind off the Laurent man and whatever his connection to Momma is. I slow Ginny and pull over to the side of the road to let the man up.

He climbs onto the bench, and as he does, Ginny turns and eyes me like she can't figure out what the hell I'm thinking, a sentiment I share once the fellow starts to jawing.

"Glory coming," he says, more to Ginny than to me. "Glory coming, and none of these here houses is in order."

"Mm-hmm," I offer, and when I do, he whips around to face me like I cussed him.

"There's a storm brewing for you up in paradise, liable to touch down any day now," he says. "And when it arrives, it's going to pick you up and whirl you all the way around. Jesus says that when the end-times come, the first shall be last and the last shall be first. And I'm here to let you know — for you, that end-time is now."

"You threatening me?"

"No, sir! I'm just a humble messenger, and the message I seen was writ in the dust you kicked up earlier, when this here wagon come through. And the terror of it lay in how your world is about to be upended. The Lord is about to come down off his throne on high and move you!"

"Move me?"

"Yes, sir!"

I turn to the man and see my mistake. He's not a white man at all, but rather a light-skinned, straight-of-hair Negro preacher.

"Let me guess. If I make a nice donation to your church's building fund, you'll see to it that the Lord sets me down someplace soft."

"A donation would be very much appreciated," he says, grinning like the tomcat who cornered the chicken. "But can't no man mitigate what all the Lord is about to bring down on your head, Bubba Laurent."

I ease up on Ginny's reins and slow her to a dead stop.

"I reckon you can make it on foot from here," I tell the preacher.

The store is closed when I return. A note from Addie, Wilkins's house girl, tells me that Mr. Wilkins had one of his spells and is at home resting. I restock the tobacco before unlocking the front door, settling into the chair behind the counter and putting the money from the delivery into the register. Wilkins hasn't made a sale all morning.

I don't foresee having any customers until the end of the lunch hour, so I sit behind the counter pretending I'm not anxious to know what all is in that old journal. That man could have found any number of ways to get this thing to Momma. But for some reason, he wants me to be the one to hand it to her. I can't shake the feeling that there's something in it I need to see, so I pick it up.

The earliest entries are from her girlhood. All of them predate the war. I skim until she mentions Jean Laurent, the man she claims is my father. She writes of their engagement, arranged by her father, and their marriage, which was loveless, owing to their difference in age, culture, and temperament. Jean was Creole, reared on a bayou plantation just north of New Orleans, and from all appearances disdainful of West Tennessee culture in general and my mother in particular.

> This is the third one. Ana screamed when the bathwater turned pink. One more, I thought after the second. One more and I'll be overcome. But I wasn't. I just sat there, watching the bath blood bloom little red flowers. It should have been a hard thing, but it wasn't. Jean brought in Dr. Bower to examine me. He said that I'm all right physically but prescribed some laudanum for my nervous temperament. I'm to take a quarter teaspoon before breakfast, and one again before going to bed. I find that I like it very much.

Another read:

> We named him Lucius. The doctor doubts he'll live very long but Jean says he has the look of a fighter about him, and I'm inclined to agree. He doesn't cry out like Ana and Maurice did as children but rather scrunches his nose up and gives a sort of sniffling murmur when he wants the breast. It's almost a coo. I'm told I'm the only one who can hear it, which is just as well because I'm the only one who needs to. Jean has been taking to the woods again. Séances, he said, are best conducted at the witching hour. He thinks I believe him.

"Excuse me, Mr. Laurent." I look up to find a young Negress at the counter. I lower my eyes. "I'd like to buy some liniment."

"Negroes order around back."

"I waited there, Mr. Laurent," she says. "I pulled and pulled, but that bell didn't make no sound."

"Pull it harder next time."

"Yes, sir."

"You have a list."

"Yes, sir."

"Leave it on the counter. I'll bring what you need around back."

"Yes, sir. Thank you, sir."

She wants a nickel's worth of flour, sugar, some thread, and a plug of tobacco to go with the liniment. I gather it in a sack and bring it out back to her. After she disappears around the corner, I pull the length of twine hanging from the bell. No sound. Someone has snipped the clapper.

I make a point of closing late every day to prove to Mr. Wilkins just how far I'll go to help him turn a profit. The day leaves me feeling funny, though, so I close at six and walk home.

Ana has cooked salt pork with corn bread and greens for dinner. Momma wants ice cream for dessert, but we're all out of rock salt, so the ice melts before Ana can get it churned good. Me and Ana sit at the table sipping cold sweet cream with no complaints, but Momma is sullen. Her mood sours the after-supper talk. I study her face as she sulks. The man was right about me having her eyes.

I lie down in my room, thinking I'll have a nice nap before going off to meet Myra, but Momma's journal won't let me, so I return to it. She talks a good deal about the old days, but when it comes to my father, she's silent. According to Momma, when my parents' house burned down, she was living here, at her great-uncle's house, not with her husband. She says it was to help take care of Uncle Elbert, who was on his deathbed. But apparently there's a lot more to the story.

He won't meet my eye, hasn't called me mother once. You'd think he'd be grateful. Jean says for me to be patient, that the boy can't yet know what all he's been given, but I'm not certain he can be broken. He's determined to maintain his heathen ways. Just the other day, the floor of his room was covered in salt, and when I checked under his bed to make sure there were no more stores of it, I found a sewn pouch of burlap that stunk of God knows what. One look at it, one look, was enough to tell me it was HER doing. Straightaway, I flew out the back door, past the quarters, down to the creek, and on further to Her cabin. Upon my approach, I heard the softest murmuring cry. I saw through the window of the cabin and found the other child, the girl, sobbing in the corner alone. I listened. I would have sworn that it was Lucius, were he still alive.

I close the journal with more questions than answers. On paper I'm a Laurent, but everyone around town considers me a Talbert, because, for whatever reason, they don't believe Jean Laurent is my natural father, and that my mother has reason to be ashamed of whoever is.

I find Myra sprawled in the hay, twirling her hair between her fingers with one knee pointing up at the purple-tinted sky. The sight of her laid out like this would have inspired a masterpiece.

I lie down and try to pull her into my arms, but she pushes me away.

"I don't mean to sleep in this barn every night for the rest of my life. I want to sleep in my own house, in my own bed, next to my own husband."

"You know I can't be that for you," I tell her. "Not right now, at least."

"Then maybe I should go out and find somebody who can."

My throat catches. "Nobody's stopping you from doing what you need to do."

I take her hand in mine, and she lets me. I kiss her, and she lets me. I pull her hand across my chest, where it belongs. We lie in the coming dark, watching one another breathe and fall asleep under the stars, like we always do. Only this time, when I wake up in the morning, I'm all alone.

* * *

I beat Mr. Wilkins to the store and open up on my own. After about an hour, Addie drops by to let me know he's not feeling well. I send word that I can manage. The place pretty much runs itself so long as there's somebody to take money and restock. Francine Whitman comes in around about noon, wanting to know if we can take on some of her eggs. I tell her I'll have to check with Wilkins first, but like as not it'll be fine. Things pick up after lunch, and for a while, it's rough going. I hardly have time to fill one order before somebody comes in wanting a plug of tobacco, coffee, or a hunk of cheese, and for the first time in a long while, there's an honest-to-God line along the counter, blocking the first row of dry goods and running out the door onto the main thoroughfare. Usually, we sell a bag of feed here, some seed and flour there, but today it seems like everybody, white and Negro alike, got together and decided they all wanted all their provisions at once.

When I get home, I find Momma sitting in the parlor in her favorite chair under the painting of her grandfather, knitting out a frantic blue-and-white pattern. I can gauge Momma's mood by how hard she's working those needles. I look around for Ana, hoping for a hint of what's got Momma so worked up. The journal is on the end table beside her. I can tell from the length of her pattern just how long she's been sitting there trying to suss out how I'd come by it and what all I might have learned from it.

"I had a delivery over in Laurent the other day," I tell her as I hang my coat up and brush the dust off my pants. "I come by it out there."

"How?"

"Does how matter?"

"Of course it matters!" she yells, hands shaking those needles like she's itching to stick me with one of them. I sit down across from her, let her simmer until she boils over.

"A man over in Laurent," I finally reply. "Says he knows you from the old days. I didn't catch his name, but I imagine you know just who I'm talking about, don't you?"

She sets her needles down, picks up the journal, and flips through the pages. "How much of this have you read?"

"Enough."

Her eyes buck, and all the fight goes out of her. She drops her pattern and relaxes back into the chair. "How is he?"

"Seemed all right."

"Good."

I lean forward, try to meet her eyes, my eyes. "Anything about him you want to tell me? Anything you think it's my business to know?"

"I won't be spoken to this way. Not by my son, for whom I've done nothing but sacrifice."

"And just what have you sacrificed for me?"

"Everything. I gave up everything I ever loved for you."

I go upstairs and change out of my work clothes. I want to have a word or two with Ana about all this, but she, no doubt sensing that, has made herself scarce. I get cold chicken out of the icebox for supper and have it out on the back porch. I don't see the candle, but once night falls, I light out for the barn anyway. Myra doesn't show. I lie there nearly shivering in the cold until around about midnight. There's no way I'll be able to close my eyes without seeing her.

The moon is waning but shines brightly enough for me to make it to the Mullinses' house. Their property borders ours to the south, so all I have to do to get there is cut through the thicket behind the barn. A lone coyote yips a ways off, but besides him, nothing's out here but me. I can't remember the last time I went to sleep without Myra by my side.

The Mullinses' house is dark, save Myra's room up on the second floor. Candlelight and shadows flicker behind her floral-patterned lace curtains. I find a few rocks in the yard, but I can't bring myself to lob them at her window to get her attention. The candle goes out, the shadows come to a rest, and I'm still standing there, trying to find the words that might could set things right. They won't come.

* * *

I don't hear a thing about Mr. Wilkins's passing until Skip Bragg, surprised to see the store open, pokes his head in and offers me his condolences. Just then, Addie comes in with a note from Mrs. Wilkins. "Of course," I tell Addie. "Anything she needs."

As I lock up, I lament the fact that Wilkins's death is going to be what breaks the ice with Myra. Though I hate to admit it, part of me brightens at the prospect of her coming sympathy. She'll look me in the eye, I imagine, smooth back my hair, and smother my grief with her comforts. She can't deny me her company, not now, I think as I catch sight of Myra coming toward me in the reflection of the shop window. I hang the sign about Wilkins's passing and I fix my face to smile before I realize Jeff Morris has her arm. Jeff was in school with me and has always been sweet on Myra. He and I were friends before he went to read law down in Oxford. I stand there facing the store, waiting for them to pass, but then Jeff sees me and ups his step.

"Closing awful early, aren't we?" he says, grinning. "We were just coming over to see if you had some chocolate bonbons."

"We don't sell bonbons."

"I could've sworn I'd seen them in here. Myra just loves them. But I guess that's some other store I'm thinking of. Myra, what's that other store I'm thinking of?"

"Pearson's."

"That's right, sweetheart. Isn't that around here somewhere?"

Myra won't meet my eye.

"Pretty early for courting, isn't it?" I say, though I can't figure why.

"It's over in Lakeland," Myra says. "Like I told you."

"I'm sorry, sweetheart." He beams. "I guess I've led us on a bit of a goose chase. But I promised you sweets, and sweets you shall have. Bubba, you mind opening up for a few more minutes for us to look around?"

I draw his attention to the sign. It's only after Myra reads it that she bothers to acknowledge me, but there's no sympathy in her eyes, only pity. Jeff drops his oily smile just long enough to murmur condolences before taking Myra by the arm again and walking away.

Momma's gone when I get home, which is odd for her. She has people she visits from time to time, mostly older folks, but none of them are receiving this time of day. I find Ana in the kitchen, cutting biscuit dough. I ask her where Momma's gone.

"I can't say," she says, brushing flour off the table. "I promised I wouldn't say."

She walks out to the hallway, covered in enough flour to pass for white. I follow her. She tries to go out the front door, but as she starts to open it, I stand behind her and force it shut. She takes a deep breath.

"I been nothing but good to you, Bubba Laurent," she says, still facing the door. "Don't make me regret it."

I back away from her, close my eyes, and feel myself crumble.

Ana kneels down beside me, puts her hand on my back, and rubs slow circles into it, like she did when I had nightmares as a child.

"What am I?" I ask her.

She wraps her arms around me, brings her forehead down to meet mine. She has the same eyes as Momma, the same eyes as me.

"What you are is my Bubba. Lillian may have carried you, but you been in my hands ever since you came out of her. The minute I saw you, I knew you were mine."

In the washroom, I look at myself in the mirror. All I see is what I've always seen. Ana brings butter-fried pork chops, mashed potatoes, and biscuits up to my room. I stare at the plate for a while but can't bring myself to eat.

Later, I hear Momma clamor through the door and, without a word, bound up the steps and lock the door to her room behind her.

Around about dusk, the doorbell rings. I doubt Momma plans on leaving her room, and so I assume Ana will turn whoever it is away, but she doesn't. Instead, she calls up the steps for me to come down. I pull on my pants and find a decent shirt, figuring that it's a condolence call on account of Mr. Wilkins, but it isn't. It's Myra.

It's funny seeing Myra there, framed by the arch in the foyer with her hair pinned back. She's never set foot in my mother's house before. She's wearing a red broadcloth dress. When Ana leaves, Myra pats the place beside her. I move my mother's knitting pattern and sit down in the chair across from her instead.

"It was Daddy's idea," she says. "I came down the steps, and Jeff was already standing there waiting. It was just easier to go."

"You don't have to explain anything to me," I tell her. "It's your business."

"I don't want him, Bubba."

"You wouldn't know it from the way you carry on with him."

"I only do what I have to do to have peace. You know I'm waiting on you."

I laugh.

"What?" she asks, halfway smiling. It's painful for me to see just how ready she is to be in on the joke.

"You really think I'd marry you? After all I know about you?"

She glances down at her skirt and smooths the wrinkles out with her hands like she's making ready to stand. "You don't mean it," she says. "You're just upset with me."

"I aim to have a respectable wife, one that ain't been ruined."

Myra stares at me, eyes darting back and forth across my face like there's something written there she can't quite make out. I stare straight ahead, my hands gripping the armrests. It's all I can do to keep them still. Myra starts to open her mouth to speak, then doesn't. Instead, she takes a deep breath, stands, and smacks me so hard that, for a minute, I think my jaw might be unhinged.

"There's a limit to how much I'll put up with, Bubba Laurent. Even from you."

Then she cuts across the room to leave. I let her.

Ana barges in from the kitchen as soon as the door shuts. "You've got no cause to treat her that way."

"She's a good woman," I say, my jaw still hot from Myra's hand.

The whole town, save Momma, who still won't leave her room, turns out for Mr. Wilkins's service. Reverend Meyers preaches on how there never lived a better steward over what God gave him than Mr. Robin Wilkins. Near about everybody in the church nods in agreement. After Reverend Meyers invites friends and loved ones to say a few words, everyone cuts their eyes at me. I stand and talk for a few minutes about how good Mr. Wilkins was to me over the years. What all he taught me. I never had a father, not really, but Wilkins came pretty damn close. After I sit down, Myra catches my eye. Her look lets me know I have her sympathies but not her forgiveness.

I wait for Myra leave to before I tell Mrs. Wilkins that if she needs anything to just let me know and I'll sort it out. She has on a black veil and the bearing of a thoroughbred who's just run her last race. She hugs me close, rocks me back and forth, cups her cold, soft hands to my cheeks, and tells me I was the closest thing Mr. Wilkins ever had to a son. Then she looks over to the casket, nods as if she and the old man had been carrying on a conversation, and turns to me.

"You should take over the store, Bubba," she says.

"I will," I say. "Just as soon as I can get the money raised, I'll write you a check."

"I don't need a check. Just have it. It's what Robin would've wanted if he'd have thought about it for more than five minutes. It's what I want."

"He was thinking, Mrs. Wilkins," I say. "He was thinking about you. He wanted to lay something by in case anything happened to him.

Those were his wishes. I couldn't look myself in the mirror if I didn't abide them."

I don't know if any of what I said about Wilkins's wishes was true, but he worked hard to keep that store running, and he deserved to have it pay out for his widow.

At the cemetery, I study the Negroes shoveling dirt onto Wilkins's grave. They tip their hats to me in turn. I wonder if they know. If all the Negroes I've ever come across have always known, always seen, what I couldn't.

Momma clears out before I can question her. I stand in front of her empty closet in my suit, hardly believing it. According to Ana, who, now that Momma has packed up and gone, is extraordinarily forthcoming, Asa, the man from Laurent, arrived with an empty wagon not an hour after I left for the funeral and, without a word passing between them, started helping Momma fill her trunks.

"They always had a funny sort of hold on one another," she says, squeezing my shoulders. "Unnatural. I've never seen anything like it."

I turn to go to my room, and Ana follows me. Stands there as I undo my tie. I put my cuff links away and notice the bank papers, a letter, and the journal. I pick up the journal; nearly half of it has been torn out, which is fine by me. I already know more about my mother than I want to. I close it, hand it to Ana, and tell her to make good use of it next time she needs to stoke a fire, then head out to the barn, even though Myra won't be there.

All that night, I lie awake staring up at the stars. In the morning, I light a candle and leave it in the loft so that I'll feel what I felt when I used to come home from the store knowing Myra was waiting on me.

I wash up and sit down to breakfast. Ana has laid the journal, bank papers, and letter out beside my eggs and rye toast. I look them over as I drink my coffee. The bank papers belong to an account at Memphis

Trust that, as of two days ago, has been signed over to me. I put the papers aside and pick up the letter, surprised to discover that it is from Asa Laurent, not my mother.

Son,

I cannot tell you how many mornings I awoke resolved to break my silence. After I received word of your birth— after I felt the swelling of pride which surely must alight upon every father's breast— my world was upended, and for quite some time I was lost. My life has been a series of vicious cycles from which my only refuge is the knowledge that the revolution of one may, to whatever degree possible, prepare me for the next, engendering me with the unerring belief that, just as the world spins on an axis, making on each return a new day, we advance only by removes and revolutions, moving forward only to look back, trudging out of one storm only to find ourselves in the eye of another. Progress is merely the name of the carrot preceding the stick. When I returned to Laurent, your identity as my father's son was well-nigh established and I thought that, owing to my Negro blood, his name could do more for you in death than mine could in life, so I allowed your mother to believe I, along with him, perished in the fire.

By now I'm sure that Ana will have told you a fair amount about me, and that you are, to some degree, shocked at the revelation of your true parentage. But I want you to hear the facts from me. I was born a slave, my father's, your grandfather's. Around the age of nine, after the passing of his white son, my half brother, Lucius, I was removed from my mother's care, made to live in the great house with him and your mother, and raised to take my brother's place as heir to the Laurent plantation, becoming then, and remaining for some time after, a slave owner of the planter class.

By secrecy, I had hoped to spare you the burden of race. This world has contrived by every means conceivable to instill within you, within all of us, the idea that the Negro is inferior. After the War, I watched Negroes rise to heights I had never thought possible, but the once-at-hand dream of social equality, at least in this nation, is a farce. Indeed, I fear that, in the aggregate, there was more freedom in the bygone years of this century than there will ever be in the next. One feels with each passing year the once pliable laws governing Negro mobility coarsening to iron. And with the Freedmen's Bureau going under, much hard-won wealth, the only means through which it is possible to attain what men have taken to calling freedom, has been irredeemably lost. I once believed with all sincerity that your life, whether you lived as Negro or white, would be far freer than mine, but for every step forward this nation takes in the direction of Truth and Righteousness, two are taken back. With each passing day, the chasm between the races grows wider.

I have no doubt that you are plagued by questions: What does it mean to be a Negro? When, upon what day? What hour? What gesture will out the black of my blood? Am I Negro or white? Allow me to put the matter to bed as earnestly as only one who has lived as both white and Negro might. You are both and neither. To indulge unquestioningly in the privileges of the former is to fall into a web of silken fetters that will rot your soul from the inside out. To imbibe and live within the propaganda entrenching the latter is to condemn yourself to a lifetime of self-doubt. Both are part of the same snare, one in which I myself have been doubly caught. Know this: Whether the mask you wear in public is black or white, it will forever belie the finer aspects of the self that will ultimately determine your lot in life.

But race is not my principal aim in writing.

Before I left my mother's care, she told me that Lucius's soul might seek a new home within me. She herself housed the souls of several departed kin within her. Such a thing was common

among her people in Africa. Often, my sister and I were held in
thrall as she conversed animatedly with some presence, invisible
to us but set clearly before her. But such moments were a rarity.
She was well practiced at keeping her selves in abeyance and
could exhibit each individually, employing them in the making of
medicines and the reading of signs.

On the eve of my departure, my mother gave me a store
of salt and a root poultice to put under my pillow so that if
Lucius's spirit returned, he could not find me. I did so and slept
peacefully for months, mindful not to disturb the salt circle upon
waking and doing the same before I lay down to rest. But then
one evening, I came back to my room and discovered that the salt
had been swept away and Lucius haunted first my dreams and
then, later, my waking mind. I know not whether such spirits
have beset you, or whether they ever will, but if I did not at least
try to impart some means of defending yourself against them, I
would never forgive myself.

Son, the age of miracles is not past; it is not sealed, as the
proponents of the Good Book profess, but upon us always. All
that was possible then is possible now. Even as you read this,
there are very likely forces at work within and about you. I know
just how cruel such influences can be. Even now, in my nephew,
Walter, who, astonishingly, is as light as you, I see the signs of
it, and I'm certain that once you make his acquaintance, if you
make his acquaintance, my meaning will be made plain. It is the
peculiar habit of some minds to alight upon some far-flung object
without which, they believe, their lives are found wanting, and
so has it been with Walter. The unquenchable thirst with which
he pursues religious feeling has consumed him in much the same
way drinking consumes a drunk.

I fear greatly that one day you will be beset by such influences
and have no earthly purchase. If ever you begin to see things
not of this world, go to the woods behind the house where you

first laid eyes upon me. Just beyond it, but before you reach the creek, there is a great sycamore tree. Near its base, there grows a certain plant, the root of which you should make into a tea. You will know the plant from its pink-and-purple pentagonal bloom. If you do not wish to drink its tea, dry it, put it in a cloth bag, and put it behind your head before going to sleep.

 This will not cure you, for there is no cure, but it will provide you with strength enough to endure, to discern what is undue spiritual influence and what is of yourself alone. It would also be good for you to sprinkle salt around each entrance of your home. These actions will do much to protect you from the worst of the terrible gift of sight from which I hope you have been spared.

 I have not been a father to you, and I will not do you the disservice of pretending to be one now. In my father, in place of love, I found expectation, disappointment, and shame. Upon learning of your birth, I feared this cycle would repeat itself. Who in this country would willingly claim an ex-slave for their father? But, if I may, I would like to offer some fatherly advice: Live not for ideas or fashions or whatever politics are in vogue, but for those you love.

 Once upon a time, it was my greatest dream to own myself and, for a while, I believed I did. But, with time and experience, I have come to see that true freedom lies not in independence, but rather in having the opportunity to decide to whom your life will belong. Your mother and I have decided, rather selfishly, that every minute we have left belongs to each other. Forgive me. There may come a time when you will have to choose between your own happiness and what the world says is right or wrong. If that time comes, I pray you will make the right choice.

I fold the letter up, put it in my breast pocket, and set out for the store. But as I begin to walk, my feet carry me across the field to the

Mullins place instead. I stand in the front yard for a while, but I can't bring myself to ring the bell.

It's a slow day at the store. Slow enough to make me wonder if people are keeping their distance out of respect. I close up early, go around back, and saddle up Ginny. I haven't run any deliveries since Wilkins passed, and so I imagine she needs the fresh air and change of scenery as much as I do. I don't have my mind set on going anywhere in particular, but before long, Ginny's ambling down past the houses lining Lucille's Lane.

There are fewer Negroes out on the road than there were the day we came through here with the wagon. Women and children working in their gardens, and men, here and there, coming in from the fields. Some wave. Most keep to themselves.

I stop in front of what used to be my father's house, half expecting to see him. A woman, my father's sister, comes out onto the porch. We stare at one another. I make to dismount Ginny, but before I can, she waves me off and goes back inside, closing the door behind her.

I drive Ginny until the packed dirt of the lane gives way to trampled grass. A structure peeks out from behind a stand of sweet gum and beech trees. The Laurent plantation was around here somewhere, and at first I believe what I see are its ruins. But as I approach, it becomes clearer that it's a half-built A-frame church. Wind rustles the leaves. Water babbles somewhere nearby.

A loud series of thwacks peal in the air. I turn back, squint into the structure, and see a man in rolled shirtsleeves and suspenders. I dismount Ginny, amble closer, and see the preacher I picked up in the wagon the other day.

"Little late to be working, isn't it?"

He pauses, glances in my direction, and then picks up his hammer.

"I slaughtered a hog yesterday evening. Spent all morning smoking him down. And then, soon as I sat down to the table to say grace, I heard this blue kind of ringing in my ear. I jiggled it, but all the jiggling did was shift the sound from my hearing to my vision. It was the Lord calling me, saying, 'Walter, by whose grace were you allowed to fix this meal?' 'Yours, my Lord,' I says back. 'And whose house is sitting out there in the woods unfinished?' And so I stood right on up and come out here to finish it."

"You got all that from your ear ringing, did you?"

He cuts his eyes at me. "The Lord's always talking. It's on you to figure out how to listen."

A breeze kicks up, blowing Walter's oversize shirt back and prompting a bobwhite quail to cry out.

"You knew who I was to you when you saw me on the road the other day, didn't you?"

He nods his head like he's still listening to me well after I finished talking. Then he shrugs, rolls his shoulders back, and reaches into a bag of nails.

"Blood always outs," he says, not meeting my eye.

I watch him work for a while. His silhouette could be mine. If anyone were to happen upon us, they might mistake us for brothers.

Smoke billows out from as far as a mile away from the house, and Ana is standing in the yard with her hands on her hips. The barn is a crackling wall of flame. The barn doors blow open, and I half expect to see the ghosts of those requisitioned Confederate horses, manes ablaze, come galloping out of it.

"You want me to run over to the Billings place and tell Flip to get the brigade up to wet the house?" Ana asks.

In my mind, I see a lone ember, carried on the wind, falling softly onto the roof, burrowing bright into the attic, lapping its tongue down the bare wood wall to devour Uncle Elbert's wardrobe before fanning out over the red baroque rug and settling into the floorboards to blacken the ceiling above my room, Momma's room, Ana's room, and the room where Aunt Jessup, after Rich's and Caleb's haversacks, overstuffed with religious tracts, hardtack, and unread letters from her, returned home without them, spent the last ten years of her life murmuring to herself the words to "Amazing Grace." It would blaze through the hallway quick and slow, scorching the blue-green damask wallpaper and saving the walls until it could gather up enough heat to melt the plaster and get at the lath beneath it.

By then, all the windowpanes on the second floor would've given way, releasing enough rolling plumes of smoke to blot out the stars and allowing into the house enough fall air for the fire to roar its way down the Persian runner that carpets the landing and stairs, open out into the great room, and rise up into the parlor to balk at the incombustible brick hearth before snaking its way around it to raze the oak table in the kitchen.

Whether or not this house catches fire, I will use the money my father left me to build a new one to suit Myra.

"Naw," I tell Ana. "There's nothing for them to do."

Once the fire dies down, I walk deep into the woods to watch the sun set over the creek, like me and Myra used to do before we discovered the hayloft. I come to the water's edge, where the reflection of the tree limbs yearn toward one another but never touch, and squat down to get a better look at my reflection. Soot from the fire has blackened my face. "I'm Bubba Laurent," I tell my reflection. "Who the hell are you?"

The Ties That Bind

LOUIS EARL LAURENT
(1885–1980)
Son of Reverend Walter Laurent
Father of Robert Laurent and Benny Ross

THE DEVIL FIRST appeared to Louis in his father's church. It was while he was on his knees, praying for the strength to quell the lust he carried in his heart for his brother's wife, that the Devil whispered to Louis the same words of comfort he'd imparted to Cain when God unjustly favored Abel, to David the evening Bathsheba tempted him, and to Judas the day he learned Jesus would rather perfume his feet than feed the poor. "Everything you got in you, God put there," the Devil said. "He wouldn't have put it in you if He didn't want you to act on it." In all his years, Louis had never once strayed from the path his father set him on, the straight and narrow path of righteousness. But when Ernestine, the woman his adoptive brother and best friend, Junior, was to marry, locked eyes with Louis over his mother's pecan pie, all that righteousness went right on out of him.

Louis and Junior had met in children's Bible study but didn't get to knowing one another good until the latter saved the former from drowning. It had been during a game of hide-and-seek. Church was

141

over, and so, while the grown folks traded lies by the cemetery, all the children whose parents allowed it left their good shoes by the back door and walked barefoot through the woods to the creek. The water wasn't deep that time of year, and so drowning was the last thing on anyone's mind. Besides, most of the children were content to stand on the bank, splashing each other's legs, dipping their toes in the water. Only Louis, who was Reverend Walter's son and so did as he pleased, thought it a good idea to hang his clothes on the low branches of a river birch and doggy-paddle out.

The Sunday before, Louis had discovered that if he lay flat on his back with his arms spread, his legs extended, his head back just far enough for the water to tease his ears, he could float. It was a kind of peace, this floating. A drowsy wakefulness that allowed Louis to, for a moment, forget what all lay before him, what all he was to inherit. And so when the bee first landed on his forehead, he did not move.

By then, Buddy McCaffery was ten Mississippis off from seeking out his first hider, and Louis, loving the cool of the water, the warmth of the sun, and the exhilaration of rule-breaking, decided to stay right where he was. Clementine, whom Louis would one day marry, had a bad feeling about leaving him there, but the badness of the feeling did not outweigh her desire to be up a tree and out of sight well before Buddy called "olly olly oxen free," and so by the time Louis began to thrash, she was up in the thinning branches of a live oak tree, looking down at the sorry sight of him, powerless to help. Years later, after Louis started sleeping around and coming home drunk, she would remember this day and know her punishment far and away outpaced her crime.

At first Louis thought the bee was a leaf and tried, without opening his eyes, to blow it away. It moved, but slowly, deliberately, and not at all how Louis reckoned a leaf ought to. With less effort than the bee had spent the whole of his life imagining it would take, he embedded his stinger into the tender tissue just under Louis's eye. The swelling began even before Louis brought both hands to his face to swat at the bee, who by then was already halfway to the base of the river birch that was to be his final resting place. The reverend had taught his son to swim, but Louis was too startled by the water he'd already breathed in to do anything other than splash about, gasping. Junior, seeing all this from the bank, jumped in.

An arm fastened around Louis's waist, and for a moment, it seemed as if water itself was what pulled at him. There were people under the water, his grandmother had told him, spirits who claimed the living as their own, dragging them down into the water until they passed out and awoke on the other side of life. It was only as the hand attached to the arm pulled him up out of the water that he knew it came from this world and not the other.

He thought then of his father, of the day he was called to preach, the blood, the fire, the angel who'd wrestled Reverend Walter to the ground and compelled him to call on the Lord. "You been anointed," Reverend Walter had told Louis as he dressed for church. "It come down through the blood. Ain't no question as to if He'll call you." Louis lay there on the bank wondering if this was it, if who- or whatever had pulled him from the creek would hold him down and make him give himself over to God.

"Why the hell ain't you just stand up?" Junior said, chest heaving. "It ain't but 'bout four feet of water."

Louis had seen Junior around, but never this close up. Like Clementine's parents, Junior's people were also members of Mount Carmel, but they were not dyed in the blood of the lamb. Junior's father, Virgil, was on at a sawmill just north of Memphis when he heard tell of a Black preacher leasing good land at a fair rate to members of his congregation. Now, Virgil had always thought that Jesus was fine and was generally thankful that he'd died for our sins, but he didn't feel the need to be reminded of it every Sunday. Virgil grew up sharecropping in Mississippi but left home to find wage work in Memphis in lieu of taking over the lease of the land upon which his father and grandfather had been enslaved. What he had not known about wage work, and soon came to loathe, was that wage workers had to look their bosses in the face and be told what to do and how every hour of the day. Compared to that, sharecropping was a dream. And so every Sunday, Virgil went miles out of his way to hear sermons on cleansing fires and healing waters until enough time had passed for him to feel comfortable asking Reverend Walter if he had any land to let.

Junior mostly kept to himself. Virgil Sr. was a hard man, and the less Junior spoke, the easier his days went, and so he dug down into himself, cultivated a rich and imaginative inner life filled with jokes at which he could not help but laugh. Which was the reason other children found him strange. It was strange for a boy as big and black as Junior to be silent and then, for no apparent reason, break out into fits of laughter. As Junior's broad shoulders and barrel chest heaved, Louis became aware of his own body, of all it lacked. Junior was black and brawny. Louis was light and spindly.

"You hungry?" Louis asked.

"Always," Junior said.

And so they walked, down the length of the creek and on past a clearing of trees, to Louis's grandmother's house, where there was always corn pone, or fatback, or freshly picked blackberries waiting to be boiled, skimmed, and preserved.

"You live here?" Junior said, seeing the conjure woman's house through the trees.

"Naw," Louis said. "My grandma does."

Junior took care not to disturb the bundles of herbs and weeds splayed out on the table while Louis grabbed a plate and heaped bacon, still-warm johnnycakes, and a pat of butter onto it.

"You sure she won't mind?"

"I'm sure."

As Junior sandwiched the bacon with johnnycakes, slathering on molasses, Louis watched him, wondering still if he was one of God's angels in the guise of a boy with whom he was only passingly familiar. Louis did not want to preach, and woke each morning half-afraid that this day was the day upon which he would be called. He'd brought Junior to his grandmother's house, knowing that if there was any-one who could cast out an angel, it would be his grandmother, whom everyone knew to be in league with the Devil, the only person who'd told him he didn't have to preach if he didn't want to.

"I won't say it," Louis barked. "I'm not ready. You can't make me call on him if I'm not ready."

"What?" Junior asked, swallowing.

"Jesus. You want me to call out his name and give myself over to right, don't you?"

"I don't want nothing but to eat and get out of here before your grandma puts a root on me."

Louis laughed, but then, after Junior came to live with him, that's exactly what she did.

Folks had told Eliza to go see Ms. Lucille, Reverend Walter's mother, as soon as Virgil took sick, but in the end, she decided it was better to let the Lord take her husband's soul than to consult a conjure woman and condemn her own. Yellow fever was no joke, but she'd heard tell of enough people getting by on pot liquor and prayer to feel comfortable putting it in Jesus's hands. But she worried enough for their son, Junior, to send him to stay at Reverend Walter's while his father convalesced; of course it wasn't until after she came down with her own chills and body aches that she thought of herself. Virgil recovered just in time to bury Eliza but was too out of his mind with grief to feed himself, let alone Junior. And so, within a few months of his wife's passing, Virgil found himself buried beside her. After his parents' deaths, Junior's brief stay at the reverend's took on an unofficial permanence. Louis had a bit of a mean streak, and, when Junior's parents passed, Reverend Walter took the boy, hoping his tenderheartedness would rub off on his hardheaded son.

Unlike Eliza, Louis didn't think twice about seeking the help of his grandmother. That morning, when Louis awoke to Junior's heavy breathing, he rose from his cot, touched the back of his hand to Junior's forehead. The same disease that had taken Junior's parents had come for him.

Louis pulled Junior from bed, hefted him up, and hobbled the half mile along the creek to Lucille's cabin with a feverishly uncooperative Junior slung over his shoulder. When Louis arrived, he found the door open. Louis set the half-conscious Junior at his grandmother's kitchen table, and before he could open his mouth, she handed him a bucket and told him to go back to the creek to fetch her some water. When he got back, the air was dense with smoking herbs, and his grandmother had lifted Junior up onto the table.

"Here," she said. "Take this rag and wash everywhere on him you feel fever."

Louis took the rag, dipped it into the creek water, and wiped Junior down, making sure to wring out the rag after wiping under his armpits. Lifting him up partway, Louis washed one side of Junior's back and then the other, but he stopped once he reached Junior's waist.

"You don't think he sweats down there?" his grandmother asked.

And so Louis peeled back Junior's trousers, trying his best not to be shocked by the sight of his friend's pubic hair, and ran the rag over and around his manhood, averting his gaze only when it began to stir.

"That's good," his grandmother said. "Means his blood is moving."

Lucille's gift was sight. She could take the measure of a man by his shadow, gauge the tone and tenor of his soul, and manipulate the tendrils of light that, like a spider's web, spread themselves out, unseen, across the ether, connecting one person to another, or as was the case with her father and, for a long while, her brother, to what they owned. Most of the time, people formed and broke these bonds to one another on their own. One neighbor would help another with the harvest, and between them a band of yellow would form, waxing with each meal shared, each favor repaid, and waning with each slight, real or perceived, and if not nurtured, dissipating completely. Others were so strong, so thick and enduring, that they had to be put there by a higher power whose intentions Lucille, unlike her son, Walter, dared not claim to know.

Like her mother, all Lucille did was use herbs to loosen here, tighten there, and, if need be, cut and retie so long as it did not disrupt the greater pattern. Each plant, animal, and person had its own kind of energy. Some pushed and some pulled. Some stuck to you like burrs and others slipped through your fingers like fresh-caught fish. All pulsed with their own vibrant color. To Lucille, and her great-great-granddaughter Cassandra, the only one of her descendants to inherit the fullness of her and her mother's gifts, the world was one bright burning bouquet.

The day Junior pulled Louis from the water, a blue burning had called out to her, but by the time she reached the spot near the creek from which it emanated, it was gone. For a moment, she'd thought it was her twin brother, Asa. But he'd left. Abandoned her for that white woman just as Franklin, not long after Walter came into his manhood, abandoned her for his boyfriend, Elijah.

The day Lucille woke up and found her brother gone was the same day that the Devil first called on her. The Devil told her that she wasn't fit to be around people, that everyone she gathered around herself would leave, save him. He'd always be by her side. Years later, as she lay in her estranged son's bed dying, she'd think back to the Devil's words and know them to be right, but on the day Junior pulled Louis from the water, she still nursed a vague hope that her brother would return to her.

"Louis," Lucille said, "you see that woman standing there by the window?"

Louis, like his father, had no sense of the greater pattern within which Lucille worked, but he was keenly attuned to the presence of spirits.

"Yes, ma'am."

"You know her?"

"Yes, ma'am. That's Ms. Eliza, Junior's mother."

"Do me a favor and ask her to leave, like how I showed you."

When Louis first brought Junior in, she saw gray where before, on the day Junior had pulled Louis from the water, there had been a rich brown, ripe as planting soil, meaning that, though he would never know greatness, he had it in him to help others realize it.

After Louis washed Junior, she saw two threads not of his color—one sky-blue, the other bloodred—winding themselves around his throat. So that's what it was. The boy's mother didn't know how to let him go, and now he was stuck somewhere between this world and the other. The blue thread, attached to his father, was easily undone; the river washing had loosened it, and the tobacco had all but untethered it. But the red one, the one belonging to his mother, was another matter altogether. No root or tonic could appease it, and by the time the sun was high, Lucille knew it would need to be snipped and retied somewhere else along the greater design.

"She won't leave," Louis whispered into her ear.

"I figured as much. Do you know where she's buried?"

Louis nodded.

"Good. Bring me some of her dirt."

"Yes, ma'am."

Once Louis left, Lucille sat down in her spindle-backed rocking chair, the one Robert Reeves had carved for her mother, and wiped her brow. Her mother had always made the work feel easy, and maybe with the two of them coming at it together, working alongside one another, it was. Or maybe Lucille was getting old. By now she had almost twice as many years behind her as her mother did when she burned Laurent's house. Years before, the Devil had told Lucille the day and hour he'd return for her, and by now it wasn't as far away as it had then seemed. She knew when she arose that morning and smelled wormwood that the work before her, whatever it entailed, was going to be her last great effort, her big push, but she could not have foreseen how her decision to bind Louis's fate to Junior's would affect her grandson and his generations. Otherwise, she would have let the poor boy perish.

"Junior's lucky," Lucille said. She was looking at the boy, but her words were directed to his mother. "It's not everybody that has a mother like you. But what he need now is for you to leave. You did all you could for him in life, and now it's time to take your rest."

"I can't," the spirit replied. "I don't know how."

"Sure you do, sweetheart. Just let go. It's as easy as breathing."

Eliza's ghost walked over to where Junior was laid out and kissed him on the forehead. But she didn't leave until Louis returned, nearly breathless, holding out in front of him with both hands her grave dirt. Lucille took the dirt from Louis, mixed some with the creek water, and rubbed it onto Junior's chest. The rest she put in a glass jar.

Lucille's work did not, as some believed, reorder fate. Fate was like the current of life's rushing river. If you did nothing, it carried you along. But if you built up your strength, kicked a bit, and swam to where the strength of the current waned, you could chart your own course. What Lucille did was attune herself to that current, feel out where it eddied, note where it pooled, and gather up enough of what she could from the earth to help those who came to her navigate it. By pairing this plant with that one, collecting this dirt from that place, waiting for the sun to be here before moving Junior there, Lucille made her intentions for the boy known to the greater power she dared not name. In this way, her work was more like prayer through action than magic. When Lucille worked, she didn't see things as they were physically but only the kinds of energy they manifested, and so by the time she got going on Junior, verbena was no longer verbena but merely loving-purple. The sage that filled the air was a mending-brown, good for clearing out unwanted presences and bonding things together. And Louis was just the right kind of green to pair with Junior's rich brown.

Louis was, by then, standing by the window, frozen. He wanted to help Junior, but everything in him was telling him to leave, to run. When Lucille worked, the part of her Louis knew and loved receded, and those who had come before her stepped forward. Sometimes, he'd walk into Lucille's house and she would be there in the kitchen, stirring a pot, and then, the very next minute, she was gone. It was this aspect of the work that most frightened Louis, why he would never carry it forward, never teach his children what she taught him. Still, he didn't fear her half as much as the fire that burned in Reverend Walter's eyes, the fire Louis feared would one day burn in him.

"Fetch me that knife," Lucille called out to Louis, "and bring yourself with it."

Had Lucille been just herself, she might have thought twice about tethering the raw, newly snipped red tendril emanating from Junior to Louis, but she wasn't herself alone. She wasn't one; she was many. White went with blue. Brown went with green, and so when Louis approached with the knife, she snatched it, grabbed him by the neck, and used the knife to cut away a tuft of his hair. After she let Louis go, she did the same with Junior. Blue with white, green with brown, red with yellow; otherwise the connections wilted and withered like grapes too long on the vine.

"He'll make it," she told Louis after she'd woven their hairs together, cut her hand, dripped onto the braid some of her blood, and burned it, and from then on it was as if one was the shadow and the other was the substance; you rarely saw one without the other. If Louis fell off a wagon headed into town, it was Junior who felt it in his hip all the rest of that week. If Junior, who was never mindful enough of those hateful seeds, cut his hand picking cotton, it was Louis who lost his grip strength. If Louis went down to the juke and started a fight, Junior was there to finish it. But when Junior laid eyes on the woman working the lunch wagon around the corner from the sawmill, Louis was surprised to find that, even though he was doing nothing more than sitting on the porch snapping peas, his heart got to fluttering. "But you need to watch out for one another. Y'all brothers now."

Ernestine was not a stop-in-the-street-and-stare kind of beauty. If you had asked anybody who knew her and Louis's wife both, they would have told you Clementine—whom Reverend Walter all but forced his

son to marry—had more to offer in terms of temperament and appearance. But something about the way Ernestine carried herself made
Louis want to look and keep on looking. For Junior, it was the way her
hazel eyes fixed on him every time she handed him a sandwich. Which
is why, though she was surly with him, he came to her lunch wagon
day in and day out for the better part of six months before summoning
the courage to ask after her.

Ernestine knew from the way Junior cut his eyes from her to the
menu and back that if she took him up on his offer to take a stroll, it
would be the end of her life as a single woman in the city. And so she'd
put him off, hoping that he would give up, and then one day, much to
her dismay, he did.

That day, her uncle had parked just around the corner from the
sawmill, and so she'd already prepared and laid aside Junior's dry
roast beef sandwich. Junior was always the last in line, hanging back
to have time enough to ask how her day was. But then the lunch rush
came and went without him, and so she gave his sandwich to the little peanut-headed boy who ran up every day to see if there were any
leftovers. After the third day of not seeing Junior, the boy grew bold
enough to ask for mustard.

"Where you been?" Ernestine asked when Junior finally came
back.

"Sick," Junior said, casting his eyes down.

"Well, next time send word by somebody. Uncle Zeke was over
here worrying himself sick about you."

"Oh yeah?" Junior said, brightening. "Maybe I should come back a
little later and let him know I'm feeling better. "

"I think you should," she said. "I think he'd like that."

They courted some months. A picture show here. A night out to
the juke there. But what Ernestine really loved were the walks they
took by the river. Every Friday she helped her uncle close up, knowing
Junior was waiting for her just around the corner. She'd bring along
sandwiches, and the two of them would take them down to the bluffs

and watch the wind worry the water. Junior wasn't much for talk, but he never grew tired of listening. Her sister Alice had been the same way. Quiet. Liable to say more with her eyes than her tongue. Before Alice followed that no-good husband of hers up to Chicago, Ernestine and her would stay up half the night talking. It was owing to Alice's husband that Ernestine vowed never to marry. He was all the time bossing Alice. It had been the same with their mother and Alice's father. She didn't see how anybody could want to saddle themselves with a husband. But if it was somebody like Junior, somebody sweet and quiet, then maybe, Ernestine thought when he invited her home to meet his family, maybe she could see her way around to it.

Something funny happened the night Junior brought her around to his people. The dinner itself was pleasant enough, pretty much what she'd expected when he told her the Reverend's family took him in after his folks passed on. Reverend Walter asked whether she'd accepted Christ into her heart. She had. Cora, the reverend's wife, asked where her folks were and what they did. They were down in Mississippi. Her mother took in washing, and her mother's husband, her half sister's father, cleaned the high school.

"Junior's folks come from around Jackson," Cora had said. "Be sure to ask around. Make certain y'all ain't some kin." Cora's younger sister had let a boy she met uptown put his hand up her skirt once, and later it came out that he was their cousin by way of a roving uncle, her mother's brother. Ever since then, she'd been quick to warn folks to check whether someone they wanted to court was kin.

But none of the questions Junior's adoptive parents put to Ernestine unnerved her the way Louis's staring did. She could feel his eyes on her all through the dinner, but whenever she turned to face him, he either cast his eyes down at his plate or over at his wife, Clementine, who was sweet, Ernestine thought, but terribly dull.

It's just nerves, Ernestine told herself, remembering the jolt of electricity that shot through her when, once Cora's pecan pie had been served, she and Louis locked eyes. "I know Junior's going to put the question to me, and so my mind's doing whatever it can to ruin it."

At first, Louis attributed his inability to turn away from Ernestine to her novelty. Ernestine's voice, soft and low, was only as sweet as honey because he'd never heard it before. He'd known Clementine all his life, and so had never had the chance to feel that way for her. Once his heart got used to Ernestine, Louis lay awake at night hoping it wouldn't beat so goddamned hard every time he saw her. But then the wedding happened, and as he watched Ernestine walk down the aisle in what had to be the prettiest white dress anybody had ever seen, his insides seized up. He looked from her to Junior and back, walked around the side of the pulpit, and vomited, feeling that the burning ache occasioning the call, the awful moment his father had warned him of, the instant in which he would be brought low by God's awful power, had finally come. Only it didn't want him to preach. It wanted him to bed his brother's wife.

"Something's got to be done," Clementine told Junior not more than a month after he and Ernestine were wed. Louis was no great prize, this Clementine knew. Knew it even the day he'd asked her to come with him to see the turtles drink water. But the day before he'd taken her hand, as she was going down the cotton rows filling her sack, she had a terrifying revelation. All she had seen and done was all she would ever see and do. After harvest season was over, there would be canning. And after winter had come and gone, there would be planting, and so on and so forth for as long as the good Lord saw fit to give her breath.

Earlier that summer, Eula, Clementine's father's youngest sister, who, because she had been born with a clubfoot and was unfit for farm labor, had been given an education, wrote to her about attending the Chicago Normal School, where she taught. In the letter, Eula had offered to board Clementine and help her pay for school in exchange for helping around the house. Her father refused to let her go, remembering the way all those books had turned his baby sister's head away from God.

"You really want to be that long away from your family? Away from everybody you know and love?" he'd asked. "What about your mother? Who's going to help her around the house?"

Of course not, Clementine had told him, of course she didn't want to leave her family.

And so when Louis offered, not for the first time, to take her to the clearing out beyond the creek and make her feel like a woman, she relented, not because she fancied Louis but because fooling around was a thing to do that she had not yet done. It was uncomfortable at first, but it felt all right enough in the end. But no matter how good it felt, it was not worth Louis's sweat, feeling him writhe all over her. And so she slipped back into her Sunday best and thought no more about it until a little over a month later when she went to change her sanitary napkin and, for the third day in a row, it was clean.

Clementine's mother, who insisted on doing her daughter's laundry, was the first to notice and, remembering the way she'd slipped off with Louis that one Sunday, went to Clementine's father about it. "He'll do right by her," Clementine overheard Reverend Walter assure her father over Sunday afternoon sock it to me cake. "I'll make certain of it." And just like that, the door to that other life, the one in Chicago Eula had written to her of, closed, leaving her with a shiftless husband and a colicky baby.

Now, all Clementine wanted was to live decently, to make a good home for herself and her son. But Louis couldn't even allow her that. Couldn't do her the courtesy of at least pretending to love her. By the time Clementine took it upon herself to confront Junior, Louis was dropping by his house to gawk at Ernestine damn near daily. Nothing out of the way had happened yet, but it was clear to everyone that Louis visited for no other reason than to take whatever pleasure he could from Ernestine's company.

"It's disrespectful," Clementine continued, shaking her head. "Disrespectful to you and me both."

"I know that, Clem," Junior said. "Don't you think I know that?"

The way Louis ogled Ernestine hadn't escaped Junior's notice, but as was often the case with Junior, it took a while for his thinking mind to catch up to what his heart knew. After the death of Junior's parents, the part of him that felt things slowed. Everything registered eventually, but he had trouble connecting his inward feelings to outward causes. When Junior first introduced Louis to Ernestine, and Louis ran his eyes over her, Junior felt his stomach lurch, but it wasn't until he saw Louis throw up behind the pulpit that Junior understood the scope of the situation. If it had been anybody other than Louis sniffing around his wife, Junior would have already cut him. But this was Louis he and Clem were talking about, his best friend, his brother.

"What you keep coming around here for?" Junior asked Louis flat out one day. Louis's pretense for dropping by was that he needed a hand with a farrowing sow, which was ridiculous because no sow Junior ever knew needed help in labor. "What's over here you ain't got at home?"

"I-I just come to look in on y'all," Louis managed to stammer out. "See if anything was needed."

"Look in on your own house," Junior said, slamming the door. "Look in on Clementine if you want to be helpful. See what she needs."

Junior stood for a moment, his chest heaving with anger, the heat of it. Ernestine touched his shoulder, tried to comfort him, but he turned and walked away, so she just stood there at the door, feeling in her bones that Louis was still standing on the other side of it.

When Junior proposed, the idea of settling into a life with him in the country seemed romantic, but with each passing day, Ernestine felt her world grow smaller. She hadn't met a new person in weeks. Whereas, when she was working the lunch wagon with her uncle, there was at least one new face every day. The only real benefit to life in the country was that she had a yard to call her own. In Memphis, she'd boarded in a tiny room with nothing more to it than a bed, a hemp rug, and a chair. What was more, Junior didn't boss her, did his own mending, and even cooked dinner on the days he was off from the sawmill. But she was bored, and gradually her desire for novelty, for disruption, the thing that made her leave her mother's house and try to make a go of it alone, awoke. What if I just walk down that road and keep walking? she often found herself wondering.

At first, she tried to satisfy this urge by going into the woods out back of the house and seeing what she could see. But there were only so many animals, only so many trees. She didn't want to hurt Junior, but if things kept going as they were, she would have to leave him.

The lust to wander, to experience novelty, had always been with her. After Junior died, she would find that giving herself over to Jesus sated it, but before her marriage the only reliable remedy was sex, preferably with a man whom she'd never before seen. Of course, she gave all that up for Junior and was, at first, happy to leave that life behind her, happy to not have women whisper behind her back, to have and to hold only Junior, but, eventually, she found that she missed the thrill of bedding a new man. Missed meeting a handsome man at the grocery, asking him to help carry her bags home, and knowing anything might could happen once the door to her apartment closed behind them. This is what first excited her about Louis's unexpected visits.

The first time she'd let Louis in while Junior was out, she thrilled because even though nothing happened, she knew that if she wished it, anything could. And later, when she found herself naked with Louis in her and Junior's marriage bed, she felt relief instead of the shame she'd been expecting. She could love a man, be his wife, and not allow that love to define her.

* * *

The night Junior came home and met Louis leaving out of his front door, he didn't think much of it. He'd been drinking and shooting dice uptown. America had entered the war in Europe and they planned to use colored boys, which meant army pay, army benefits. He wasn't in any rush to go fight, but he was happy for the men he worked with, and so, for the first and only time, he'd gone out drinking with them. Before that day, he'd never drunk, and if it wasn't owing to his mule knowing the way, he wouldn't have made it home. He looked up from the porch where he'd fallen out and found his brother stepping over him.

"Louis," Junior called up, "how the hell you get all the way up there?"

"It's not that I'm up," Louis said. "It's that you're down."

"Huh," Junior said, laughing. "I guess that's one way to look at it."

It wasn't until the next morning, after Ernestine had cooked up sausage, scrambled eggs, and flapjacks, that Junior put together what all Louis and Ernestine had been up to. If he were another kind of man, the kind of man his father had been, he might have raised a hand against her, but he wasn't. He was Eliza's son, the first born of her to draw breath after two stillbirths, and Eliza's son would never raise his hand against a woman. And so, though he could not help but see on Ernestine everywhere his brother had touched, Junior sat at the table across from his wife — the only woman he had or would ever love — and shared his thoughts on the coming war.

"You come to cut me?" Louis asked the night he found Junior leaning up against the side of his barn with his switchblade drawn. He'd come out to milk Beulah, the only heifer who was not then pregnant.

"You ain't left me much of a choice."

"I won't fight you," Louis said, dropping the milking pail at his feet.

"I know you won't."

Junior walked up to his brother, took his switchblade, and with one swift swing, sliced a red line from the bottom of Louis's eye to the top of his jawline. Junior didn't want to hurt Louis, he loved his brother, but something had to be done. The situation had gotten away from him. He felt like he was on the back of a galloping horse that didn't know what whoa meant. It was like that fever dream he'd had after his mother passed. In it, he was laid out on a table, and she was standing over him. She leaned down to kiss him, but no matter how hard she strained, she couldn't reach him. That's how he felt with Louis. He could see him but not reach him, not with the switchblade, nor with the poorly aimed rifle shot that followed it months later.

After Clementine had stanched the bleeding in Louis's shoulder — Junior's bullet had only grazed him — Louis found himself drunkenly jimmying open the back door of his father's church. Had Lucille been alive, Louis would have laid it all at her doorstep, found the right root, and used it to fix him. There were other root workers, of course, but with Louis being the reverend's son and all, he was too ashamed to go to them.

In the afternoon before the evening Lucille was to close her eyes to life, she set out to make peace with her son, Walter. "I got a brother and a husband I'll never see again," Lucille told Cora when she opened the door. "I can't bear to say the same of my son." Cora invited Lucille in and served her the tea cakes she'd been saving for Walter, who, that afternoon, was out visiting the sick and shut-in. Lucille and Cora had not spoken since the latter came to the former begging her to fix it so that Walter would make her honest. Lucille, who didn't like the way the girl had thrown herself in front of Walter, turned her away. No words had passed between them since.

"I was thinking of putting in some tulips when it warms," Cora ventured. "I got some nice bulbs from Ms. Reed. I can see about getting some for you, too, if you want."

"I don't have no use for tulips," Lucille said, glowering down at the cherubs carved into her son's coffee table and wondering how a boy she raised could stomach such frippery. "Where's my son? I need to see him."

"He's out doing his visiting. He'll be back directly. Are you feeling all right, Ms. Lucille?" Cora asked, seeing that the woman had paled. "Would you like to lie down for a spell?"

"Yes," Lucille said, for all of a sudden she had grown terribly cold. "Yes, I believe I would."

Cora showed Lucille to her and Walter's bedroom—the poor woman was shivering—pulled the quilt over her, and fetched her a hot toddy.

"You love my son, don't you?" Lucille said after Cora took her hand and rubbed it as no one had since her mother passed.

"Dearly," Cora said.

"That's good," Lucille said, closing her eyes. "Real good. Be sure to do for you as much as you do for him. You somebody, too."

The Great Maker, looking out over all His children from on high, saw Lucille laid up, shook His head, sat back on His throne, turned to the angel Gabriel, and said: "Call me Death." Like a clap of thunder, Gabriel's voice boomed out all through the halls of the Father's mansion and echoed all through the streets of heaven until it reached that black, shadowy place where Death stood brushing down his pale white horse, his scythe at the ready. "Go down," God told Death. "Go down to Laurent, fetch up Lucille, and bring her home." And so Death took up his pale horse's reins and rode on past the pearly gates, on past the bright line of sky that separates Earth from heaven, on over the Mississippi, on past Walter, who just then was making his way up the lane, and did not stop until he met his brother at the crossroads.

"Stand aside," Death cried. "I'm about my Father's business and I will not tarry."

"I know whose business you're about," the Devil told Death. "I was there when the plans was laid out in the beginning. But that woman, that woman He's sent you after, I'm the one who watched over her. It ain't on you to see her to the other side. It's on me."

And so Death, taking pity on his poor, misguided brother, climbed down out of his saddle and, out of the ghostly hollow of his farseeing eyes, watched as the Devil made his way to Walter's house, where by now Walter had taken his wife's place at his dying mother's side, reached down into Lucille, lifted her up out of her body, and flew her home on his own wings.

It rained the day they laid Lucille's body to rest, but still the people of Laurent, the Black people at least, came. They came because she had brewed the tea that eased their mothers' passing. They came because she'd cured their firstborn's colic, stilled their tired wombs, and kept their husbands from straying. They came because, when everyone else thought they had lost their minds, she'd crossed the threshold of their houses, searched behind their woodstoves, under their sofas, between their mattresses, and did not stop until she found whatever charm had been laid against them. They came because they had not believed witches in league with the Devil could die. They came because she was their pastor's mother. They came because she was one of the last living among them to have known slavery.

"Say what you will about my mother," Walter said, leveling his teared eyes at the congregation, "but she knew Jesus. She wouldn't call him by name, but still she knew him. You know how I know she knew Jesus? Because Jesus is love, and nobody loved like how my mother loved. She was a powerful woman, my mother. I've seen her do things no one living should have the power to do. But you know what, church? Every one of those things. Each and every one of those miraculous things was done in service to somebody else. Yes, it was. Even now, my mother is up there with Saint Peter, laying all her sins up on one side of the scale and her good works up on the other, and I don't need to see it to know which way it's gone tip. No, church, I'm not worried for my mother one bit because she took all that power God gave her and put it into this here community, into us. Yes, church. My mother knew Jesus because Jesus is love, and nobody loved like how Lucille Laurent loved, and so I know just which way that scale's gone tip. But the question I have for you, church. The one I want to put to you is this: Do you know? Do you know which way your scale is going to tip? One day, church, one day soon, Gabriel is going to blow that horn. He's going to blow that horn, and each and every one of us is going to account for how we spent our time here on Earth. My mother spent all seventy-seven of her years serving. How will you spend yours?"

Walter's question resounded in Louis's mind as he and Junior, alongside the deacons, hefted his grandmother's red oak casket onto their shoulders and carried it out the front doors of the church and down the hill to the sycamore tree. As they shoveled the overturned dirt that, owing to the rains, was now more mud than anything else, he vowed to honor Lucille's memory by staying true to the brother Lucille had gifted him all those years ago. And now, months later, as Louis knelt before the altar, all the shame of being too weak to keep his vow came down upon him. It was in this pitiful state that the Devil found Louis and, after Uncle Sam called both Louis's and Junior's numbers, answered his prayers, doing for him just as he had done for David.

"Shell shock," they said of Louis, shaking their heads, after Junior's memorial service. "That's why he won't never speak on it. The boy's shell-shocked."

"But they say he didn't see any action. Wasn't even issued a rifle."

"I don't care what they say. All you got to do is look at that boy to know he seen something."

After the service, Ernestine cornered Louis to ask him just what had happened; all the letter from the army had said was that Junior had been killed in a training exercise. But Louis just stood there staring past her. What he wanted to say but couldn't bring himself to was that Junior — his nose broken, his eyes wide — was standing just to the right of her.

*　*　*

Louis and Junior had reported for duty at Camp Logan early Monday morning after not having spoken a word to one another for one train ride, two buses, and a night at the YMCA. No one who met them at camp would have thought they knew one another, and yet they were put on the same work detail and assigned bunks next to each other. By Friday evening, they'd helped clear more than an acre of trees, raised the mess hall where, months later, the Third Battalion of the 24th Infantry would dine the morning after the night they marched on Houston, and were told by their commanding officer, Jeb Talbert, that this was the most action they'd ever see.

"The army needs men who know how to work just as bad as they need soldiers," Jeb told Junior when he asked how long it would be before they shipped out. "If I were you, I'd consider it an honor. But if you're itching to fight, it's my duty as your CO to put that to use."

Like his grandfather, Jacob Talbert, first cousin to Captain Jack Talbert, Jeb felt most himself when he was watching one man pummel another. Before answering his country's call, Jeb spent his Saturday nights taking bets on which one of the Negroes he put in the ring could whip the others. The winner got twenty percent of the proceeds, which, on a good night, was upwards of fifteen dollars, a far cry from what any of the slaves his grandfather made fight got. After getting permission from his superiors, Jeb blindfolded ten recruits, put them in the ring, and charged the officers a dollar a head for admission.

It had rained the night before, and so the ground within the fenced-off area where the battle royal was to take place was muddy. By then, Louis and Junior had managed to go two months without speaking to one another, but before their blindfolds were put into place, the latter nodded to the former. Louis, for his part, was too panic-stricken to notice his brother's gesture of goodwill. He'd been in fights before but never with jeering spectators, never without Junior to back him up.

The first blow to Louis's face stunned him, and before he knew it, he was on the ground tasting copper. He tried to stand, but once he got to his knees, someone kicked him and he was back in the mud. He crawled until he found a post and clung to it until someone kicked him again.

"Ain't you never fought before?" a voice whispered into his ear.

Louis shook his head.

"The fight's almost over," the voice said. "Get after it."

Louis stumbled into the center of the ring, swinging as hard as he could, and eventually, after taking a few licks, tripping over someone, and standing back up, his fist connected with one of the posts. His hand cried out in pain, but he kept swinging anyway. After a while, he didn't feel anything. Not the pain in his knuckles, nor his anger at Junior over marrying Ernestine and then all but stepping out of the way, nor the interminable agony of knowing God had cast him to the wayside and would never take hold of him the way He had his father.

Louis swung and kept swinging until, finally, he landed a blow. A roar went up through the spectators and then gave way to silence, to gasps. Let that angel come find me now, Louis thought. Let him try to put his hands to me. It was only after Louis took off his blindfold and saw Junior on the ground that he realized the voice in his ear hadn't been an officer's.

Years later, as Louis lay upon on his deathbed, the Devil appeared to him one last time. Seeing his approach, the old man would reach back in his mind over the years for a memory to carry with him to the other side. He'd seek first the birth of Robert, his son with Clementine, and then of Benny, his son with Ernestine, who, though Louis would never formally claim him, was his favorite. But the only memory he'd want to carry with him was of Junior.

After the fight, Louis learned that the other men in the ring, at least the ones who were savvy enough to raise their blindfolds, saw that Junior was the strongest, and ganged up on him to have a better shot at the prize money. Junior fought them all off, which was why he and Louis were the only ones left standing.

"Well, Louis," the Devil said, "I reckon you know what I come for."

At the infirmary at Camp Logan, just before Death raised his scythe, Junior looked up at Louis like he pitied him, even though he was the one who was dying. There was a glint in his eye, a bright knowing that filled Louis with hope and dread. It was to this bright knowing that Louis turned when he wanted to sink further down into his whiskey bottle, and again when he needed to climb out of it. In the latter instances, the look recalled for Louis what he'd felt the day Junior saved him from drowning.

They were laid out on the bluff opposite the church, trying to catch their breath, when Junior turned and fixed his eyes on him. Louis's blood stilled and then, all at once, started pumping. He averted his eyes to the sky, but even though the light was mottled by the leaves of the river trees, it hurt too much to keep looking up, and so he turned his head back to Junior. By then they'd caught their breath. Neither bothered to look away from the other.

There is something more to that look, Louis would think as he closed his eyes to this world and opened his heart to the light of the other, but he would be too close up and far away to see what all was in it.

Spare the Rod

ROBERT LAURENT
(1915–1996)
Son of Louis Laurent
Brother of Benny Ross
Father of James Laurent, Mary Laurent,
and Porter Bland

YOU CAN NEVER just call up one ghost. You get one, and before you know it, all the others are there, listening in on everything you got to say. It's like back when I was a boy and the only kind of phone service folks out in the country could get was a party line. If you called one house on our street, you called them all. I can't tell you how many times I picked up Ma's rotary and ended up having to run out into the field behind Mr. Gibson's to tell him his sister was on the line, just for him to say, "Aw, Lula Jo don't want nothing," and go right back to driving Apollo, his mule. Apollo was half-blind and, supposedly, only kicked if you came at him from the left. Seemed to me he kicked no matter which way you came at him. The day they shot Dr. King, Mr. Gibson was at the plow, trying to wangle one more row out of that hateful mule.

Anyway, that woman come to me again last night.

She sat down at the kitchen table across from me just as soon as my son James got up and went to his room. This time, the skirt of her yellow dress was damp enough to drip water all over the floor. She comes every now and then, not wanting anything more than to sit and enjoy my silence. She doesn't carry on like some of the others do, not anymore, anyway. All she does is sit and look and say the same words over and over again. I think mostly she comes around just to be seen. James won't half talk to me, and Catherine, saying she needed some time to think, took our daughter, Mary, up to Ripley to see her folks, so I didn't mind the company.

I was sitting up trying to figure out what to do about James. He was getting picked on over at the school on account of the stitches running down along the side of his face. Truth be told, it was a pretty bad cut. An accident, of course, but a bad cut all the same. Catherine treated it with honey and put some potato slices on it to bring the swelling down. It looked a lot better the next morning, but he didn't want to go to school with his face the way it was. I told him he could sit out awhile, so long as he made up his lessons. It's been a week and the boy's still shuffling around the house like a turtle what won't come out of his shell. After he finished his dinner, I told him he'd have to find a better way to deal with folks not liking his face than hiding it. He stood and cleared his plate without so much as a word.

It had been a long day. I felt in my bones when I woke that it would be. The hogs had gotten loose the night before, and running them down in the dark had left my legs achy as shit. It's fall, and they can sense that pretty soon more than a few of them are going to be split down the middle, salted up, and smoked over coals.

Ma phones as soon as I finish getting my coffee creamed up and sugared, and before she can get out what the trouble is, I hear Pa in the background tearing shit up and hollering for his pistol.

"I'm on my way," I tell her.

"Don't let it burn you," the woman in yellow says as I raise the coffee mug to my lips. I chug it down, lace up my boots, and yell for James to stay put while I go see about his grandparents.

When I get to my folks' house—they don't live but about a mile down the road—they're airing it all out in the front yard. Pa gave up on the pistol and settled for his rifle. Ma is on the porch in a blue housedress.

"Go on, then," she yells. "Go on and get yourself killed. I don't give a good goddamn if somebody puts a bullet in you."

"I'm going to be the one what's doing the shooting," Pa says, laying the rifle down in the bed of his truck. "Ain't no use in you trying to stop me," he says to me.

"I'm not here to stop you," I tell him. "I'm here to help you do it." Sometimes it helps if you play along.

"You do what now?"

"I said I want to help you do it."

By now, Benny has pulled up. I passed him on the road and waved for him to turn around and follow me. He was coming to help me put in my sweet potatoes, but now I need him to shame Pa into calming down.

"You don't really want to hurt anybody, do you, Mr. Louis?" Benny says, getting out of his truck. He has on a rumpled white shirt and flea market jeans.

"It ain't about what I want, Benny," Pa says. "It's about what needs doing."

Pa gets like this from time to time. He drinks away half the night, drunk-dreams up some slight from before I was born, and wakes up wanting revenge. Even if what he's mad about actually happened, there's no making him see that nobody but him cares enough to remember it.

"Y'all boys go on home now," he says, patting down his coverall pockets, searching for his keys. Between Benny's car and mine blocking him in, there's no way for him to back out of the driveway. "This ain't got nothing to do with either of you."

Him knowing Benny is usually a good sign. If he was still in his dreaming mind, he wouldn't know anybody outside of me and Ma. It might mean he's snapping out of it. Used to be he could work out for himself what was dream and what was truth before breakfast. It's only in the past few years that he's gotten to where he wants to be outside and violent. He never actually gets to where he can hurt anybody, most times because there's nobody living to hurt. Most people he wakes up wanting to kill are already dead. But, yet and still, it's right worrisome for him to be riding around with a loaded gun in his lap.

He narrows his eyes. Things are going the other way. It's rare for him to make a go of it on foot, but the set of his gaze says he just might. Benny closes the door to his Dodge and walks around back of Pa's Chevy. He sees what I see. We have to get him to the ground, and it won't be easy. Pa's old, but he's every bit as strong as I am, stronger when he's out of his mind. Luckily, he makes for me before he thinks to reach for his rifle. I plant my feet and hunker down. He lowers his head, makes to run at me. He can come, but I won't let him past me. Before he does, Benny wraps him up from behind and lifts him into the air. Pa kicks his feet out. I grab his legs. This is how we get him back into the house.

Ma holds the door open, and me and Benny wrestle him onto the couch, managing, to Ma's relief, not to break the marble table she had shipped from Memphis back when she thought her life was going to be bigger than what it was. Pa doesn't fight as hard once we get him down, but he don't make it easy to keep him there, either. Now he's fighting us more out of spite for being manhandled than anything else. After we tussle, I tell him we're not leaving until he calms himself.

Ma gets her overnight bag and I walk her out to the car. I maneuver her car around Benny's truck.

"You don't have to come back if you don't want to," I say as she puts her bag in the passenger seat. "Benny and me can get your stuff."

"This is my house, too," she says. "I'll be back tomorrow."

Inside, Benny is standing over Pa, and Pa is staring up at him. I smell food burning. In the kitchen, I find a skillet of half-fried eggs on the stove and a cast-iron pan full of smoking black biscuits in the oven. He couldn't even let her get through breakfast.

"Mr. Louis," Benny says. "What they do to make you want to hurt them so bad?"

This is how days like this usually go. Pa gets violent and then starts to feeling bad, wanting to make nice, but it's not long before he resents everyone he felt he had to apologize to, sorrier for himself than anybody else, and takes to drinking again. Today, I tell him I don't want no apology. What I want is for him to talk out whatever foolishness he's cooked up so we can put it to bed and get back to work.

Pa looks over at me and Benny, then down at his feet. He's calm now, but the anger has yet to leave his eyes. Benny glances around at the pictures of Ma and her side of the family before taking a seat in the wingback chair across from the couch. I stay standing.

"I ever tell you how I know your people?" Pa says to Benny.

Benny shakes his head no before I can catch his eye, and Pa starts in on the fires, about his grandfather Franklin casting off the yoke of slave with both arms, about Junior. I close my ears. I've heard these damn stories a thousand times.

"Pa," I break in. "We know all this already."

"I don't," Benny says. He might not. Ms. Ernestine, Benny's momma, is funny-acting. I've known her all my life, but when I try to speak, she looks right through me like she doesn't know my face. At first I thought it had to do with Pa and whatever it was they had going way back when, but it's not just me she turns her nose up at. There's no telling what she has or hasn't told Benny about her husband, Junior; Pa; or anything else, for that matter, but the fact that Pa is Benny's real father is an open secret.

Outside, Pa's dog is barking up a storm. Ain't no way in the world there's anything out there bad enough to make him carry on the way he is. It's only after he shuts up that Pa finds his way around to making some sort of point.

"Our families got history, so it does me good to see the two of you getting along. The man I need to kill, he took my best friend from me, your mother's husband," he says to Benny.

Pa turns to me, and his eyes tell me all the words his mouth ain't saying. What riled him this morning wasn't just a dream. I walk back over from the window and stand beside Benny's chair.

"Benny," Pa says, "your mother's husband didn't die in no training exercise like they told your momma."

"So that's who come to you?" I ask. "The ghost of the man who killed Junior?"

"No," Pa says. "Jeb ain't no ghost."

The dead come for all kinds of reasons. They come with warnings, wants, and every manner of grudge. Most of the ones haunting Pa are soldiers he knew from Camp Logan. They come to learn what happened and why. Why did they have to die, and what was it all for? He tries to tell them that he doesn't understand it any better than they do, but they don't believe him. If he's living and they're dead, he's got to know something, don't he? The dead want everything you have and can't give.

I started seeing Yetunde when I was just a boy. I woke up one night, peeped out from under the covers, and there she was in the chair by the window, calm and cool as all get-out, rocking and smiling, rocking and smiling. I pulled those covers right back over my eyes and acted like my great-great-grandmother's old spindle-backed rocker wasn't creaking away until dawn. When I got up the next morning, the afghan draped over the back of the chair was damp to the touch.

At breakfast, Pa asked me how I had slept. I lied and said I'd slept fine. He said it didn't seem like it. I ignored him and tried as best I could to eat my oatmeal, but it caught in my throat. Nothing I ate that day went down right.

The woman came regular each night after the first. Early on, she was silent, content to rock and hum with no more consideration for me and my sleep than the man in the moon. Then one night, I peeked out from under the covers and asked her if she was living or dead. I didn't know which answer I was more afraid of.

She said she hadn't thought about it in a long while, which probably meant she was dead. Though sometimes she forgot and thought she was alive.

I asked her how she died.

She said she'd rather not say, but if I really wanted to know, she would tell me.

I told her she didn't have to tell me if she didn't want to.

She started to explain, but I couldn't make out what she said over the sound of Ma busting through the door.

"Robert, who are you in here talking to?" Ma asked.

"Nobody."

"Don't sound like nobody," Ma said, stepping into the room. When Ma's eyes fell on the rocking chair, the woman put the black of her finger to the pink of her lip.

"Myself," I said. "I was talking to myself."

Ma studied the room like she knew I was guilty but didn't have enough evidence to convict me. Later, I asked the woman why I could see her but my momma couldn't. She said it was because I was hers and Ma wasn't.

"You're not nobody," Ma said finally. "You hear me?"

"Yes, ma'am."

"You can't hoot with the owls at night if you want to soar with the eagles in the morning."

"Huh?"

"Go to sleep. It's late."

"Burning is one thing," the woman said after Ma left, "and drowning is another. But to have the sky enter you is something else altogether. You look into that blue and you feel like you're falling, but you ain't.

171

The sky is the one doing the falling. It's the one making its way into you. I let the sky in to have its way with me, and then I couldn't figure what was me and what was it."

"What do you mean you let the sky 'have its way' with you?"

"I mean just what I said. I flew."

She didn't say anything else. She just kept rocking and staring off into the distance. I couldn't sleep for fear of the sky entering me, and for a long while after, I refused to look up at it.

"Your momma says you were talking to yourself," Pa said the next morning. It was a Saturday. I was slopping the hogs while Pa leaned on the fence post, watching me do it. That day he made me do all the work. Claimed he had to stand still to figure out what the weather would allow us to plant that spring. Said the air had to have a certain feel to it before you could seed.

"It wasn't nobody there," I said, remembering the way the woman had looked when Ma entered the room. "I was just making conversation with myself."

The hogs were in a pen out in a clearing in the woods behind the backyard. After we finished up with them, there was a cow out to pasture Pa wanted to check on. If she was ready to birth, Pa was going to show me how to help her. I can't tell you how much I didn't feel like learning.

"They come to me, too," he said after a while. "They don't come to your momma or near 'bout anybody else you might meet, but they sure as shit come to me."

It's a three-hour drive to where Jeb lives in Dyersburg, two if we take 51, but Pa says he'd rather stay to the back roads. We take my car because I'm the only one who bothers to keep the registration up, and the last thing we want is to get pulled over. Pa is up front with me, Benny is in back with the woman. Whenever I check the rearview, she levels her eyes at me.

After about an hour, Benny says he's hungry, so we stop over at a gas station in Henning. I fill up while Benny's inside and then get back in the car with Pa. The question I want to put to him but can't find my way around to is: Why now? For over fifty years, Pa has suffered this man to draw breath. What I don't have to ask is how much of a mess of things Pa might make, setting out to kill a white man on his own, if I don't keep an eye on him. Last time he got like this, I wrestled with him half the day and then, thinking I'd gotten through to him, went home. I'd barely had time to get in the house and get my boots off before Eva Watson called, saying she'd seen Pa drive by — rifle hanging halfway out the passenger side window like an old bluetick — just before she heard a shot. By the time I caught up to him, he was at Blake Rogers's old place, sitting on the rotted-out porch, looking lost to the world. Blake had been dead going on five years. I hid his guns, but he just went out and bought new ones.

"It was Junior come to me," Pa says. "I hadn't thought about Jeb in a good long while, but when Junior come, he reminded me it wasn't my grudge to forgive."

"You have to do it now, though? Why don't you take a couple of days to think it out?"

"It's gotta happen today," Pa says.

You see them first out of the corner of your eye, like a shadow flitting its way across a well-lit room. You blink and they're there, as live-seeming and whole as any person you'd want to meet. They come to loved ones if their loved ones can see them, but if their loved ones can't, they come to anybody who can. If you're lucky, you'll blink again and they'll be gone just like they never was. But if you're like me, if you're like Pa, they never leave.

"It takes a good while to get used to," Pa said as he watched the game. "But after a time, seeing them won't bother you no more than a mosquito will. You might even learn a thing or two if you pay attention."

We were listening to the Cardinals play the Cubs on the radio. Ma had gone into the bedroom to read because she didn't, and never would, trust the radio. The news was just about the only thing you could get her to sit still for. This was back when Ma worked at World Color, dyeing magazines on the assembly line, before the ink started to dull her sense of smell and stain her hands green. When I was small, I wanted to work at World Color so that my hands could be green, too.

"I was five when they first come to me," Pa went on. "I couldn't tell no difference between them and living folks and caught hell for it from everyone but my grandmother, God rest her soul." Pa was in his favorite chair. I was on the floor.

"You're lucky," he said. "You got most of your growing up out of the way before they come to you."

There's not much to see between here and Dyersburg besides cotton. Every once in a while a new business pops up, a restaurant, a bar, a bowling alley, but you can pretty much set your calendar to its closing. The only thing I've seen have any staying power, outside of the gas stations, is McDonald's. They crop up like ragweed, while good restaurants go under.

Benny stares out the window, gets antsy, and then starts fiddling with the funeral programs in the pocket behind the passenger seat. I never planned on putting them there, but after each funeral, I reach around and slide the program in. I don't know what I would do with them if they ever made it into the house. Right now, he's bending back the front cover of Mr. Gibson's program, then watching it spring forward. It shouldn't bother me, but it does. Mr. Gibson died peaceful, in his sleep. When he comes, it's always through the front door with his hat in his hand, offering me molasses candy in exchange for snapping a bucket of peas, just like he did when I was a boy.

"Keep straight," Pa says.

"I'm keeping straight."

The sun is just shy of making it up over the tops of the trees. When I was younger, you could hardly see the sky for all the overgrowth, but ever since Clayton Cotton bought up all the land on either side of Highway 14, clearing out everything that refused to grow a white boll, it's gotten bigger and bigger, and today there's not a cloud in it.

"No, you're not. You're wobbling. You're all over the paint."

I make a right and it puts us directly in the path of the sun. Part of me wonders if it wouldn't have been better to make this trip under the cover of night.

"Daytime's better," Pa says, reading my face.

I don't ask why.

Pa never spoke of his time in the army when I was coming up, except to say I should never join. But then, after the ghosts of the servicemen started coming to him more and more, he let slip that he was at Camp Logan the day they marched on Houston. I'd always assumed Junior died in the riot.

"I shouldn't be dragging y'all into this," Pa says. "Y'all don't have no place in it. Just drop me off down the road and I'll figure it out. You won't have to be there. You can just park a ways off and I'll find you. You don't have to be there."

"Mr. Louis, we not letting you do this alone."

"You won't have to do anything," Pa says. "Just leave it to me."

After another hour, we turn off the highway onto a side road. Benny leaves the programs alone and starts fiddling with something I can't see, and the woman in yellow is watching him like she's never seen anything like it. Pa is half-asleep.

"I'm awake. Just resting my eyes."

"Nobody said you weren't."

"I could feel you staring at me. You should be watching the road."

"I am watching the road."

"Could have fooled me."

We pass the turnoff for Jackson, and I almost take it out of habit.

"You get up this way a lot, don't you?" Benny says, eyeing my reflection in the rearview mirror.

"I don't know what you mean," I tell him.

"Don't Lorraine and them live out this way?"

Benny likes to play like this sometimes, but right now, with Pa in the car, it's too much. I don't give him the satisfaction of a response.

"Eunice's niece?" Pa says, turning to Benny. "What she got to do with any of this?"

"Nothing," Benny says, turning from Pa to grin at me. "Just making a little conversation is all."

I turn, and in another mile or so, we reach Dyersburg proper.

"Now, if we really gonna do this," Benny says, leaning forward over the console, "we need a plan."

Pa nods.

"The way I see it, we got a few ways to get this done. We can leave him where he lays, take a few things, and make it seem like a robbery. Another way to go would be to make it look like he did himself in. Make him swallow some pills and lay him out on his bed all nice and neat. Or we could bring the body with us and take care of him at home. If we do that, it gives us a little bit more time before folks start looking at it funny. Of course, that means some liability on the back end, but I'd much rather that than waiting around to make sure the police see things how we need them to. But I think with us being from out of town and all that, we can get this done nice and quiet with nobody looking at us sideways."

Pa turns around to face Benny, then cuts his eyes at me. He cuts his eyes at me because he doesn't know that Jeb won't be the first white man Benny and I have killed.

*   *   *

It was my sophomore year of high school and Candy Smith, a white woman not too much older than Benny and me, got caught with a man her husband thought might be black. Before she married, Candy was a Laurent, one of Bubba's grandkids, and being a white Laurent meant something, even though her branch of the family had only known hard times. Her husband, Ken, was one of the people for whom the name Laurent still carried weight. Ken's father delivered milk for Laurent's Dairy for thirty years, and Ken's first paying job was at Laurent Farms picking strawberries, and like everyone else in the county, they went to Laurent's Grocery for all their sundries. So when Candy Laurent agreed to go with him to the drive-in and then, a year later, to be his wife, Ken — a high school dropout who used his brother's license to get a job as a long-haul trucker — could hardly believe his good fortune.

Everybody in town knew Candy kept a boyfriend or two while Ken was out on the road, but nobody ever felt it was their place to say so. When Ken pulled up, thinking, knowing, how nice a surprise it would be to Candy for him to arrive a day early, he saw a man walk right out of his front door, glance at him, and then take off into the woods. The first thing Candy thought to say was that someone had broken in and tried to have his way with her.

Ken called Sheriff Potts that very night, and the next morning, Sheriff Potts, his deputies, and a band of overzealous volunteers — the likes of which are never in short supply — invited every colored man fitting the description down to the station. But when it came time to pick one of us out to punish, Candy came clean, and Sheriff Potts, shaking his head the whole while, let us all go.

Only Ken didn't want to let it go. Even after Candy had laid the truth of it out and told him all about her boyfriends and how she met most of them at the diner she waitressed at, and how she loved Ken, loved only him, just lonesome was all, he couldn't let it go. He'd fixed it in his mind that a nigger had run up in his house and laid hand to what was his.

"Candy just a good-hearted woman," Ken said to us the next week out in the woods.

Benny and me were walking back home from school when Ken called out to us from the road. Benny used to could sing, and a lot of people thought he might have a future in it, so white folks were always going out of their way to talk to him in case he got famous. I assumed this was what Ken wanted. Him pulling a gun and walking us into the woods was the last thing I expected him to do. By then, Benny and me had put all that foolishness with Candy behind us. You can't carry everything with you.

"Too good-hearted even to see justice. Too good-hearted for her own good. But you niggers know what's what, don't you? You know justice ought to be served."

Benny and me just stared down at the gun.

"Yeah, it was you I seen running. Yeah, you, the light one. I thought it was an awful pale nigger. Maybe that awful pale nigger was you. You got anything to say for yourself?" Ken said, the water in his eyes thickening to tears as he pointed his pistol at me. "You know what it's like to go out and work for something. Hmm? No, no, you don't. You niggers got it easy. Got everything handed to you. Especially you."

He was talking about me. Pa's family had always had land, and poor white folks, especially those coming up from Memphis trying to find a cheaper way to live, resented it. That he was alone and carrying a pistol was a comfort. I'd seen black folks die in ways much more painful and public.

"Good white folks out there working like dogs, and here you got everything handed to you. It's a damn shame."

"Mr. Ken," Benny said. "Ain't nobody out here touched your wife but you."

"Ain't nobody out here asked you to put your goddamned two cents in, either."

Benny put his hands down and took a step toward Ken. The leaves were dry enough for you to hear each footfall. We were in a clearing just shy of Pa's property line. Not a month before, Pa and I were down here breaking up a whiskey still. Nobody was foolish enough to hide one on their own land, but the law was allowed to arrest anyone within a hundred feet of a working still, so if you came across one, especially as close as this one was to the cow pasture, you pretty much had to bust it up. If one of the hogs hadn't have gotten out, caught the scent — there wasn't much hogs loved more than sweet corn mash — and led us to it, we might never have seen it. My ears were just past ringing with the sound of axes striking metal.

"Ken, if you gonna shoot us, then go on and shoot us, but I ain't gonna stand out here in the sun all day, catching your spit."

I put my hands down. I saw what Benny saw. Ken either forgot or didn't realize he'd left the safety on. Benny speared him. He drove his head into Ken's gut and took him to the ground. Ken dropped the gun, and while Benny was laying into him, I picked it up and flicked the safety off. But before I could think about whether I wanted to pull the trigger, whether I had in me what Pa has in him, a shot rang out and the gun recoiled. Benny stood, breathing hard and heavy, and Ken, he was lying flat, eyes open, arms out like it was a white Christmas and he was about to make himself a snow angel. He was staring up at me like he wanted me to watch him die. When Ken's ghost comes, when he lays himself out on the carpet, when he plants himself in front of the wheels of my truck, he looks up at me just like this.

We pull up to Jeb's house near about noon. It's a good ways from downtown, and his closest neighbor, from what I can tell, lives about two miles up the road. We park behind a stand of live oaks and track how many cars drive by. In the span of half an hour, we see one. We work out that Benny is going to go up to the house first. He's going to knock on the door to make sure Jeb is home and no one else. He's going to say he's got car trouble and needs to use the phone. If Jeb's a good Christian, he'll let him. If he knows his way around an engine, he might even offer to take a gander.

"There's things you need to know," Pa says once Benny's gone. "There's things you need to know I haven't found a way to say. I done things I'm not proud of," he says. "There's people I haven't done right by."

"I already know enough about what you have and haven't done," I say. "Whatever other dirt you're holding in, save it. I got enough of my own to carry."

Pa lets out a sigh, bites his lip, and turns toward Jeb's house. From the driver's seat, all I can see is trees and brush, but on the other side of the ditch, I notice blackberry brambles. My son James won't eat fresh blackberries, but he'll eat them in a cobbler. I asked him why once when we were sitting down to a cobbler his mother made, and he told me he didn't like the seeds. I told him that they still had seeds in the cobbler. But when I said this, he just shrugged and went back to eating.

"What's your wife up to today?" Pa asks.

"She's out visiting some of her folks."

"She does that a lot," he says.

I don't say anything to that.

Benny makes his way back to the truck. He's eating something, but he's holding it in a napkin, so I can't tell what it is.

"He in there," Benny says, chewing. "Don't seem like he's expecting anybody anytime soon."

"What are you eating?"

"Biscuit and bacon," Benny says, and as he says it, a piece of bacon falls out of his mouth and onto the ground. Seeing it makes me think of how fat Benny's dog, Tyson, is. There are probably people who don't eat half as much as what that dog picks up off the floor.

"He made you a sandwich?" I ask.

"Yeah," Benny says. "What of it?"

I don't say anything to that either.

"How did he seem?" Pa asks.

"Seemed like an old white man," Benny says.

Pa turns toward the house again. I crane my neck to get a better angle, and I can see it now. It's nice but not too nice, set a ways off from the road. If nobody does anything about the trees, in a few years' time you won't be able to see it at all.

"I told him I had to lock up," Benny goes on. "He's in the house waiting."

Pa gets out the truck and walks around to where Benny is.

"You boys don't have to do this," Pa says. "I can go in alone."

"Is that what you want?" I ask.

Pa nods.

Benny claps Pa on the shoulder and walks around to the passenger side. He's still eating. I try not to think about how I'm going to be the one digging the crumbs out of the seat cushion when we get back. Pa starts up the driveway, glances back at us, and keeps walking. He's not carrying his gun, but his gait seems off. He's different from how he was this morning, though. Benny brushes off his pants, sticks the napkin in the cup holder, and asks about turning on the radio, but music on top of the woman in yellow's humming would be too much for me, so I tell him no. Ghosts don't care anything about where you are or what you're doing when they come. All that matters to them is what they want with you. I still haven't figured out what the woman in yellow wants with me.

"Let's go watch," Benny says.

We walk around the side of Jeb's property, making our way through the brush and blackberry brambles. The berries stain Benny's shirt like dried blood as we wade through them. I'm more careful, and so my clothes come out clean.

A window around back allows us to peep into the living room. Jeb is smaller and weaker than I'd imagined. He's wearing a green flannel shirt tucked into a pair of pleated tan slacks. He seems to be a few years older than Pa but in better health. He's sitting and Pa's pacing back and forth, talking.

"What's he jawing about?"

"I don't know."

Pa sits down on the couch beside Jeb, leans forward, and glares down at his hands like he's frightened at the sight of them. Jeb puts his hand on Pa's back.

"What are they doing?" Benny asks.

"I know as much as you," I tell him.

Pa turns to the window. He sees Benny and me and makes to stand up. Benny starts walking around to the front, and I follow him. Pa meets us at the door like it's his house and we haven't been invited.

"Jeb is a good man," Pa says, simpering like a chastised child. "I just got a little mixed up is all."

"These your boys?" Jeb asks, coming over to the door. His face just cries out to be punched.

"Yeah," Pa says.

"They seem like good boys," Jeb says.

"You the man that killed Junior?" Benny asks.

Pa shoots a startled glance at Jeb.

"Why don't y'all come in and have a seat?" Jeb says.

On the wall facing the door are pictures of Jeb's children and grandchildren. Every one of them has Jeb's scrunched, bat-like face and scarecrow frame. I hadn't thought too hard about what I would find here, but this is not what I expected.

"I got a pot of coffee on the stove," Jeb says. "You boys want any?"

Benny says he'll have some.

The place smells almost nice, kind of like cinnamon but with a tinge of cat urine. There is a litter box by the door, but I don't see a cat anywhere around. On the coffee table is a half-built ship in a bottle, a schooner.

"That's just a little project I've been working on," Jeb says, handing

Benny an orange mug of black coffee. Benny always drinks his coffee black. I don't see how he can stand it.

"You can just push it on over to the side. It won't hurt nothing, and please have a seat. My wife would turn over in her grave if she knew I had company and left them standing."

We sit.

"You boys are the spitting image of your father."

I turn to Benny. His eyes are staring down into the black well of his coffee.

"What are we doing here?" Benny asks.

"I'm sorry," Pa says. "Sometimes I just get a little confused is all."

"Confused?" I ask.

"Yeah," Pa says, cutting his eyes at me. "Confused."

I'm a pretty good judge of when Pa is in and out of his mind, and right now he's in. There's something else going on here.

"So what happened?" Benny asks.

Jeb tells us all about their unit, how a sort of informal boxing tournament came about between the draftees. It started as a way to settle disputes during basic training. Junior knocked out just about everybody he was pit against due to the strength of his left jab.

"It was almost like fighting a man with two right hands," Jeb says, rubbing his jaw.

A large glass placard on the mantel above the fireplace reads "Salesman of the Year." Behind it, there's a cross, the Catholic kind with Christ nailed to it, only the expression on his face refracted through the glass is one I've never seen before. It's almost like he's angry, and while Jeb's speaking, it's all I can see.

"Nobody was supposed to be hurt. Not like that."

"So who killed him?" Benny asks. He's holding his coffee with both hands, gazing into the black of it.

"It was an accident, you see—"

"Junior got knocked out," Pa says. "We got him to the infirmary, and for a while it seemed like he was going to be all right. But when the doctor checked in on him the next morning, he was dead."

"Any white soldiers die that way?" I ask.

"No," Jeb says.

"Seems strange to me," I say, "that someone could just knock him out like that. Him being such a good boxer and all."

"Me, too," Benny says.

"The other fellow was a good fighter, too," Jeb says. "I haven't seen anybody who can hit like him in a good while."

Pa glances down at his hands. His knuckles are knotted up and scarred. In them is everything he didn't let himself remember until now.

I start to speak, but before I can, an orange-and-white cat winds its way around my foot and blinks up at me. When I nudge it away, it trots over to Jeb's outstretched hands.

"Come here, Josie," Jeb says, scratching it between the ears. The cat is as smug as a child spared the rod.

"I don't think he meant to hurt him," Jeb says. "Just didn't know his strength is all. We were all just boys. We didn't know what we were doing."

"Who was he?" Benny asks.

"It's not my place to say," Jeb says, turning to Pa.

Benny sets his coffee mug down beside the coaster Jeb laid out for it, stands up, and walks out the door. He hasn't smoked all day, so I imagine he's going to light up a cigarette. That's probably why he's been so short and antsy. I don't allow smoking in my car.

"Is he gonna be all right?" Jeb asks.

"Yeah," I say. "He'll be fine."

Jeb picks up Benny's half-empty coffee mug and places it on the coaster.

"Is he mad?" Pa says.

"He'll be fine," I say. "Are you okay?"

Pa leans forward, makes like he's going to cry, and seeing him do it makes me want to reach across the table and give him a good lick to the back of his head like he'd have done to me when I was a boy. But before I can, Jeb takes Pa's hand in his and squeezes it. The sight of it makes me sick to my stomach. No one was there to hold my hand when Pa smacked me.

"I'll be outside," I say, standing up. "Let me know when you're ready to go."

I find Benny smoking a cigarette under a sycamore tree halfway between the house and the road. He's smoking it nice and slow. It's his second. He'd have burned through the first one already.

"Anything I want to know?" Benny asks. He grinds the cigarette into the tree. The red ashes linger on the bark. I wonder for a second if the grass underneath will catch.

"Naw," I say. "There's nothing you want to know."

There's a flash of movement in the sycamore tree above Benny's head. I can't make out what it is.

"My grandmomma used to say owls carry death," Benny says, pointing up at the tree, "so when you hear them, you know it's somebody's time somewhere. When I was little, I used to sit up by the window and try to figure out who they was hooting about. One night I slipped out of bed, went out the back door, and cut across the yard to try to track it. But the closer I got, the less I could hear it. I caught up to it up in a pecan tree, but it wasn't alone. There was a whole mess of them up there, and when I walked up to that tree, all I could see was those big moony eyes of theirs peering down at me. When I saw it, I knew she was right."

"What are you trying to say, Benny?"

"I'm saying I seen an owl."

I look over my shoulder. Pa's still inside.

"I think Pa has a few more good days left in him," I say.

"He might," Benny says, lighting another cigarette. "And then again, he might not."

* * *

Nobody is in a talking mood, so we ride home in near silence. I drop Benny off at Ms. Ernestine's house and tell him we'll plant the sweet potatoes tomorrow. As I pull out, Cassandra, Benny's daughter, peeks out through the blinds in the living room. There's something funny about that girl. When I drop Pa off, I tell him to lay off the liquor. I don't want any more calls from Ma like the one I got this morning.

"I'm not your child," he mutters, slamming the door.

When I pull up to my own house, I find a white-tailed doe standing in the middle of the driveway. She doesn't want to move; I have to damn near nudge her to get into the garage. I wait for a minute before getting out of the car in case her mate is anywhere near as bold as she is. By the time I get into the house, the sun has gone down.

James is at the kitchen table with a bowl of cornflakes and an almost empty box. If I let him, cereal would be the only thing he ate all day every day. From the side, it seems like the stitches are bleeding, but when he turns his head, I see that it was just a trick of the light.

"You hear from your momma today?"

He shakes his head no.

"You want me to make you something else to eat?"

He shakes his head again. It's a wonder how he got to be such a quiet boy. He certainly didn't get it from my people.

"Look," I say, "I'm sorry about what happened to your face. I wasn't trying to hurt you. You know that, right?"

"I know," he says, looking down at his bowl and stirring the sugared milk into a whirlpool.

"You still hungry?" I ask him.

He shrugs.

"Tell you what. I'm going to make two bologna sandwiches. If you want one, then you can have one. If not, I'll have both. All right?"

"Yes, sir."

"Good. Now go turn on the radio or something. I don't see how you can stand all this quiet."

*   *   *

The day we killed Ken was the day the woman in yellow quit talking and started repeating those words, the same ones over and over again. We left Ken's body in the woods, went to my house, and waited for Sheriff Potts to come pick us up. Only Sheriff Potts never came, not then or on any of the slow, flutter-hearted, over-the-shoulder-glancing days that followed Ken's death. I gave Benny a change of clothes and put the bloody ones in the barrel behind the house to burn with the leaves.

"Set the fire but don't let it burn you," she'd said to me as I put the flame of Pa's lighter to Benny's shirt and dropped it in, along with his pants and shoes. As the fire spread out across the bottom of the can, the heat of it rose to kiss my face. After it burned down some, I took off my own shirt and fed it to the dying flame. I searched the yard for something else to feed the fire, but I couldn't find anything. I reached my hand out to it. "Don't let it burn you," she said again.

I try to show my son that life's not about doing what you want to do. It's about doing what needs to be done. That's why I go out of my way to teach him how to protect himself. He knows when to run and when to fight. He knows to get close when he sees a gun, to back up when someone flashes a knife. Try to pin my boy down. See if he knows how to kick. Try to grab ahold of him. See if he knows how to bite. I don't go easy on him. I come at him like someone who means to take his life. I've never been one for the by-and-by, and I can't claim to know what this life or the next is all about, but if my son were given the choice Ken gave us, I'd want him to choose his own life. I'd want him to choose his life again and again and again.

BOOK III
Troubled Water

ONE DAY, WHILE the Devil was out walking the West African backcountry—land that passed back and forth between the Oyo Empire and the Kingdom of Dahomey so much that, in a given year, most villagers didn't know which king their crops were to be given to in tribute—a woman in labor called to him. He looked left and he looked right but he didn't see nobody, and so he started back to walking. She called his name three times before he found her laid out in a charred field. Her knowing him by name was a bad sign. One of God's favorite tricks was to let folks see in death all they'd been blind to in life.

"I know you got it in you," the woman begged the Devil with her dying breath. "Please take care of my baby."

By then, the number of people the Devil had watched Death come for was greater than the grains of sand blowing about the Sahara, but he had a soft spot for the discounted, the abandoned, the orphaned. And so when he saw the gleam of his eldest brother's scythe flash across the horizon, he took the newborn, a baby girl, up into his arms, and when he did, she fixed her eyes on his, blinked, and then closed them back into sleep.

"I've come for the both of them," Death said, descending his pale horse. "Hand her over."

"This one's mine," the Devil told his brother. "I'll see to her."

"There's nobody left on this side of life for her," Death said. "It's a mercy."

"I'm here," the Devil said. "She's got me."

"A place has been made for her," Death said. "She don't have power enough to stay on this side."

"I got power," the Devil said, and when he said this, the Devil touched his fingers to her forehead and gave her some of his power, not knowing that what he gave her here would come down through her generations. Or that watching her children contend with it, each in their own way, would forever endear them to him, that the woman's descendants were the closest thing he would ever have to children. "I got power enough for the both of us."

For three days and three nights, the Devil walked with the girl in his arms. War was the order of the day, and Death had swept his scythe over half the countryside. Seeing this, he held fast to the sleeping baby, walked on, and kept walking until he found a village by a river isolated enough to feel like it might be safe.

He heard tell a rich man lived there whose wife had just lost a twin girl in labor. When the Devil arrived at the man's compound, he saw through the window of one of the structures a woman breastfeeding the surviving newborn.

"I found this little one by the side of the road," the Devil told the woman. "Could you see your way to providing her some comfort?"

The woman set her own daughter down in a basket and took the motherless one from the Devil. She put the baby to her breast and nursed her as if she were her natural daughter. And so he left the girl there and made for Haiti, where the conditions were ripe enough to stir up some good trouble, but his mind never strayed from her, never ceased to wonder what would become of her. He would see a slave ship in the distance and wonder whether it held in its dark belly the girl he'd help birth.

And so, years later, after whispering into Nat Turner's ear about what all the coming eclipse might mean, he returned to check on her. He'd gotten as far as the river that bordered her village when he saw the smoke and knew that the hell on Earth that Jesus had tasked him with abolishing had already visited her. He sat down by the bank of the river with his hat in his hands and, for the first time since falling to Earth, did what he'd once teased his brother Jesus for doing. He wept.

Why couldn't his Father God help? the Devil wondered. How had it come down to him to be the one to do the saving?

As the Devil turned to leave, twin cries pealed out from under a bush. One look was enough to tell him the children belonged to the woman. He scooped them up, determined to find a safe place to set them down, but there was no such place. Not for them. Not on Earth.

And so, for the first time since his fall, he walked to the water, where the line between this world and the next was thinnest, and called on Father God. When he spoke the name for God that only angels know, the skies opened up and he could see the other side of Creation, his Father's house, in the water. Seeing this, the Devil took the children and dove up into the water that was the sky and the sky that was the water.

"Are these your children?" Saint Peter asked once he'd arrived at the pearly gates.

"If they are, will you let them into where they can be taken care of?"

"The young'uns can't stay here, Devil. They got to go back down and be reborn."

"It ain't safe down there for them. Can't we work out something?"

"I never thought I'd see it," Jesus said, clapping the Devil on his shoulder. "Father's been watching you. Says He's forgiven you. Says you're ready to come home."

"What happened to the little girl I rescued?" the Devil asked. "Is she up here or down there? These are her children."

"I don't know," Jesus said, taking the babies from the Devil. For Jesus loved little children, all the children of the world. "But what does it matter? All that's troubled on Earth will have salvation here in the by-and-by."

"Not everybody can wait for the by-and-by," the Devil said. "Folks need saving right now."

"You been too long on Earth," Jesus said, looking his brother over. "You can't get caught up worrying about each individual person. You got to look at the big picture. You got to look at it through God's eyes."

"I don't got God's eyes," the Devil said. "The only eyes I got is my own, the ones God gave me, and so far all they've seen is suffering. Let me see this thing through. Then I'll see about coming home."

"All right," Jesus said, shaking his head. "But I can't promise that this door will open for you again. You know how Father God is. That's twice you've denied Him. Ain't no guarantee there'll be a third."

"I know," the Devil said, spreading his wings, readying himself to fly back to Earth, for he was already seeing in his mind's eye the woman, shackled and confused in the bowels of a slave ship headed for New Orleans. "I'll just have to take my chances."

Precious Blood

CASSANDRA ROSS
(1960–1983)
Daughter of Benny Ross
Natural Mother of John Laurent

HERE'S A STORY Gram used to tell me: Once upon a time, there were two sisters who'd married two brothers and lived across the street from one another. Each morning they rose early to work in their gardens, and in the evenings, they sat out on their porches, put their feet up, and hollered across the road to each other. One day around this time, a man with a wide-brimmed hat and a crooked cane came limping down the road. He walked slow and cocked low to shade himself from the setting sun. The sisters were too caught up in their talk to see him before he was upon them. Had they known the man they would have spoken, but neither had ever seen him before.

After, the one sister called across the road to the other and said: In all my life, I ain't never seen a man so black.

The other sister bucked her eyes and said: Black? The man I saw come down through here was pale as I don't know what.

And when the one sister said this, her sister knitted her brow and peered at her like she was a wolf dressed up in people skin. She'd known her sister to tell a lie every now and then, but never one so bold.

You must think I'm some kind of fool, she said.

I didn't before, her sister replied, but I sure do now.

At this, the one sister huffed. She'd always suspected her sister thought she was smarter than her, and now she'd finally admitted it. She stared for a full minute across the road at the woman she thought she knew before turning her back in anger and slamming her front door behind her.

Then the man came back down the road, walking the other way. The sister who'd stayed outside gasped. Where before she'd seen white, now she saw black.

The man stopped, looked the woman over, and decided she was someone he might want to meet. He limped over to her fence post and rested his crooked cane against it, tipped his hat, and said: Now, ain't you something to see.

The woman grinned up at the man, for he was head and shoulders taller than her, and said: I might be.

Here, the story changes based on what kind of mood Gram is in when she tells it. Sometimes the man lies his way into the woman's house, claims to be in dire need of her facilities. The version I like best is the one where the woman just invites him inside of her own accord. But in the one I'm telling you, they don't do no more than stand outside talking.

After, the man tipped his hat and walked on, leaving the woman dumbfounded. She hadn't known what all a man's words could make her body feel. How could a man talk to a woman like that, a married woman, no less, make her feel all kinds of ways, and then pick up and leave?

She was getting ready to cross the road and apologize to her sister, to tell her it was all a misunderstanding, when she saw the man's crooked cane still leaned up against her fence post. She picked it up. The handle was still warm with his touch and, when she put it to her nose, smelled like linseed oil and man-musk. The man never came back for his cane, and the woman spent the rest of her life wide-nosed with the scent of him.

The moral of the story, according to Gram at least, is if you want to be happy, and stay happy, don't touch no man's crooked cane, no matter how good he smells. But that can't be why the first teller, whoever she was, told it. Sometimes I think the story's telling you to be happy with what you have and to not let your mind get further down the road than your feet can carry you. Other times, I think it's saying you got to get what you want while you can. Mostly I feel sorry for the woman, though. I can't imagine spending my whole life wanting something and never doing anything about it.

Porter and me started up on an Easter Sunday. Gram took me to church to hear Reverend Powers preach the Word. Gram liked Reverend Powers because he was old and used to be the assistant pastor to Reverend Walter, who, according to Gram at least, really used to carry the Word. I liked him 'cause every once in a while he slipped up on a sermon that sounded like it might could be halfway right but more often than not he got sidetracked by pettiness. One Sunday he spent the whole service preaching on how black folks shouldn't air their dirty laundry on account of some woman named Celie, and books turning black women against black men. That Sunday, Gram sat there with her face scrunched the whole sermon. Said she'd come to hear tell about Jesus. I'd come to see Momma. Momma was dead and buried in the graveyard behind the church, but everything about her grave was alive with her scent. Momma was most always purple, but the night she died she was strawberry drifting into shamrock. Your true color comes back after you're buried, though. Each grave is bathed in its own bright scent. I loved visiting the graves, but every night I prayed for living hands to touch me.

Gram thought my hair needed flat-ironing, but then, after I got the iron hot, she decided we didn't have enough time, and so, instead of straightening it, I undid my plaits and picked it out into a natural. We ended up late to church anyway, and by then the only open pew was the one in front of Porter and Ms. Lorraine. Even from the aisle, I could see the hymnbook in his hands growing strong with the scent of him. I'd never smelled his kind of blue before, but by the time Reverend Powers finished preaching the Resurrection, it was all over me.

Alton Reeves was leading the choir in "He Never Said a Mumbalin' Word," and everybody else was on their feet, feeling right thankful for the blood, when God put it on Porter's spirit to run the back of his hand along the base of my neck, fiddle with the ends of my hair, curl my locks around his fingers, and tug. One minute I was facing Reverend Powers, and the next my eyes were level with Porter's parted lips. My head went back, and all I could feel was cooling blue. It was like that time Benny had won some money gambling and drove me and Gram to Biloxi to spend the weekend at the beach. Porter pulled my hair, and all of a sudden, I was splashing around in that good clean water, feeling whole again. I'd needed a blessing. I'd needed a blessing something awful, and when Porter pulled my hair, I got one.

When I came back to myself, the Communion tray had passed me by and Gram was hectoring Porter for an apology. I turned around to see him better, but all my eyes would allow me to focus on were those lips. Porter's tongue was telling Gram all about how he had no idea what she was on about, he'd just been sitting there trying to get his Bible lesson. But his lips told another story. Porter's lips were the pink of budding sweet pea, and looking at them was enough to make you want to wait around for the bloom. And so while his words denied all the things his hands had made me feel, his lips teased out all the ways they might could make me feel those things again. By the time the Communion tray had made it around to him, Ms. Lorraine, Porter's momma, had convinced him to apologize, regardless of whatever he might or might not have done. He said he was sorry, but I didn't want no apology. I wanted him.

Gram was mean and sweet—somewhere between blood and berry—and depending on the day, her hue could be loving or hateful or both. Porter pulling my hair brought out the hateful. She said a mannish boy like him, a boy who was all hands, was no kind of company for a young Christian lady like me to keep.

Church was the only time I got to see any boys. Gram had schooled me at home because the schoolteachers were dumb twice over: They didn't know the Bible and they didn't know how to treat me. Then, after I turned eighteen, I put in an application at World Color, but Gram wouldn't drive me to the interview, said she'd miss me too much if we ended up working different shifts, so mostly I just sat at home, thinking of how nice it would be to have someone call on me.

No, Gram said, reading my thoughts.

Why not? I asked. She hadn't even pulled the Skylark out of the church parking lot.

Because you're my grandchild.

Gram always said that when she didn't want me to do something but couldn't think up a good enough argument against it.

I might be your grandchild, I said. But I'm not a child. I'm the same age you were when you got pregnant with Benny. Benny is my daddy.

I know that, she said. You don't think I know that?

Back before Gram sat him down in her kitchen and told him he had to choose between liquor and living with her and me, Benny smelled green like sun-drenched dew grass. Now, the house Benny stays in is robin's-egg blue with a rotting-away porch, and when I'm out walking down the street and he hangs his head and waves to me, what's wafting off him is turned stomach-green. Sometimes I wave back and sometimes I act like I don't see him.

Most times when we pass Benny's house, Gram turns but don't never say nothing. But the day Porter pulled my hair and awoke the woman in me, instead of looking and going quiet, she asked: You know the one thing I don't regret about having Benny?

Him buying you this car before he lost all his music money?

No, Gram said. The only thing I don't regret about carrying Benny to term is Benny growing up and having you, and I don't want you wasting what little time God gives you running up behind a damn near man who don't know no better than to pull your hair to get your attention.

I looked out the window. What I didn't say to Gram but will tell you is that, in the Bible, love is a doing thing. What Porter made me feel in church was the Lord doing His work. God had used Porter's hands to touch me.

When we pulled into the driveway, Gram turned the engine off, took a deep breath, and said: Promise me. Promise me you won't go running behind that boy just 'cause he's the first one to sniff after you.

I promise, I said, because I had decided already to wait for Porter to come to me.

Before she passed, Ms. Maybelle was on the mothers' board of the church, smelled like how pennies look at the bottom of a fountain, and baked the nastiest lemon cakes anybody had ever tasted. Gram said it was because she was getting up in years and sometimes couldn't tell the difference between sugar, salt, and baking soda, but really she was just hateful. Every repast, she'd eat a sliver of everything, save her own baking. But I went to her service anyway, because I wanted to see and be seen.

Most folks wear black to funerals, but I prefer to put on something with a little life to it, so, after fixing a basket of sweets — tea cakes for Momma, fry bread for Mr. Jean, biscuits for Ms. Lucille, who didn't like sweets, and a slice of Gram's fresh apple cake for Reverend Walter because, when he was living, apples was his most favorite thing — I slid into a nice blue curve-cut dress. You don't have to tell me dead people can't eat. I know that. But if I were to die, I would like for some-body to sit by my grave, bring me sweets, and remember I was a living body with wants and needs. The first time I brought food, it was just for me to share with Momma. I put a tea cake right where her head-stone and the green met, and as soon as I did, this furry-footed warm feeling tiptoed up my spine. The tea cakes must remind Momma of life before she met Benny, because she was never that happy with him.

I tried to tell Gram about how the graves smelled and the furry-footed feeling they gave me the day we bought Momma's head-stone, but she wouldn't listen. She thought I was missing Momma and talking nonsense. But I wasn't missing Momma. She was her own pur-ple self in the ground. I could find her whenever I needed. Gram just shook her head and said I was starting to sound like Benny. Benny drinks because his sober mind is much too loud for him.

I was at Reverend Walter's grave, which smelled like red clay after summer rain, when Porter found me. I'd seen him earlier during the service. He came in just as Alton Reeves hit the high note in "Goin' Up Yonder," wearing a baggy mud-brown suit. Gram cut her eyes at me when he took a seat in the pew across the aisle, but I didn't pay her no mind.

What are you doing all the way back here? Porter asked.

Being friendly, I said, and he must have liked the way I said it, because he laughed.

You don't seem too heartbroken about Ms. Maybelle passing.

I wasn't. The Lord has made a beautiful day.

The Lord make that dress, too?

Then it was my turn to laugh. He liked my dress 'cause it was blue, and people liked seeing their own scent come back to them. Makes them feel complete. It hugged my figure so good that Deacon Watts made the sign of the cross when I walked past him.

Anything in your basket for me?

Only thing left is whiskey, I said. But that's for pouring out.

I'll pour it out sure enough.

Up in the sycamore tree, a crow cawed and flapped his wings.

I don't think he likes you, I said.

Do you like me?
I might.

Porter came over in the evenings when Gram was at work. Gram worked the line at World Color, dyeing magazines and pamphlets. Sometimes she came home with her hands so red, they dyed the dishwater pink. If it was Tuesday, Porter and me would watch *The A-Team*, because he liked hearing how Mr. T pitied the fools. Otherwise we'd sit on the couch and I'd lay my legs across Porter's lap and let him play with my feet. He said he'd never known anybody to have feet as pretty as me. On Friday afternoons, I had him pick me up from the graveyard so we could visit with James. James and Porter worked together down at Laurent's Grocery. Now, you see, I liked James because he was loving-yellow and let his eyes do his talking. I say James talked with his eyes because I would see him looking at something and know he was seeing more in it than he could put words to. But if you looked where he looked, most times you could see it, too. He was quiet. Not because he didn't have anything to say, but because there was just too much in his head for his mouth to get around. When Porter had James in the truck with him, we would go around his people's land to pick berries and chase baby goats. Afterward, Porter would drop me off down the road from Gram's and I would walk home. But then one day, he cut the engine and said:

You must not like me all that much.

What do you mean? I asked. Of course I like you.

You don't ever want to spend any real time with me, he said.

He was talking to me, but he was facing forward like he was embarrassed to be feeling all of what he felt. It was enough to make me want to cry. Porter was real sensitive, but his mind wouldn't always let his body show it, so sometimes I cried his tears for him.

All you have for me is an hour here and there, he said. It's like you don't want me around at all.

I want you around, I said. I put my hand on his shoulder, but he wouldn't look at me. I wanted him to look at me.

It's all right if you don't like me, he said. Lots of folks don't like me. I'm used to it.

But I do like you, I told him. I like you a lot. It's just that Gram doesn't like me being out and about so much. She just doesn't want me to get in trouble.

What if your Gram didn't know? he asked, turning to look at me, finally. What if we hung out while she was asleep?

That night, Porter drove me to the river, took the key out of the ignition, unbuckled his seat belt, climbed over the console, and pecked the sweet pea of his lips down the length of my neck. I put my hand to his chest and pushed him back. Solomon was right. A woman's tresses have power enough to capture a king, but before I allowed Porter to climb the tree of my body and lay hold of its fruit, I had to ask whether the water was enough for him.

He pushed my skirt up to the part of my thigh the sun never sees and said that if it was enough for me, then it was enough for him. His thumb grazed my panty liner.

But the water wasn't enough, because if the water was enough, then John the Baptist would have been enough, but he wasn't enough. You need Jesus. You need the blood to be saved. That's why they say blood is thicker. That's how you know God anointed women. Women bleed but don't die to give life, just like how Jesus bled and didn't die to give life, just like how I was bleeding then.

Porter pulled his hand back, but by then it had already slicked his thumb and forefinger.

It's not a lot of blood, though, I said. You won't hardly notice it.

He kissed me and said that he could wait until my monthly was over.

I put his hand back on my thigh. I couldn't.

*   *   *

One time, I dreamed that the river was Porter. Not him himself, but his self-same scent. The color I smelled on him ran all the way to where the Hatchie meets the Mississippi. There are times, though, when the Hatchie really does smell like Porter. I first saw it on one of those bright fall days that look like summer but aren't; you know, like the day got switched at birth and went home with the wrong season. I was walking along a line of poplars when a cloud decided to give way and let the sunshine on through. When the rays hit the water, it was like the sky had ridden down on the sunshine's back to find a new home on the river. It was all I could do to keep myself from diving in.

After we finished, Porter wiped himself off with a towel he kept behind the seat. Once he got his pants back on, I asked him if he didn't hear the things people said about me.

He said he wasn't worried about what other people said, that most folks round here wouldn't know their asses from their elbows if it wasn't for shit.

I laughed and told him that Momma had said the exact same thing just the other day.

Porter asked me if Momma always talked back when I visited her grave.

Most times, I said.

That must be nice.

I laid my head down on his chest. It was nice to speak to Momma from time to time, but I still missed her living self.

He stroked my hair and said that made a lot of sense. Porter missed his momma, too, even though Ms. Lorraine was still living. Ms. Lorraine liked to drink, and just like Benny, once she found her way into a bottle, she couldn't never seem to climb out of it. Sometimes it'd be days before Porter heard tell of her.

I took Porter's hand, raised it to my lips, and kissed it. He wouldn't ever have to worry about knowing where I was. I was ready to be the only home he ever needed. He beamed, kissed the top of my head, and hugged me so close that if anybody had peeped in on us, they wouldn't have been able to tell where I stopped and he started. His scent was my scent.

Gram could be evil-mean when she wanted. I once saw her throw a frying pan at Derby. Derby was picking pecans out of our yard like he does every autumn, and any other day she might have said bless his heart, invited him in, and sent him home with a full belly and a plate of ham for his aunt Sally. But that day, I don't rightly know why, she lit after him with a frying pan. She didn't hit him, but it was a hot minute before he passed by our yard in anything other than an all-out sprint. Gram was wearing her pan-throwing face when she caught me climbing back into my window.

You been out with that boy, haven't you?

I might have been, I said, swinging my other leg in from out of the window. Every place on me he'd put his hands to still tingled.

Didn't I tell you not to mess around with him? she asked like she was really trying to remember. Didn't I say to let him be?

I sat down on the edge of the bed, took my shoes off, and waited on Gram to light into me. But she didn't. Instead, she sat down and put her arms around me. She smelled like the Noxzema she rubbed on every night before going to sleep.

He do something to you?

No.

Don't lie to me, little girl.

He ain't do nothing *to* me, I told her. What we did, we did to each other.

Gram took her arm off from around my shoulder, leaned forward, and put her head in her hands.

Jesus, Gram said, lifting her head to the ceiling. Tell me what I done to deserve a granddaughter who sluts herself so.

Gram.

Jesus, Gram said, raising her hands. Please, Lord, find it in your heart to forgive my granddaughter for defiling your temple.

Gram.

Don't talk to me, Gram said. Talk to Him. Pray to Him for forgiveness.

I got down onto my knees and bowed my head, but I didn't pray for forgiveness. I prayed for Porter to touch me again because I liked it when Porter touched me, and I couldn't understand why letting him do it was wrong. If Jesus was love and I loved Porter and he loved me and Jesus loved the both of us, how could Jesus not love the way we made each other feel? Porter's touch was my blessing, and I knew better than to hide my blessings under a bushel.

After Gram left, I pulled the covers back, climbed into bed, and closed my eyes, but there was too much color in me to sleep. I'd never had a hue all to myself before. Some days I didn't smell like anything, and other days I was my own rainbow, but now all I could smell on me was blue. Porter had marked me, and the next morning, when I went to the bathroom and saw the dried blood on my inner thigh, I knew I had marked him, too.

When sleep finally came for me, he brought with him a woman. She had on a yellow dress and her hair came down past her elbows in long black waves. The dress was lace-trimmed, belled at the cuffs, and silky with the kind of shine that catches the moonlight in its folds and throws it back at you. She had to lift it up to walk, and when she did, I saw her blistered feet. She lifted her wrists to me. There were scars from where she'd been shackled. She tried to say something, but every time she opened her mouth, water trickled out instead of words. The yellow of her dress reminded me of James. I sat up and watched the shapes her mouth made. She seemed real sweet.

Gram woke me the next morning by kicking up an awful ruckus in the kitchen. I tested the doorknob to see if I could get out. Sometimes, when Gram got mad, she locked me in my bedroom to give me time to read Scripture and think, but that morning it was open. By the time I'd dressed, unplaited my hair, and made my way down the hall, Gram had set out biscuits, scrambled eggs, fatback, and sliced peaches with clotted sweet cream. A peacemaking breakfast if I ever saw one.

I ever tell you how the Lord saw fit to bring me your father? she asked, sitting down to the table. I shook my head no, and when I did, she set a teapot to boil and told me this:

Once upon a time, Gram was married to a good man named Junior. He had been raised up in the church and taken in by Reverend Walter after he lost his parents to the yellow fever. Now, Junior had a brother by way of his adoption named Louis, and sometimes when Louis looked at Gram, her cheeks grew hot and her heart fluttered. She couldn't eat. And in bed, when Junior started kissing on her, she pretended he was Louis.

Then one night, in a dream, she felt herself rising up, and before she knew it, her dreaming self was high above her house and drifting, faster and faster, slowing only once she caught sight of Louis's house. She sifted down through the roof and snuggled right up next to Louis, and in the morning, her hunger was sated.

But her dream visits had the opposite effect on Louis. Each morning, he rose up bedraggled. Wouldn't work. Couldn't eat. And found himself dropping by his brother's house just to catch sight of her.

One day, Gram opened the door and found Louis standing there about to knock. She told him his brother wasn't home, and he said he knew exactly where his brother was.

If you know he's out, she said, then why did you come by?

You know, Louis said, stepping into the house and closing the door behind him. You know the reason I come by.

Go home, Gram said.

I will, Louis said, just as soon as you answer me this: Why you smile the way you do? Don't you know a smile like that makes a man lie awake dreaming?

Don't do this, Gram told him, backing away, all but tripping over the coffee table Junior had made for her. It ain't right.

I know it ain't right, Louis said, taking his hat in his hand and looking down at his feet. I come over here today to apologize for trying to put it all on you. It ain't on you. This here weight on my heart is from the Lord. God's testing me same as He tested David. But I'm weak, Ernestine. I'm so weak. You make me weak.

I haven't done nothing to you.

I know, he said, shaking his head. I just can't stop thinking about you. I thought that if I came over and talked to you, got it all out in the open, maybe even prayed with you, then I could start trying to put it all behind me. Will you pray with me, Ernestine?

He reached out and grabbed hold of her hand, but he didn't pray.

Quit it, she told him, once he'd brought his other hand up and rubbed the top of hers. But she didn't pull her hand away. And when he lowered her hand, leaned forward, and pressed his lips to hers, she didn't step back. And when he pulled the strap of her housedress down to kiss her bare shoulder, she closed her eyes to better feel it. She opened her mouth to tell him to stop, but then, almost as soon as she parted her lips, his lips were there again. They were everywhere at once, those lips, and by the time they were walking their way back down her neck to kiss away the strap on her other shoulder, she was drunk with the touch of them. She couldn't breathe. Was aware only of where his lips had and had not yet been, but soon would be. She raised her hands to push him away, but then they, like her lips, betrayed her. Her mind thought, Push, push hands, push him away from me, but then, in pushing's stead, her hands unbuckled, unbuttoned, and caressed, and then, as if this had been her hands' plan all along, pulled him down to the davenport on top of her.

The worst part was all the guilt she didn't feel. She pulled her underwear back up from around her ankles, helped Louis button his shirt back up, and, later that night, slept next to Junior.

Love can be like that sometimes, Gram said. Sometimes it burns so bright in you that you can't see your way around to feeling anything else. It don't matter what's right and what's wrong. Course, after I turned up pregnant with Benny, Louis's love wasn't nowhere to be seen.

I looked down at the flat of my belly. One time, a lady at revival who was pregnant let me touch my hand to her hard, hairless belly. I couldn't help but wonder if the woman's belly was always hairless. If the little ring of hair around my belly button would fall off if I ever got pregnant.

Are you listening to me? Gram asked.

Yeah, I said, raising my head up to meet her eyes. I'm listening.

The teapot whistled. Gram stood and picked it up off the stove with her bare hands, forgetting that the handle gets hotter than the water. When she dropped it, water sloshed out all over the floor, sending these little hot-pink sparks bouncing up every which way. She reached to grab a dish towel from on top of the fridge, slipped, and fell bottom first. I jumped up to help her, but when I held my hand out to her, she pulled my arm down, forcing me to bend over until my forehead was level with hers.

No man will love you the way I do, Cassandra, she said. Not even your father. All you got is me.

When she let go, I took a step back and looked at her, and then, because I didn't know what to say, I grabbed the mop from the corner and started sopping up the hot water.

I do wonder sometimes, though, Gram said to my turned back, where all the love he said he had for me went. All the love I had for him is still here in me.

I was in Gram's garden working off breakfast when I saw James walking up the road with a handful of daisies just yellow enough to match his scent. The garden was around back, so he couldn't see me yet, but

I could see him. When he got to Gram's gate, he looked up and down the road both ways before unraveling the rope, dragging the gate over the gravel, and stepping into the driveway.

Those flowers for me? I called out.

Sort of, he said after he walked over to me. They're for your momma's grave.

I took the flowers, raised them to my nose, and sniffed. They were loving-yellow, rich and buttery. A little white ribbon was holding the stems together and I could tell James had tied it himself. I was going to invite him in for some sweet tea, but then the living room blinds flashed closed. Gram was watching us.

You want to walk me to the church to give them to her? I asked.

He said he did. He was trying to work himself up to telling me something. James never wanted to visit the cemetery.

When we got there, James opened the gate and let me lead him down the rows to Momma. She was in one of her moods, so I just laid the flowers up beside her headstone and kept walking to the big sycamore, where there was shade and folks who were always happy to see me.

I asked James if he was willing to sit in the grass, even though he had on them nice pleated slacks he always wore.

He sat down smiling and said, I don't mind the grass. Sometimes, when everything's quiet and I'm sitting in the grass not doing nothing, I get this peaceful feeling, you know? Like the little things I'm worried about don't seem so bad, and the longer I sit there not doing nothing, the better I feel. Why is that?

It's God. That's Him blessing you.

You think so?

I know so, I said. God didn't just make everything, He is everything. And if He is everything, then you and me are part of Him. Everything is. And when you think on it that way, it's blasphemy to not love anything just the way it is, even if parts of the Bible say you're not supposed to. We're all one and the closer we get to each other and everything else that is God, the better we feel.

Huh. I've never heard that preached, James said, but I like the sound of it.

There's a woman who comes to me from out of the water, I said. Sometimes it seems like she wants me to go with her, but if I go with her, I won't be able to come back.

James got real quiet because he knew what all my words weren't saying.

I'd prefer it if you didn't go with her, he said after a while. I'd prefer you to stay.

I don't know if it's up to me, I said. But if it is, I'll try to.

I'd like it if you tried, he said, and when he said it, I could tell there was more to his words than what his mouth was saying, too. I wondered what it would have been like if God had sent James to pull my hair instead of Porter, to have been bathed in James's sunshine instead of Porter's cooling water. But I couldn't see God calling James to do anything like that. He was a blessing, but not the kind I needed.

I got something to tell you, he said, finally. The flowers ain't from me. They're from Porter.

No, they're not, I told him.

You're right, he said, I bought them. But Porter did ask me to come talk to you.

He sent you to break up with me for him, didn't he?

Yeah, James said, more to the sky than to me, I'm real sorry.

Why did you say you'd do it? I asked, really wondering. Why did you tell him you'd talk to me for him?

I don't know, he said, pulling up a blade of grass and fiddling with it. I don't know why I do anything he asks me to.

*   *   *

Later that night, I awoke to the yellow-dressed woman watching from the hallway. She crossed her arms, the same way Gram does when she wants something from me. I closed my eyes, and the room went away, but the woman stayed. I opened my eyes, and the room reappeared around her, only now she was sitting at the edge of the bed, one leg bent under her, the other hanging off the side, letting the yellow of her dress spill off the bed and onto the carpet. She was smiling like she had news she couldn't wait to share with me. I closed my eyes again and we were at the river. I could feel mud under my feet, and the feel of the mud was so nice, it made me wonder why anybody ever bothered with shoes.

She waved me over. I shook my head no. I liked the view from here, and I didn't see any reason to get closer. There was light enough from the stars to give the river a glow all its own. It was too pretty to touch, like this woman at church. Her skin is the color of a Hershey's Kiss, but her eyes are homemade caramel. Her voice sounds like how beech tree bark feels, and her smile is every good and brown thing on Earth rolled up in sweetness. Whenever the pastor asks us to turn to one another in fellowship, I never turn to her because giving her a hug would feel too good, and too good was just what the river and the yellow-dressed woman looked to me to be.

But then the woman came over to me, took my hand, and walked me down to where the water rose above my ankles. She let go of my hand, bent down, cupped some water up, and held it out for me to drink. I pursed my lips tight, but the water went in anyway. It tasted cleaner and sweeter than water from the river should, and by the time I drank it down, she'd cupped up more.

More, she said.

I drank more, and the more I drank, the more she held out to me.

I backed away. She stepped closer. I tripped and fell back into the mud, and she knelt down beside me.

More, she said. More.

I told her my stomach hurt.

She told me the water would help.

I covered my mouth with my hand; the taste of the river mud was sweet.

More, she said. Just drink a little bit more.

I did, and when I did, she sat down beside me and told me her story.

Her mother died in labor, and if a stranger hadn't have happened by, she'd never have known life. The stranger gave her to a couple who had just given birth to twins—one living, one stilled—and the couple treated her like she was their own. She even grew up calling them mother and father, just like their natural daughter.

When the woman and her sister were old enough to understand, their mother took them to the river and showed them the water and the dirt and how they were two things coming together as one. A few years later, after a suitor proposed to one and not the other, the one sister refused the suitor until he agreed to marry them both. On the day of her and her sister's wedding, the stranger returned and called to her from the road with a wedding promise.

Anything you need, the stranger said, leaning over the fence post of her new husband's property. Anything at all. Just call my name and it'll be yours.

He had power in him, this stranger, but she didn't need anything until the day her village burned and she had to leave her children in the water.

Sometimes you have to leave what you love, she said. But that don't mean that what you love leaves you.

What happened to them?

The stranger took them to where slavery could never touch them.

Where was that? I asked.

I don't know, he never said. But if you want, he can take yours, too.

I don't have no babies.

Yes, you do, she said, pressing the cold of her hand to my belly. He just ain't been born yet.

There's nobody in there.

The woman laughed. I was the same with my twin boy and girl. First, I tried to will them away, owing to the fact their father was a slaver, but they wouldn't quit me. Go back, I told them. Go back and find somebody else to be your mother. But they wouldn't leave. I bet this one's like that, too, she said, rubbing my belly. If you want him to find another mother, you should let him know now.

I called Porter to see if he had it in him to tell me to my face what he said through James. But he wouldn't answer. Every time I phoned, Ms. Lorraine picked up and said he was out. I called all that next week, but I was never able to catch hold of him. I knew he bagged groceries over at Laurent's on Saturdays, so I walked there and waited for him.

When I made it up to the town square, I found James out front, sweeping the sidewalk. He said Porter was busy doing something for Mr. Laurent and might be a minute. The white Laurents had owned this grocery and every store in the county worth going to for as far back as anybody bothered remembering. Mr. Laurent was the only store-owning Laurent living, and most folks said he'd be the last on account of him liking men. But Gram said folks had it wrong. She didn't think he liked men, women, or anybody who wasn't himself.

I told James I didn't mind waiting for Porter to finish up Mr. Laurent's business.

James cocked his head to the side and stopped sweeping. He fixed me with those knowing eyes of his and asked if he could ask me a question.

I told him to go ahead.

What makes you so sure about Porter?

I grinned but didn't say anything. What he really wanted to ask was what did I see in Porter that I didn't see in him. James was handsome in a shy sort of way. He was broad in the chest but slumped his shoulders like he was trying to hide himself.

He's your friend, I said. Why do you hang around him so much?

He looked down at his broom like he knew the reason but was too ashamed to tell it. Just as he opened his mouth to try, a crow cawed and I caught sight of Porter peeping out through the window at us. I fixed him with a look. If he didn't come out, I was going in. He hung his head, pulled his apron over the top of it, and came out to where me and James stood.

I wanted him to say something about my dress. It was the same one I'd worn to the graveyard the day he asked me to take a ride with him, but if he noticed, he didn't say anything about it. He just nodded his head in the direction of his truck and started walking toward it. I followed him. When we got there, he opened the door and waved his hand for me to get in.

I put my seat belt on just to keep my hands from reaching out and grabbing hold of him.

Porter scrunched himself up against the car door like he didn't know what it felt like to have his hands on me, while I sat on the passenger side, remembering with my body what all his hands could do.

He asked if I knew we were cousins.

I said I did. I know all my people.

Apparently, Gram had called Ms. Lorraine and told her my daddy and his were half brothers. Said it might be best for everybody if we didn't see each other anymore.

But us being some kin was no kind of reason for him to break up with me, and I told him so. I scooted over and put my hand in his lap and told him I would miss how good he made me feel. Wouldn't he miss how good I made him feel? He pushed my hand away.

It's not right, he said.

I put it back and I told him it was. I told him all about Isaac and Rebekah, Jacob and Leah. We're all brothers and sisters through Christ, so what difference did it make if we shared a little blood?

That was olden times, he said. Now they have laws and such to keep what we did from happening.

I don't care what laws they have on the books, I said as I kissed his neck. God is the one who put us together, and His laws trump man's.

What if I don't want to see you anymore? he said, shrugging me away. Did you ever think of that? What if all I ever wanted from you was what you got between your legs, and now that I've had it, I'm done with you?

He was lying. There was no way in the world he would have been able to make me feel all the things I felt if he didn't love me.

He tried to say more, but before he could, I leaned over and hushed his mouth with mine. I was tired of his words. I wanted to see what his body had to say for itself. At first he acted like he didn't want me to touch him, like it didn't feel good to have my mouth on his. I unbuttoned his pants and reached my hand around until I found him. He tried to push me away, but he was too weak with need to do it. I brought my mouth to his fruit and his fruit was sweet to my taste. He bucked his knees and tried to kick me off of him, but I kept at it anyway. I kept at it until his legs went still and his hands found my hair and pulled it like hair-pulling was the thing his hands were made to do. The Word of God is a living, breathing thing, and His will makes itself known to us in the way our bodies become one. The blood brought Porter and me together when he laced his fingers into my locks. We were our own Communion. We were Christ's body made new.

For the Love of Money

PORTER BLAND
(1959–1996)
Son of Robert Laurent
Brother of James and Mary Laurent
Natural Father of John Laurent

IT CALLED TO Porter, the housecleaning money tucked away under Lorraine's mattress; it called to Porter with the promise of mornings on which he would not have to rise with the rooster to meet the mule. Porter did not then know the sounds of the city, of sirens, the honking of horns, street corner conversations, and cries of *Yes, yes, yes*, bouncing up bricked alleyways at dusk, sifting down from the apartment above like popcorn ceiling dust at dawn, but if you'd asked him the day he died if he'd have traded them for the chirping of crickets, he'd have told you no.

As he counted and folded his momma's hard-earned money, Porter thought to ask, but didn't, how the stack of bills had come to know him by his Christian name. Had he been sanctified, like his great-grandfather Reverend Walter, he might have known the voice of the Devil and rebuked him, but Porter wasn't the churchgoing boy his half brother, James, was, Easter being the exception. The week prior, when Cassandra, the girl-cousin with whom he'd fathered a child, came to him in what wasn't a dream, he hadn't asked questions and he didn't see any reason to start now.

All during Cassandra's funeral, Porter sat staring into the open casket—his ears not hearing the wail of the newborn baby, his own and her own, and whom he had not even so much as seen in passing snatches, but rather was blind to, as mangy dogs and diseased cows appear to be blind to the flies milling about the corners of their very eyes—watching to see whether the heaving of her breast was a trick of the light or his guilt-ridden imagination. Later, after he'd climbed into Lorraine's poorly hidden bottle of white dog, he was not only not surprised to find Cassandra's ghost lying in his bed, but had opened the door to his room half expecting it, seeing in his mind's eye her arms akimbo behind her head staring up at his ceiling, the way one might lie in the grass and stare up at the stars.

Porter had heard the stories about Cassandra, had seen from afar the girl who, though she appeared sane, spent hours in the grave-yard behind the church talking to herself, but he was not prepared for the physical fact of her, her pull, the ineluctability of her gaze, which could not, would not, be denied. One Easter, when Cassandra and her grandmother had sat in the pew in front of him, her hair—the long unruly corkscrew waves of it—drew his eyes up, down, and around. He followed each, trying and failing to discover where one or another of them ended, but there weren't any endings, only beginnings. That Sunday, he looked and kept looking until his hands had no choice but to follow his eyes.

Long before Porter stuffed his clothes into the blue floral-patterned carpetbag Lorraine's aunt Eunice had gifted her years before, hoping, praying, her favorite niece would let both Talbert County and Robert Laurent alone and come back to Jackson, where folks knew how to act, he'd suspected he was meant for more than what he'd so far seen and known. And so, upon hearing what all the money had to say on the matter, and without a thought for the son he hadn't even so much as held, Porter rose, pushed aside the poultice of roots and herbs Lorraine had known would not cure his lovesickness—for they had not cured her of Robert—took what little money the white folks paid his mother to scrub their toilets, and caught the first train north.

There were streets in Chicago that Porter could walk without seeing anybody who remembered which white family his great-grandmother had belonged to, the family his mother still cleaned house for. In looking first for the YMCA and then for work, he walked them all. Eventually, shoe-shining, which he'd only taken up after being put off from factory work by the striking unions, put him in Thomas's eyeline.

When Porter asked what kind of polish he wanted for his wing tips, Thomas heard the way that little bit of down-home country dumb rounded off his questions, and he knew his own customers would love it, trust it, just as they had loved and trusted their parents, grandparents, and all the other Great Migration Black Southerners who raised them.

"What's your name, son?" Thomas had asked Porter as Porter shined his shoes.

"Porter."

"Any trouble with the law?"

"Nope."

"You wanna come work for me?"

Porter peered down at the shine of Thomas's shoes, raised his eyes to the gold rings on his fingers, met the gleam of the man's eye, and reckoned he would like to work for him.

Then, Thomas operated Lazarus Life Insurance out of a rented storefront most passersby took for abandoned. Porter reported there every morning before being sent off on supply runs, collection calls, bank drops, and errands for Thomas's wife, Cheryl, that took him all over the city. After a while, people got to knowing Porter, liking his face, and so it wasn't long before he was able to bring in a few clients of his own, afford to pay someone else to shine his shoes. Porter didn't love the work, but it beat the mule. Besides, there were not all that many legal jobs that would have provided a Black man with no education enough money to send home and dress respectably.

Now, more than a decade after Cassandra's funeral, when folks see Porter in a nice Italian suit, hat tipped to the side, leaning on a high-top table, country dumb is the furthest thing from their minds. At least until he opens his mouth.

"Where you from?"

"Tennessee."

"My grandmother's folks are from there."

"You want to get out of here?"

"Sure."

Yes, Porter thinks, looking out over the blur of city light through what of the window is not obscured by the woman's grin, I've come a long way from Laurent. What the mattress money had not allowed him to escape, though, were the visions of Cassandra sitting in his lap, tilting her head back, wrapping her arms around his neck, and appraising with wild, disapproving eyes the immodesty of the woman's red-sequined, low-cut, black-belted minidress and shaking her head. No matter where or how Cassandra appeared, she never failed to pluck the country boy he was out of the man-about-town he thought himself to be.

After the taxi pulls up to Porter's apartment building, he steps out onto the curb and walks around back of the car to open the door for the woman in red. She holds out her hand all ladylike and he uses it to help her out of the cab. There, under the streetlight, the woman is not nearly as attractive as the strobing shadows of the club had made her seem, and Porter wonders for a moment if he chose wrong. Before the woman in red approached his table, he'd exchanged glances with a woman in yellow. Her dress didn't catch the light and tease the mind the way the red sequins did, but the way she stared felt intimate, familiar. Part of him wanted to go over to her, lift her chin up to what light there was, and see why. But then this woman, whose name he hadn't quite caught, approached him, and in the time it took Porter to lean down to better hear her, the woman in yellow had disappeared.

After Porter pays, the driver turns on his blinker, makes a U-turn, and guns it. Porter and the woman watch him run one red light and then another before making their way into the building. If you had asked Porter before he died what about the city he loved best, he would have told you it was the way folks never felt the need to oblige them-selves to one another. You could walk past people, see them every day, and never greet them. He didn't give the driver a tip, because he knew he'd never see him again.

The light in the hallway of his apartment building, Porter thinks as he turns to the woman, is much more flattering than the streetlight. The only problem is that once he crosses the threshold of his unit, the ceiling lights in his living room blink, even though the switch is off. He flicks it back and forth for a while but gives up once he hears the laughter.

The woman in red, upon seeing the flickering lights and hear-ing the laughter, picks up the heels she just took off and quickly, qui-etly backs her pretty self right on down the hall and out onto the street, remembering as she ascends the steps of the L something her grandmother — who had once seen Reverend Walter, Porter's great-grandfather, preach a sermon on backsliding at a tent revival outside of Jackson — told her about the dangers of the Devil's music, strange men, and what all might befall her if she continued to walk disorderly.

Inside, Porter hangs up his hat, kicks off his loafers, and lies down, leaving space enough for Cassandra, still laughing, to crawl into bed next to him. Cassandra laughs because once you've died, and all the rows you had to hoe in life have gone to seed in death, the everyday things people do to stay and feel alive are funny. Cassandra often thought — and Porter knows Cassandra's thoughts because she likes to whisper them in his ear as he falls asleep—Porter could use a few laughs. Life was the only thing standing between Porter and the funniest joke he'd ever heard.

"I'm not saying it won't hurt," Cassandra tells Porter as he lies in bed staring up at the ceiling, "but it's nowhere near as bad as folks make out."

Porter closes his eyes.

"There's pain, of course, but sometimes that pain's good. Sometimes it's just what a body needs. Like how when they killed Jesus. It was painful, but it was just what was needed."

When Porter first got to Chicago, he marveled at the way people did their drinking in bars as opposed to living rooms and front yards. Before he hopped the train north, he'd never purchased alcohol from a store. All wine came from fresh fruit fermented in a shed-cooled tin tub. All whiskey was clear because no bootlegger Porter knew had time or patience enough to barrel-age it. But drinking home brew had less to do with growing up in the South than it did with being poor. If you had asked Porter before he died what he'd have wanted for his last drink, he'd have said the strawberry wine his uncles in Jackson fermented in his aunt Eunice's garage every summer.

Today, the bar is in Edgewater, off the Red Line somewhere between Howard and Bryn Mawr. Granville? Berwyn? It doesn't matter. What matters is that no one Porter associates with ever has reason to take the train north of Clark and Division. What matters is a question Porter no longer bothers asking himself. There is beer on tap and a wall behind the bar with alcohol that, like Chicago, is shelved and segregated according to class and color.

Porter catches the bartender's eyes, a hippie type with a ponytail who went to Oberlin for two years before dropping out and, for a semester, had a melanated roommate, and so prides himself on knowing enough about African American culture to nod up in greeting Porter instead of down, a gesture Porter fails to notice. Porter does notice the extra finger of whiskey go into his Bourbon Rickey, though.

"Much appreciated."

Porter downs his drink. The bar is dimly lit, and in the back corner, near the restroom, there's an older couple arguing. The woman has come to drink and the man has come, once again, to bring her home. "I'm not asking you to have dinner ready," the man says. "I just want you to be home when my shift's over." In reply, the woman looks the man up and down as if to say, If it comes to it, I can take you.

"Murder-suicide."

Porter, engrossed as he was by the couple, didn't notice the woman now sitting next to him walk in, take off her coat, and decide, out of all the empty stools along the bar, to take the one next to him.

"Excuse me?" Porter says, turning to her.

"How it will end," she says, gesturing to the couple. "Murder-suicide. If I were a betting woman, that's where my money would go."

"What are you having?" the bartender asks the woman.

"Gin and tonic. Also, another of whatever he's drinking."

"I'm fine. Thank you."

"What? You don't want to drink with me?"

"You shouldn't joke about suicide," Porter says. In the back of the bar, the man scoots his chair back but does not get up to leave, as Porter surely would have. The woman was deep into a hole of her own digging, and one day her husband, if he wasn't careful, would find himself down there with her.

"Why not? Are you thinking of killing yourself?"

Porter considers his drink. The bartender put more ice in this one than the one before.

"My father killed himself when I was twelve," the woman says, glancing off the side of Porter's face. "Joking was the only way I got through it. Some days I think it's all that's keeping me from joining him."

"I bet he shot himself," Cassandra, putting her hand on Porter's shoulder, says. "Ask her if he shot himself."

"I'm sorry."

"Why? You didn't know him. He could have been an asshole for all you know."

"Was he?"

"Not to me. The fuck do I care how he was to everyone else?"

After the bartender sets the woman's drink down, she stares into it. There's a tan line on her ring finger. At the back of the bar, the man stands, trips over a chair, and falls face-first onto the floor. His wife sits at the table and stares at him.

"Who was it for you?"

"My girlfriend back home. She didn't kill herself, but she may as well have."

"How old was she?"

"Twenty-three," Porter says, eyeing the door. The bartender clears the empty glasses and wipes down the bar with a bleach-soaked mildewy rag. The scent makes the back of Porter's hand itch.

"That's rough," she says, taking a sip of her drink. "I bet you're great at sex, though. Most emotionally unavailable men are, at least in my experience. I've always wondered if the same is true for women. What do you think?"

"I wouldn't know," Porter says, standing.

"Wait," she says, taking hold of his hand. "Don't you want to find out?"

"I have a thing I have to get to."

"Don't you find me attractive? I find me attractive."

"Of course," Porter says, "but I have to get going."

"I don't believe you," she says, taking a pen out and writing down her number on a napkin. "But I'm betting that's not a huge barrier for you. Call me when your thing is over."

Porter reads the napkin. Bianca. He's never slept with a Bianca before and probably never will, he thinks, as he folds the napkin and puts it in his pocket. He's wrong. Bianca hands the bartender a hundred-dollar bill before he can loose a twenty from his money clip.

Porter steps out of a cab, pays the driver, and walks up to Thomas's house. Thomas lives in a sky-blue two-story in the southern suburbs. The summer after Porter moved to Chicago, he'd climbed up on top of the roof of the garage and repainted an exterior wall damaged by a winter storm.

"You don't look like a painter," Patrice had said when she found Porter helping himself to a glass of lemonade in the kitchen.

"I work for your dad."

"Doing what?"

"Whatever needs doing."

Patrice had just graduated from Spelman and was kicking around Chicago while she figured out what she wanted to do. She'd wanted to be an architect, to put her mark on the Chicago skyline, but Cheryl had talked her out of it. It was Patrice who'd asked Porter to take her out and she who, a few years later, after she got into law school, ended it.

From the sidewalk, Porter can see Cheryl in the living room talking to guests. He walks up, lets himself in, and waits in the foyer for her to greet him.

"Porter!" Cheryl says, wrapping her arms around him. "I'm so glad you could make it."

"It's good to see you, too, Cheryl."

"You know," Cheryl says as she takes Porter's coat and scarf from him, "Patrice is up in her old room and she would just love to catch up with you."

"Thank you, Cheryl," Porter says, searching out Thomas, "but I don't want to bother her while she's dressing. Is Thomas in his office?"

"If she's not ready by now," Cheryl says, taking Porter's arm and guiding him into the living room, "she'll never be. Did you know Patrice has been offered a job at a firm here in Chicago?"

"I didn't."

"Well, she has and I'm pretty sure we can convince her to take it. Now, I don't know what happened between you two before she went off to school, and I don't care. When you get to be my age, you'll see that the little things that break you up when you're young don't matter when you're older. Love is what matters. Don't you agree?"

"I don't know if it's that simple."

"Of course it is," she says, turning to Porter. By now they've passed the other party guests and reached the base of the stairs. "Life is too long and short to not have someone to share it with, especially in this economy."

Over Cheryl's shoulder, Porter spies Peggy, Thomas and Cheryl's other daughter, setting a tray of deviled eggs down on an end table, and tries to catch her eye. When he does, she shakes her head and walks away. There's no one else with the power to deter Cheryl, and so when she places her hand on the banister and starts up the stairs, still talking, he has no choice but to follow her.

"Cheryl," Thomas calls after them. "Now, I know you're not trying to use this poor boy to convince Patrice to come back home."

"Nonsense," Cheryl says. "I was just showing him the remodel we did on the bathroom last year."

"Sure you were."

"Thomas," Cheryl says, descending the stairs. "Are you calling me, your wife of thirty-five years, a liar on the evening of our anniversary?"

"Is fat meat greasy?"

"Thomas Ezekiel Bishop, I have guests to attend to. I can't stand here all evening defending myself against baseless accusations," Cheryl says. And then, turning to Porter, "Be sure to find me before you leave."

"Come have a seat," Thomas says, opening the door to his office.

Porter regards the wood paneling, crown molding, and Thomas's various degrees and certificates—undergrad at Morehouse, MBA from Booth, Black Businessman of the Year—before his eyes alight on the bar cart.

"I would offer you a drink," Thomas says to Porter after closing the door, "but judging by your breath, I'd say your liver's had a rough enough go of it today."

"It doesn't affect my work."

"That's true enough," Thomas says, pouring himself a whiskey. "It hasn't."

"I'm not an alcoholic."

"I know," Thomas says. "That's what makes it so sad."

"Are you firing me?"

"You know me better than that," Thomas says, raising his glass and taking a sip. "Now sit. I'm trying to tell you something."

Porter sits down in the leather chair across from Thomas.

"I don't have a son, but if I did, I can't imagine liking him any more than I do you. There was one while where I thought maybe you and Patrice would, but, well—"

"Thomas, I—"

"Don't interrupt me," Thomas says. He takes a deep breath and stares down at his hands. "I'm getting tired, real tired, and I think it's time for me to stop and enjoy what I have before I get too old to do anything with it. If I were to put Lazarus up on the market, sooner or later it'd end up in the hands of the white boys. I'd rather burn it to the ground. Those big firms don't do right by our folks, never have; they'll void a black policy before the ink on the death certificate's dry. Now, Patrice and Peggy, they don't have any interest in insurance, which is fine. I raised them to be whatever it is they wanted. Patrice followed her mother into law, and Peggy, well, Peggy's still figuring it out, which is why I want to give it to you. Have you run it alongside me a while as part owner and then, when I retire, let you buy me out."

"Thomas, I-I don't know what to say."

"Say you'll get your shit together. You say you're not an alcoholic—well, fine, you're not an alcoholic. But you need help, son.

Get it or I'll hold out until I can find somebody I can trust to not pour my legacy out with a bottle. You understand me?"

"Yeah," Porter says, "I understand."

"Good," Thomas says, patting Porter on the back. "Now, let's get going before Cheryl sends a search party after us. Oh, and before I forget, Peggy told me to tell you someone named James keeps calling the office, wanting to talk to you. Won't leave a message. You know what that's about?"

"Naw," Porter says, eyeing the bar cart. "I don't know any James."

Thomas and Cheryl's backyard is strewn with white lights for their anniversary party. During the dinner, Porter sits at the main table with the family, but after it is his turn to toast the couple, he tries as best he can to fade into the background.

"If you're hoping he'll take it back if you sulk long enough, you're out of luck," Patrice tells Porter after she finds him alone in the kitchen, trying to ignore Cassandra, who is picking up deviled eggs, licking them, and making faces.

"I'm flattered. I really am."

"But?"

"I don't deserve it."

Patrice sighs.

"Nobody deserves anything," she tells him. "You get what you get and you make what you can of it."

Porter grins, remembering why he likes her. Patrice doesn't judge, not even after he told her about Cassandra. She just takes Porter as he is and never tries to change him.

"Remind me again why we couldn't make long distance work."

"You didn't love me," Patrice says, smiling. Cassandra sets a deviled egg down and places a hand on Patrice's shoulder.

"That's not true."

"It is," Patrice says. "You only ever loved her."

"You leaving already?" a woman calls out to him as he reaches the foyer. Porter, slipping his coat onto his shoulders, turns to her. It's the woman he saw in the club the other night. The one in the yellow dress. When did she get here? "Seem to me like the party's just starting."

Had Porter been sober, he might have found her bare feet and centuries-old dress strange.

"I got work to do."

"This time a night?"

"Yeah, I do."

"Thomas and Cheryl are good people," the woman says. "They took you in when you didn't have nobody else. Least you could do is help them celebrate."

"What's it to you?"

"More than nothing," the woman says. "More than nothing."

The diner where Porter catches up to Bianca doesn't pay their staff well enough for them to take an active interest in the arrival of customers, so they seat themselves at a table in the back corner. Once they sit, Porter considers Bianca, finds something striking in her features, and can't identify what it is. At first he thinks it's the prominence of her nose, but as she turns to face the window, he realizes it suits her profile.

"You're trying to figure out whether I'm white," Bianca says, eyeing Porter. "I'm not. People think I am, but I'm not."

"I know you're not white."

"Oh yeah? How do you know that?"

"Your nose."

Bianca laughs, raises her menu to cover her nose, and leers at Porter over the top of it. He grins because that's what he's conditioned himself to do when people stare directly at him.

"Can I ask you something?" she says.

"Sure."

"If I were white, would you have met up with me?"

"Maybe."

"Why maybe?"

"I never thought you were white, and so I'm not sure how I would have acted."

"I'd like to think a man like you would be more careful," she says, considering the menu. "There are some white women who go around pretending to be light-skinned to pick Black men up, bring them home, and watch their husbands get violent."

"I've never heard of that happening."

"People don't talk about it, but it happened a lot back in the day. It happened to pretty little black boys like you all the time."

"What do you do when people think you're white?" Porter asks. "Do you correct them?"

"Sometimes. Mostly I just let people think what they want. My husband thought I was white when I met him, and so for a long time, I just let him."

"How did that work out?"

"Not great," she says, looking down at the table.

Cassandra nestles her head on Porter's shoulder. He tries, discreetly, to shake her off but can't, so by the time the waitress comes to set down napkins and silverware, she's wrapped both her arms around him. Bianca orders cornflakes with no milk. Porter gets a cheeseburger.

"There must be something in the water today," Bianca says once the waitress leaves.

"What do you mean?"

"Look out the window."

At first, Porter sees only the Ford and not the couple inside it.

"They've been arguing in there the whole time," Bianca says.

"What do you think it's about?"

"I'm not sure. He's pretty pissed, though."

"Maybe he came home and found her with a pretty little black boy."

Bianca throws her head back and laughs.

The waitress returns with Bianca's cornflakes and tells Porter it'll be a few minutes before he gets his burger. Bianca eats her cereal, picking the cornflakes out of the bowl with her fingers. Porter can't help but notice the deftness with which she does this, eating one flake at a time, never disturbing more than what she means to put in her mouth. The considered and effortless movement of her fingers seems, to Porter at least, uniquely capable of unthreading reality.

Once, Patrice invited Porter to an interpretive dance performance, part of an end-of-year show for a dance class she'd taken on a whim. It was at a small venue a few blocks away from his apartment. In the dark room, each of her movements, the intricate articulation of her limbs rising to meet the music, entered him, and for the hour or so she was onstage, he had no clear sense of himself as someone who existed before he saw the way her body moved. After the show, Patrice had asked Porter what he thought. He'd started to answer but ultimately didn't have words for it, what she'd made him feel. It had been the same with Cassandra. He'd never found the words for how she made him feel.

"If you're interested," Bianca says, "I know someone who could help you with her."

"Help me with who?"

"Your little girlfriend situation over there. The one shooting me all those dirty looks. I didn't know until we got here if you could see her."

"You can see her?"

"Better than I can make out the fine print on this menu. I see all of them. Always have. It's annoying as fuck. My godmother was always saying it was a gift. Said she wished she could see my dad. Well, let me tell you, she doesn't. If she woke up to go to the bathroom in the middle of the night and saw him sitting on the couch loading his pistol, she'd shit herself."

"I knew he shot himself," Cassandra says.

"Well, sweetheart, you were right. Congratulations. Anyway," Bianca says, turning back to Porter. "What's your story? Were you born with a caul?"

"I only see her."

"Then there may be hope for you yet."

"What do you mean?"

"Your connection might be what's holding her back. I can help you sever it if you like."

"We don't need any help," Cassandra says, stroking Porter's cheek. "I'm what's best for him. We're what's best for each other. He doesn't see it now, but he will. He'll see it one day real soon and then we'll have a good laugh about how long it took him to come around."

"I think the gentleman can speak for himself. What do you want, Porter?"

The first thing Bianca has Porter try is setting boundaries, telling Cassandra when her company isn't welcome. "You can't come in," he tells her after unlocking his door, only to find her sitting on the couch, waiting for him as soon as he finishes changing out of his suit. Then Bianca suggests he clean his apartment, get rid of any relationship reminders, and burn sage. He cleans, but everything he owns reminds him of her, and so he doesn't get rid of anything. The sage just triggers the smoke alarm and makes him choke. The last thing she tells him to try is asking her what she wants from him and giving it to her.

"What do you want?" he asks Cassandra one night after she climbed into bed with him.

"I want you to join me. I want us to be happy. When was the last time you were happy?"

* * *

When none of her suggestions work, Bianca invites Porter to see her godmother, Therese. The outside of Therese's house is painted sunshine-yellow, setting it apart from the redbrick houses lining this and every other street on the South and West Sides of Chicago. Porter finds the shade unnerving. He arrives early and, not wanting to go in without Bianca, stands out on the sidewalk, toeing a weed that had lain dormant under the concrete for more than twenty years but had, the week prior, shot up through a crack after a heavy rain. Lorraine, Porter's mother, had once gone to see a root worker about luring Robert, Porter's father, away from his wife. It didn't work but Lorraine paid the woman twenty dollars a month for three years to keep the charm going, anyway.

"Your cock better be worth it," Bianca says after she knocks on the door.

The inside of the house is as colorful as the outside: Every other wall is painted blue or green or red or yellow. Therese gestures for them to sit on a plastic-covered couch and disappears around the corner into the kitchen to make tea. She isn't as old as Porter thinks she should be. Bianca has spoken of Therese as if she were a grandmotherly figure, and everything he sees of the house—the way it is kept, the knickknacks, the '50s furniture—reinforces this notion. But the woman flitting back and forth from the kitchen to the living room seems young.

"Bee," Therese calls from the kitchen. "I had a dream about a white rose last night and woke up knowing I would see you today. But then, as I cooked breakfast, I thought, That can't be right. Bianca never comes to see me anymore."

Bianca rolls her eyes at Porter.

"Tell me, Porter," Therese says. "What do you do with a goddaughter who doesn't visit?"

"I was here last weekend, Therese."

"A goddaughter you raised because she had a gift her mother didn't know what to do with? You teach her everything and then she grows, marries a white boy, and poof! It's like you don't exist."

"She's lying. I come see her every Sunday."

"It may be a lie, but it's also the truth," Therese says, placing the tea on the coffee table and sitting down in a chair across from Porter and Bianca. "Now, tell me about this girl who refuses to cross over."

Porter tells Therese about Cassandra, omitting the fact of their kinship and the son he's never seen. He heard from Lorraine that James and his wife, Twyla, are raising him. Lorraine sent Porter a picture of the boy but he couldn't bring himself to look at it, so he put the unopened envelope in the shoebox in the top corner of his closet where he kept his vital papers.

"Think of your life like a web," Therese tells Porter after he explains Cassandra's haunting of him. "All around us, there are these tiny little threads tethering us to one another, fixing us in place. Some last only for an afternoon. Others last lifetimes. Those threads are thick. Those threads, not even death can sever."

"What can I do about it?" Porter asks.

"You? Nothing. Me? I can perform a ceremony to help loosen her hold on you, but it won't be easy, and it won't be cheap."

"How much?"

"Not more than what your life is worth, which, from the sound of it, is what this girl wants."

Outside, Bianca offers to walk Porter to the train. Once they get to the station, she walks him up to the platform, saying she'll wait awhile with him for his train. After a few expresses pass them by, a local heading south pulls up in front of them. Porter says goodbye and steps on. Bianca grins and follows him into the car.

"Are you following me home?"

In lieu of an answer, Bianca sits down in a handicap seat by the door and pats the one next to her. Porter opts to stand and hold the handrail. They ride to his apartment in silence. Every once in a while,

Bianca looks up at Porter, but when he turns to her, she lowers her gaze. Cassandra, who took the empty seat beside Bianca, also looks up at Porter. When he peers down at her, she doesn't bother looking away.

"It's not like I expected it to last forever," Bianca tells Porter once they reach his apartment. "But I thought we could limp along for a good twenty or thirty years, you know."

They are sitting on the floor of Porter's living room. On the coffee table in front of them is a half-empty bottle of whiskey and two coffee mugs. Cassandra walks back and forth across the floor, then sits down in front of the couch to sulk.

"It's not right," Porter says after Bianca tells him why she left her husband. "What he did, it's not right."

"Shut up," Bianca says, pouring herself another mug of whiskey. "You don't care."

"I care," Porter says, putting his hand on Bianca's shoulder.

"Don't," she says, shrugging Porter off. "That's not what this is. Not what you're for."

The next morning, after Bianca dresses and leaves, Porter awakes with a terrible hangover. If he were his half brother, James, he would've arisen from bed feeling disgusted with himself. He would have gotten up, told his reflection it was time to turn his life around, to do better. But since Porter isn't his brother, he picks a suit up off the floor of his closet, hangs it in the bathroom to steam while he showers, and goes to work.

As his office sways and rocks like a tethered boat rising to meet the tide, Porter lays his head down on his desk, ignoring first the persistent ringing of his phone and then the knocking he thinks is in his head. It's not until he smells the Paco Rabanne and hears the rustling of polyester that he knows the knocker is Thomas.

Porter raises his head as high as he can stand to. Thomas leans over, reaches behind Porter, and opens the shades. The night prior, Thomas had a dream in which he attended Porter's funeral, and so he drove in to work anxious to check up on him. Like his grandfather on his mother's side, Thomas was gifted with future-seeing dreams and had seen the deaths of his aunt Genie, his childhood friend Cecil, and Mrs. Parsons, the teacher who taught him to read, in his sleep.

"Your phone's ringing. You plan on answering it?"

"You want a lie or the truth?"

Thomas leans over Porter's desk, picks up the receiver, and holds it to his ear:

"Lazarus Life Insurance, Porter Bland's office...He's not in today. May I ask what this is regarding?...My condolences. I'll let him know to call you back...Have a blessed day.

"It was that fellow you don't know, James. Says he wants to talk to you about Robert Laurent's land. That mean anything to you?"

"Nope."

"James seems to think different."

"He's mistaken."

Thomas shakes his head, knowing both what's to befall Porter and that there's nothing he can do to stop it.

"You know why I got into life insurance?" Thomas asks.

"If I say yes, will you tell me anyway?"

"My father was a mortician on the South Side. Ran his shop right out of his basement for more than forty years. You can't even imagine the kinds of things he had to put up with, but he took pride in what he did. Used to say, 'I can't give people back their dead, but I can help them get on with life.' I like to think we do the same. Insurance isn't everything, but it's not nothing."

Porter sits up and readies himself for yet another speech leading, inevitably, to an invitation to join Thomas at the Million Man March.

Thomas had been beating the race drum ever since he'd seen a video of a Black man beaten by the police on the news a few years earlier. Porter was outraged by the video, and by police brutality in general, on an intellectual level, but inwardly, emotionally, the video provoked nothing in him. But, in watching everyone around him fall to pieces, in hearing them tell each other enough was enough, he wondered, not for the first time, if he was dead inside. He'd felt next to nothing for the man in the video and can think of nothing he wants to do less now than ride a bus for sixteen hours, stand in a crowd, and listen to people shout at one another in an open-air echo chamber.

"He took me with him to pick up a body once," Thomas continues. "I knew before the coroner pulled the sheet back, it was a child. Whoever lit into that boy didn't want his momma recognizing him. His face was all mangled up. Pop worked all night trying to give him back his face. Later, Pop took me aside, told me the only way for me to survive this world was to know it wanted me dead."

"What happened to him?"

"Pop? He passed away in his sleep, the way the good Lord intended."

"No, I mean the boy. What happened to the boy?"

"I don't know. Pop never said. But that's not the point. Every day we get on this Earth is a gift. Now, you've never told me what all happened down home, and I've never asked, but whatever it is, you can't keep letting it eat away at you like this. You got to find a way to live, son."

"Yeah, I hear you."

"I wish you did," Thomas says, standing up. "I wish to my soul you did, but you don't."

Later, at Therese's house, Bianca leads Porter through the front room, past the kitchen, and into a room with burning candles and statues of Black men and women presiding over large bowls of oranges, sweet potatoes, grapes, and apples. One statue in particular, a Black woman in a yellow dress holding peacock feathers and a mirror, draws both Porter's and Cassandra's attention. If the house were a store, he'd have bought it. There are no tables or chairs in this room, only a bare hardwood floor on which Bianca, Porter, and Therese sit.

He's felt the spirit before in church, in the shouting, in the sermon on the Resurrection Reverend Powers preached the day he pulled Cassandra's hair, but he's never had a name for it and doesn't know to connect it with what he sees in Therese's face after she says the words, pours the water, drinks the rum, and lights the candles.

"There's something very old here," Therese, looking at Porter and glimpsing, vaguely, the tie that binds Porter and Cassandra, the same tie that bound Louis and Junior, says. "Something very old and very strong."

"What do you mean?" Porter asks. "What is it?"

"I don't know," she says, returning to herself. "But whatever it is, it doesn't want me to help you. Some bonds are too strong to be broken."

Porter takes the train a few stops south to a Caribou Coffee. He goes in and buys three donuts and a black coffee, no cream. No cream, Porter repeats. The boy working the counter reminds Porter of someone, but he can't place who it is. He picks up his coffee. They added cream to it. In fact, there is more cream than coffee.

He doesn't complain.

As Porter is leaving the shop, he sees the woman who argued with her husband at the bar the afternoon he met Bianca. She is in the corner eating alone. Porter waves at her, but she just stares at him. Why would she wave back?

Porter is up the platform at Monroe and on a northbound train headed back to work when his pager buzzes. He unclips it from his waistband.

It's a West Tennessee number. James. Thomas must have given James his number.

"You see that boy down there?" Lorraine had said, pointing toward the creek the day they moved from Jackson to Laurent. "Your father picked him and his momma over me and you."

James, as if he'd heard his name called, looked up at Lorraine and Porter and waved. It was the first time Porter had ever laid eyes on James and Mary, his father's other children. Lorraine had seen Robert's truck from the road, parked by a church on a hill overlooking a creek. When Lorraine pulled the burgundy Plymouth Robert had bought her the year prior up beside it, Porter looked down the hill and saw his father there with a boy about his age and a young girl he knew, even before Lorraine told him, were his half siblings.

Porter had not known he and Lorraine were moving from Jackson to Laurent. Lorraine hadn't, either, but rather had up and decided that very morning she could no longer stand her aunt Eunice's nagging. Porter had awoken, as he had awoken on other mornings, to his mother and his great-aunt arguing. He had not known and had not cared what about until his mother screamed, "Not one more minute, we're not living for one more minute under this roof," as she packed what few belongings they had into Aunt Eunice's old carpetbag. And because she had no one to watch him, and had cared, then, at least, whether or not he was watched, he went with her to clean the white folks' house and then, later that day, on to Laurent. He'd stolen the toy from the white folks. It was just lying there among dozens of others for anyone to take, and so he took the multicolored cube, twisted it, shuffled it, and reshaped it into new patterns as James waved. If James had merely stared as Mary had, Porter would not have hated him, but he'd smiled and waved, and so Porter had no choice but to hate him.

The sight of James, the boy his father called son, waving at him from what could have been a Norman Rockwell painting, inspired in Porter a cool, subterranean contempt for James beyond even the unrealized loathing he held in reserve for Robert—who, even as James waved, was ascending the bank to protest their sudden appearance, this man in fishing waders who, all throughout Porter's childhood, had called, promising to visit, sending his mother and aunt into tizzies, and then rarely, if ever, following through — and matched only by the unconscious hatred he harbored for himself.

Porter did not want, did not desire in any conscious way, to bring about James's humiliation but rather knew — as Cain, in seeing Abel's offering to God, knew already the feel of his brother's blood on his hands — he would be the agent of such humiliation. And so a few years later, after they'd both taken jobs at Laurent's Grocery, Porter invited James to Bo's party, not knowing, but rather sensing, as a fox, in scenting chickens and seeing between the trees a henhouse, tastes already the feathered flesh between his jaws, that James, who was charming to old folks but awkward with anyone their own age, would find a way to embarrass himself.

And because James had waved at him, Porter relished the sight of a drunk James soiling himself on Bo's mother's couch, even as he shouted down the laughter, even as he stooped down, put James's arm around his shoulder, ushered him into his truck, and drove him to their father's house, a house Porter had never so much as set foot in, savoring the memory of it even as their father emerged, half-naked, dead sober, pistol cocked, eyes burning not with disdain for Porter but for the sorry state of the son who bore his name. At Porter, he did not even so much as glance, shooing him home to Lorraine with a wave of the hand in the same manner as a man might shoo a stray dog. And because James had waved, Porter showed up to Laurent's Grocery the next day with an apology pint, hair of the dog, envying even then the bruises Robert had left upon James's face, because he had never known love without violence or violence without love.

"You don't have to do it, you know. Just because you didn't do right by her then doesn't mean you have to abide by her will now."

The woman in the yellow dress had boarded the train and sat down beside him without him noticing. The ruffles at the bottom of her dress brush against his ankle.

"I don't know what you mean," he says, standing.

Howard. He missed the stop for his office by a mile. Oh well, Porter thinks as he prepares to get off the train, may as well stretch my legs. He takes a sip of his coffee—which is not to his taste and has long grown cold—sets it down on his seat, and steps out onto the platform. There is a Catholic cemetery Porter sometimes visits just a few blocks up from the L on the Howard stop. To the south is the CTA train yard. To the east is Lake Michigan. Walking along the coast of the lake brings to mind the Saturday nights he spent with Cassandra at the river. They would drive into Memphis, cross the bridge over to Mud Island, turn the engine off, and sit. There were no streetlights, and so, after the sun set, it was only him, Cassandra, and darkness so black you couldn't see your hand in front of your face. Looking at the lake now, he thinks about wading out into it, swimming out far enough for the water to cover his head.

The gate to the cemetery is open. The fence around the cemetery is wrought iron and Porter wonders as he walks along the inside of it whether the fence is meant to keep the dead in or the living out.

"Jeffrey!" Porter hears. "Jeffrey!"

A woman jogs over to Porter's row, stops three graves shy, and tilts her head at him.

"I'm sorry," she says. "I thought you were somebody else."

There are graves with artisan stonework, crosses, angels, and saints whose colorless eyes are wide with judgment. Even here, it's clear who had and who had not. As he wanders the graves, reading the headstones, Porter hears laughter and turns to see a man in a wide-brimmed hat and black boots.

"Are you Jeffrey?" Porter asks.

"I might could be," the Devil says.

"There's a woman over there searching for you."

"It's folks searching for me all up and down the Mississippi."

Porter shrugs and turns to go.

"Wait," the Devil says.

Porter turns back.

"There're other ways, you know. Over there ain't the only one. You can choose different."

"I don't know what you mean."

"I think you do," the Devil says. "I think you know just what I mean."

Porter leaves the graveyard and walks out onto the beach. The shore across from the cemetery is too rocky for his loafers, and so he takes off his socks and shoes, sets them down by the road, and walks barefoot along the coast until the rocks give way to sand. Farther up, near the water, there are a couple of teenagers, a girl and guy, snickering to themselves on an overturned rowboat. Porter takes off his suit jacket, unknots his tie, places them on a rock jutting up out of the sand, and watches the couple until the girl, seeing Porter, whispers into the guy's ear. They stand and walk away, hand in hand. Once they're out of sight, Porter walks over to the rowboat. He can tell it belongs to a rental company near Navy Pier, and as he turns it over, he wonders if whoever first rented it just lost their deposit or had to pay for the boat outright. There is a set of oars attached to the boat, which is unfortunate. Without the oars, he would only have been able to drift along the coast, which was his original plan, but once he sees them, he has no choice but to roll up his sleeves and use them. The blue gray of the water is only a shade or two off from the slate gray of the sky. He doesn't have wings like the people in the stories, like his great-great-grandmother, but if he can row out far enough to touch the spot on the horizon where lake gives way to sky, he'll be able to set the oars down and dive up into it. The Devil waves to Porter from the shore. Porter waves back.

BY THE TIME the Devil had caught up to her, the girl he'd helped birth in Africa was a woman and God had abided chattel slavery for over four hundred years. The Devil wandered all about the South, inquiring if anybody had seen a woman whose eyes were farseeing. When he made port in New Orleans, he was directed to Marie Laveau. In Memphis, he was pointed to Uncle Dub, Cat Strong, and Mrs. Millie. But he didn't find her and her children until he hit backcountry.

"Do you remember me now?" the Devil asked, taking his hat into his hands.

"Course I do," the woman said. "You're the man who saved me."

"Anything you need," the Devil said. "Anything at all. Call me and I'll come running."

The last time the woman called for the Devil, he arrived at the Laurent Plantation smelling already the fire that was to burn. He was in Washington, fomenting war between the states, when she called him, and by the time he reached the creek near her cabin, she'd already told her daughter, Lucille, goodbye, and given Franklin, the man she'd all but adopted as a boy, instructions to keep her son, Asa, away from the fire.

The Devil went to the woman's cabin and knocked three times. Lucille answered the door.

"You know me?" the Devil asked.

"I'd know you by the color of your scent if not by your reputation."

"Where's your mother?"

"You want some pie?" Lucille asked, swinging the door wide. On the bed in the corner, he spied her brother, Asa, passed out. "She made it special."

"Is she settled on it?"

Lucille sighed. "It's been a long time coming. She says she should have flown back a long time ago."

The Devil hung his head.

"Did you try to stop her?" the Devil asked.

"I been stopping her from doing it ever since they stole Asa. It's only so much you can do to keep somebody from doing what they want."

The Devil stood there in the doorway of the cabin, letting the night blacken, not knowing quite where to go or what he would do with himself if she followed through with it. The woman was the only human the Devil had ever truly loved. He was waiting on her to go back to his Father's house. But if she went through with this, she'd be stuck here on this side of life until Judgment; not even Saint Peter would be able to sneak her in.

"If you go now, you might could catch her before she flies back to Africa."

And so the Devil turned on the heel of his boot and crossed the creek, following the scent of almost flame, of almost smoke. It was still early evening and yet no one was out and about. Folks must know, the Devil thought as he made his way up to the house. They weren't going to help the woman, but they weren't going to stop her, either.

The Devil eyed the house warily, the whiteness of it reminding him of the one his Father had built for Himself up in heaven, a house with many rooms, one of which, before the Fall, had been promised to him. He opened the door, trying not to count how many years it had been since he'd been home. It was on the other side of that door, standing alone in the marble-paneled foyer, that he found the woman. She was standing there in a yellow dress, a glass jug of kerosene in one hand and a lit candle in the other. She grinned when she saw him. In her eyes, the house was already burning.

"There're other ways to get this done," the Devil told her.

"There ain't," she said. "I done looked every which way and I ain't seen one."

"Does it gotta be with you in it?" the Devil asked.

"My people in Africa been waiting on me," she said. "This the only way to get back home."

"If you wait just a little while longer," the Devil said, "I'll take you to the by-and-by, where nothing that happened on this side matters. We can wait out time there together."

"I don't want no by-and-by. What I want is the then-that-was. But that's not why I called you here. I called you here because I want you to look in on my children, the grown ones I got to leave behind. Their wings never come. They can't go where I'm going. They don't know how. And so I need you to look after them."

"That's not why God made me," the Devil said. "I'm not supposed to look after people, to care for them. It's not in me."

The woman put the jug of kerosene down, walked over to the Devil, and put her hand to his chest.

"Yes, it is," she said. "It's right here. I feel it. Everything in you, God put there. He wouldn't have put it there if He didn't want you to act on it."

And when she said that, the Devil, for the second time ever, was struck dumb. Never before had anyone used the truth of his lie against him. And so the Devil, knowing his Father's hand was on the woman, stepped back and watched as the fire that burned in the woman's eyes spread throughout the house.

At first, the fire followed the trail of kerosene, blooming out over the wood floors, arcing its way up and down the walls, burning the dark red wallpaper sunset-orange. In the shadows that traced the fire, the Devil saw faces singing, only in place of words there was crackling, instead of song there was flame, but this didn't stop the woman from dancing to it. The first time a flame threatened to nip at the yellow of the woman's dress, he left. The Devil knew better than most what fire could burn, and for the first time ever, he wanted no part of it.

And so the Devil walked outside, went down the stone steps, and looked back at the house. By then, folks had come out from their cabins to stand and stare. It would be another hour or so before the fire would grow bold enough to lap the white walls of the exterior black, but the Devil sat looking at the house all the same. He wanted to see her take flight, watch as the black of her wings cut across the black of the sky. The Devil had been there in 1803 at St. Simons Island when the newly arrived Igbo had looked to the left, looked to the right, spread their wings, and taken flight. Maybe Jesus was right about Black folks, the Devil had thought as he watched their shackles fall from the sky. It was then that freeing Black people stopped being a chore and became a calling.

"Remember to look after my children," the woman said to the Devil before she spread her wings. "I'll look in on them when I can, but when I can't, I need you to do for them like you done for me."

By the time the woman rose up out of the house that, by morning, would be a husk resting upon a bed of ashes, the smoke from the fire had just about blotted out the moon and the stars, and so the Devil couldn't be sure which way she flew, back to Africa or up to heaven. And so the Devil traveled back to Africa, over to Europe, and all across the Americas, telling lies to spread the truth, using crooked sticks to hit straight licks, and watching out for the woman's children, their children, and their children's children, and so on and so forth, doing whatever he could to guide them, teach them which of God's rules were meant to be bent, help them avoid His wrath when those rules were broken, seeing all the work he put into freeing Black folks in one generation evaporate within the span of the next, and he was tired, real tired. There was no place on Earth he could put his feet up, and so he walked, kept walking, trying as best he could to atone for the sins of his Father and do right by the woman.

My Brother's Keeper

JAMES LAURENT
(1955–2019)
Son of Robert Laurent
Brother of Mary Laurent and Porter Bland
Husband of Twyla Laurent
Father of John and Lucy Laurent

HAVE YOU EVER seen a seed through to harvest? If you have, you know all about how you can see the seed in the plant. I don't have to tell you that the beige stripes running down the middle of a black watermelon seed are the same white stripes you see in its sprout and then—after a growing season—its ripening gourds. It was Grandpa Louis that first showed this to me. Back then, there was nobody I liked better. Nobody I wanted to be more like than him. Most people move through the world; Grandpa Louis moved with it. He could look to the sky today and know whether it would rain tomorrow. Watching him was its own education.

Each summer, I stood at his side, helping coax sprouts from the ground that gave way to creeping vines bearing leaves and yellow blooms that closed themselves up into tiny green gourds. Each time I filled his watering can and helped him hoe the rows, I saw a bit more of

247

the seed in the growing plant, and come harvest, I helped him heft the full-grown gourds into the back of his truck to take to town, knowing the thing sowed was the thing reaped. I think people are the same. What went into you is what comes out of you. No matter how hard you fight to try to get away from it.

I tried to put what all happened with Cassandra out of my head the day I met Twyla. When I drove up to Jackson to stay with my sister, Mary, and met Twyla, it was like some future self reached back across time to pull the man I am out of the boy I was. I told all this to John when he was old enough to start asking after what love might could be. You might not know the why or the how of it, I told him. All you know for sure is the *is* of it. All you know for sure is that who you thought you were isn't who you are at all. Everything from my life before him and Twyla—the drinking, the fighting—felt childish, and I knew the moment I held him in my arms that it was time for me to put away childish things.

After Cassandra died, everybody had a lie ready to tell about how they saw Death's shadow upon her. Evie Sharp, who was an usher at Mount Carmel, said she saw the pale horse's footprints leading up the road to the river toward where Cassandra had been headed earlier in the evening. Nobody put much stock in this, though. Even though Evie was twenty years sober and, praise Jesus, hadn't looked at a bottle sideways since, she still had a drunk's imagination. Everett Harding told folks that any woman who frequented the cemetery as much as Cassandra did couldn't help but to become Death's mistress. Mary said all the talk was just folks trying to wrap their minds around a tragedy that, even to the grandchildren of slaves, seemed unreal.

I haven't been able to fall asleep without dreaming I was back there in that water since I quit drinking. I close my eyes and see Porter sitting up on the bank, turning up a bottle, while I splash around half-drunk, trying to fix my hands to where my eyes had last seen Cassandra. I put Lucy to sleep. Check under John's door to make sure the lights are off. Say my prayers and lay my head down to sleep, and by a quarter past three I'm up gasping, not knowing for certain until I see Twyla if the damp of my nightshirt is sweat or water from the creek.

It's dark out tonight, but there's enough of a moon for me to make out Twyla on her side, eyes open, facing me. She could have been a model if she wanted to, Twyla. It's not just how pretty her face is. It's this way she has of making each room she enters her own. Twyla walks in and everything else in the room strains toward her. It's her silhouette, the lines she makes with her body, that draws you in. The one I'm following now starts at the top of her hip, curves down toward her midsection, and then glides up her arm to round out her shoulder.

"You were doing it again," she says.

"I know," I say. "I'm sorry."

"Sorry doesn't get me my sleep back."

I reach my hand out to touch her face. She groans and turns over.

"I think maybe I should sleep on the couch," I say.

"I think maybe you should," she says.

I swing my feet over the side of the bed, slip on my house shoes, and make my way to the living room. My wife, like my God, is jealous. Assurance usually creeps into marriage with time and children, but none has made its way into ours. If a woman Twyla fancied to be my type was on the television, like Anne-Marie Johnson, who plays on *In the Heat of the Night*, and my eyes lingered a beat too long, I'd hear days later how she was too skinny and not nearly as talented as folks let on. Knowing there's a woman waiting for me in my dreams that she'll never be able to weigh and find wanting makes Twyla more jealous than me flirting with a living one ever could. Sometimes, when I'm in the water, I reach my hand out and feel the tips of Cassandra's fingers brush mine. I wake half believing she's still alive.

*   *   *

The first time the water called to me was the day I met Porter. Our father was to one side of me, baiting hooks, and Mary was up near the tree line gathering rocks, minerals, and pieces of petrified wood in her upturned skirt. I was standing on the bank, staring at the water, when it whispered to me. I stepped into the stream and bent down to hear better, but before I could make out what it was saying, my father called to me.

"You come out here to fish or to ruin those trousers?" he asked.

"Fish," I said, trudging back up to the bank.

"All right, then. Come learn something."

The crunching of gravel meant someone was pulling into the church parking lot up the hill behind us. I turned around. A Plymouth had parked next to Dad's truck.

"Let me go see what these folks want," he said. "Stay here and keep an eye on your sister. Don't let her get too close to the water."

Mary sat down in the grass, crossed her legs, and held a piece of quartz up to the sky. I turned and watched Dad climb the hill. By then, the woman I didn't yet know was Ms. Lorraine had gotten out of the car and was leaning on the hood. Her hair was up in a beehive, and she was smoking a cigarillo. The brown of the cigarillo was the brown of her skin, and when she stared down the hill at me and inhaled, it looked like a tiny sun was burning between her lips. The boy I didn't yet know was Porter sat in the front seat, tinkering with a toy, not at all interested in the conversation his mother was having with the man who'd just come up out of the woods in waders. Dad looked down at me and Mary, turned back, grabbed Ms. Lorraine by the elbow, and dragged her out of view. Porter fixed his eyes on me. I waved to him. He didn't wave back. He just stared for a moment and then went back to whatever it was he had in his lap. Mary tugged my arm, calling my name, all forty-odd pounds of her pulling at me. I was knee-deep in the water. I must have backed into it while I was staring up at Porter. I stepped up onto the bank and told Mary not to worry. It was only a few feet of water, but nothing I said calmed her. She was terrified. Said she thought I was going to drown.

Each waking holds its own risk. There's a slippage. A break between the person you were before you went to sleep and the person you are after your dreams have had their way with you. You go to sleep hoping you'll wake, knowing you might not. But, even if you've made it through the night more or less intact, you can't shake the feeling that the room you woke up in isn't the same one you went to sleep in. Some days I like the world I wake up to better, but I know before I open my eyes that this day isn't going to be one of them.

The phone rings and the pain in my lower back keeps me from getting up to answer it. At some point in the night, I managed to roll off the couch and onto the floor. I lie there, trying to feel out how far the pain in my back will allow me to lift my head. I barely clear the carpet. I close my eyes, half hoping for a reset, as Twyla clip-clops down the hallway. I know it's Twyla because I've taught both John and Lucy to pick up their feet.

"Turn over," Twyla says.

I do as I'm told. Twyla lifts up my shirt. The cream is cold when she first squeezes it onto my back, but it warms as she rubs it in. It smells like menthol and horse liniment.

"I knew this was going to happen," she says. "We need a new couch."

"The couch is fine. The floor is what got me."

"We need a new one of those, too."

I hear what sounds to be an owl outside, but that can't be right. It's too late in the morning for owls to be out.

"What are you doing up so early?" I ask.

"Mary called," Twyla says. "The phone woke me."

"Oh. What did she want?

"Have you been doing those stretches the doctor prescribed?"

I shake my head no.

"It's only going to get worse if you don't do them."

"I know."

With Twyla's help, I make it back down the hall to the bedroom. I can't remember the last time I was so helpless.

"You want your back pills, the muscle relaxers?"

"No. I'm all right."

"If you were all right, you'd be standing. Want some orange juice?"

"Yeah, I'll take a little. Thank you."

Twyla leaves and I stare at the wall opposite the bed. Hanging there, just above the dresser, are the words "Don't forget the bridge that carried you across." The black letters are set against the blue of either a cloudless sky or calm waters. It was a Father's Day gift from Twyla and the kids. When Twyla comes back with the orange juice, I take a long swallow. The aftertaste is chalky.

"What brand is this?"

"The same brand I always buy."

"It tastes different."

"That's the back pills you're tasting."

"I told you I didn't want them."

"Yeah, well. You needed them."

"What did Mary want?" I ask.

Twyla sits down on the edge of the bed and takes my hand in hers. She's looking down at our hands. Somebody's died. Somebody close.

"Who was it?"

"Mr. Robert," Twyla says. "They called here first but they couldn't get through, and so they called her. He passed away late last night."

"No, he didn't. I was with him just yesterday. He was doing fine."

"I'm sorry, James. I'm so, so sorry."

* * *

Once, when I was running the push mower across the yard, a dust devil kicked up just ahead of me. As I stood there watching it lift and spin and scatter the fresh-cut blades of grass, it was like I was it. Some part of me had stepped outside of myself to twist and turn in the wind, and if I stared long enough, I'd lose myself to it. This is how I felt from the time I started hanging around Porter up until he left for Chicago. Everything around me spun while I stood stock-still.

I didn't really get to knowing Porter until after Mary grew up and went off to school and I got a job working the register at Laurent's Grocery. Porter bagged groceries, and both of us swept up and re-stocked.

"You don't say much, do you?" Porter asked one day as we were closing up.

"Naw," I said. "I guess I don't."

"I like that about you," he said. "You doing anything later?"

I shook my head no.

"You want to go to a party with me?"

I knew folks my age went around to each other's houses to drink every other weekend, but I had too good a reputation to be invited. The party was at Bo Everett's place. I knew Bo, but I'd never been to his house, and he'd never been to mine.

"He with you?" Bo asked Porter after he'd opened the door.

"Yeah," Porter said. "He with me."

Bo stepped aside and let us in. There were people milling about in the kitchen, but most folks stood around the bonfire in the backyard, drinking. Bo's mother, Ms. Everett-Reed, who wore a hat with a bird on it every Sunday, was nowhere to be seen. The kitchen counter had a bottle of Jack flanked by two handles of grain alcohol and a punch bowl of Kool-Aid.

"You want a cup?" Bo asked me.

"Naw," Porter answered. "He good."

"You his daddy?" Bo said, already filling a white Styrofoam cup to the brim. "He old enough to drink if he wants."

"I ain't," Porter said. "But you should ask your momma about me. See what she has to say."

Bo laughed with everything but his eyes. "I won't, 'cause I done already heard tell about what all you get up to. But the boy's got mouth enough to speak for himself."

"You sure about that?" somebody asked. I didn't see who.

"I'll have some," I said.

Bo handed me the cup.

My dad couldn't stand the smell of liquor, so before then I'd never even had a taste. I took a swallow. It burned something wonderful. Until then, I had no idea I was only ever a few swallows of throat burn away from the sweetest peace I'd ever known.

"Now, I know you not gone let your boy drink alone," Bo said to Porter.

"Fuck it," Porter said. "Top mine off with some whiskey."

"I won't. I done already mixed this so it'll taste good, and if I add anything else, it won't taste right and you'll waste it."

"What I drink make you piss?"

"I'll pour it, but I promise you won't like it, and you better not waste it."

Porter took a sip, eyeing Bo. You could tell from the way his face scrunched up as he drank that it didn't taste good. He and Bo stood around talking over my head for a few minutes, and then me and Porter made our way out into the backyard. I don't know what the hell Bo used to start that bonfire, but it smelled like skunk spray and diesel.

"You don't have to finish it if you don't want to," Porter said, pouring his drink out into the grass.

"I know," I said, taking another long swallow and watching the flames from the bonfire billow to smoke and spread themselves out across the night. As we stood there not talking, two girls I'd never seen

254

before drifted over, stood a few feet away from us, and waited for Porter to notice them. He acted like he didn't see them right up until the moment they eased their way over and stood between us and the bonfire.

"What's that smell?" the tall light-skinned one asked.

"What smell?" Porter said, staring through her into the fire. "I don't smell nothing. James, you smell anything?"

I shook my head.

"Are you serious? You don't smell that fire?"

"If you knew it was the fire," Porter said, turning from her to grin at me, "why'd you ask?"

"Just making conversation."

"Well," Porter said, smiling at her now. "You're doing a piss-poor job of it."

"Hey," she said, smiling, because once Porter smiled at you, you couldn't help but smile back. "Be nice."

"What will nice get me?" he asked.

She took his hand and they went back into the house. Leaving me and the girl's friend, who was a bit shorter, dark-skinned, and probably twice as beautiful, alone together. She shrugged as if to say, Well, I guess I'm stuck with you. If it had been any other night, my heart would've been pounding, my palms would've gone sweaty, and I would've tried to strike up a conversation about the stink, but by then I'd tasted bliss, and all I wanted was another cup of it.

"I'm going to go get another drink," I told her, which must have been the right thing to say, because she stayed by my side the whole rest of the night.

Bo was at the kitchen counter, still pouring drinks. He smiled when I came over; he knew I'd be back for more.

"The first one's free," Bo said. "You gotta kick in if you want more."

"How much?"

"How much you got?"

* * *

255

Sunk deep into Ms. Everett-Reed's sofa and lying a little to the side, I felt like everything blended into everything else: the beige of the shag carpet, the people, the pictures of Jesus and MLK up on the wood-paneled walls.

"What am I again, James?" Bo asked.

"You's a son of a bitch," I said, and folks just busted out laughing. "Everybody in this motherfucker is a son of a bitch, but I loves y'all anyway. I loves y'all dearly."

By the time Porter came back, I was right popular.

"Am I a son of a bitch, too, James?" Deborah asked. Dark and Lovely's name was Deborah. At some point, I don't rightly remember when, she'd made her way into my lap. I sat up a bit and her face came into focus.

"Yeah," I said. Her hazel eyes were set against her skin like milk chocolate swirled into dark. "You the prettiest son of a bitch in here."

She leaned down and kissed me full on the mouth. Everybody just loved that.

"You want to show me how pretty I am?" she leaned down and whispered into my ear.

"I see just now why you brought him," Bo said to Porter. "This nigga's Richard Pryor when he drinks."

"You all right, James?" Porter asked from somewhere in the blur of color.

"Is that how pretty I am?" Deborah said, feeling how excited I was.

"Where'd you find this one, Porter?"

"He been here all the time," Bo said. "That's Mr. Robert Laurent's son."

"Laurent? The folks who own that land?"

"Yep, the black ones, though. He ain't kin to the white ones that own the groceries, least I don't think."

"The boy who walks with his head down?"

"Yep."

"I'll be damned. I thought he was special."

"You want to go somewhere?" Deborah asked.

In my mind, Deborah stands and takes my hand, the same way her friend took Porter's. We stroll past the kitchen and on down the hall to Ms. Everett-Reed's bedroom. There's a picture of Ms. Everett-Reed and her late husband on the nightstand. I think to lay it face down but don't. I unbutton my pants and Deborah takes her underwear off but leaves her skirt on. My hands find her hips and it's so dark that all I can see are the whites of her eyes moving up and down, up and down, lowering only when Deborah decides her lips need to be on mine.

After dreaming all this up, I opened my mouth to tell her yes and vomited all over the both of us. Deborah shrieked. Everyone else laughed. I laid my head back and closed my eyes.

The next thing I knew, my arm was slung over Porter's shoulder, and he was walking me. My feet were hitting the ground, but my legs were wobbling. First they went one way, and then, without any kind of warning, they'd go another, one stepping firm, the other just kind of dragging.

"You got a key?" Porter asked.

"Yep," I told him. "Mr. Laurent wants me to open."

"That's swell, James, but we're not at the store."

I looked around. I was home.

We got to the front door. He let me go to search my pockets and I slumped right on down to the ground. The porch light came on. I turned and saw Dad standing in the doorway in a T-shirt with his pistol leveled.

He lowered it when he saw me on the ground.

"What the hell you doing down there?" he said. "What's wrong with you?"

"Nothing," I said, smiling. "Just happy is all."

"Aw, hell, you're drunk. Why'd you get him drunk?"

"He got himself drunk."

I threw up again, mostly in the flower bed, but a little bit on the porch.

"Get up."

I turned over onto my side. It took me a minute to remember how to stand up from lying down. There're a lot of different ways to go about standing up from lying down, but you have to pick one and commit for it to work. I couldn't pull it off. I'd get one leg under me, forget what I was doing, and try to raise the other.

"You know better than to show up here," he told Porter.

"Yes, sir," Porter said.

"Go on home."

I could hear Porter crank the engine as Dad dragged me into the house by the ear. The headlights of his truck fanned the living room as Dad stood me up to give me a punch to the gut. I responded with more vomit.

"So you want to go out and get yourself drunk, do you? Is that what you want to be? A drunk, like your grandfather? Like Benny?"

I didn't respond. He'd already made up his mind about what he wanted to do to me.

"You want to drink like a man, you can get hit like a man. Stand up!"

I thought I was standing until he grabbed me by the throat and raised me up against the wall. Once I got my legs under me, he laid into my face. Luckily, I was still so drunk that it only hurt about half as much as it should've. He must have left me there when he was finished, because I woke up on the floor the next morning.

"You can't stay here with him like this," Mary said when she saw my face a few days later.

"Where am I supposed to go?"

"Somewhere," she said. "Anywhere."

All during my father's funeral, I stare at the double doors in back of the church, waiting for Porter to walk through them. I listen to Reverend

Powers's eulogy, the songs, and Ms. Lorraine, reeking of white dog, shouting about all the ways my father did her wrong, and taking it as proof that she must have, had to have, called up her son and told him the details regarding our father's homegoing. After the burial, I stand around the parking lot, letting folks pat me on the back and bend my ear, expecting, all the while, for a car that might could be Porter's to drive up the tree-lined driveway. When I get home, I pick up the phone to call him, only to realize I don't have his number.

Ironically, the last time I saw Porter was at Cassandra's funeral. As Ms. Ernestine stood over the mound of newly turned earth, Porter watched Cassandra's grave from the back steps of the church like he was waiting for her to rise out of it. I sat in Dad's car, waiting to drive Ms. Ernestine and John, who was asleep in a borrowed car seat, home. When she saw Porter standing in the shadow of the church, she turned tight-eyed, took her shoes off, and lit out after him. There was no one there to keep her from pummeling him but me. I hopped out of the truck, knowing I wouldn't reach her in time.

"You're just like him," she shouted as she brought the heel of her shoe down on his head. "You just Louis Laurent all over again."

It took Ms. Ernestine yelling that for me to notice the family resemblance. He couldn't have been Benny's son, so he must have been Dad's. We were brothers. Of course we were brothers. After I bear-hugged Ms. Ernestine away from Porter, he wiped the blood from his brow and walked away without so much as a wave. That was the last I ever saw of him.

"Don't you bring that baby in here, either," Ms. Ernestine said after I drove her home. "I don't want to see another Laurent bastard for as long as I live."

Ms. Lorraine lives in a yellow shotgun house with a blue door in the part of Talbert County everybody calls the Thicket. All the houses are set off in the woods, accessible only by a gravel road that washes out every time it rains. A few years ago, there was talk of paving the road and running a sewer line out there, but nobody's gotten around to it yet.

Ms. Lorraine's house is flanked by two crepe myrtles, and when I pull into the driveway, both are in full bloom. Out from her front door juts a prefab concrete step-up porch Benny installed. It has just enough clearance for Tyson Jr., Benny's cataracted rottweiler, to squeeze under. The last time I visited this house, Tyson Jr. was a pup. When I cut the engine, he raises his head, tilts it, and considers me. Ms. Lorraine steps out of the house with her pistol and squints at me. I lean my head below the windshield visor so she can see my face.

Whenever I run into Ms. Lorraine at the grocery store or, as is the case more and more, funerals, she's cordial, always sure to ask after John and Lucy. But after the ruckus she kicked up at Dad's wake, I don't rightly know how she'll act toward me. She just stares at first, but then, after a minute, her eyes soften.

"You're the spitting image of Robert when he was your age," she says as I make my way to the porch. "Anybody ever tell you that?"

"Evening, Ms. Lorraine."

She wraps both arms around me, squeezing tight enough for me to feel the cool of her pistol through my shirt.

"Come on in," she says once she pushes herself back from me. "Come on in and jaw with me a minute."

Pictures of Porter line the walls. The biggest one is a twenty-four-by-twenty-four grade school picture of him holding a rolled piece of paper meant to resemble a diploma. He was the same age then as John is now, and the resemblance is strong.

"Can I get you anything to drink?" Ms. Lorraine asks, already heading into the kitchen.

"No, ma'am."

When she doesn't respond, I assume she's bringing me a drink, anyway.

"You and Mary figure out yet what y'all want to do with Robert's land?"

"No, ma'am."

"You know Benny could be some help if you plan to keep it. He's been wanting to work around here. Says the road is eating him alive."

"He's still driving that truck?"

"For as long as they pay him, he is. But like I said, he's about ready to put the road behind him."

She comes back with two glasses of whiskey. Hands one to me and sets the other down on the coffee table.

"No iceman today, so you'll just have to drink it straight."

"Ms. Lorraine, you know I don't drink."

"Still? I thought you gave up preaching."

"I did."

"You had the Word. Not everybody can say that. Reverend Powers sure can't say that."

I tell folks I don't drink because I'm saved, but the real reason is I can't stand to face them angels. At first it was just the woman, but the more liquor I drank, the more I saw. Black angels in buckskins, white angels in waistcoats with sugar-rotted teeth, and everything in between would crouch down low to wherever Grandpa Louis's moonshine had laid me and start to whispering.

"It's bad luck to let it go to waste," Ms. Lorraine says, picking up my glass and downing it. "Lord knows I don't need no more bad luck."

I glance up at the picture of Porter. Ms. Lorraine follows my eyes.

"I know what you're thinking."

"You do?"

"Yep. I saw John after the funeral and had to do a double take. He could be my boy."

My throat tightens. I try to swallow but can't.

"When's the last time Porter came down to see you?"

"He sent me a check a few weeks back. But you know I can't hardly ever get him on the phone."

"You think I could get his number?"

"Of course you can. I can't promise you he'll pick up, but you can try him."

Ms. Lorraine reaches under the coffee table, retrieves her address book, and copies out the number for me.

"This is the number to his office. You'll have an easier time getting ahold of him there than you will his home phone. He don't ever pick up his home phone."

After I left Ms. Lorraine's, I drove to the church, parked, and walked toward the creek for no other reason than it was nice out and I wanted a little bit of scenery. A short cool spring was giving way to a long hot summer, and all the flowering trees were casting off their petals, letting the current carry them downstream. I walked down to the creek's edge, peered down at my reflection, and saw Porter and my father both staring back at me. Nothing ever goes away; it just goes around and around in you. All you can hope for is to fare a little bit better than you did before.

The next day, I rose early to work the fields. I'd spent the whole week prior plowing Dad's fields, and now it was time to do some planting. Mary and I didn't know what we wanted to do with the land just yet, but I figured I might as well use it in the meantime. I was going to put in corn, but after having a talk with Mary, I decided to grow bush beans and cantaloupe to have an earlier harvest. As I walk the tree line edging the rows, I come across the clearing where Grandpa Louis kept his goats. What made these goats something to see was that they froze up and fell out every time they got scared. Once, when I was little, a handful of them squeezed up under the wire fence and made their way up to Grandma Clem's flower bed. She hollered at them from the kitchen window and all of them dropped where they stood. Up until

I showed them to Porter and he told me different, I thought all goats fainted.

I got to know Cassandra after Porter brought her by to see the goats. I'd seen her before but never out of her grandmother's company. Ms. Ernestine kept Cassandra on a tight leash. I couldn't believe she let Porter anywhere near her granddaughter. Cassandra wasn't what you'd call pretty, but she drew your eye. Part of what made her face stay alive in your mind were her eyes. One was hazel and the other had a greenish tint to it. The hazel eye met your gaze the same way as any other person's might, but the green one stared right through you to your soul.

"What makes them faint?" she'd asked after Porter felled one with a loud clap.

Grandpa Louis told me once toward the end that if people took the time to get their heads around what all God has given us, the rich brown earth, the blue sky above, we'd be falling out every day just like those goats.

"I don't know," I told her. "They just do."

After that, Cassandra took to coming by without Porter to feed and play with the goats. She'd call up to the house and ask if I'd watered them yet, and by the time I'd filled their buckets, she'd already be there. Once, when I went to get water from my grandparents' spigot, I caught Grandma Clem staring at Cassandra through the trees.

"Is that Ernestine's granddaughter out there fussing with those goats?" she asked.

"Yes, ma'am."

"That girl's off. You keep an eye on her."

"She won't hurt them goats."

"I'm not worried about the goats."

I left Grandma standing in the yard still staring, made my way over to the clearing, emptied the buckets into the trough, and stood back as all the goats ran over, save one kid playing with Cassandra, trying his level best to get at her hair. I'd never known anyone to enjoy rolling around in the grass as much as she did.

Twyla doesn't like for me to touch a thing in the house when I come in from working the fields. I go into our bedroom to get changed for dinner and find Twyla curled up under the covers, staring at the wall. I get dressed, lean down to kiss her forehead, and turn off the lights before getting dinner started.

I first bore witness to one of Twyla's spells a few weeks after she and Mary took me and John in. By then, Porter was long gone, Cassandra was in the ground, and Benny and Lorraine were too bottle-sick for anybody to even think about asking them what should be done. Dad wanted to turn John over to the state after about a week of hollering, but I wasn't going to let him out of my sight until I found somebody trustworthy to take him. Dad said it was his house and he wouldn't stand for one more night of that goddamned baby waking him up every goddamned hour of the goddamned night. I packed up my things, borrowed a car seat from someone at church, and drove up to Mary and Twyla's the next morning.

"Can I ask you a question?" Twyla said one day, putting her book down. By then, I'd been there a month. I thought she was going to complain about John.

"Sure," I said, bracing myself, already thinking up other places where John and I might be able to stay.

"How do you feel when you look in the mirror and see that scar?"

"I've had it a long time," I told her, touching the raised spot just below my cheek. "I don't think much of anything about it anymore."

She nodded as if my response was just what she'd expected, then pulled her skirt up to just above her knees.

"Do you see them?" she asked.

I didn't see anything but her legs.

"Do I see what?"

"Look at my kneecaps."

After I leaned down, they came into focus. They looked almost like brown freckles at first, the little pockmarks, but they were not quite even with the rest of her skin. They dipped like divots. I reached my hand out to touch them, and then, remembering myself, I pulled back.

"Go on," she said.

They were rough, like goose bumps with calluses. Even still, something in me went electric. Twyla had asked me to put my hand on her knee.

"I can't feel it," she said. "I know your hand is there, but it doesn't feel like anything."

It saddened me to know she'd felt nothing when I touched her.

"How?" I asked, pulling my hand back.

"My mother," she said, fixing her skirt back into place. "Whenever I think about going back to Richmond, I put my hand here and my homesickness clears right up."

I wanted to ask her more about it, but just then, right as she finished talking, John cried out from the other room. I excused myself to go settle him, and when I came back, I found Twyla curled up on the couch, staring at the chair. I sat down across from her, knowing she either wouldn't or couldn't answer me if I called her name. Later, when Mary got home, she helped her to bed.

"She's just like that sometimes," Mary said. "Don't worry about it."

The next time was after her boyfriend, Clay, hit her. I don't know the details of what they were arguing about and didn't feel the need to ask after them. All I knew was he put his hands where he shouldn't have.

I waited for Clay outside of a bar the football players liked to frequent and leaned on the hood of his black Chevelle for I don't know how long before he stumbled out, half carried by a woman in blue heels.

"I know you," he said once they made their way around the side of the car. "You're that country nigger what likes to hang around my girl, Mary's brother. What you doing out here?"

I stood up from the hood of his car.

"Clay," the woman said. "You might not want to fool with him. You know them backwater boys be wrestling hogs and shit."

"Look," Clay said. "I done already said sorry. What else you want me to do?"

I told myself I'd only come to talk to him. To warn him about what would come his way if he hit her again. I couldn't see how anyone could find it in themselves to raise a hand to Twyla.

"She told me you was sweet on her," Clay said, squaring up. "Says it's cute."

I strode up real slow. Let him see me coming. Growing up in my father's house was enough to teach me that violence could be a kind of drug, but I didn't know how strong it was until I was standing over Clay, holding his collar with one hand and laying into the side of his face with the other. I'd been hit before, hard, but I'd never been the one doing the hitting, had never felt my knuckles split and not know if the blood on them belonged to me or the man beneath me.

The woman took it upon herself to try to get me off of him. She reared back and swung her purse at me so hard that later, as I was cleaning the blood off my face, I found a blue sequin embedded in my cheek. When the purse didn't stop me, she bent down, tried to grab my arm, and after she caught an elbow, fell back against Clay's car with a thud.

I knew then how my father came to be the kind of man he was, and if I didn't stop right then, I'd be just like him. The thought of it was like bile on my tongue. I stood up, took a few steps back from Clay, who'd turned over onto his stomach and was pushing himself up off the ground, and went over to see if the woman was all right.

She was all right enough to push my outstretched hand away and cuss me. I turned back to Clay just in time to catch an uppercut. I fell back against the car. Clay cocked his fist back to hit me and I let him. I let him until my bottom lip burst and my left eye swelled shut.

"Just how many times do you have to call him before you take the hint?" Twyla asks after I put Lucy to bed. I've called Porter's office every day for over a week.

"I don't know," I say, getting up from the chair. "As many as it takes to get ahold of him."

"Why?"

"Because Porter was Dad's son, too. He deserves to have a say."

Twyla's got her hair wrapped in a black silk scarf and is wearing the red nightgown I like, a gift Mary gave her a few Christmases back. She's on her side, facing me with her head in her hand.

"What if he decides to come back here?"

"Would that be so bad? Maybe he and John should meet."

"Why?"

"You know why."

"I don't want him around John," Twyla says, sitting up.

"What if someone else tells John the truth?" I ask, closing the door. "What if he figures it out?"

"We'll cross that bridge when we come to it."

"Sometimes there's no bridge," I say. "Sometimes you get to the river and there just ain't no way across the water but through."

"What?"

"I'm saying it might be better to have it out in the open is all. The truth has a way of coming out, and I'd rather he hear it from us than from somebody at church. I don't want anybody to have the power to make him look at us sideways."

"We're his parents," Twyla says. "We raised him. That's the only truth that matters."

"Nobody's saying you're not his mother, Twyla. Him knowing where he comes from don't stop you from being his mother."

Twyla turns her back to me. I get into bed and put my arm over her shoulder. She shrugs it off and scoots away. It's all just so fragile, this life I've built with her. I try to hold on to it as tight as I can, but every time I turn around, something comes along threatening to shatter it.

In the morning, I awake to the sound of a truck engine rumbling into the driveway and then cutting off. I turn, expecting to find Twyla asleep, but to my surprise, she's gone. I rise out of bed, pull on some clothes, and hear the bell ring as I make my way to the door.

Benny wears a black hat, light-wash jeans, and a blue-collared shirt. He steps in and stares at the couch like he can't figure what purpose it serves. I invite him to have a seat. Twyla drifts by.

"Lot's changed since last I been by," Benny says, taking his hat off.

"It's been a good while," I say, though I have no memory of Benny ever setting foot in my house.

"Lorraine told me you stopped to see her the other day. I didn't know if I believed her. I thought she was seeing things."

"She seemed pretty sharp to me."

"Yeah, and she made me know it, too."

"I imagine she did."

"You can't always go by that, though," Benny says, scratching his head. The year prior, Benny put Ms. Ernestine up in Talbert Manor after she'd gotten lost and was found driving twenty miles per hour the wrong way down the interstate. "Momma has her sharp days, too. Sometimes that makes it all the worse."

I nod.

Benny looks down at his hands. He's holding one thumb down with the other like he's trying to suss out which one is stronger.

"Lorraine said you were asking after Porter. Is that right?"

"It is."

"I don't rightly know how to tell you this, especially on the heels of

Robert's passing. Lorraine got the call about Porter late last night. I'm heading up to Chicago to see about the body today, and I was wondering if maybe you wanted to drive up with me."

I don't trust Benny's truck, so we take mine. Benny offers to drive and I oblige him. After we get a few miles out of Dyersburg, I offer to take over. He tells me he wouldn't know what to do with his hands if they weren't touching the wheel.

A soul music station out of St. Louis acts like it wants to carry us all the way to Illinois. It's mostly Motown, but every now and then a Stax record slips in.

"I opened for Johnnie Taylor out on Beale once."

"You're kidding," I say.

"I'm not," he says. "Some of his businesspeople wanted to sign me, but I didn't have my head on straight. I was a bitter man. I didn't understand what sweet could get me until I got older."

"What made you give up music?"

"You wouldn't believe me if I told you," he says.

"You don't have to say if you don't want to. I was just making conversation."

He glances over at me like he's sizing me up, then cuts his eyes back to the road.

"If I put words to it, you'd think my mind wasn't right."

"Try me."

"It was the Devil," Benny says after a while. "I give up the guitar so he'd leave me be."

"Dad used to see people that passed on," I tell Benny. "Said it happened sometimes with folks in our family, talk to them even. So if he saw ghosts, I don't see any reason to doubt you saw the Devil."

"He never told me."

"He might have thought you wouldn't have believed him."

Benny shakes his head and laughs. "I didn't say nothing to him about the Devil for the same reasons."

"You mind if I ask you a question?"

"Ask."

"Whatever happened between you and Dad? Used to be ya'll was attached at the hip. Then one day I looked up and y'all weren't even speaking to each other."

"It was Lorraine. I told him how I felt about her. I'd always had a thing for her."

"What did he say?"

"He didn't say nothing. Just laughed at me."

"Dad hardly ever laughed at anything."

"I know," Benny said, grinning. "That's what made it so spiteful."

"I'm sorry."

"A man can only put up with so much."

"I'm real sorry."

"Nothing to be sorry about. I could count on him if needed. He knew he could count on me, too. Just because you can't stand to be around someone doesn't mean you won't die for them."

There's a sign for a rest stop a few exits away. I need the bathroom, but it doesn't seem like the right time to say so. Benny must have read my mind, though, because he takes the exit anyway. We pull into a space between two Chevy Impalas, one black, one white, both with Louisiana plates. The floor of the bathroom is filthy, but at least there's toilet paper in the stalls and soap in the dispenser. When I get back into the truck, Benny tells me he wouldn't mind resting a spell, and so I take the wheel and drive us the rest of the way.

Down the street from the coroner, we find a hotel that's much too nice for the occasion. It has a view of Lake Michigan and a minibar that proves too tempting for Benny. I go to the bathroom and come back to find him pouring a tiny bottle of gin into a can of Coke. As wary as I am of him drinking, I don't feel it's my place to speak on it. To my relief, he passes out before he has a chance to do too much damage. I mute the television and flip through the channels. I think about calling Twyla, making sure she's all right, but I'm too afraid of disturbing Benny's sleep, so in the end I settle for pulling a chair up to the window and looking out over the lake.

The next morning, I wake to Benny on his knees praying for forgiveness. I turn over. Make a little noise so he knows I'm up. He asks me to get down on the floor with him. I haven't prayed aloud in a good long while, but when I reach for the words, they find me.

"You sound like Reverend Walter," Benny says after my prayer. "If I weren't looking right at you, I'd have sworn you were him."

We have a few hours before the medical examiner's office opens, so we go downstairs to have a look-see at the complimentary breakfast. Neither of us can stomach more than a muffin. As we sit there, drinking our coffee in silence, I think again about Twyla. She's been trying for years to get us up to Chicago, but there's never a good time. I promised her we'd get around to it one day, but Lord only knows how many we have left.

The coroner is a lot younger than I expected. As she stands there telling us all about how the water entered his lungs, the state of him when he washed up on the beach, I can't figure how someone so young can stand to live so close to death. But really, that's all life is. We move from one death to the next, hardly leaving one funeral before getting ready to go to another, until it's our turn to lie down for good. When she asks us to identify him, I squint into Porter's face, searching out the boy I used to know. I don't see him. No matter how hard I look, I don't see him.

It falls to me to fill out the funeral program and make the preparations because Ms. Lorraine is too out of her mind with grief and Benny's pretty much useless. Reverend Powers gives the eulogy. Mary comes home. Twyla won't let me tell John and Lucy anything about Porter, let alone bring them to the funeral, and so I sit beside Ms. Lorraine, put my arm around her shoulder, and let her cry into me while Benny sings. We bury Porter out back of Mount Carmel, near

Cassandra, under the sycamore tree. "One day," I tell Porter as I lay a white carnation on his casket. "One day I'll sit John down under this here tree and tell him all about who you and Cassandra are to him, who you are to me."

The last time I drank was the night John was born. That evening, Porter pulled into our driveway. He'd been drinking, planned to do more, and wanted to see if I'd join him. We got a couple of burgers, drove to the creek, and wolfed them down with our legs dangling over the tailgate.

"Ain't you never going to ask me what's wrong?" he said after we finished eating.

"It ain't for me to ask after what you don't want to say," I said, pouring the pint of whiskey up. It had a sweetness to it. I wanted to ask where he'd gotten it from, if there was more of it, but I had to wait for him to finish complaining first.

"You know it already, don't you?"

He'd meant Cassandra being pregnant. Ms. Ernestine had taken her up to Jackson after she started showing because she didn't want folks in her business, but everybody already could tell she was pregnant.

"Yeah, I know it," I said, though by then I was more interested in what was happening on the other side of the creek. There were angels there. Dozens of them dressed in white, quietly milling about in the woods.

"I don't know how she keeps getting back down here. Must be hitching rides. But it's already all been decided. As soon as she has it, Ms. Ernestine's going to turn it over to the state."

"You'd let the state have your baby?"

"They can't do no worse by it than I would."

On the other side of the bank, there was a woman carrying two bundles. She was powerfully dark. It was as if night had gathered all the shades of herself together and taken human form. All the other angels stopped what they were doing to watch her baptize her babies.

"Do you see what she's doing?" I asked Porter.

"Yeah, I see her," he said. But he wasn't looking at the water. Cassandra was walking toward us. She saw the woman, too.

"Fuck," Porter said. "I don't know how the hell she always knows where to find me." But Cassandra wasn't studying him. Her eyes were set on the other side of the river. The congregation of angels had surrounded the woman and were holding hands. Cassandra stepped into the water. I jumped off the truck and started toward her. Porter caught my arm.

"Where are you going?"

"To stop her."

"She pulls stunts like this all the time," Porter said. "Plays like she's going to drown just so I'll save her. I'm not playing chicken with her tonight. I'm not freezing my ass off in that water."

It didn't look like she was playing.

On the other side of the water, the woman was holding her arms open while the other angels joined hands. I turned back to Porter. He shook his head and turned up the bottle.

I'd swum this creek before and knew it couldn't be more than six, maybe seven, feet deep, but when I waded in, I lost my footing almost immediately.

I swam and looked and swam and groped, but I couldn't find Cassandra nowhere and then, after a while, I quit trying. By then, the liquor had caught up to me, and the angels were rejoicing. There was a light on the other side of the creek, and if I let them, the light and the water would wash all those backbreaking years I would spend working my father's land out from under me. If I wanted, the light would fly me away from here. I wasn't smart enough to go to college like my younger sister. I didn't have nothing much ahead of me to look forward to. There was no one in my life aside from Dad, Mom, Mary, and Deborah, and most days I didn't feel like any of them liked me all that much. All I'd done was all I'd ever do, save for that light on the other side. That was something new.

I woke to Porter breathing whiskey into my lungs. I sat up, coughed, and searched the bank for Cassandra. She was up near the truck with her hand on her belly, breathing quick breaths.

"She says her water broke," Porter said. "I don't know whether I believe her."

I stood up and walked toward her. She seemed sick.

"We need to get her to the hospital."

Porter threw me the keys to his truck.

"You can drive her down there and wait all night for nothing, if you want. I done just about all the saving I'm going to do."

The keys landed on the ground in front of me. There was moon enough for me to see only half of Porter's face, but from where he stood, half in the dark, half in the light, he could see the whole of mine. He had a kind of smirk on his face, a smile that stopped just short of his eyes. It was the same look my father got whenever word reached us of a black boy being killed over nothing. He'd shake his head, put on that smirk, and talk about needing to teach me to defend myself. But I could see behind the smile. See how scared he was of all the ways the world might hurt me, which is why I could never bring myself to hate him, why I couldn't blame Porter for running off and leaving John behind. Porter was just a boy, and the difference between a boy and a man is how much he's willing to do for those he loves, not only in spite of fear but owing to it. The night John was born, I became a man.

I picked the keys up and then turned to help Cassandra into the truck. She had a look on her face I'd never seen before, like she was scared, more scared of going to the hospital than she had been of drowning in the creek.

"You ever been to the hospital?" I asked her after I got in and buckled my seat belt.

She shook her head.

"It's going to be all right," I told her. "They know what they're doing at County. It's not like how it used to be."

She closed her eyes in response, and so I turned the ignition and pulled out, trying as best I could to keep Porter's truck on the dirt trail that led from the creek to the road. Once I made the road, I turned to Cassandra. She lurched forward and vomited.

I drove up to the emergency entrance, hopped out, and ran around to the other side of the truck to help Cassandra out, but before I could get her door open, the guard told me to clear the way in case of ambulances.

"I'll just help her in and then run back out," I told him. "She's having a baby."

"And she'll still be having it by the time you park like you're supposed to. Move it."

I ran back around, jumped in, and drove around to the parking lot. The lot was full so I parked on the grass, hopped out, and ran back to the entrance to get a wheelchair.

"Those are for admitted patients," he said. I ignored him.

I wheeled the chair around to the side of the truck and opened the door. She didn't seem to know who I was or what I was trying to do.

I got her into the wheelchair and pushed her through the doors of the hospital. The waiting room was half-empty, and at the nurse's station there were three nurses, two white, one black. I went up to the black nurse, tried to tell her what all I thought might be wrong, but she just handed me a clipboard with some forms and told me to fill them out.

"Is it raining outside?" one of the white nurses asked.

I shook my head, wheeled Cassandra around to beside one of the rows of chairs, and tried as best I could to fill them out, but I didn't even know what her birthday was and had serious doubts as to whether she and Ms. Ernestine had any insurance.

"Terrence," the other white nurse said. "Go get a mop and clean up that mud."

The man made a big show of running the mop all around my feet and up under my chair.

I asked Cassandra about the insurance. She said she couldn't see anything, and the matter-of-fact way she said it, like sight coming and going was an everyday thing, terrified me.

I went to the nurse's station, handed back the empty form, and told the nurse what Cassandra told me. She stood, looked at Cassandra slumped over in her wheelchair, and sat down.

"Someone will be over to look at her in a minute."

If I'd been a better man, a stronger man, I would have thrown open those doors, wheeled her back there, and yelled and fussed until some-body took a good look at her, if for no other reason than to shut me up. But I wasn't a better man, and so I waited. I think back to this moment a lot, and when I do, I can't help but marvel at how I just sat there, too ashamed to make a scene. It was another hour before the nurse called her name and two more before somebody figured out what was wrong. Her blood pressure was too high.

They rushed her back behind the doors. Someone asked if I was family. I didn't know what to say and so I said nothing, which made them think that I was the baby's father.

"How long do you think it will be?" I asked the black nurse. Her name was Pam.

"It could be any minute or it could be tomorrow."

I used the pay phone to call Ms. Ernestine. She didn't pick up. Then I called Ms. Lorraine, to try to get word to Porter. She didn't pick up, either. I called my father after trying both numbers three times.

"What's she got to do with me?" he rasped.

"She needs somebody, Dad. Somebody who can advocate for her."

"People have babies every day, James," he said. "She'll be fine."

I hung up. Regretted wasting my quarter on him. I waited for what felt like half the night.

Around about three o'clock, Pam told me to act like I was going to the bathroom and find room 106.

"Where's the baby?" I asked. Cassandra was sitting up alone in the hospital bed. I was worried she'd given it away already.

"They took him to clean him, and I'm fine, thank you."

"Him?"

"Yeah. It's a boy."

I sat down in the chair beside her.

"You know what you want to call him?"

"John, like the Baptist, only he won't need water to be reborn, because he was half born in the water, so now all he needs is the blood."

I put my hand to her forehead. She was burning.

"Is this the happy father?" a doe-eyed nurse said as she came in. She walked up to me and put the baby in my arms. His face was all scrunched up. Bruised from the birthing. He was as warm to the touch as his momma, and so I thought it was normal.

"He likes you," Cassandra said, closing her eyes. "You and him are going to be friends. I can already tell." Those were the last words she ever said to me, and because they were the last words she ever said to me, when her heart stopped and the monitor started beeping and the nurse ran to her side and the alarm sounded and the doctors rushed in, charged up the paddles, and tried and failed to shock her back into herself, I held him.

I can't understand why I'm here and she's not. If it weren't for John, I half believe I might have found a way to join her. It's hard for us to see outside ourselves, what it all means. Sometimes life feels like it's just one terrible thing after another. But every now and then, when you least expect it, some sweet bit of brightness cuts through the dark days, opens your eyes, and grows you until you're bigger on the inside than you ever thought you could be. That's what John did for me.

That night, as the doctors worked to try to bring Cassandra back, John opened his eyes but he didn't cry. I reckon he was too young to comprehend what all he'd lost. He looked up at me, furrowed his brow, narrowed his eyes, and parted his lips like he had more questions on his mind than his mouth could fit around. I've seen this look cut across his face time and again over the years. Once when he was five and he found out bacon came from the pigs he'd helped his grandfather feed, and once more the day I told him my father passed. I'll probably see it again when I tell him the story of how he came to be. I hope to God he forgives me.

The Prodigal Son

BENNY ROSS

(1916–2013)

Son of Louis Laurent

Brother of Robert Laurent

Father of Cassandra Ross

CASSANDRA, THE DEVIL come for me three times in my life. The first time was after Momma give me over to Grandmomma to raise. I was about ten and getting to be too much trouble for her, so one Saturday morning she packed up what little I had to call my own and carried me over to Grandmomma's. Grandmomma was Momma's momma and had come up from Mississippi after her husband passed and bought a piece of land down a ways from us. I learned from Grandmomma that the real reason Momma give me up back then was because she couldn't stand the look of my real daddy's face on me. That very evening, the Devil stopped me coming out of Laurent's Grocery.

He said I was a very handsome colored boy and he'd been watching me a good long while. I looked powerful lonesome. Didn't I have nobody to look after me?

He had on a wide-brimmed hat, like how the cowboys used to wear in the picture shows, and tan boots longer in the foot than any natural-born man's foot ought to be. That was the first thing that clued me in to him being the Devil.

I told him I didn't need nobody to care for me. I could care for my own self just fine.

He said he'd seen me stealing penny candy and that I ought not to have done that. Didn't I have nobody to buy it for me?

I told him he must have been watching some other colored boy, 'cause I never stole penny candy.

He laughed and called me a little liar but said it was all right because he liked little liars. He said they had a special place in his heart, and when he said it he cupped both hands to his heart like he was going to open it up and show me the chamber he kept all the little liars in.

I'm the patron saint of lost and lonely thieving boys, he said. If you come with me, you can have all the penny candy you can eat.

I told him thank you kindly, 'cause that's how you used to have to talk to white folks back then, but if I wanted something I could get it myself.

He just threw his head back and laughed.

When Sunday come, I just knew I had to give my soul over to right. Grandmomma walked me down the road to the church, and before we turned the corner, I could hear that organ ringing out. It was rolling over those notes nice and slow, building up to something grand. Soon as we walked through the door, the choir kicked in like they'd been waiting on us all along. They had on these purple-and-gold robes and were singing and swaying something awful. Everybody was standing around with they arms out like they was waiting on hugs. Something in me moved, started squirming like it wanted to get out. I'd only ever gone to church with the Reeds. They was Primitive Baptist and didn't allow no music during the service, so before Mount Carmel, I had never felt the spirit before. When Ms. Maxine started to jumping and shouting to where couldn't nobody calm her down, I thought, That's just how I feel. That right there is just how I feel.

Then Reverend Walter came out the back in a robe of his own, except his was purple where the choir's was gold and gold where theirs was purple. He jumped into that pulpit and said:

Young Man. Young Man. Your arms is too short to box with God.

And when he said it, the organ player struck up them thunder chords and I knowed he was talking to me.

He started telling about this man's two sons. You see, this man, he had a lot of land and money and the youngest son was greedy, and he wanted all he could get before his daddy passed on. So he asked for his share while he was living and took it to the city. But once he got there, he got all caught up. Wanted to live like how folks in the city lived and lost his way, spending up all the money his daddy give him on women, liquor, and gambling. Ended up sleeping with the hogs, and the hogs ate better than he did. But then, you see, this young man realized that even the poorest servant in his father's house had it better than he had it in the city, so he decided to go back to his father and beg to be his servant. But his father wouldn't hear it. He didn't want no servant, he wanted a son.

It was a right powerful sermon, and when he was finished, I had tears in my eyes. I mean, I was brought low. It was like the music had broke my soul open and Reverend Walter's Word rushed in and filled it.

Reverend Walter ended by saying the father in the story was our Heavenly Father and He had prepared a place for us. It didn't matter what we did, or whose child we were, our Heavenly Father would always have room for us in His house. Boy, did them words hit me.

You see, I never had no father to call me his own. And when you don't got no father on Earth who'll claim you, having one up in heaven sounds right nice. My momma's husband, Junior, was killed in the war before I was born and rumor was I wasn't none of his no way. William Reeves, her boyfriend, was always around, but he let me know early and often I wasn't none of his blood.

The doors of the church are open, Reverend Walter said. And if there is anybody under the sound of my voice, anybody at all who is ready to accept Jesus Christ as their Lord and Savior, come and stand before this altar.

I rose up out of my seat, and before I knew it, his hands was on my shoulders.

Did I accept Jesus Christ as my Lord and Savior?

I did.

Did I renounce Satan?

I did.

My heart was wide open and all I wanted was for Jesus to come down from on high and make it his home. Everybody was crying and hugging one another and laying their hands on me and thanking the Lord. I'd never felt so good before. I been trying to work my way back around to that good feeling my whole life.

After the service, Reverend Walter walked me down to the creek behind the church and dipped me in that cooling water.

Something bound up in me came loose out there in that creek. Whatever it was had been sunk down low in me all along, just waiting for good clean water to let it rise.

Baptism, Reverend Walter told me as he toweled me off, opens a door in you that can't never be closed.

Later, I told him about the Devil coming to me outside of Laurent's Grocery.

He said it was good that I'd rebuked him and that the Devil came to him from time to time, too. But if I stayed on the straight and narrow, then I'd have nothing to fear from spirits trying to hold themselves upright with crooked sticks, and the best way to stay out from under the Devil's thumb was to find a ministry.

I told him I liked music, and so he brought me over to the choir director and I practiced with them that very next week.

At first I was just singing along with everybody else, but then the choir director stopped practice and made me carry "I'll Fly Away" by myself. I closed my eyes, opened my mouth, and just let that old song have its way with me. When it was over, everybody was standing back staring. From then on, the choir director had me lead all the songs.

A few months later, a man from another church came to play the guitar alongside me singing. I'd heard guitars on the radio before but had never seen one up close. The man let me fiddle with it a little and showed me how to strum out a few notes and when I came back for practice, Reverend Walter had a six-string waiting for me. He said it was old and that somebody in the church just had it lying around, but later I found out he'd driven down to Memphis and bought it himself.

Baby Girl, you wouldn't believe some of the things I used to could make my guitar do. Reverend Walter would preach the Word and I would get to feeling good and start playing chords after him and by the end of the sermon, me and him would just be cutting up. You know that feeling you get when the music starts beating your heart for you and it makes you just want to stand up and dance and jump and shout? That's the spirit. Reverend Walter's Word would call it down, and me and my guitar was what was moving it all through the church house, all through the people.

I didn't hear from the Devil again until I got to knowing Robert. Reverend Walter brought him up to church one Sunday and thanked the Lord for allowing him to bring his grandson back into his humble house of worship. I watched Robert close. I wanted to see what made him get to be Reverend Walter's grandson and not me. I was powerful envious until I realized he didn't care nothing 'bout the Word or the Bible or Reverend Walter and would just as soon get up and walk out in the middle of a sermon as he would fall asleep, but then I got jealous twice over when he started courting Lorraine.

It was Palm Sunday, and between services I caught Robert out back woofing at her. Lorraine sang in the choir with me and sometimes when I hit them notes, I wasn't thinking 'bout Jesus, I was thinking 'bout her. That Sunday, her green velvet dress just drunk up all the sun. Robert had on his black suit and had her pressed against the outside wall, teasing her with an orange pop he'd stolen. Every time she got ready to fix her lips on it, he'd pull it away and act like he was going to spill it on her.

Robert Laurent, she said. If you don't quit playing with me—

You'll what, Robert said, and as he was saying it, Lorraine knocked that soda pop clean out his hand. Her face was pulled tight in meanness, but even that meanness had loving to it. That bottle of pop may as well have been my heart spilling out all over the cement. Aside from all that, though, me and Robert got to be pretty good friends.

But then there was that business with Ken.

I scrubbed and I scrubbed but it seemed like I wasn't gone never get clean of all Ken's blood. It was as I was trying to wash that the Devil come back to me.

He said he had no idea my voice was so pretty and wanted to know just where I got it from.

I told him all things come from my Father God who strengthens me.

Do it, now? he said, smiling that grin. What about all that blood? That blood come from God, too? Because it look like it come from that white man y'all boys kilt dead.

We were by the water spigot. Robert was out there standing over an oil drum, burning our clothes.

You like that fire, don't you, boy? the Devil said, putting his boot up on the spigot. You come with me, you can watch all the fire you want.

Our Father, who art in heaven—

God don't want you, boy. God likes Him them pretty white souls. Your soul's all black and blue and bloodred. But I don't mind that. I don't mind that at all. Thems just so happen to be my favorite colors, black and blue and blood.

I looked down at my hands. By then, all the blood was gone, but it seemed to me like I could still feel dregs of it clinging to my fingers. An engine rumbled and I just knew it was the paddy wagon coming for us. But it was Mr. Gibson hauling a load of turnips.

I guess you worried about Buckra now, the Devil said. If you was my friend, you wouldn't have to worry none.

I wouldn't?

Of course not, the Devil said. I take good care of my people. Always have. Always will.

Me and Robert didn't have no more trouble, but I still felt off. I couldn't find that good feeling in church, no matter how good I sung. I told Reverend Walter about it, and he said that what I needed was the love of a good woman.

I first met Shirley Ann down at the post office. Reverend Walter had took to giving me a few dollars every Sunday, but it was barely enough to help Grandmomma with the bills, so I got a job loading delivery trucks. I liked the work fine. Only problem was they kept putting me down for Wednesday evening shifts, and I needed Wednesday evening free so I could lead Bible study.

You really that much of a choirboy? Shirley Ann asked me the day we met. She had some papers on her desk. She was shuffling through them and stamping on the date. She was eighteen and sweet. Just up from Memphis. I must have been about seventeen by then.

Yes, ma'am, I told her. Sing there every Sunday.

And when I said that, she laughed. Shirley Ann had a gap between her two front teeth. It was that gap what made me know I was going to love her and she was going to love me.

Shirley Ann was a good mother to you before she caught hold of that stuff. I remember she used to take you out to walk by the river and sing the same song to you over and over. She had a voice like a song-bird humming out the morning. I tried to get her up onstage once, but she wouldn't sing for nobody but you. If I could just play it for you, I could make you feel all I been trying to say.

You know you met Reverend Walter once? You was just an itty-bitty little thing at the time. He was laid up and low sick. I put you in the bed with him and you crawled right on up to him and tried to put your hand in his mouth. You were always trying to do that. I guess teeth must be powerful interesting to a baby who don't have none. He didn't mind, though. He popped them right on out and let you play with them. You were just as happy. Like it was all you'd ever wanted. You looked over at your momma and me like, See how easy it was? Just take your teeth out and let me play with them from time to time. It done me good to see you and Reverend Walter enjoying one another's company, hearing his voice sound out all the syllables in your name.

Too soon after, his heart give out on him.

Folks told me I ought to rejoice, that the Lord had called home His best and biggest trombone, but I couldn't take not seeing him in that pulpit. It was Reverend Walter who'd brought everybody together in love, not Jesus. I tugged at that pain and pulled out a song for his homegoing. After the funeral, Grandmomma took me aside and told me Reverend Walter was my folks, that I was his grandson.

I had a set at Bubba's the night the Devil come for me the third time. After Reverend Walter died, I left the church and I started to playing guitar at the jukes. The music didn't feel like it did in the church, but between the liquor and the women, it was almost as good. I didn't have to go to Memphis to play back then; people would drive up from Memphis to hear me. There was a white man who kept coming round one while, tried to get me to make a record. But I wasn't studying him. Grandmomma used to tell me how Grandpa lost his land signing an X to some papers, and I had that in my mind all while he was jawing. Besides, it was enough for me just to play and know folks liked it.

That night at Bubba's, I had played so good everybody and their brother wanted to buy me a drink. I'd drove to Bubba's but his son Jacob, who ran the place, wouldn't let me drive back on account of how much I'd been drinking. I had run off the road a few times, so I couldn't be too mad at him. I didn't live but 'bout six or seven miles away. I'd walk home and come back for my truck in the morning.

I got 'bout halfway home when I seen a man bathed in leaf-mottled moonlight beneath a sycamore tree. He was chewing on a stalk of wheat. Had his hands behind his back, studying his boots. They were black this time. If he'd have been going one way or the other, I wouldn't have thought anything of it, but the way he was standing there made my short hairs stand on end and my hands itch. So I called out to him to try to make friends, but he acted like he didn't hear me. He just stood there shifting his weight from one foot to the other like the ground was hot on them. I upped my pace to put some distance between me and him.

After 'bout a half mile, I looked back to see if he was still standing there, but he wasn't. He was walking close enough to reach out and touch me.

You got a light? he asked.

Naw, I said. I don't got no light.

Liar, he said, laughing.

I turned around and swung on him, but I didn't connect with nothing.

Come on now, Benny, he said. I thought you and me was friends.

I don't know why, but the only thing I could think of to save myself was Reverend Walter's old Bible. He give it to me before he passed on and I kept it in my nightstand.

Shirley Ann must have heard me coming in, and I guess she could tell I was drunk from the way I bust through the front door. I never could fiddle with that lock when I was drunk. By the time I finally got in the door, she'd gone and locked herself in the bedroom with you, which is just where I most needed to be.

It made me powerful angry.

I started beating on the door, trying to break it down, but she had shoved a chair up against it and that made me all the angrier. She'd run 'cause I had a tendency to beat on her, but I wasn't studying her. I was trying to get at that Bible. Anyway, the Devil must've got into me, 'cause the next thing I knew I was standing over her and she was all bloodied up. You were in the corner, fussing and hollering, and my momma, your grandmomma, was in the doorway with her pearl-handled pistol. It took her shooting a hole in the ceiling for me to come back to myself. It was a good many years before I realized there was no use in running from the Devil 'cause the Devil was already in me.

I used to blame Junior for dying in the war and Mr. Louis for never claiming me, but it was my own selfishness that kept me from giving you what you needed. I saved every bit of tenderness I had in me for myself. My own hurt was too big in my eye for me to see anybody else's.

It was Lorraine that brought me back around to myself. I'd been furloughed from driving and was hanging around the hardware store to see if anybody could use me, when she come in wanting to see about a new porch. There was a government program that give older folks money to make improvements around the house and somebody had put Lorraine down to receive some of it. I rode with her back to her house to see what could be done and we got to talking about old times. When you get to be a certain age, it's not all that many people you can talk to who know what all you used to be. While I was taking the measurements, she asked me if I was still singing.

I said I hadn't for a long while.

You had the prettiest voice I'd heard in real life, she told me. Used to give me chills to hear you.

Don't tell me that, I said.

It's true, she said. All the girls in the choir was just wild about you.

Not all of them, I said, turning to her. I don't know what I was hoping to see.

Please, she said, smiling. You were Mr. High and Mighty. You wasn't studying me.

You can't tell me you didn't know how I felt about you back then, I turned and told her.

Benny Ross, she said as she put her hand on her hip. How's anybody supposed to know how you feel if you don't tell them?

You saying you would've courted me? I asked.

I might've if you had've told me how you felt.

What if I told you how I feel now? What would you say then?

That depends, she said, grinning. Will you sing for me?

I quit drinking after Lorraine and I moved in together. Not for any particular reason I can point a finger to; Lord knows Lorraine didn't mind it. I just kind of wanted to see what the world was like when I wasn't staring at it through the bottom of a bottle. It's hard, but it's hard in a good way. Like how when you work a plow in the spring knowing you'll have watermelon and tomatoes in the summer. I haven't tasted any of the fruits yet, but I can see the sprouts. I wish I could have had the courage to quit when you were alive. Back then, I thought I was the sickness and drink was the cure. I'm not saying I would have been perfect, I'm still me, I can't put it all on the liquor, but I probably would have been a lot better off without it.

I know that love cut you deep. If I was a better man, I would have been around to warn you off Robert's boy. By the time I come to know 'bout it, it was too late. I've seen what the wrong kind of love can do to a person. Your grandmomma loved Mr. Louis and he wouldn't pay two cents to see her fed. There must be something to it. Starting up in church like y'all did. Like the Holy Ghost spills over and the love you have for God carries over into the love you have for them. Maybe that's the whole point of church. For everyone to see the Lord in one another. But then again, I met most of my women at the juke, so what do I know?

Speaking of church, I saw your son in Bible study the other day. He gets his lesson just as good as you used to. Soaks it all in. Don't you worry your pretty little head about that one. James is raising him up

289

right. Doing a better job than Momma did with me, a better job than I did with you. I keep my distance. He's got a better grandfather in Robert than he'd ever have in me.

My grandmomma used to say owls come carrying two things, love and death, and when you hear them you know it's going to be one or the other. When I was little, I used to listen for them. I'd sit up by the window wanting to know which they was who-ing about. One night after one hooted, I went out the house to try to find it. It was summer and the night was hot, so I was having trouble getting to sleep, anyway. I slipped out of bed and put on my outside shoes. Grandmomma was fast asleep. She could sleep through anything, so more often than not I had the night to myself. I cut across the yard tracking the sound of that owl, but the closer I got to it the quieter it was. I found it in a live oak tree about a mile from the house. But it wasn't alone. There was a whole mess of them up in that tree. When I walked up, they all glowered down at me with those big moony eyes of theirs. I stood there for a long while, seeing them see me. I thought about what I must look like to them. A black boy out in the night all alone, standing there peeping in on their business. What's he doing out there all by himself? I bet they wondered. Owls are probably about the only animal I'd feel bad about killing. Who? That's the question those owls are all the time asking. Last time the answer was you, and one day soon the answer's going to be me.

The last time the Devil come for me was right after I come and left them flowers for you. I remember you like the purple ones best because they remind you of Shirley Ann. I got home and the Devil come in right behind me before I could get the door closed.

Well, Benny, he said. I reckon you know what I come for.

By then I was too tired to run, so I told him to come right on in and have a seat. He took his hat off and set it down beside him.

He told me he missed my playing and asked me if I wouldn't give him one last song.

I told him it had been so long since I played that I didn't even know where my guitar was.

That's all right, he said, reaching into his hat and pulling out a brand-new dreadnought, a Gibson Hummingbird with gold trim. You'd have been playing this at Carnegie Hall if you hadn't have rebuked me and quit singing.

I took it and strummed out a few notes. It sounded right nice.

I asked him what he wanted to hear.

He told me to play a song my baby girl might like.

I told him no and started to hand it back.

Keep it, he said. Just in case you change your mind. I know where to find you when I want it back.

A little while after he left, I picked it up. I picked it up and wrote out a song for you.

Listen.

I'm starting up them chords right now. I'm stringing those notes out long and slow so when you hear it, you'll know it's building up to something grand. Are you listening, Baby Girl? I'm stringing them notes out nice and loud because I want this song to ring out to you over the years. I'm stringing it out nice and slow because I want them notes to wrap you up in father love the way I never could. I want you to hear it when you're rocking away in that crib. I want you to hear it when you're at that middle point in life, not going forward or backward but just round and round in circles. I want you to hear it when you're old and thinking over all you've done in life. I want you to hear it so you'll know you'll always have a place in my house. Baby Girl, I'm praying this song will reach you wherever you are. If it don't get there in time, don't worry. I'll sing it for you in eternity.

BOOK IV
All God's Children Got Wings

Robert Laurent's Last Day

ROBERT LAURENT
(1915–1996)
Son of Louis Laurent
Brother of Benny Ross
Father of James Laurent, Mary Laurent,
and Porter Bland

WHEN THE DEVIL came for Robert Laurent, the fallen angel found him dressing for a funeral he'd attended years earlier. As Robert straightened his tie in the mirror, he noticed that his hair had grown long on the sides and thin at the top. Robert's father, Louis, had a full head of hair the day the Devil came for him. Had his wife, Catherine, been alive, she would have sat him down at the kitchen table, wrapped a worn tablecloth around his neck, and cut it herself. Robert, not acknowledging the Devil's sudden appearance, stared at the mirror's reflection of the water mark on the ceiling above his bed. A water mark he'd been meaning to have fixed and would have if the thought of it did not leave his mind every morning upon waking. As the Devil took a seat in Catherine's old chair—a chair that was, more and more, occupied by the nurse Mary had hired—Robert stared at this water mark and allowed his mind to make and remake it the way his children used to do with clouds. The water mark most resembled a ship with large billowing sails, but under his eye, it became a house on fire. "Set the fire," the woman in yellow had told him all those years ago, "but don't let it burn you." He placed his hand on the mirror. It warmed to his touch.

"Nice suit," the Devil said, admiring the black-and-gray chalk-stripe pattern.

"Gift from my daughter, Mary."

"She's got good taste."

"What are you doing here?" Robert said, turning to look at the Devil full on.

"I reckon you know already," the Devil said. "I reckon you know well enough the reason I come."

The last time Robert spoke to Mary, Vic Talbert was out on his tractor plowing the fields Robert leased to him for half the crop yield. Vic had planted soybeans, and on his way home from the cemetery one day, Robert had noticed that they were almost ready to harvest. Though Vic Talbert was white, he and Robert were second cousins once removed owing to the fact that Robert's great-grandmother Lucille and Vic's great-great-grandfather Asa were siblings, though neither Vic nor any of his progenitors, save Bubba Laurent, knew of the connection. Mary had called to see whether Robert knew what became of the mink coat Catherine inherited from her grandmother. He didn't. Robert asked if she was coming home for Thanksgiving. She wasn't. Each year, Robert thought as he considered the picture of Mary tucked into the corner of the dresser's mirror frame. Each year she looks more and more like Catherine.

The first time Robert saw Catherine was the summer of '46. That year, he and Benny had found work at Jones's Concrete and Masonry, doing colored jobs Turner Jones deemed beneath him. That day, they were pulling concrete at a corner store just north of Ripley. The cement mixer poured the slurry, and he and Benny used their hoes to pull and spread it out over the gravel parking lot. Once they'd worked their way around to the drive-up window, Robert stopped, wiped his brow, turned toward the shop, and saw through the window the most beautiful woman he'd ever seen staring back at him. "Catherine," she told him after he'd strutted into her uncle's store to buy a Coke. "My name's Catherine." It sounded like what somebody might call an angel. He could never, not in a million years, have imagined her face repeated in a daughter who couldn't stand him.

Robert and Mary had never been close. She didn't need the doors to her closet thrown open to check for monsters, never craved her father's attention. Had she been a boy, he would have appreciated her independence. Would have taught her how to bait a hook, clean a fish, shoot a gun. He would have done with her all he had tried and failed to do with James.

Robert, misremembering the morning's purpose, left his bedroom with his shoes in hand because Catherine didn't like for anything to touch her white shag carpet save socks, house slippers, and bare feet. He searched the hook by the door. They weren't there. He checked the kitchen counter, where Catherine used to leave them, and found a year's worth of Sears catalogues piled up. How did those get here? he wondered. He checked the bathroom. There was nothing there but his razor and a bar of Dial. Catherine preferred Ivory and would only use Dial if there was nothing else. Forgetting, for a moment, that Catherine had passed years before, Robert made a note to himself to pick up some from the Dollar General on his way to the co-op, despite the fact that both the co-op and the Dollar General had shuttered years prior. It happened like that sometimes; he'd remember some little thing about Catherine, and it was like she was right there, like she never left. The dead had always come to him, but for some reason, Catherine never did.

"You could have called," Catherine had said the day he drove up to Ripley to tell her she was too good for him. "You could have called if all you wanted was to break up with me."

"I'm not a good man," Robert told Catherine. They were sitting on the bench swing on her parents' front porch. "I've done things I ought not to have."

Catherine looked down at her dress. It was red with white polka dots, her best one. She'd put it on because Robert had said on the phone the week before that he wanted to talk, and she'd thought that meant a proposal. Seeing Robert's muscles working beneath his shirt as he pulled concrete had made her feel things between her legs she'd never felt before. No one had told her what love was, but she'd heard tell of it at the picture shows her aunt and uncle treated her to and so she assumed love was a warm feeling between your legs. Catherine was known for a mean streak when she was younger, and it was owing to that that Robert had been the first man to ask after her. He drove up from Laurent every other weekend to bring her little gifts and pass time on her parents' porch with her. She'd never been doted on before, never had anybody pay her special attention. Her mother warned her about men who said nice things and made you feel a certain way. "They get what they can get from you," she said, remembering how the first boy who'd touched her moved away to New York and then enlisted in the 369th Infantry. "And then they leave you." But Robert had never even so much as tried to kiss her.

"I don't understand. You saying you don't want to see me anymore?"

"I'm saying you're too good for me. You deserve to be with somebody as good as you."

"So you met somebody you like better. Is that it?"

"No, I like you better than anybody I ever met. I'm saying I don't deserve you."

Across the road, Miss Lula Jo, who used to babysit Catherine and had never married, was bent over in her front yard tending to her azaleas. Sometimes, when Catherine was little and nobody was around to see, Miss Lula Jo would pinch Catherine's forearm so she could watch her cry. One day after doing this, Miss Lula Jo bit off more of an apple than she could chew and choked. Catherine watched as Miss Lula Jo gasped for air, clutched at her throat, pleading with her eyes for help. Even to this day, Catherine relished the sight of that mean old woman on the verge of death, begging for her help.

"I don't care nothing about what you done before, so long as you're good to me. You plan on being good to me?"

Robert nodded.

"Good. Now shut up and go ask Daddy for my hand before I change my mind about you."

In the living room, Robert caught sight of his reflection in the mirror again. Between now and the moment he realized his keys were missing, his suit had grown looser and his face had wrinkled. He stared, half believing he was looking at his grandfather's face.

"Time slips in the end," the Devil told Robert. "One minute you're here and the next..."

When the Devil came for Reverend Walter, Robert's grandfather, he was rebuked so vociferously that the poor Devil had to come back later and collect the old man in his sleep. Walter's father, Franklin, Robert's great-grandfather, had made his peace with the Devil when the plantation upon which he was enslaved burned to the ground, and so at his appointed hour he was so full of gratitude that he took the Devil's face in his hands and kissed it. Franklin's only dying regret was never having slit the throat of the man who'd shot Opa, his first mother. Reverend Walter refused to speak on the father who'd abandoned him and his mother, and so Robert had never heard of either Franklin or the Chickasaw woman who found him in a burlap sack by the river. Reverend Walter's only dying regret was not baptizing his mother, Lucille, in the name of the Father, the Son, and the Holy Ghost so that she might know Christ's love and through his mercy be saved.

"You can't put it off forever," the Devil said, following Robert into the living room, seeing as he went the blood vessel in Robert's left temple that, at any moment, would rupture. "If you come with me now, there won't be no pain in it."

"That a threat?"

"Naw, I don't make threats, only promises."

"I aim to live out every moment I got," Robert said, brushing past the Devil.

"All right," the Devil said. "Have it your way."

Did he leave the keys in the truck? Robert wondered as he went out into the garage in socks and peered into the passenger side window. They weren't in the cup holder, on the floor, or in the ignition, and so he went back inside, knowing there was no good reason for them to be in the glove box.

Robert was pulling the plastic on the couch back and checking in between the cushions by the time James let himself in. Ever since James had hit puberty, Robert found it harder and harder to look the boy in the face. He was so much like Louis that Robert could hardly stand it. It was James who had sat in the rocking chair of what used to be Robert's room as the Devil reached down into Louis and pulled him up out of himself.

"What happens now?" Louis had asked the Devil.

"You can fly up to heaven on my wings or you can stick around here."

"Grandpa, you all right?" James, who had not inherited his father's and grandfather's gift for sober second sight, stood and asked what was left of Louis.

"Where's Junior? Is he down here or up in heaven?"

"I don't know, and if I did, I wouldn't say. This your decision to make. You can't put it on nobody else."

"Dad!" James yelled to Robert, who was going through Louis's papers in the living room. "Dad!"

"I guess I'll stick around for a while. See what kind of man my grandson grows up to be."

"All right, then," the Devil said as Robert crossed into the room and, upon seeing the Devil, stopped. "Come find me when you're ready."

"How you doing, old man?" James asked Robert.

"Fair," Robert said, still searching the couch. "Just fair."

"You finally got sick of sitting on plastic?"

Catherine had covered the baby-blue paisley couch in plastic after

James, a two-month-old at the time, smiled his first-ever smile, gurgled, and then spit up on her. She'd picked the upholstery out of a catalogue over her mother's objection that it would show dirt.

"Naw," Robert said to James. "I can't find my keys. Something must have eaten them."

"You don't need your keys anymore, Dad," James said as Robert put the couch plastic back how Catherine liked it. "I'll drive you anywhere you want to go."

Robert regarded James warily. He was older than he remembered, rounder at the belly.

"What's that?" Robert asked, pointing to the bags in James's hand.

"I brought you some groceries."

"I can get my own groceries."

"Well, now you don't have to."

Robert picked up the bag and ran his hand over the mule that had been Laurent's Grocery's logo for as long as he could remember. Robert had fixed his eyes on this same mule the day Catherine confronted him over Porter.

"Who's that rude bag boy over at Laurent's Grocery?" Catherine had asked one evening after he came in from feeding the hogs. Robert laughed.

"You mean your son? I didn't think he had it in him to be rude to anybody, let alone his mother."

"No," she'd said, leveling her eyes at him. "Not James. The other one. The dark-skinned one. The one that has your face."

"What's this?" Robert asked James, lifting a plastic-wrapped sweet potato out of the bag.

"It's a sweet potato."

"I know it's a sweet potato. Why is it wrapped up like this?"

"I don't know, Dad. That's just how they came."

"Organic?" Robert said, reading the sticker. "They charge you extra for it?"

"Probably."

"You don't grow your own?"

"I do, Dad, but sometimes it's just easier to buy them."

Robert set the bag down on the table, remembering that he'd yet to find his keys.

"You can put those up in the kitchen," Robert said to James. "I got to find my keys."

"Where is it you want to go? We can take you."

"We?" Robert asked, seeing for the first time the little girl behind James's leg.

"Mary," he barked. "Where did you slip off to?"

The girl eyed him warily. Lucy wanted to like her grandfather, really, she did, but she didn't like the way he talked to her father, the way he talked to her.

"This is Lucy, Dad," James said, trying his best to peel the girl off his leg. "You remember Lucy, don't you?"

"Of course I do. I'm not senile."

Lucy stepped from behind James's leg and smiled the way her mother had taught her to use on strangers.

"Go on," James said. "Say hello to your grandpa."

"Hello, Grandpa."

"Where's John?"

"John has chores he needs to finish. I'll bring him by tomorrow. In the meantime, why don't I fix us some breakfast?"

"I don't have time for breakfast," Robert said. "I've got to get to the church."

"It's still pretty early. When do you have to be there?"

"Eleven. The service starts at eleven."

"All right. It's nine now. There's plenty of time to eat."

"Listen to your son," the Devil said. "This very well may be your last meal."

"Yeah," Robert said, eyeing the Devil, who, by then, had put his feet up in Robert's recliner. "I guess that's enough time to eat."

James defrosted the bacon in the microwave while Lucy cracked eggs into a bowl. Lucy's haughty airs, the same airs Twyla put on, had always unnerved Robert. Robert couldn't fathom how or why James had fixed his mouth to say "I do" to a dicty little debutante wannabe like Twyla after being reared by Catherine. Catherine was the last real woman, Robert thought as he watched the fire dance beneath the skillet of frying eggs.

"Don't let it burn you," Robert said as the image of the fire flaring up and consuming them all in a flash danced before his eyes.

"Huh?"

"The fire. Don't let it burn you."

"I know how to use a gas stove, Dad."

They ate, and before Robert knew it, he was strapped into James's road-eating machine, flying like a bat out of hell over the gravel, seeing the dust fly up behind them.

"I told you it skips toward the end," the Devil said from the back seat as the image of James taking a curve too fast, losing control of the car, flipping them over into a ditch, flashed before Robert's eyes.

"Slow down," Robert said, holding on to the armrest for dear, dear life.

"I'm only going forty, Dad."

In the back seat, Lucy crayoned wide looping scribbles over the image of a cartoon turtle while the Devil looked on in fascination. Robert wondered how she kept her crayons from flying everywhere at this speed.

"You're not on the highway."

"All right, Dad. I'll slow down."

"What will it take, Catherine?" Robert had asked Catherine, who, after learning Robert had another son, had been in Ripley for the better part of six months. "What do I have to do to get you to come back home?"

"I won't be made a fool of." It was the first time he'd been able to get her on the phone in over a month. "I won't walk around Laurent with folks staring at me like they know more about my business than I do."

"I'll do anything, Catherine. Anything. I can't go on living like this. I miss you something terrible. I don't know who I am without you."

"I miss you, too."

"Then come home."

Catherine held the phone to her chest. Robert could hear, faintly, her heartbeat. The sound of it brought him back to their wedding night, back to how, after, he'd laid his head on her chest and listened as she talked a mile a minute about what all in life they would have and do together.

"Here's what I want. I want you to break off all ties with that woman. I don't want to hear that you shopped at the same store or even pumped gas at the same station."

"Done."

"If she sees you in the street and calls out to you, don't turn your head, don't acknowledge her. If she's on fire, I don't want you to even so much as piss on her."

"I won't see her ever again. I promise, Catherine. Not ever again."

"I don't want you talking to that boy, either."

Robert fixed his mouth to assent but then stopped short.

"He didn't get to pick how he was born. A boy needs his people to know his place. I hardly see him as it is."

"You asked me what it would take. I'm telling you what it would take."

Headlights flashed the windows and the truck pulled into the driveway. Mary was off at school, and as far as he knew, James, who still lived at home, was asleep in his bed. Nobody else had enough salt in them to show up at this hour unannounced.

"Somebody's outside, Catherine."

"Don't shoot them."

"I won't if I don't have to," Robert said, throwing a robe on over his T-shirt and boxers. "I love you."

"I love you, too."

He replaced the rotary phone's receiver, opened his nightstand, retrieved his pistol, and went out into the hall. Hearing voices, he peeped through the living room blinds and spied two shadowy figures, one sitting, one standing, at his front door. He turned on the porch light, opened the door, and found James sprawled out on the ground, laughing, with Porter standing over him. It was the first and last time Robert would ever see his sons together.

They arrived at the church, Robert, James, and Lucy. After they parked in the empty lot, Robert realized his mistake. There was no funeral today. The person he was thinking of had passed a long time ago.

"That's all right, Dad," James said after Robert apologized. "While we're here, though, we may as well make use of these flowers."

There were lilies in the back seat beside Lucy.

"Your mother loves those," Robert said, thinking of the bouquet he'd given Catherine after they found out she was pregnant. "Be sure to save her some."

The distance between the church and the cemetery was farther than Robert remembered. The air was green with the scent of fresh-cut grass. Lucy ran, stopping only once she reached a climbable sycamore tree. Robert, spotting his mother's grave, halted. After more than a decade of soap operas and contented solitude, Clementine had passed away peacefully in her sleep. Reverend Powers gave the eulogy, which had a might too much sermon in it for Robert's taste. The bereaved don't want no sermon. Nobody sick with grief wants to be preached at. They want to hear a few nice words, reminisce if they can stand it, and go home.

"You okay, Dad?"

"I'm fine."

A breeze rippled the blades of grass and worried the leaves in the trees. By then, Lucy had climbed halfway up the sycamore. Robert imagined her falling up into the clouds, letting the sky take hold of her the way the woman in yellow had described to him all those years ago.

"Little girls ought not to be climbing trees. It's not safe."

"She's fine, Dad."

James was the first baby Robert had ever held. The day he was born, Catherine was salting water for a mess of sweet peas he'd picked when she dropped the Morton's, held her stomach, and let out the most awful cry he'd ever heard. For the next twelve hours, he sat in a wooden rocking chair in the den while neighbor women talked at him about what it takes to raise a child, ceasing their chatter only to listen and comment on his Catherine's screams, until, as if in sympathy with her plight, a quieter, though more piercing cry accompanied and then replaced it. Later, the midwife came out of the sick-and-lying-in room and placed the now too-quiet newborn into Robert's cradled arms. James's eyes were closed when he was handed to Robert. But, after a few minutes, they opened, locked onto his, and did not blink. The room was overfull with friends and family, most of whom had attended his own birth, or babysat him, or given him a nickel for every bushel of shucked corn or snapped peas. All of them had quieted to better watch the baby watch him. Now his mother, father, wife, and everyone else who shared this memory with him was here in this cemetery.

"It won't be long before you join them," the Devil said, seeing Robert's thoughts.

"You want to meet the woman who gave you your name?" Robert asked Lucy after she climbed down from the tree.

"Momma gave me my name."

"This is your great-great-great-grandmother Lucille," Robert said, ignoring the girl. "She was my grandfather's mother."

Lucy touched her hand to the gray of the stone and felt an electric chill.

"She was born a slave, but she died free."

Lucy took her hand away from the grave.

"Twyla and I haven't taught her about slavery yet."

"She needs to know her people. Her and John both need to know their people," Robert said. And then, kneeling to level his eyes at Lucy, "All this used to be a plantation. My people, your people, were owned by a man named Laurent. It's from him that we got our name."

"I'd like to go home now," Lucy said to James.

"In a little bit, sweetheart," James said, handing her the keys. "Why don't you go back to the car and wait for us?"

"Why does she talk like that?" Robert asked.

"Twyla's working with her on her diction. Says she doesn't want her to sound ignorant."

"You think the way I talk is ignorant."

"You asked why she talks that way. I'm telling you."

"One day you're going to regret letting your wife run roughshod over you."

"Let's head back."

They left the shade of the sycamore and walked back toward the church, which seemed small to Robert from this far back. The wind changed direction and carried with it the scent of hogs and late pollen. The woods between here used to be so thick you couldn't see the water for the trees.

Once they reached Cassandra's grave, James peeled a couple of lilies off of the bouquet and placed them at the base of the headstone. It took a year for her grandmother Ernestine to scrape together enough money to give Cassandra a proper headstone. Some of the church folks offered to help, even took up a collection, but she would take none of it. In the end, one of the deacons took the money to the stonecutter directly and convinced him to tell Ernestine a story about mixing up the estimates. The deacons patted themselves on the back for being so slick about it. But, one Sunday, after the stone had been in place for a few years, Ernestine put all of what the church paid on it right back into the collection plate.

"Dad," James said, stopping short of Catherine's grave. "I'm going to put these flowers on Momma's grave. Do you want to come with me?"

Robert tried to read what was carved into the heart-shaped stone's reflective surface, but his mind wouldn't allow his eyes to process the name etched into the granite.

She came back in the end, Catherine did. It took a few months, but she came back. By then, both of their children had moved out. Mary had gone off to the city to do God knows what and James had taken up with Twyla. She showed up late one night with a suitcase. Said she was tired of depending on her sister. It was her house as much as it was his. She pushed past his astonishment, leaving her bags for him to carry in. She slept in Mary's room the first couple of months, but then, one night, after he'd showered, he walked into the bedroom and found her lying on her side facing the wall.

Robert dried himself, replaced the towel, slipped on his nightshirt, and lay down next to his wife, feeling, knowing, any chance he had at happiness depended on how he handled the next few moments. She wasn't asleep. He'd have heard her breathing if she was asleep. She knew he was next to her and yet she did not move. Robert turned over on his side and faced her. Her hair was wrapped up in a scarf, but he could smell the Pink lotion she'd used on it. How long had it been since his nose had found her scent? He scooted closer to her, reached his arm out, and snaked it around her midsection. She grabbed hold of his hand and squeezed it.

"I didn't deserve her," Robert told James as they stood before her gravestone.

"I know," James said, and then, after a minute, "none of us did."

Robert had been the first to feel the lump on her breast. She was in the kitchen doing the dishes and he'd sneaked up behind her to run his hands over her. "This is what I missed most," she told him as she kissed his hand the night they'd reconciled, "these hands. I missed the feel of these hands on me." And so, up until they found the cancer, Robert had made a point of touching his wife every day.

"I don't want no more treatment," Catherine had said after the first round of chemo failed to shrink any of the tumors. "I don't want to be poked and prodded in no hospital. I want to die in my own home. I want to die natural."

Later that night, after eating the dinner of pork chops and sweet peas James had prepared for him, Robert lay down in his funeral suit next to the space where Catherine wasn't, closed his eyes, and, as the blood vessel in his left temple ruptured, saw himself riding the air on his own wings high above a blazing fire. As the vision came to him, the Devil took Robert's hand and pulled him up out of his body.

"Wherever Catherine is," Robert told the Devil when the Devil put to him the question he'd asked each of Robert's ancestors. "I don't give a damn whether it's heaven or hell. Take me to Catherine."

The Wayside

John Laurent
(1983)
Son of James and Twyla Laurent
Brother of Lucy Laurent
Natural Child of Cassandra Ross and Porter Bland

YOU HEAR TELL devils are ugly, but the one who took hold of me is sweet-faced. She's got this long wavy hair and her skin is brown. If I were a girl, her body would be my body. She was in the creek behind the cemetery. Dad took me to fish and see the turtles take water. I watched the turtles stretch their necks into the warmth of the sun as she stared at me from the place in rippled water where my reflection was supposed to be. I turned to the side; she turned to her side. I raised my arms; she raised her arms, too. I frowned down into the water, and she grinned at me. One of her eyes is hazel and the other is green.

Now whenever I go to look at myself, I see her. She smiles and this warm red feeling starts blooming up in me. No one's ever spoken to me about the birds and the bees, but I know good and well what happens when a bull preens and struts his way around to the back of a heifer to take in her scent, and so I'm not surprised when, after I catch sight of her in the mirror, what happens to that bull happens to me.

"Son," Dad had said when he walked in on me wiping the shame up off my comforter. "You're getting to be a man now. And so I'm not going to stand here and tell you what you can and can't do with your body, but I'll say this: God gave you seed to sow generations, not to cast by the wayside."

"Yes, sir."

"And since you have so much time on your hands," he said, "I think it might be a good idea for you to take on a few more chores."

"Yes, sir."

"You can start by washing these sheets," he said, glowering at the wet spot on my comforter.

Dad handed me his Bible and told me to read Luke 8, the Parable of the Sower. I found the answer to my ailment in verse two, right at the beginning of the chapter: "And a certain woman, which had been healed of evil spirits and infirmities, Mary called Magdalene, out of whom went seven devils." I set the Bible down, stood up, and paced back and forth across the room. It didn't say nothing about how them devils got into Mary, but whatever it was happened to me, too. Which was why I felt the need to cast my seed to the wayside at every opportunity.

All through the summer, I washed up while taking care not to look in the mirror. I fished and pretended I didn't see her smiling up at me. I kept my hands busy and my mind clean. Mornings, I woke up early to feed and water the hogs. Afternoons, I split, quartered, and stacked the wood. Evenings, I sat up at the kitchen table reading the Bible for as long as my eyes would let me. And at night, I laid myself down to sleep praying she wouldn't shame me. I did any and everything I could think of to keep my mind off of closing the door to my bedroom, turning off the lights, and allowing that devil to work me. And I was clean up until the day Angela sat down beside me.

Angela used to live down the street from us. Our mothers were best friends until right after her parents got divorced. Momma and Ms. Deborah, Angela's mother, used to talk on the phone every day, but then one day, Momma slammed the phone down and didn't answer when Ms. Deborah called back. I don't rightly know why, but I haven't heard Momma mention Ms. Deborah since. Before then, everybody used to joke about Angela and me marrying. Dad was the only one who didn't think it was funny.

Sometimes, when Angela raises her hand, the back of her shirt rises and the she-devil starts whispering about the pink lacy underwear curving her waistline. Making me wonder about how pink lace would feel against my skin. And so, before I see her, I make sure to get my Bible out and thumb through a few verses in Corinthians to still my blood and stifle that blooming.

"Son," Principal Moss says. "It's all well and good you want to read the Bible, but there's a time and place for that, and biology ain't it." Principal Moss used to be Coach Moss, and there's a way he has of speaking that lets you know it. On his desk, there's a picture of his wife and daughter, and while he talks, I stare at it instead of him.

"I know it don't always seem like it, but what you come out of these halls knowing and not knowing is going to determine how far you get in life. You know what I'm saying?"

"Yes, sir."

"You're a good kid, John, and I don't want to punish you for doing right, but if I hear about you not getting your lesson again, for any reason, we're going to be having another kind of conversation. You understand?"

There's a poster of the football schedule on the wall behind Principal Moss. This is what I turn my attention to after I tire of his family portrait. I look at any- and everything in his office but his crossed eyes, because once I focus on them, I won't be able to look away.

"Yes, sir," I say to the wall.

"Good. Now get your ass on back to class."

"Yes, sir."

"And look people in the eye when they speak to you. You kids never look anybody in the eye when they're speaking to you, and it's rude."

"Yes, sir."

When I leave Principal Moss's office, I find Angela outside waiting to go in. She gets sent to Principal Moss's office at least once a day. Angela's real smart but she doesn't like being told what to do, which is a real problem because being told what to do is pretty much all there is to school. None of the teachers like her because she's always taking the lessons further than teachers think they ought to go and asking questions they don't know the answers to.

"You mean you got in trouble for reading the Bible?" Angela says. She has on blue jeans and a black T-shirt airbrushed to say "No Scrubs" in green bubble print. Her hair is braided into a ponytail and pulled around to the front of her shirt. I follow the weave of her hair, and my eyes run right back on around to the words "No Scrubs." I get caught up in this loop two or three times. "That's the most *you* shit I've ever heard."

"I try," I say.

From where I'm standing, I can smell the coconut oil her mother used to braid her hair, and the sweetness of it is just enough for that devil to start up in me again. I just know her scent will find me in my dreams.

"Did you forget my phone number?" Angela asks, looking down at her shoes.

"No," I tell her. "I remember it." Angela's number was the only number besides my own I knew by heart.

"Then call me."

That next Sunday, I play sick to skip church and meet Angela down by the creek. God would forgive me because it was Him who put it on my heart to bring Angela back into the fold. Angela and her folks used to go to church with us every Sunday. We'd sit beside one another in Bible study, and when it was time for church to start, she and her mother and father would take the pew in front of us and, sometimes, her hair would fall over into my open hymnbook. But after her dad left, her mom stopped going to church and Angela stopped believing in God. "That little bit of water Reverend Powers splashed didn't mean anything," she told me one night over the phone. All that week, her words sat on my heart like a stone. I could guide her back onto the straight and narrow if only I could get that devil to stop whispering to me about how pretty she is.

Angela has driven her mother's red Honda through the grass and all the way up to the edge of the water. It's a wonder she didn't tear it up. Angela has a hardship license because her mom has two or three jobs and is always working. I lean my bike up on an oak tree a little ways up from the bank and walk down to her.

Angela is lying across the hood of her car with her head propped up against the windshield. I can see the reflection of the clouds in the sky on the glass behind her, and the sight of it is so pretty it could be a calendar picture. She doesn't turn when I walk up, but she knows I'm there.

I sit down next to the tire, kick my legs out in front of me, and lean back on my elbows.

"It's nice out today," Angela says from the hood of the car.

"It is," I say.

It's warm out but most of the leaves are already starting to turn. When the wind blows, you can hear how dry they are.

"You're really not going to join me up here?"

"I didn't want to presume," I say. Sitting on the hood of someone else's car is like putting your feet up on a friend's coffee table. Even with their say-so, it never feels quite right.

Angela swings her legs over the car, walks around me, and then sits her coconut-oil-and-sweet-sweat-smelling self down just close enough to make that she-devil whisper. It was the same smell as when Angela's mother used to plait her hair over at our house.

She lies back and puts her hands behind her head. Our elbows touch.

"What would you be doing right now if you were out here alone?" she asks.

I think for a moment but can't come up with anything better than the truth, which I decide to keep to myself.

"Probably this," I say.

"Me, too," she says.

I think about leaning over and kissing her but don't because I don't know what I'll do with myself if she gets mad at me over trying something. For a minute, it seems like maybe she feels the same as me. Maybe when our folks fell out of favor with each other, she cried herself to sleep, missing me the same way I missed her.

"What do you want from me, John?"

"Nothing. I don't want anything from you."

"Liar," she says, glaring over her shades at my pants.

That devil, she just won't leave me be.

"I'm sorry," I say. "I can't help it."

"You want me to touch it, don't you? Is that why you invited me out here?"

"No," I say. "I just wanted to see you."

"You and every other boy."

I didn't know there were other boys.

"What do you even like about me?"

"I like everything about you."

She snorts and shakes her head. I look to the sky, hoping to find the words somewhere up there for what all she makes me feel.

"Hey," Angela says. Her hand hovers over my pants.

"What are you doing?"

"What do you want me to do?" she asks, pulling my zipper down, reaching her hand in, and pulling out my shame.

"Tell me to stop."

"Huh?"

"Tell me to stop."

"Stop."

"You don't mean it. Say it like you mean it."

I try to say it again, but I can't. I seize up and it's over before it even begins.

"You talk a good game, John," she says, wiping her hand off on my shirt. "But you're just like everybody else, aren't you?"

I don't say anything.

"That's what I thought," she says, standing up.

I search for the words to stop her, the words that will keep her here with me, but I can't find them. After she leaves, I lie back down. If I don't get the devil out of me, I'll be damned for all eternity.

That night, I wake up to find my tighty-whities sticky with shame. I peel them off, put on another pair, and decide then and there to get rid of that she-devil once and for all. The sky is bright with the moon, but I could make it to the horse apple tree that shades the water troughs and back to the house in the dark. Sometimes Lucy comes with me because she likes to see, but not touch, the pigs. Tonight, all I have is the Word of God for company. In Luke, when Christ cast out the unclean spirits they went into the swine, and so I'm hoping I can do the same with the she-devil, try to get her into one of the runts that's going to die anyway.

I step over the gate and walk up to the horse apple tree to where a sow is resting with her sucklings. All of them are wedged up under her, save one runt who's off to the side, shivering. I pick him up and bring him over to the other side of the fence with me. Dad says it's more humane to wring a runt's neck than to let it starve. The runt wakes when I pick him up, but he doesn't squeal or anything. He just noses my hand, grateful for the heat. I know then how much weaker I am than Jesus. I'm not even strong enough to damn a piglet. I put him in my coat pocket. It won't hurt nobody if I feed him some leftover corn mushed up with cow's milk, name him Luke, and let him spend the night in my closet.

Angela doesn't come to school the next day, so I write a note and leave it in her locker, even though she hardly ever uses it. That afternoon, they announce over the intercom that Principal Moss is no longer allowed on school grounds. When I get home, I go straight to my room and relive my shame. I am still in bed, trying to figure out what I could've done different, when Momma calls me downstairs to tell me Angela is out front.

The inside of the car smells like Starbursts and feet. Angela wears long baggy pants and a thick sweater, even though it ain't cold out yet. She probably wore it so she wouldn't have to worry about me lusting after her. I stare straight ahead because I don't want to be disrespectful. She raises her bare feet up into the driver's seat and rests her head on her knees. Her toenails are blue.

"I'm sorry about the other day," I manage.

"You're not the one who needs to apologize," she says, staring through the windshield. The blinds in the living room are open and Lucy is peeking out at us. Angela waves.

"I love your little sister," Angela says. "She was the first baby I ever held. Nobody had ever looked at me the way she did."

"I remember that," I say, glad to have her eyes on me.

She puts her feet down on the floor and turns the stereo up. Anita Baker belts out "Sweet Love," which had always been Angela's favorite song.

"We got some history, don't we?" Angela says. "I don't have to tell you this is my favorite album. You just know it."

I nod along and don't say that's why we should be together, always.

"You remember when we were playing dress-up and your dad walked in and you had on your momma's lipstick and high-heeled shoes?"

"I don't."

"Yes, you do, John! Don't lie. Oh my God, your dad's face! If I could bottle his expression, I would keep it on my nightstand and spritz it into the air every morning right when I woke up. I think the lipstick was what sent him over the top. You were so pretty!"

"You were a bully."

"I was a little bit bossy, yeah."

"You made me eat dirt."

"I did not!"

"You did. You said it tasted like candy."

"That was red clay, and it *was* sweet!"

"It didn't taste like candy."

"Well, yeah, it's still dirt, but it's sweeter than other dirt."

Angela faces forward. I follow her gaze. This time it's my mother who's staring through the blinds at us. When our eyes meet, the blinds flick shut, and when I turn back to Angela she's crying.

"What's wrong?" I ask, reaching my hand out to rub her back the way I've seen Dad do when Momma's having one of her spells. My hand grazes her bra strap. An electric thrill runs through me. I hear a thumping sound and it takes me a second to realize my heart is making it.

"I like you," she says. "I like you a lot."

"What's the matter with that?" I ask, grinning. "I like you a lot, too."

"My mom is sending me to Chicago to stay with my dad."

"Oh," I say. "For how long?"

"For forever."

I pull my hand back. She turns to me, red-eyed, and I feel like I've been sitting at the bottom of a pond, holding my breath for a very long time.

"When do you leave?" I ask.

"Tomorrow," she says, more to the dashboard than to me.

"So you came to say goodbye?"

"Yeah," she says. "I came to say goodbye."

I don't cry; even though I want to, I don't. Dad says a man needs to hold himself together, otherwise the world will tear him apart, and so, instead of crying, I say goodbye and open the car door to leave.

"Wait," she says. "There's something else you should know."

The cassette stops. Angela wipes her face, takes a deep breath, and starts it over. Then she reaches into her pocket, pulls out a crumpled picture, and hands it to me. I squint at it. I recognize my dad right off, but it takes me a moment to place the woman in his lap. There's a man who resembles my dad next to them.

"That's my mom," Angela says, pointing to the woman. As soon as she says it, I recognize Ms. Deborah.

"Why is she sitting in my dad's lap?"

"They used to date, if you can believe it."

"That's crazy."

"I know, right?"

"Why did you want me to see this?"

Angela sighs, tilts her head back, and stares up at the car headliner. Outside, the antlers of a buck peek over the top of the picket fence. It'll be hunting season in another week or so.

"I don't know if I'm doing the right thing," she says, still looking up at the ceiling. "I don't know if there is a right thing. But if you found out something important about me, you would tell me, because that's the kind of person you are."

"What is it?"

"Do you know the man in the picture? The man sitting beside your dad?"

"No."

"That's your dad's brother, Porter."

"My dad has a brother?"

"A half brother, yeah."

I hold the picture up to my face. The resemblance is undeniable.

"So I have an uncle I don't know about? That's weird."

"John," Angela says, grabbing my hand and squeezing. "I don't know how to tell you this."

"Tell me what?"

"He's not your uncle. He's your father. At least according to my mom."

"Why would she say that?"

"I don't know, John. She might be mistaken. But just in case she wasn't, I thought you should know. She says you were adopted after your birth mother passed away."

My legs go numb. The buck is nowhere to be seen.

"Please don't hate me. Like I said, I don't know if any of it is true, but I felt like you should know."

But it is true. I don't know how or why I know, but it is.

"I don't hate you. I have to go back inside, but I don't hate you."

I open the car door.

"Wait," Angela says. "Before you go, can I have a hug?"

I let go of the door, scoot toward the console, and wrap my arm around her shoulders.

"No," she says. "I want a real hug."

The living room blinds flick open and closed again.

"Let's go around back," Angela says. We walk around back of the house. Angela wraps her arms around me and squeezes tight. The smell of her hair wafts into my nose and my shame rears its head.

"John?"

"Yeah."

"The other day at the creek."

"Yeah."

"I wanted to do that. I just wanted you to want me to do it more than I wanted to. I wanted you to want me so much you couldn't help yourself. If I were the boy, I would have laid you down in the back of the car. I would have said you were so pretty. I would have said I had to have you. That I couldn't help it, because sometimes men can't. You would pretend you didn't want me, but you would. You wouldn't know it, because girls don't always know it, but I would reach my hand down and feel you and know you wanted me as bad as I wanted you."

I don't know what to say to any of that.

"Here's my dad's number and address," she says, wiping her eyes. "I want to call you, but you have to call me first. Can you call me first?"

"Yeah," I say. "I'll call you first."

"Promise?"

"I promise."

The day after Angela leaves, I call the number she gave me to see if she's made it. When I do, it rings and rings. I try again the next day and get static. The third time I try, I look the numbers over real close and press them in slow. It rings again but no one picks up, and so I call Ms. Deborah, Angela's mom, to make sure I have it down right.

"What?" she answers.

"Hi, Ms. Deborah. This is John, Twyla and James's son."

"Oh, hi, John. What can I do for you?"

"Hi, I was wondering if you could give me Angela's dad's number. She gave it to me before she left, but I think she might have written it down wrong."

"I have his number, but I left my address book at work. Why don't you swing by there after school tomorrow? I should have it with me then."

"All right," I say, not thinking until after I hang up to ask why she couldn't just call me back with it, but then I decide I don't mind. The more reasons I have to not be at home the better. Lately, everything out of my parents' mouths sounds like a lie.

After the school bus drops me off, I feed Luke some milk and a can of creamed corn, hop on my bike, and ride over to Talbert Manor, the nursing home where Ms. Deborah works as a receptionist. The hill it sits on is rough going, and by the time I'm halfway up it, my quads ache and my calves burn. Once I get to the top, I rest my bike against the side of the building. When I walk in, Ms. Deborah is on the phone. I take a seat in one of the chairs across from her desk.

The reception area opens out into a large living room with tables, a few couches, and a large TV playing on mute. At one of the tables, three men play what looks to me to be either rummy or three-handed spades. Two of the men have on velour tracksuits—one red, one black—with matching Kangol hats. The other man is in a hospital gown and keeps looking over his shoulder down the hallway, like he's waiting on somebody to bring him the card he needs to make his hand.

"John," Ms. Deborah says, laying the receiver flat on her chest, "can you do me a favor and take a cup of ice over to Ms. Ernestine in room 5?"

I get up and walk down the hallway to the kitchen. There, I find a white woman in a hairnet chopping lettuce. She watches me fill one of the Styrofoam pitchers on top of the ice machine but doesn't say nothing. Room 5 is across from the water fountain, just off the main hallway. The door is cracked open. No one answers when I knock, and so I open it a teeny bit wider and ease my way in. The lights are off but there's just enough sun coming in through the window for me to see a woman lying on her side, staring at the wall. I set the pitcher down on her nightstand beside an old-timey picture. The she-devil stares at me from out of it, only this time her movements don't mimic mine. She sits so still that if I didn't know any better, I'd have thought it was actually a picture of her. When I lift my eyes from the frame, Ms. Ernestine's eyes are on me.

"What are you doing here?" she asks. Only the right side of her mouth moves.

"Ms. Deborah told me to bring you some ice."

"If I want ice, I'll ask for ice."

"Yes, ma'am," I say, turning to go.

"You don't have nothing to say for yourself?"

"No, ma'am."

"I'll give you one more chance to explain yourself and then I'm coming to cut you."

"Ma'am?"

"There it went," she says, sliding a neon box cutter out from under her pillowcase. "Now, are you coming to me or am I coming to you?"

I freeze, not knowing whether to run or to stand there and let her try to cut me, out of respect. She pushes the hospital bed railing down and swings her right leg over it. It's as black and smooth as petrified wood. She tries to lift her left leg, but it won't go.

"Shit," she says. "I guess you're coming to me."

I back out of the door.

"Where you going?" she calls after me as I close the door. "It won't take long if you hold still."

I walk back over to the reception desk. By then, Ms. Deborah is off the phone.

"You know what, I can't find his number anywhere around here. I think I might have left it at home after all."

"That's all right," I say. "You can just call and give it to me later."

"Nonsense. We'll just swing by my house and pick it up. Then I can drop you off at home. How's that?"

"What about my bike?" I ask.

"You can come back for that later."

* * *

I knew the car Angela drove belonged to Ms. Deborah, but I'm still surprised to see it. She lets down the windows and we descend the hill in silence. She drives with just her left hand at the bottom of the steering wheel, just like Angela. When we reach the stoplight, Ms. Deborah glances at me, smirks, and then turns back to the road. Before Ms. Deborah got divorced, she lived in the house down the street from us. Now she rents an apartment just outside of town. Inside, all the walls are white, save the burgundy one behind the oversize brown leather couch.

"Have a seat," she says.

I take a seat.

"Can I get you a drink? I have to make myself a drink as soon as I get in, otherwise I just can't get settled."

"I'll have some water," I say.

She comes out of the kitchen.

"Just water?"

"Yes, ma'am."

"You don't have to act all innocent with me," she says, laughing. "You been running around with my daughter, you must be into all kinds of shit."

The clock above the TV reads five.

When Ms. Deborah comes back, she has with her a loud glass of I-don't-know-what in one hand and a bottle of beer in the other. She hands me the beer and sits down beside me. I set the beer down on the table.

"You really don't drink?"

"No, ma'am."

"*No, ma'am*," she mocks, crossing her legs. Her socked foot lands on my knee and rests there. A warm shiver runs up in me and I try not to feel it.

"Here," she says, holding her glass up to my lips, "take a sip."

It tastes like lime, sugar, and gasoline.

"Did you even taste it? Here, try again."

I take a swallow. It burns.

"Pretty good, right?"

"Mm-hmm."

"Your daddy used to love these. You used to couldn't hide no liquor from James Laurent. It could be up under the bathroom sink and he'd sniff it out like a bloodhound. Course you wouldn't know it now."

In front of me is a glass-top coffee table with family pictures pressed under it. Most of them are of Angela when she was little. I catch myself in the background of one of her at the bottom of a slide. I'm standing behind the ladder, peeking at the camera.

"You know I was his first and only before you were born. Used to be he would do anything for me. Anything. He'd have drunk my bath-water before you came along," she says, shaking her head. "Do you have any idea what it feels like to be loved like that and then thrown away?"

"No, ma'am."

"It makes you sick. Makes you sick to your soul. I never would have given Angela's father the time of day if I hadn't been so soul-sick."

"I'm sorry."

"You should be. It's all your fault."

The she-devil is in the mirror. She gestures for me to stand up.

"Ms. Deborah, you think I could have that phone number now?"

She lets out a sigh, sits up straight, and downs her drink, eyeing me all the while.

"What do you need to talk to my daughter so bad for?"

"No reason in particular. We're just friends is all."

"Yeah, she was getting to be real *friendly*, wasn't she? I thought I was going to have to call the cops on your principal. You think he'd be too shamed to come sniffing around after her. I guess he figures he's got nothing left to lose now."

I lean forward. My stomach lurches. It's all I can do to keep from vomiting.

"Here, have a sip," Ms. Deborah says, holding the beer out. I wave it off.

"I guess you weren't as close to her as you thought you were, huh?" she says, putting her feet up on the coffee table, stretching her arm out, and resettling it behind my head. She has on the same deodorant my mother wears. "You can be close to me, if you want. I could use a new friend."

"I think I have to get going," I say, standing up.

"Suit yourself," she says, sitting back. "You know where the door is."

I stand up, step over her legs while she eyes me, and walk down the hall to the front door, trying as best I can to avoid the mirror.

"Ms. Deborah?" I call out after I open the door.

"Yeah."

"Before Angela left, she showed me an old picture of you and Dad. What you said about Porter, about my parents, is it true?"

"Nobody's told you?" she says, standing up from the couch and coming into the hall. "You mean after all this time, they haven't said anything? I never would have showed Angela his picture if I thought you didn't know. I'm sorry, sweetheart. You want a hug?"

"No, ma'am," I say, backing out the front door. "I should get home."

"All right, well, don't tell your parents what we talked about," she says. "I'd hate for them to think I was trying to stir up trouble."

I keep to the shady side of the street on the walk back to Talbert Manor. It's only a few miles, but there's no sidewalk, and so whenever a car comes, I have to step into the ditch. By the time I get back to my bike, the sun has set.

When I get home, everyone is already at the dinner table. We have pork chops and greens for dinner. Lucy spreads the greens around her plate to make like she's eaten more than she has. Dad's staring out the window like he's waiting for somebody to rescue him, and Momma's eyeing me like she's trying to read on my face where I've been.

"You stink," Lucy says when I sit down next to her.

"Lucy, what did we just talk about?" Momma asks.

"What happens at home stays at home."

"That's right," Momma says. "But not that, the other thing."

"Just because it's true doesn't mean it's nice to say it."

Momma nods and goes back to cutting around the red parts of her pork chop.

"Dad, did you have a brother?"

He doesn't look up from his plate.

"What makes you ask?"

"Ms. Deborah."

"Deborah says a lot of things, John. I wouldn't put too much stock in most of it."

More lies. I screech my chair back and go into the kitchen. I turn the faucet on and splash water on my face. Out of the corner of my eye, I catch sight of a sock it to me cake on the counter and wonder whether Momma would notice if I pinched off just a little bitty piece. The she-devil is in the glossy black finish of the refrigerator. She looks at me, and her look lets me know she's been wanting a slice of sock it to me cake, that a slice of sock it to me cake would make her day. I can't explain how I know her thoughts. I just know they aren't mine. It's like her thoughts and mine are two trains running on parallel tracks.

I step over to the utensil drawer, grab a butter knife, and step back over to the cake plate. The cake plate is crystal, and the cover handle is a naked baby angel. Momma sent away to the Swarovski catalogue for it. Grabbing hold of a naked baby to get cake always makes me feel ashamed. I place the top on the counter, cut off a little sliver, and bring it to my mouth. It's sweet. I cut another piece off. It's bigger than the first one, but eating it makes me even hungrier.

More.

It's more than the sweetness of it, or the fact that I'm having cake by myself while everybody else is in the dining room raking their forks over salty pork, watery greens, and canned corn, it's that I need it in me. My cheeks get hot and the she-devil's smile wears my face.

"John!" Momma yells. "Just what do you think you're doing?"

I look down at the cake, only there's no more cake left to look down at. All of it is in me, and my face and stomach are warm with the sweetness of it. I wait for the shame of it to wash over me, but it doesn't. I don't feel anything.

Early the next morning, I take Luke out of my closet, walk him down to the hog pen, and put him back with his brothers and sisters. He's big enough to eat from the trough now. After I come back to the house, I pack my backpack full of Pop-Tarts, granola bars, cans of apple juice, and gas money, take the keys to the truck, and ease it out of the garage. It stalls when I kick it out of reverse, but otherwise it rides fine. I printed the directions out in study hall. If I take the back roads to Memphis, I can take I-55 north to I-57, just over the Missouri Bootheel. From there, it's a straight shot to Chicago and I won't have to check the directions again until I see the city. Only the car doesn't make it to Memphis. Dad told me the gas gauge wasn't working right, but I don't remember it until the engine cuts off. I coast until there's enough room between the road and the trees for me to pull over. It's light out, but the sun hasn't made it all the way up yet. It's cool, but my jeans and windbreaker are enough to keep me warm, at least while I'm walking. I passed a gas station a few miles back. If it had been open, I would have stopped and filled up then, but it was too early. I'm hoping it will be open by the time I get there. If not, I'll just have to wait outside until it is.

I make it to the last road I turned off of, the one with the gas station, only I don't remember which direction I was coming from. There are no landmarks other than trees, and I wasn't paying close enough attention for them to be of any use to me. If I was thinking, I'd have brought the directions with me and worked my way back from them, but I wasn't thinking.

"Lost?"

I don't see anybody.

"Hello," I call out.

Nobody answers.

It's not until the man strikes his lighter and holds it to the cigar between his lips that I see him standing beneath the tree on the other side of the crossroads. I can barely see through the haze of smoke he's puffing.

"Do you happen to know which way the gas station is?" I ask.

"I might," he says, stepping forward out from under the shadow of the tree. He's a lot taller than he first seemed. I wait for him to say more, but then he doesn't. If I'd been thinking, I'd have grabbed a knife before I left, but I didn't.

"Can you tell me which way it is?" I ask.

"I could."

"Will you?"

He laughs a laugh that makes me want to take a step or two back.

"You're a little young to be on the road this early by yourself, aren't you?"

"I'm not," I say, knowing now how Momma and Dad lie so easily. All you have to do is pretend the lie is the truth. Simple. "My dad's half a mile back, in the truck with the rifles. We were going hunting but then we ran out of gas."

"Hunting, huh? Killing make you feel like a man?"

"No, sir. We just hunt to eat."

"Hunts to eat. He says he hunts to eat." The man says the words over and over again like he can't parse their meaning.

"Well," I say. "I guess I'll go get that gas now. If I take too long, my dad will come looking for me."

329

"It's good you and your daddy do things together. All my old man ever gave me was grief. Even kicked me out. His own son. Can you believe that?"

"No, sir."

"Yeah, I don't imagine you can. Your daddy takes you hunting. Your daddy would never kick you out of his house. Would he?"

"No, sir."

"But then, what I can't quite figure is why he sent you off all by yourself while he sits up in his warm truck, hugged up with them rifles. It just don't sit right with me. If I had a son like you, I'd keep an eye on him. I'd keep him close to me."

"I volunteered."

"You know, I saw a truck coast by here not too long ago. Looked like it was stalling. Was that you? If so, it might be more to it than just gas. Maybe I should run on down to where you pulled off and offer your daddy and his rifles a hand."

"It's just gas," I say.

"You sure?"

"I'm sure."

"Well, then today's your lucky day. I just so happen to have a full can of gas right here," he says, switching his cigar to his left hand. He leans down and picks up a red gas can from behind the tree.

"That's all right," I say. "I'd hate to trouble you."

"No trouble at all," the man says, walking past me toward where the truck is. He has a wide-brimmed hat and hair down to his shoulders, like the portraits of Jesus they put up in white churches. He walks on past me, and since he's headed to Dad's truck, I have no choice but to follow him.

"I know what you're thinking," the man says as we walk. "You're thinking what's this man doing out here so early with a full gas can. Well, yesterday I was brush-hogging that field over yonder for a friend when I got stuck in a mud rut. I gassed it and gassed it and by the time I worked myself out of there, my poor tractor was all gassed out. It was already dusk by then, so I figured I'd just leave it till morning."

"Sounds reasonable," I say.

"It do, don't it?" he says, laughing that creepy laugh again. This time it's pitched somewhere between a howler monkey and a hyena. "But in my limited experiences, lies often sound more reasonable than the truth."

We get to the truck and the man makes a big show of searching for my dad.

"Now, where did he get off to so quick? You reckon he seen a buck so big he needed both rifles to take it down?"

"Maybe," I say.

"Yeah," he says, opening the gas cap. "Or maybe you're just a little liar."

My throat catches.

"That's all right," he says, lifting the can up to the tank. "I like little liars. Little liars have a very special place in my heart." He looks down at his chest when he says this, like he wants to make sure his heart is still there. The cigar is still in his mouth, and in my mind's eye, I see a smoldering ash falling into the open gas tank and flashing us both out of this world. When it doesn't, he empties the can, closes the gas cap, and throws the can in back of the truck.

"The least you can do is take me to refill it," he says.

I swallow and nod. He runs around to the passenger side and hops in. By then, the sun is up. I hop in, turn the engine on, and hold my breath. The air inside the truck is thick with cheap gasoline, cigar smoke, and body odor. I roll both windows down and he does me the courtesy of blowing his smoke outside.

"Chicago, huh?" he says, glancing at the directions. "That's one hell of a drive, especially in this raggedy old beater. There's only one thing that'll get a boy your age up out of bed this early. What's her name?"

"I don't know what you mean."

"Is it a him? You can be honest with me. I won't judge. My Father might would judge, but I won't. No, sir. It's all the same to me. I don't care one way or the other."

We get back to the crossroads.

"You know, you got a really pretty face. Anybody ever tell you that?"

"No."

"Touchy about that, are we? All right, I'll let it be. No shame in being pretty, but I'll let it be. Take a right here."

I do as he says.

"So, this somebody you're sweet on. You love each other so much you're gonna run off to Chicago and start a new life, is that it?"

I don't say anything.

"Be careful, boy. Be. Care. Full," he says, tapping his ashes out to the rhythm of his speech. "Be careful of love, because love will mess you up worse than meth. That's what got my brother killed, loving too hard. Me, I love myself. Nobody puts you up on a cross for loving yourself."

I nod.

"I bet love is turning your rifle-toting daddy inside out right now, making him sick with worry. 'Where's my son? Where's my son?' Oh, I can just hear it!" he says, grinning. "You got a momma, too?"

I keep my eyes on the road.

"Yeah, you got a momma, and I reckon she's just as strung out on loving you as your daddy, only with no rifles to keep her company. I bet all she sees in her mind right now is you turned over in a ditch somewhere. I bet she turns into one of those milk carton mommas on the evening news, standing in you all's front yard, pleading through the camera to them other mommas sitting on their couches watching the TV, just knowing she must have done something to run that boy off. Children just don't up and leave without cause. They just don't."

There's nobody out on the road but us.

"But they don't have to worry about you, right? You're a smart boy. I bet you know better than to talk to strangers. Know to keep the gas tank full. To not pick up hitchhikers. They needn't worry themselves over you. Pull over here."

I turn into the gas station. It's open now.

"Listen," the man says, taking the lit cigar and crushing the ember out on the dashboard. "It's rough out here. Not everybody you meet is going to be as sweet as me, you hear me?"

"Yes, sir."

"Next time this old beater quits on you, who knows what'll happen? One of those ditches your momma's steady dreaming up might jump up and meet you. Young, handsome man like you bleeding out on the side of the road... That would be terrible, wouldn't it?"

"Yes, sir."

He opens the door, and my heart starts beating again.

"Oh yeah," he says, turning back to me. "I reckon you owe me for gas."

I reach into my back pocket, open my wallet, and pull out a five. The man sucks his teeth.

"Them's gas station prices, boy," he says. "I gave you roadside service."

I put the five back and take out a twenty. He shakes his head like he's truly disappointed in me.

"They say the love of money is the root of all evil."

I hand over everything I have.

"God bless," he says, tipping his hat and walking away.

I used to like to listen to the old revival preachers talk about how they were called. There was one older preacher who used to talk about the day the sky broke open, picked him up, and set him down right in front of Mount Carmel. He was out planting beans on a back acre for his daddy, who was laid up with gout, when the wind changed, the sky turned from blue to gray, and the clouds overhead ran together into a funnel. He tried to run for shelter, but before he could get his feet under him, the wind picked him up and he was flying over the fields his father had planted, the house his grand-father had raised from nothing, the church where he was baptized. He thought then of the life of sin he'd led since leaving his father's house for the city. The women he'd lain with, the nights at the juke, the Bible in his nightstand he hadn't cracked in over a year. He knew he didn't have any right to, but he closed his eyes and prayed for forgiveness just as the ground rose up to meet him. He landed in a pile of uprooted hedges not far from the church. Everything else had been leveled. But Mount Carmel stood firm, solid as the rock Peter brought Jesus. And he just knew his life wasn't his anymore. One preacher was struck by lightning three times before he give himself over. Another went dumb at the crossroads on his way home from the casino, and the only thing he could fix his mouth to say for the next month was Jesus, Jesus, Jesus.

At first, I thought the she-devil was the yardstick by which God meant to take my measure. I thought He set her to work in me same as He sent that tornado for that older preacher, only it don't seem like I'll ever be set down. Every day, I wait for the sky to go gray, to hear His voice boom out over the thunder and know I've been called to do His work. But it never happens. I don't know why I ever thought I could save Angela. I can't even save myself.

When I pull out of the gas station, I don't drive home. Instead, I go to the creek and walk to where I last met Angela. I can't rightly say what I'm looking for, what I want from the grass when I lay my head down on it, what I hope to find in the sky when I look up at it. All I know is I need to look at something larger than me. I park the truck and go to the part of the creek where I first saw the she-devil. The sun makes a bright halo behind the she-devil's head. I glare down at her, and she stares up at me. I touch where on me her hair would be and imagine the downy softness of it, flowing down my neck, resting on my shoulders. She holds some of it out for me. I reach my hand out to touch it, but water is all I come away with.

NOW, THE DEVIL had been there in 1801 when Richard Trevithick debuted his steam locomotive at Camborne and had liked the machine so much he lent his name to it. And so when he crossed the railroad tracks in central Mississippi and saw a "Puffing Devil" barreling down on him, he knew before he caught up to the train at the station that he'd found just the thing to take his mind off a spate of recent setbacks.

The year was 1878 and the Devil had just walked from Virginia to Mississippi. In Richmond, he'd suffered through John Jasper's preaching of "The Sun Do Move" and was disheartened by the pastor's exhortations to stand by the Bible—"every word and line, read it," Jasper had said, "meditate over and believe it as a white book, unmixed of errors"—for the Devil knew the book to contain a powerful many mistruths and lies regarding hisself. What was more, the Devil was distraught over the situation in Haiti, his crowning achievement, his pièce de résistance, if you will. But since the revolution, the Black nation had suffered one coup after another, and the reparations to France siphoned every would-be surplus. Now he heard tell that Lysius Salomon, a president he'd have handpicked, both for his bigness and for his Blackness, was headquartering a new national bank in Paris. He'd worked hard to sow the seeds of freedom and now here men like Jasper and Salomon were misspending the fruits of it.

Yes, sir, the Devil was mighty depressed, and so he walked the Mississippi backcountry, because Mississippi was always ripe for good devilment. He was bound for Clarksdale but stopped over at the

Illinois Central Depot in Water Valley after hearing the call of the train whistle.

"You're an engineer?" the man at the depot had asked, skeptical.

"I know how to drive a train."

"Are you Brotherhood certified?"

"I got brothers, yeah," the Devil said.

"I see," the clerk said, opening his desk drawer and retrieving a BLET card with the name Chester Wakefield printed on it. "If anybody asks you about a union, show them this. I'll subtract your weekly dues from your check."

"That's mighty white of you," the Devil told the man. "I sure do appreciate it."

Then, yellow fever was having its way with just about every town from New Orleans to Memphis, and so the people at the Illinois Central Railroad Company were desperate. That cotton wasn't going to ship itself.

"Why's the caboose draped in black?" the Devil asked when he was shown to his train.

"In honor of the last two fellows who drove it."

And so the Devil drove his train on up into Memphis, down to New Orleans, and back again, taking every corner hard and not giving one goddamn about the many bales of cotton he left in his wake. It was around then, as he was cutting up through the middle of Mississippi, that a girl named Ida B. asked him if he couldn't give her a ride back to Holly Springs.

"Folks clearing out of there," the Devil told her. "The fever's bad down that way."

"I need to get home to my brothers and sisters," Ida B. told the Devil. "They don't have nobody but me."

The Devil turned to Ida. The way she said this, the set of her eyes, the tone of her voice, let him know this girl was going to be somebody. Years later, he heard tell of her refusing to ride in the colored coach, getting dragged off a train at Woodstock, suing the railroad company in Memphis, and winning. He'd read in *Free Speech* how a white grocer's greed had led to the arrest of over a hundred Black men and resurrected the tradition of lynching in Memphis. "The city of Memphis," Ida wrote in response to the lynching of Thomas Moss, Calvin McDowell, and William Henry Stewart, "has demonstrated that neither character nor standing avails the Negro if he dares to protect himself against the white man or become his rival." When the Devil read these words, he pictured not the woman who set out to tell truth freely, but the orphaned girl who stared down Death to watch over her family.

Without You

MARY LAURENT
(1958)
Daughter of Robert Laurent
Sister of James Laurent and Porter Bland
Friend of Twyla Laurent

YOU ASKED ME what John's birth mother was like. I told you I barely knew her. I saw Cassandra around town every now and then, but I'd left Laurent for school by the time my older brother fell in with her and Porter.

Tell me about her, you said, laying your head down in my lap. You're the only person besides James who knew her.

She was pretty.

Prettier than me.

No, I said. No one's prettier than you.

Was James in love with her? you asked.

I don't know how it started, you and James. One day you wanted nothing to do with either James or John and then the next day you were in love, first with the baby, then with my older brother, and I felt like it was me, not them, who was visiting. With you, he was more like the boy I knew than the man alcohol was on the verge of making him.

I'm not sure what James felt for Cassandra, I said. The only thing I knew for sure was what he felt for you.

What do you think? you asked. Should we tell John?

It's not for me to have an opinion, I told you. It's for you and James to decide.

But if it was you, would you want to know?

If it was me, I told you, I'd have preferred to have been adopted by you.

But would you have wanted to know the truth?

Truth is relative.

You stood up. You walked around the coffee table, went into the kitchen, and poured yourself another whiskey.

I really do like this one, you said, glancing at a dressing mannequin. But it needs color.

It was an experimental design, a black-and-white paisley print cut in the Victorian fashion: a low neckline, belled linen engageantes, and a skirt with a bustle. After you left, I cut it up, dyed it yellow, and made it into the tunic that altered the course of my career. Then, I wanted to be the next Ann Lowe. Now I just want to be able to afford to live in Manhattan.

You think everything needs color.

Because everything does.

I leaned over the side of the couch and put on a record.

When are you going to get a decent table for that thing? you asked.

I like the way it sounds from the floor.

You sat back down beside me.

Tell me something else about her.

She liked the graveyard, a lot.

James said the same thing. I didn't know what to make of it.

No one did.

What else?

That's all I've got.

You knew I was lying.

I only really talked to her the one time.

Tell me about it.

It was around the time you started dating that thick-necked football player, Clay, and seeing the way he put his hands on you made me sick. So, instead of driving down to Biloxi for spring break like we'd planned, I went home. If I had that week to do over again, I would have spent it with you. I'd have spent every moment I could have with you.

I was walking to the store, everyone in Laurent walked back then, when I found Cassandra on the side of the road beneath the sycamore tree, hunched over, clutching her midsection. There was an overturned picnic basket at her feet out of which spilled broken glass, whiskey, and cookies. She'd been standing there long enough for ants to find the cookies.

Are you hurting? I asked.

Some, she said.

I helped her stand up and didn't see the blood until I got her arm around my shoulder.

It was just a little bit at first, she said. But then it was a whole lot.

You want me to take you to the doctor?

She shook her head.

You got to go somewhere. Won't do anybody any good to have you bleed out here.

We weren't far from my grandparents' house, so I took her there. Grandpa Louis's truck was gone, but Grandma Clem's purple-ribboned gardening hat bobbed through the woods, so the back door had to be open. I helped her up the back steps and sat her down in the wicker chair while I left to get a towel. When I came back, she was facing the mirror, staring at it like there was someone there she couldn't stand the sight of.

I touched my hand to her head. She was running a fever.

I'm going to get you some help. You stay right here. All right?

She looked down at her feet. She didn't want to stay but was too weak to argue. By the time I reached the back door, Grandma Clem was in the yard, laying aside some herbs she'd gathered from the woods. She had a glove in one hand and a rusted trowel in the other.

Mary, she said, beaming, I was wondering when you was going to stop by to see me.

Hey, Grandma.

What's wrong, sweetie?

I didn't know how to explain and so I just took her ungloved hand and walked her back to the room where I had stashed Cassandra.

Oh my goodness, she said when she saw Cassandra.

She wouldn't go to Dr. Whitney.

Yeah, I wouldn't want him poking at me, either. It looks like the bleeding's stopped, Grandma Clem said, stooping down to better see her. But let's get you cleaned up all the same. Mary, she said, turning to me, set some water boiling and, if you can manage it, drag that tin tub out back into the kitchen and fetch me some soap.

I don't have time to wash up, Cassandra said. I need to try again.

Look at me, Grandma Clem told her. You're too far along to do anything with whatever you stuck up there other than break your grandmother's heart. You understand me?

Grandma Clem's kettle already had some water in it, so I just turned on the gas, lit the stove, and set it to boil. Then I went out back and found the tin tub over by the water spigot. I dragged the tub in and used the spigot to fill a couple of buckets. By the time the water finished boiling, Grandma Clem had brought Cassandra over, stripped her clothes, and sat her down in the tub.

You feeling well enough to wash yourself? Grandma Clem asked.

Cassandra looked down at the mess of herself and shook her head like she didn't know what washing was. Grandma Clem sighed, took a washcloth, and started scrubbing the dried blood from between her legs. I set a fresh bucket of water down on the other side of the tub and watched. A fine line of hair began just below Cassandra's sternum and went up over the slight rise of her belly, thickening as it encircled her navel and disappeared into the pink lather Grandma Clem rubbed in circles around and underneath her legs.

Mary, Grandma Clem said, turning to me, run and fetch me a

colored bath towel, a sanitary napkin, and some witch hazel. Then she took the fresh bucket of cool water and rinsed her off.

I backed away from the tub and went down the hall to the linen closet. Most of Grandma's towels were white, but after digging around, I managed to find a tattered blue one.

Cassandra smiled when I handed her the towel. After she dried off, Grandma gave her some aspirin for the pain and made her lie down in the guest bedroom. By the time we finished emptying the tub and drying the kitchen floor, she'd gone to sleep. She slept with her arms splayed like a child.

Grandma Clem tried to call Cassandra's grandmother, but each time she dialed the number, the line was busy.

Do you know where Ernestine lives? Grandma Clem asked.

Yes, ma'am, I told her.

Run down there and tell her to come get her granddaughter.

Yes, ma'am, I told her, turning already to go.

Wait, she said once I was halfway down the hall. Leave the what and why to me.

Yes, ma'am.

It was nearly dusk by the time I made it back to the tree. I searched the base, half expecting to see blood, but there was no trace of Cassandra, aside from the overturned basket. I picked it up, threw the tea cakes and larger chunks of glass into the tall grass.

I had to ring the doorbell three times before Ms. Ernestine answered. When she did, she told me she already had a Lord and Savior and wasn't looking to buy anything.

I come about Cassandra, I told her.

She's not here.

I know, I said. She's taken sick and is over at my grandmother's.

And just who is your grandmother? she asked, narrowing her eyes.

Mrs. Clementine Laurent.

You're Louis's granddaughter?

Yes, ma'am.

Her face soured. By then, the sun had set.

My granddaughter left here on two good feet. I reckon she can make it back on them. There's nothing the matter with her feet, is it?

No, ma'am.

Good, she said before slamming the door in my face.

I met Cassandra walking on the road not more than a stone's throw from where I'd originally found her. She was still wearing my grandmother's floral nightgown. I handed her the basket. She thanked me. I asked her how she was feeling, and she said much better now, and I knew from the way she said it that Grandma had given her more than aspirin. She started walking away but I reached out and grabbed her hand. I can't say why. She smiled at me like I was an old friend, brought my hand to her mouth, kissed it, then turned around and walked away.

You meet your friend on the road? Grandma Clem asked when I got back to her house.

She's not my friend, I told her. I barely know her.

Well, she said, you know her a lot better now. I tried to get her to wait a while after she woke up. She said she would but then, as soon as I turned my back, she was gone. The apple don't fall far.

What do you think she tried to use? I asked.

I don't know, but she's lucky whatever it was didn't land her in the hospital. If you ever get in trouble, don't try anything without coming to me first.

A faraway part of me already knew I'd never be in the kind of trouble Cassandra was in, but I told her that she would be the first person I called. And then, when it happened to you, she was.

* * *

344

You told Clay you were late. He told you to take care of it, so you did. I did. We'd just moved into the house on Bennett. You sat down at the table. I brewed the tea and poured it into your favorite cup. I set it down in front of you and asked if you were sure. You said you weren't and then you drank it. It tastes like peppermint, you said, holding the empty cup out to me with a smile. It was because of this smile that I thought you would be okay. We went into the living room. I put on a Minnie Riperton record, and you opened *Orlando*, because Virginia Woolf was on the list of writers your professor gave you to read. When the record went off, you asked me how long it was supposed to take. I said I didn't know but could call my grandmother and ask. You shook your head and went back to your book. I stood up to put another record on, and you asked if we could take a break from music, and I said we could. Then you set your book down.

Are you okay?

Yeah, you said. I'm fine. But you weren't fine.

Do you want some ibuprofen? It might help.

No, you said. You didn't like what ibuprofen did to your stomach, but then later, in the bathroom, you asked for it. You asked for it and I let go of your hand to go find it, and by the time I came back, it had happened.

Are you okay?

Yeah, you said. I'm fine.

I helped you into your bed. There was a picture of you with your parents in front of their house in Richmond. You laid it face down. I pulled the covers up to your chin. You turned over, brought your knees to your chest, and held them there.

Are you okay?

I'm fine.

I closed the door, and then later, after I lay down, I heard you crying. I got out of bed and went to your door and listened. When the crying didn't stop, I came into your room and held you. When I woke up the next morning, you were gone.

Are you mad at me? I asked when you came back later that afternoon.

Why would I be mad at you?

I'm sorry.

You don't have anything to apologize for.

I'd lost you, and later, much later, you told me you lost yourself, too. Seeing you with Clay reminded me of my mother and grandmother, and I wondered why all the women I admired seemed destined to spend their lives suffering fools.

A few weeks later, James called. When he told me about Cassandra dying, Porter leaving, and how no one wanted anything to do with the baby they'd left behind but him, I told him to come to Jackson. By then, you were spending more nights at Clay's apartment than at our house on Bennett.

Are you sure it's okay? I asked after you'd agreed to let James visit.

Yeah, you said. What difference does it make?

And so James and John came to live with us. James asked about you, why you wouldn't eat with us, why you cried so much. You didn't realize how thin the walls were, and so you didn't know we could hear you. I told him you were fine and to leave you alone.

What do you mean? he asked. I haven't said anything to her.

The way you look at her says enough.

After I finished telling you the story about Cassandra, you stood up and went over to the record player. You could have changed the album, but instead you started it over.

Are you sure he's not John's father? you asked. It was late. If you weren't there, I would have gone to bed hours earlier.

It's not like James to lie, I told you. If he was the father, he'd have said so a long time ago.

He calls her name in his sleep, you know. Has for years.

I didn't know that, I said. But I wasn't surprised.

How come you never tried anything with me? you said, sitting down beside me.

What do you mean?

I see the way you look at me, the way you've always looked at me. How come you never tried anything?

Before I met you, I didn't know that a woman could feel things for other women. Before you, I thought I'd never feel anything for anyone. But then, after you sat down beside me, I knew better. It was the first week of classes. I was in the stairwell of the student union, sitting with my skirt pulled tight over my knees, upset because the housing office had made a mistake. They didn't have a dorm room for me. I couldn't go back to Laurent, and I couldn't stay in Jackson, either. I didn't know what I was going to do.

Your heels spiraled down the stairs toward me. I didn't know anybody on campus yet, and so the last thing I expected was for whoever owned those heels to stop for me. But you're not the type to let anybody endure suffering alone, if you can help it. You sat down beside me. I told you what was wrong and you said I could stay with you. No one has ever been as nice to me as you. Grateful, I hugged you, and your scent—not the rose-shaped bottle of perfume you kept on your nightstand, but the musky peach-pit sweetness of you—found me. I caught your scent and the part of me that wanted to be touched—the part of me I thought was dead—rose up in me, lay down when you married James, and rose up again when you came to visit me alone.

I never tried anything with you, I said, facing forward, because you mean the world to me and I can't stand the thought of losing you. I need you to be my friend, Twyla. You're the only friend I've got.

That's pitiful, you said, laughing. I'd forgotten how mean alcohol made you.

I've always wondered what it was like to be with a woman, you said, sliding your hand up my thigh. When you look at me, what is it you think about doing? What do you want from me?

It's late, I said, moving your hand and standing up. I think we should call it a night.

After I had changed for bed and gotten under the covers, you knocked on the door to my bedroom, and when I didn't answer, you came in, anyway. You lifted the covers up, lay down next to me, and wrapped your arm around me.

The next morning, after I dropped you off at the airport and returned my friend's car, I went for a walk and passed a homeless man holding up a cardboard sign that read: "BE CAREFUL OF LOVE." Once I got within a few feet of him, he turned his sign over: "CHOOSE JOY! CHOOSE FREEDOM!! CHOOSE YOURSELF!!!" The pleading look in his eyes endeared him to me. I reached into my purse and pulled out a five-dollar bill to place in the overturned worn black hat. He smiled, waved my outstretched hand away, and asked me to buy him coffee and a donut instead. The shop around the corner wouldn't take his money. I bought the coffee, but when I came back to the corner, he was gone.

I still can't hear Minnie Riperton without thinking about that night. It doesn't matter where I am or what I'm doing, whether I'm on the train, at the bar on Eighty-Fifth, or at home alone. *Adventures in Paradise* plays and everything before my eyes falls away. I smell you. Feel the warmth of your head in my lap. It feels like a beginning, even though it's the end. The record stops, I lift the tonearm, and start it over again. My love for you is not all of me, but now that you're gone, I'm not sure what I'm supposed to do with the other pieces.

In the Valley

LUCY LAURENT
(1988)
Daughter of James and Twyla Laurent
Sister of John Laurent

THE SHADOWS HAVE always come for me. When I was little, the shadows rose up out of their dark corners and stood stone-still, toes on tip, backs flat against the walls of my bedroom. Some of the shadows came creeping out of my closet. Others slithered out from under my bed. All of them waited for my parents to leave my room before making nightmares of my dreams. Not every shadow is black. They can be red, blue, yellow, purple, or green. One shadow had white teeth and a yellow dress. Her laugh made my short hairs stand on end. I called her the midnight woman. Whenever John turned on the light in his room to read the Bible, she slipped out from under his door and visited me. "Lucy," she called. "Lucy." The sound of my name in the midnight woman's mouth gave me an achy-sweet tingling. When she came, I sat up in bed, because if I fell asleep with her eyes on me, she'd turn night into day, take my hand in hers, and drag me to the creek. Her hands were as rough as the bark on a sweet gum tree.

She'd lift her dress by its folds, wade in, tilt her head to the sky, let the folds drop, and then spread her arms like wings. Her stance an upright stamen. Her dress a yellow, white-rimmed water lily. I've tried to sketch it, but I can't make the picture in my mind—the sienna brown of her skin, the shine of the sun, the way her dress rose in tandem with the flow of the current—live on the page in front of me. While the woman stood there shaming nature with her beauty, I'd walk to the edge of the creek, squish my toes in the mud, and find Momma staring back at me. Somehow, I knew that if I reached my hand out to help her, she'd pull me under. And so I just stood there, watching her mouth contort into soundless screams.

The first time the shadows came for me was the day Momma abandoned me. Dad and John had gone fishing, and so nobody was home to see her go but me. After she left, I went into the den, sat down in front of the empty couch, and, not knowing what else to do, watched cartoons and plucked cream shag carpet strands. There was a bald spot in the carpet by the time the first shadow knocked.

"What they done?" the knocker called out. "What they done to make you so blue?"

I froze. Could he see me?

"I'm not trying to scare you. Just thought you might be lonesome. You want company?"

I stood and went to the door, but I was too short to see through the peephole.

"Just thought I'd ask," he said. "I'll be on my way if you don't want any company."

His boots clacked down the driveway. I went to the window. He had on a wide-brimmed black hat and no face. I peered into the window, thinking it was an illusion, but there really was nothing there. Nothing under his hat save the shadow that, once upon a time, must have been his face.

My art teacher, Ms. Oatsome, said drawing nightmares robs them of their power. I tried to draw the man, but his lines were as hard to pin down as the midnight woman's skin was luminous, and so his face, or rather the absence of it, always stuck with me. All I was able to draw of him were his hat and his boots, and so I drew them over and over again. He was the only shadow to ever knock. The rest just barged right in. I didn't see them as much after I left home, but for as long as I lived in my parents' house, the shadows, and the nightmares they brought on, were relentless.

Momma came home two days later, unpacked her suitcase, sat down on the couch, and took up a book like nothing had happened. Said it was all a big misunderstanding. She'd just gone to visit Aunt Mary, didn't Dad remember? John bought it, but I knew she was lying.

Before I left home for good, I tried to have an honest conversation with Dad about Momma leaving, how I never fully recovered from it. It was a week before my eighteenth birthday. I was on the couch, and he was sitting in the recliner with a blue beach towel rolled up behind his back for support.

"She just went to see Aunt Mary," he said, "she didn't leave."

"I'm not a baby," I said. "I'm not now and I wasn't then."

"I don't know what you want me to say, Lucy."

My mother didn't love me, she only loved John. After John left for seminary, she cried every night for a week. The only time I ever elicited any emotion from her was when she found Garrison's ring.

I was a junior in high school when I met Garrison at the library. He was at a carrel, studying for the MCAT, and I was picking up books for Momma. Momma hated driving and started sending me out on all her errands the day after I got my license. All she ever did was read, but the local branch of the library didn't carry the kinds of books she liked, and so she sent me to the university to check them out for her. I was searching for a book on her list when I turned a corner and found my way blocked by Garrison's outstretched hand.

"You must be an English major," he said. "I didn't think anybody here liked Jane Austen but me." Momma and Garrison have the same taste in books: old, dusty, and boring.

"I don't go here. I'm still in high school."

"High school? Looking like that? I don't believe it. Not for one minute."

On our first date, he took me to Steak 'n Shake and told me all about how he noticed my lips before he noticed me. Said they were perfect, plump, and pink. He couldn't believe nobody before him had tried to kiss them.

I got pregnant. Garrison proposed; he didn't believe in abortion. Said he couldn't stomach it. I said maybe, and then, before I could get the money to go to Planned Parenthood, I miscarried.

"Nothing's changed for me," he'd said, his eyes glazed with tears. I was shocked. I'd thought I was letting him off the hook by getting it taken care of without telling him. He could move to Chicago without me and not feel the least bit guilty. I hadn't realized he actually wanted the baby, actually wanted me. No one had ever cried over me before. "Has anything changed for you?"

I didn't have the heart to remind him I'd never actually said yes. Not then, at least.

"Just what does this boy expect?" Momma had asked after finding Garrison's ring in my dresser. She'd met me at the front door after school one day, holding the ring in one hand and the Tiffany Blue box in the other.

"Answer me!" Then, Momma's anger was like music to me. This particular blowup was a decrescendo. It started with a shout and ended with a whisper. "Answer me."

I walked around her, slid my backpack off, set it down on the couch, and continued on into the kitchen. She followed me.

"Don't walk away from me when I'm talking to you."

"I wasn't walking *away* from you," I said, grabbing a yogurt and an orange. "I was walking *toward* the refrigerator."

I sat down at the kitchen table. Momma stood in the archway that separated the kitchen from the living room.

"How old is this boy?" she asked, holding the ring out. "How can he afford this?"

I peeled my orange in lieu of answering. Garrison was twenty-two, a transracial adoptee whose parents patted themselves on the back for bringing home the coal-black baby—his father's words—nobody else wanted, and bound for Rush Medical in the fall. Harold was an internist at Baptist East Hospital, but to hear him talk, you'd think he hunted and fished professionally. Garrison's mother, Veronica, came from old Memphis money—meaning her ancestors owned slaves—organized events, and doted on Garrison.

"What did you tell him?"

Orange wedge in hand, I stood up from the table, went to the silverware drawer, and took my time grabbing a spoon. Momma eyed me. It was the most attention she'd paid me since I was little, and I relished it, despite myself. The night before Garrison asked me to marry him, I dreamed I was alone in a cemetery, staring up at the stars. I walked around the graves, but there were no names on them. A woman stood with her back to me, but no matter how much I called after her, she never turned to face me. I woke up knowing I had to get away from Momma, from Laurent.

"I told him I'd think about it."

"Think about it?" Momma shouted. "What's there to think about? You haven't even made it out of high school. You haven't even started applying to college. You're nowhere near ready to get married."

I peeled the top of my yogurt back, dipped the spoon in, and coated my tongue with its milky whiteness. Momma sighed and sat down across from me. I'd told Garrison I wanted to wait until after I graduated college to get married, so, worst-case scenario, I had at least until then to figure out how I felt about him, but I didn't bother explaining all this to Momma. She hadn't even noticed I'd gotten pregnant, or that I was failing every class except visual arts, or that I was drowning.

No, all she did was call me chubby and force peppermint weight-loss tea down my throat.

"He loves me," I said, stuffing the orange peel into the half-empty yogurt carton. "You only pretend to."

"Pretend? What do you mean 'pretend'? What are you talking about?"

"You may be able to fool Dad, but you don't fool me."

"Look at me, little girl," Momma said, taking hold of my hand. "I don't give a good goddamn about what you think you know, but if you ruin all the work I've put into you by saying yes to this boy, you're going to learn what it's like to not have a mother. Do you understand me? This will not be your home anymore. Your father and I will no longer be your parents. No Christmas. No Easter. No Thanksgiving. You can run off with this boy, or you can finish high school, go to college, and continue to be part of this family. Which is it?"

When Garrison and I left for Chicago, we only made two stops. The first was at a Cracker Barrel on the other side of Cairo, his favorite restaurant, and the second was in Effingham for gas. Garrison insisted on driving the whole way, but when he nodded off just before the exit for Champaign, I made him pull over. Before then, I'd only ever driven my mother's Honda, so it took a few minutes for me to get used to Garrison's Suburban. It was so high off the ground, I felt like I was floating. Usually, I hated driving, the stop-and-go of it. But when I exited 57 for 90 and merged onto the Skyway, it was like an epiphany.

You can see the whole of Chicago from the Skyway. The road rises beneath you as the suburban sprawl, plumes of industrial plant smoke, and parking lots give way to Lake Michigan, the low-rise neighborhoods of the West Side, and then, head, shoulders, and antennas above the rest of downtown, the Hancock building, and for a moment, you feel as if you're just as tall. You cross the bridge and then, all of a sudden, you're in the city.

Once we got downtown, I got off the highway at Thirty-Ninth and took Lake Shore north, passing first Grant Park and then the river. I didn't mind the stop-and-go so much here. It gave me a chance to see Millennium Park, enjoy the sight of people jogging and biking along the water, catch sight of the Art Institute for the first time. After I turned off Lake Shore and onto Sheridan, Garrison woke up and asked me to let him drive. I didn't mind driving the rest of the way, but he said that getting to the apartment might be tricky, so I pulled over.

Instead of taking Clark or Sheridan north, Garrison drove west and ended up getting on the Dan Ryan, even though our apartment was right off the lake in Rogers Park. "If I hadn't let you drive," he muttered under his breath, "I wouldn't have gotten so turned around." By the time we made it to the apartment building, the super, who was supposed to meet us out front with the keys, had left, so we spent our first night in Chicago at a motel down the street.

The air was dense with stale cigarette smoke. The bathroom smelled of bleach and urine. The windows were painted shut. I asked Garrison to go see the man at the front desk about getting another room, or at the very least fresh towels, but he said he didn't see any point, they were probably all like this. I stewed for a few minutes before resolving to go down myself. But before I could, Garrison got up, pulled on his jeans, and left.

While he was gone, I sat down on the bed, picked up the phone, and called John. He answered on the first ring, which startled me; I usually had to call two or three times to get him on the phone. Most times he was at the library, nose-deep in some theology book.

"Where are you? Dad said you ran away. They've been worried sick."

"I didn't run away. I'm not a little kid. I left."

"Adults don't leave in the middle of the night without saying good-bye. Are you in some kind of trouble?"

"I just had to get away. I couldn't take living at home anymore."

John sighed, and in my mind's eye, I could see him scratch his head, stand up, and walk over to the window. I'd only ever been to John's apartment in Nashville once. The walls were bare, save shelf after shelf of books, a few pictures of us Dad gave him, and one framed poster of Martin Luther King Jr., John's actual hero.

"All right, I'll tell them. But first I want to know where you are, what you plan on doing, and how I can reach you."

I stood up and walked over to the window. The room was on the second floor and faced Sheridan. From there, I could see Garrison pacing back and forth with his hands in his pockets.

That night, I dreamed I was driving a wagon, watching the sun rise over the horizon. Beside me was a woman. All the world was open, and a part of me that was small and quiet had now grown large and loud. I was leaving everything behind to be with her. At first, I thought the dream was about me and Garrison. Then I watched him cut a waffle into perfectly symmetrical squares the next morning and knew I'd never feel for him what the man in my dream had felt for the woman.

We were able to get into the apartment the next afternoon. After Garrison left to go to the hardware store, I sat down at the kitchen counter and began to draw the woman in watercolors. She was older, white, dignified yet reserved. She seemed happy, but at the same time nervous. Her hair was a coppery gray, but you could tell it used to be red. I was shading it in when I heard a knock at the door. It was my father. He had to have started driving within an hour of my hanging up with John to have made it so quickly.

Our apartment was large, just under a thousand square feet, but my father's presence made it claustrophobic. His boots didn't even fit under the coffee table. I had to move it in order for him to sit on the couch comfortably.

I asked if I could get him anything. He said he was fine. I brought him a glass of water, more so to give myself a moment in the kitchen to think.

"I didn't come to bring you back or anything," he said, staring down at the coffee table. "You woman enough to make your own decisions. But I want you to know that no matter where you go or what you do, you'll always have a home with me."

"Did you give Dad my address?" I called and asked John after Dad left.

"I did, yeah. I'm sorry. He was just so upset. I thought if he knew where you were, he'd feel better. Are you mad?"

"No," I said. "I'm glad you gave it to him. Thank you."

"You should call Momma, too," John said. "She misses you."

"When you gave Dad my information, was she there?"

"Yeah," John said.

"She could have come up with Dad, or even called, but she chose not to."

"She's hurt, Lucy. You leaving hurt her feelings."

"Yeah, well, she hurt mine first."

At first, I spent my days home alone, pretending to study for my GED while watching daytime soap operas. At night, I flashed cards with medical terms in front of Garrison's face while he did squats, power lunges, and sit-ups. Someone had told Garrison exercise improved memory, and so, after dinner, I quizzed him on anatomy while holding his ankles.

When I tired of soap operas, I took my sketch pad into the city, found a coffee shop, and drew people. Most of my sketches were of the barista who worked the morning shift. My eyes were drawn to her because she never smiled. I drew her pulling shots of espresso, making change, and microwaving pastries with downcast eyes, a knitted brow, and pursed lips.

"It's customary to pay your models, you know," she said one day, looking over my shoulder. Her name was Tash. She'd come to Chicago from Gary the year before with only a suitcase and a camera.

"You're a photographer?" I asked, amazed. "What do you photograph?"

"Whatever I want."

It was Tash who first took me to the Art Institute. She met me in front of the stone lions after her shift, holding with a caramel macchiato and blueberry scone. In exchange, I paid our entry fee with the credit card Garrison's parents gave him.

Tash walked me past the displays of African and Indian art—relics of colonial conquest—to the back wing, where an exhibition of Gordon Parks's work was on display.

"He directed *Shaft*, you know? Weird, right? It's watchable if you ignore the plot, though. The visuals are amazing. Have you seen it?"

I hadn't.

I liked the pictures, especially the ones of people on the streets of Harlem, but they didn't move me the way Tash hoped they would, and try as she might, she couldn't make me understand why they were so important to her. I had disappointed her. This was a friendship test and I'd failed it. As we left the photography wing and walked around the other galleries, I could tell she'd cooled on me. I was trudging through the museum, already mourning the death of our nascent friendship, when I saw the ballerina.

Her back was to me, but her head was turned. I could see her profile, even though she was lightly drawn. Her eyes were downcast, but nothing in particular held her gaze. Her toes were on tip. Not much more than a sketch, but her lines, rendered midmovement, showed something of her personality. Her back was twisted, strained to hold the awkward position. She was in pain; she was ecstatic. She wasn't alone. The gallery was full of dancers stretching and twirling in stilled motion. The same, but different.

"He was a misogynist," Tash said.

"Huh?"

"Degas. He called the women he painted animals and made them hold those awkward poses for hours. It had to have been excruciating."

"Maybe they thought the pain was worth it."

Tash cocked her head, baffled.

Later, when I came to see this exhibit with Caroline, I asked her what she thought of Degas, whether or not he was a misogynist. She laughed.

"Do you like his work?" she asked.

"I do," I said, admiring *Dancers in Blue*, on loan from the Musée d'Orsay. "I like it a lot."

"This inspires you," she said, reaching her hand out to the canvas. "The man's been dead for almost a hundred years. What difference does what he thought make? In the end, all that matters is the art."

The sight of Caroline's pale finger against the brightly colored canvas sent an achy thrill down my spine.

"What are you doing?" I asked as she ran her finger along the outer rim of the ballerina's tutu. The motion detector buzzed, but no one paid us any attention. The detectors were always going off. They were sensitive.

"I'm getting a feel for the brushstrokes," she said, holding her finger out to me. I was breathless. I wanted to put her finger in my mouth. I wanted her to touch me with it.

"Do your other professors do stuff like that?" John asked me later. "Take you to museums?"

"She's not just any professor, John. She's Caroline Collodi. If Caroline Collodi asks you to meet her at a museum, you go."

Caroline was not only an art historian, but an artist in her own right. She was one of the youngest Guggenheim grant recipients ever, had recently sold a piece to MoMA, and regularly published art criticism in magazines and scholarly journals. She taught painting at both Loyola and the School of the Art Institute of Chicago, and for some reason I couldn't fathom, she'd taken an interest in me.

"I don't know, Lucy," John said, typing. He was googling Caroline. "I think you need to be careful."

"Are you worried because you think she's going to turn me into a lesbian?" I asked, figuring he'd clicked on the famous article that alluded, obliquely, to her sexuality.

"I'm worried because you're twenty years old and you don't know yourself yet."

It was Caroline who helped me understand what art meant to me. "The evocative force of the painting," Caroline had said in her lecture on Georgia O'Keeffe's *Black Iris*, "lies in the productive tension between the light and the lines. The brightness of the outer petals pushes the eye outward to the white edge of the canvas as the lines draw the eye in, past the muted maroon, into the dark center." Caroline paused, turned, and faced me. "The petals open not to expose but to obscure, intensifying desire by hiding what the lines compel the eye to see." I'd applied to every school in the Chicago area, but I only got into two, Loyola and, by some minor miracle, the University of Chicago. In the end, Garrison thought it would be better to go to Loyola because of the tuition and the commute. "He's holding you back," Caroline said, shaking her head, after I told her this. "You're lucky I discovered you." UChicago was where she had gone for undergrad.

I knew that when I drew, the part of me I thought was dead came alive, but I'd never dreamed of becoming an artist before Caroline's Feminist Forms in American Art class.

"Art's not always about beauty," Caroline told me after I'd gotten a B, my first ever, on my Adrian Piper paper. We were sitting side by side at a table in her office. She was explaining the critical implications of Adrian Piper's *Catalysis*, a series of performance pieces that included passive public transgressions—wearing a shirt that read "Wet Paint," wearing clothes soaked in sour milk, eggs, vinegar, and fish oil on a train during rush hour—when her knee brushed my thigh. Each nerve in my body strained toward her. "Sometimes it's about provocation. Forcing the audience out of their comfort zone to show them who they are."

I scooted my chair back from the table and stood. My hands were shaking.

"I have to go to the restroom," I said. "I'll be right back."

In the bathroom, I saw the midnight woman in the mirror above the sink. I stared at her and she stared back at me. I turned my head and she turned hers. I took a step back and she took a step forward and blew me a kiss.

"How'd you get that?" I asked Caroline after I came back from the bathroom and found her flipping through my sketchbook. It had been tucked away in my backpack.

"I took it out of your bag. You shouldn't have left it unattended if you didn't want me to look at it."

I found the thought of Caroline pawing through my things strangely exhilarating.

"Who was your model for this?" she asked, pointing to a watercolor of the midnight woman. I'd drawn her in profile.

"No one," I said. "I dreamed her."

"Interesting," she said, holding the sketch up to her face. "You need a better grasp of technique, but you have an eye. That's rare. What's your major again?"

"Accounting."

"No, it's not. Not anymore. You and I are going to the registrar right now and changing it. From now on, I'm your advisor."

When I got home that evening, I dead-bolted the door behind me, went straight to the bedroom, lay down, and touched myself. Each stroke of my hand was a new wave of bliss. I turned over onto my stomach. Closed my eyes. Worked my hand harder. I was face down on the pillow, slack-jawed and drooling. Then, all at once, everything seized up and I was floating. My body went soft. I couldn't stop shuddering. Even after I stood up, pulled my jeans on, and went into the living room to unlock the door and wait for Garrison, I couldn't stop shuddering.

"Aren't I enough for you?" Garrison asked me one night after he'd come home early and found me touching myself. It was late and I was half-asleep. We were lying with our backs to one another in the same full bed we'd driven up from Tennessee. It still smelled like boy.

"You're enough," I told him. "I just like how it feels when I touch myself. Don't you?"

"No. Never."

"Never?"

"My mom had a cousin go blind that way, so I never tried it."

"A cousin who went blind?"

"Yeah, he wrote me a letter on my twelfth birthday warning me not to masturbate. He wrote letters to all my cousins. What? Why are you laughing?"

"Garrison," I said. "You're training to be a doctor. You know Veronica wrote that letter, right?"

He didn't know. Unlike me, he believed everything his mother told him. He was upset. I tried to kiss him, but he pulled the comforter around himself, stood up, and went to the living room. I turned over and deleted the tab with Caroline's website from my phone's browser history and went to sleep.

* * *

"A degree in art is only one of many possible starting points," Caroline told the handful of students she gave access to her personal studio. Everyone in the room was a graduate student but me. I was both touched and intimidated. "One step in a lifelong journey. The only real way to become an artist is through apprenticeship. Give yourself over to an established artist, then take what you learned and make it new. That's how the old masters did it. That's how we'll do it. For this to work, you have to do what I say. No back talk. No second-guessing. Your time is not your own anymore. It belongs to me."

The next semester, I let Caroline choose my class schedule, inhaled every book on art theory and practice she lent me, and spent every hour I could in her studio, trying as best I could to transfer the sketches she liked to canvas. I'd never worked with oil paint before, only graphite and watercolors. Caroline gave me primers on the basics, and after I mastered those, she gave me private instruction on advanced techniques. When I couldn't quite get the hang of a particular stroke, she'd pull her chair up to my easel and use her hand to guide mine through the motions.

Garrison was skeptical of Caroline's methods at first, but then, after Sharon, a woman in his cohort whose father was a famed art critic, called her one of America's greatest living artists—something I'd told him already—he endorsed them and began to praise my progress, calling himself my patron to his friends.

Sometimes, I drew Garrison while he studied. Trace anyone's lines long enough and you'll find something worth seeing. People became nothing more than shapes and colors, portraits waiting to be rendered. I worked weekends, lagged behind in other classes, and then pulled all-nighters to make up for it.

"You should come home, Lucy," John said. He'd graduated from seminary by then and was assistant-pastoring at a Nashville megachurch. "Just for Thanksgiving. It's been almost two years. Momma and Dad miss you."

"Dad knows where to find me, and Momma told me I couldn't come home anymore. She said she never wanted to see me again."

"She didn't mean it, Lucy. She was just angry. She would have said anything to keep you from leaving."

"I'll come home when Momma calls and invites me," I told him.

She never did.

In the winter, in order to put in more studio hours, I begged off Garrison's invitation to go with him to visit his parents. I painted, shaded, scraped here, touched up there. Lost weight. Developed calluses on the pads of my index finger and thumb and, on occasion, slept on Caroline's couch. I sketched the midnight woman, trying to get the lines right, capture the light, the fierce, placid expression on her face. I imagine that what I felt as I worked was akin to whatever it was that went on inside my brother when he got to thumping his Bible and calling on the Lord. "Art," Caroline liked to say, "is the closest we can hope to get to a common perception of reality, to communion with eternity."

"Don't you think you should take a break?" Garrison asked one afternoon as I headed out to the studio. He was watching *Gilmore Girls* and eating a bowl of cereal on the floor. He didn't stay up all night with flash cards the way he did when he first started med school. He was almost ready to graduate, eyeing residencies.

"No," I said. "I don't."

The day after spring break, I came into Caroline's studio and found that my work in progress was gone. The blank canvas in its place was

Caroline's way of saying try again. "Sisyphean joy," she said the first time I asked where my piece went, "the pleasure of pain that proceeds greatness."

"But Sisyphus never made it up the mountain, right? The rock kept rolling back down."

"'The struggle itself toward heights is enough ... One must imagine Sisyphus happy.' Albert Camus. Add Camus to your list." I kept a running list of Caroline's book recommendations and read all of them.

The second time I found a blank canvas where my work had been, I smiled because it meant Caroline thought I was capable of better. It took a little over a year for me to produce a piece Caroline approved of. I titled it *Unnamed Woman*. She looked exactly like the woman who appeared in my dreams, except in the painting, her back is to the viewer, the water is black, not blue, and instead of a yellow dress, she is engulfed in flames. "Pack your bags," Caroline said the day after she saw it. "I'm taking you to New York."

"It's not my place to tell you what you should or shouldn't do," John said when I called to tell him about New York. "We're long past me telling you how to live, but the fact that you feel the need to ask my opinion says something."

By then, he'd lost his job at the megachurch, owing to the videos that surfaced of him in drag. In them, John goes by the name Cassie, wears a backless blue gown, reads people's auras, makes comically out- landish predictions that people in the YouTube comments swear came true, and is gorgeous. My brother was gorgeous.

"She said she wants to take me to see her friend's exhibition and introduce me around. What's so wrong with that?"

"The trip isn't the issue. It's the fact that you're sharing a room."

"It's cheaper that way. Besides, Caroline doesn't do romantic entanglements. She says they're too messy."

"What does Garrison have to say about this trip?"

"Since when do you care about Garrison?"

"I don't. You could leave Garrison tomorrow, for all I care. I'll come help you pack if you want. I'll even help with first and last months' rent on a new apartment. If you know you don't want to be with Garrison, break it off. The sooner the better. Just make sure that when you jump out of the frying pan, you don't end up in the fire."

That night, I dreamed I was breaking into a stable. The door to the stable was padlocked. I hit it with a rock, not really expecting it to work, but then, to my amazement, it did. I eased the door open. I could hear the horses breathing, but it was too dark for me to see them. There was a lantern hanging on the wall with a matchbook on a string hanging down beside it, but I knew better than to light it. With one hand out in front of me, and the other gliding along the stable walls, I felt my way forward, counting the paces. When I hit twenty, I turned, slowly reached my hand out, and felt the nose of a horse. She startled at first. Backed away. I opened the door of her stall, stretched my hand out, stroked her neck, and then led her out. I grabbed her mane, jumped, swung my leg around, and mounted the horse bareback. There wasn't enough light or time to fuss with a saddle. I slow-trotted her on the gravel because I didn't want anyone to hear her shoes striking it, but then, once we made it to the grass, I let her loose and I was flying. Then someone whistled and the mare reared, dismounting me.

I woke gasping and turned to Garrison. John was right. I didn't want to be with Garrison. It was cruel to let him keep thinking I'd marry him when all I wanted was my freedom. I composed my breakup speech in the shower, rehearsed under my breath on the train, and turned it over in my mind during class. I would start by thanking him for supporting me. Then I'd bring up how we'd both changed over the past few years. He was applying for residencies. There was no telling where he'd end up, whereas I wanted to stay in Chicago and go to the School of the Art Institute to get my MFA. Caroline said I was a shoo-in. Our relationship had run its course. It wasn't anybody's fault. It was just life.

Most days I went straight to the studio after class, but that day I knew I wouldn't be able to focus, so I came home early. Garrison usually did the cooking, but it felt cruel to break up with someone after they'd prepared a meal for you, so I stopped by the store on the way home to pick up some crushed tomatoes, spaghetti, bread, garlic, and butter. I couldn't do much in the kitchen, but I could do pasta with red sauce.

At first, I thought the sex sounds—the mewling moans, the squeaking springs—were coming from the apartment above us. But then, as I set my keys down on the end table and continued into the apartment, I realized they were coming from the bedroom. I opened the door and found Garrison fucking a white girl. Or, rather, she was fucking him. Reverse cowgirl. A surprising choice for Garrison. He and I had only ever done missionary.

A blond mop of hair hung over her face. Probably why she didn't immediately notice me. Her body was hairless. No stubble or anything. For some reason, this, more than anything else, shocked me.

I couldn't help but wonder how long it would take me to render a realistic sketch of the circular motion of her hips with Garrison's hands on them. The color contrast of their skin stirred me. I could already see in my mind's eye her torso as the focal point of the image. I'd start at her neck and paint her hair over her clavicle at the top of the canvas and impasto Garrison's hands to stand out in textured relief at the bottom. I'd have to change the color of the wall behind them, though. Off-white would be a terrible choice. I'd go bold. Scarlet? No, scarlet was too on the nose. Too overtly sexual.

It needed to be cool but suggest drama. Seafoam? Blond against sea-foam would wash out. I'd have to make her hair color darker, like Caroline's.

"Hey," I said after both of them failed to notice me. "Hey!"

The woman screamed and, in a surprising feat of acrobatics, swung her leg over Garrison, rolled off the bed, and crouched into a defensive position on the floor. She must have had some sort of martial arts training. Not karate or anything like that. Krav Maga? Maybe? Capoeira? Certainly some sport that involved squatting. Maintaining a low center of gravity.

"Hey," Garrison said, bolting upright. "You're home!"

"Sorry." The woman stood up and began to gather her clothes. Black bra. Light-wash jeans. A white floral-print peasant blouse. She said sorry each time she stooped to grab an article of clothing, as if each was its own separate transgression.

"Sorry!" she said again as she brushed past me. I knew her. Her name was Sharon. She was one of Garrison's classmates.

"No problem," I said reflexively.

"You're usually not home this early," Garrison said, getting out of the bed and pulling his tighty-whities up from around his ankles.

"I thought I'd make dinner," I said, holding up a grocery bag. Even though I was only cooking in order to break up with him, I wanted him to feel some guilt. "You could have broken up with me, you know. You didn't have to cheat."

"I know. I know. I'm sorry. The thing with Sharon just came out of nowhere and I didn't know how to tell you. We've just kind of grown apart, you know? You have your art thing and I'm applying to residencies. There was just never a good time to bring it up."

This was my speech. I tried to summon righteous indignation, but all I felt was relief.

"Look," he said, sloppily remaking the bed. "I'm sorry you had to find out like this, but you had to know this was coming. I care about you a lot, but I barely see you anymore. I can't remember the last time we had sex. At this point, it just feels like we're roomies. You spend more time with your professor than you do with me."

Black lace. She'd left her underwear behind. If it had been me, my underwear would have been the first thing I reached for, especially if I were wearing jeans.

"Listen," I said, looking down at Sharon's panties. They were pure silk. "I'm going to New York this weekend. Let's wait until after I get back to sort this out. Okay?"

Caroline told me to pack at least one business casual outfit. Meaning a black dress, or maybe slacks and a blazer? I had both, but nothing fit right. I'd lost a lot of weight, and so everything was loose and baggy. I needed to go shopping. Only I didn't have any money. I was debating with myself whether Garrison's cheating on me justified my use of his credit card when Aunt Mary called to tell me what my father couldn't.

"How?" I asked after she told me my mother died.

"We don't know yet, sweetie. It looks like maybe it was a heart attack. I'll know more tomorrow. I'm on my way to the airport now. When's the earliest you can make it?"

I sat down on the bed beside my half-packed suitcase, calling to mind the day my mother left me. That morning, after Dad and John went fishing, she came into my room and told me she was leaving. I asked if I could come with her. She said no, I couldn't go where she was going. When I cried, she scowled and all the color drained from her face. "Be good for your father," she'd said, closing the door. After she left, I stood, went to the bathroom mirror, and stared at myself until I became nothing more than a shape in the frame. I haven't shed a tear since.

"I can't," I said, taking up a blouse and refolding it. "I'm leaving for a school trip tomorrow."

"You're going to have to cancel, sweetheart. Your mother passed away. You need to get home."

There was a Kara Walker exhibit at the Art Institute that Caroline wanted me to see. She said it would be useful for me to contemplate the "grotesque eroticism of Walker's reappropriation of idyllic plantation imagery." I would have called and canceled, but Caroline rarely, if ever, answered her phone. I put on jeans and a hoodie, set my phone on the counter, rode the train into the Loop, got off at Monroe, and found Caroline admiring *Gone*.

"Have you ever read *Gone with the Wind*?" she asked.

"I haven't, no."

"It's a horrifically engrossing book. I had to read it in school one year. I thought I was going to hate it but I ended up loving it. These pieces work the same way. You know you're supposed to hate what you're seeing, but you feel drawn in, anyway. This one," she said, gesturing to the silhouette of a young Black girl fellating a white boy. "I can hardly look away from it. The way the girl thrusts her chest forward and holds her arms back is thrilling. Even in abjection, she's defiant. A bit like your *Unnamed Woman*. And look at the expression on the boy's face. A sort of gleeful ignorance. I wish I had enough melanin to make something this racially transgressive."

"I can't come to New York with you."

"That's disappointing," she said, still focusing on the piece. "May I ask why?"

"I have to go home. Something came up."

"Lucy," she said, pinching her forehead. "I had to call in a favor from the dean to get you funding for this trip."

"I know. I'm sorry."

"I didn't want to say anything because I wanted you to act natural, but I arranged a meeting between you and Anton Kern. An artist dropped out of one of his exhibitions. Instead of filling the slot with one person's work, he wants to turn the exhibition into a showcase for emerging artists. I sent him photos of all my students' work and *Midnight Woman* was the only one that interested him. Now, it's not a lock, but he wants to meet you and see your portfolio in person. I don't want to stress you out or make you nervous, but I can't over-state how big an opportunity this is. Whatever this is back home, can it wait?"

"My mother died."

"I see," Caroline said. And then, taking my hand: "Come outside with me."

We walked out of the Art Institute, over into Grant Park, and didn't stop until we reached the Bean, which Caroline only ever called *Cloud Gate* out of respect for Anish Kapoor's vision. It was the middle of the week. The park was mostly abandoned, save a few teenagers on skate-boards. We found a bench across from the sculpture.

"I don't usually talk about this kind of thing with my students," she said, casting her eyes down at the concrete. "But let's just say my rela-tionship to home is as complicated as I assume yours is."

"What makes you think my relationship to home is complicated?"

"Lucy," she said. "You spent Christmas in the studio working with me. It's not exactly a secret."

I nodded, though I couldn't quite remember which of the days was Christmas.

"Do you know why I took the name Collodi?"

I didn't. Until then, I'd thought Collodi was the name she was born with.

"I was born Caroline Anderson. I changed it to Collodi after I started painting. *Pinocchio* by Carlo Collodi was my favorite book when I was little. A puppet who cut his own strings and willed himself to be human. I took the name to remind myself that I could be whoever I wanted to be."

I'd always hated the name Lucy Laurent. The alliteration made me sound like a DC Comics sidekick. It had never occurred to me before to change it.

"The art is all that matters in the end. All the other things—family, friends, partners, et cetera—are just strings. Cut them."

Caroline was the only person who understood me.

"Take it from someone who's been where you are. If you want to become an artist, a real artist, not just someone who draws and paints, you have to leave the girl you were behind, you have to cut the strings."

"What do you mean?"

"Forgive me if this sounds crass, but is it really necessary for you to go to this funeral?" she said, shaking her head. "If your mother were still alive, if she were on her deathbed, I would drive you to the airport myself. But this is a rare opportunity. To have the chance to showcase a piece at a major gallery at your age, in as short a time as you've been working, is...it's unheard of. I'm sorry your mother passed away, truly sorry, but I'd think long and hard before throwing this away for a ceremony that doesn't mean anything."

The skateboarders who'd been slaloming in and around *Cloud Gate* were gone.

"We're not like other people, Lucy," she said, cupping my chin in her hand and turning my face back to her. It was the first time she'd touched my face. "We know that the work is the only thing that endures. But the work doesn't come easy. It requires sacrifice. This is a golden opportunity."

Without thinking, I leaned forward and kissed her. Her tongue tasted like cinnamon. She kissed me back at first, but then, all at once, she broke away from me.

"This didn't happen," she said, panting. "For your sake, this didn't happen. At least not until after you've graduated."

*   *   *

I felt like I was drunk, and so instead of taking the train from Monroe, I decided to walk for a while and catch the Red Line at another station. As I walked, I thought about the first time I'd gone to the Art Institute. I'd never even been to a proper museum before and now I was Caroline Collodi's protégée. How many other aspiring artists would kill to be in my shoes? There was a story Dad used to tell me and John about a man who sold his soul to the Devil in exchange for talent with the guitar. It sounded ridiculous then, but now...I don't know. Maybe selling your soul was just an allegory for the work art requires. But Caroline wasn't asking me to sell my soul. Only to miss my mother's funeral. What even is a soul, anyway?

I ended up catching the 151 bus instead of the train. It jerked to a stop every other block from Division to Montrose, and so by the time I made it back to the apartment, I was dizzy. The last thing I wanted to see when I got home was Garrison waiting to ambush me.

We'd mostly avoided each other since I walked in on him and Sharon. He'd offered me the bed, but I told him he could have it, since he'd been sexing other people in it. I could hear him watching a basketball game as I fumbled around in my purse for my keys. But when I unlocked the door, he turned it off. Breaking up with someone and still having to live with them is its own circle of hell.

"I just got off the phone with your aunt Mary," he said, meeting me at the door. "You left your phone here. They've been trying to reach you. Why didn't you tell me your mother passed away?"

"I don't know, Garrison," I said, walking around him to set my purse down on the table under a print of Norman Lewis's *Girl with Yellow Hat*, which Garrison bought me after I said I wanted to be an artist. I averted my gaze, but the yellow of it wouldn't leave my periphery. "Maybe it's because I caught you fucking a white girl in our bed the other day."

"I booked you a ticket home for tomorrow afternoon," he said. "That should give you enough time to pack. How else can I help? What do you need?"

"You booked me a flight? Why wouldn't you talk to me first?"

"I thought that… I figured that you'd want to get home right away. I should have asked, though. I'm sorry. I can call and change it to the following day."

I sat down on the couch and turned the TV back on. I'd walked for at least a mile before getting on the bus. My feet were tired.

"I don't know if I'm going to be able to make it to the funeral."

"What do you mean you don't know if you're going to be able to make it?" he asked, stepping in front of the TV. He hadn't even been watching a live game. It was a re-airing of the '96 finals. Bulls versus SuperSonics. "It's your mother."

"Caroline set up this meeting for me in New York," I said, flipping through the channels. "I can't miss it."

"Lucy," he said, sitting down beside me. "I know this lady's a big-deal artist or whatever, but this hold she has over you. It's not healthy. Making you miss your mother's funeral? That's cult shit, Lucy."

"She's not making me do anything, Garrison. She's going out of her way to help me because she believes in me. You don't understand what it's like to really want something. You've always had everything you wanted handed to you. I've never had anything I wanted, ever. I want to be an artist, and I'm not going to let you, my mother, or anyone else stop me," I said, but he wasn't listening to me anymore. He was holding the phone to his ear.

"What are you doing?" I asked.

"I'm calling your aunt back. Maybe she can talk some sense into you."

"Hang up."

"Yeah, she's right here. Okay. Hold on."

He put the phone on speaker:

"Girl, if you don't quit fooling around and get your ass on that plane tomorrow, I declare before Christ I'm gone come up there and kick it."

"Mary, let her be. Lucy? Baby Girl? Can you hear me?"

"Yeah, Dad. I can hear you."

"You do whatever it is you need to do, Baby Girl. Don't worry about us. You go do whatever it is you need to. We're all proud of you down here. We're real proud. We love you. We'll be all right."

In Laurent, everyone pulls over to the side of the road for a funeral procession. If it is a long procession, some people will go so far as to step out of their vehicles, take their hats off, and bestow a sympathetic nod on any mourner willing to meet their eye. My father is one of these people. He goes out of his way to catch the eye of whoever's in the back of the limousine to let them know their loss is felt. But on the day of Momma's funeral, no one is there on the side of the road to catch his eye and nod to him because the whole of the town is driving behind us in the procession.

I called Caroline from the airport. She said she understood. It was my decision, ultimately. Even if she thought it was the wrong one.

I texted her before we left the house, asking if we could move the meeting to Sunday. There was a flight to New York early the next morning, and so, if she still wanted me, I could come. But by the time the funeral director opens the door to the limousine, she hasn't replied. Aunt Mary takes my phone and puts it in the seat back pocket.

"Whatever it is you're worrying with on that thing can wait. Your mother's in there. This is the very last time you'll get to see her face before Glory."

I step out of the limo and into the sunlight. I amble up the steps to the church porch and would have kept going if Aunt Mary didn't grab my hand and squeeze.

"Wait for your father and brother."

I turn back. John is standing on the other side of the limo, waiting on my father to get out. At first, I think his back has seized up, but he just wants to collect himself before going in.

The only other funeral I've ever been to was Grandpa Robert's. I couldn't have been much older than seven or eight. It was bad luck for little girls to wear black, so Momma bought me a purple dress with Juliet sleeves. John said funerals were like church, except there was a dead body and people fell out from crying instead of catching the spirit. This made me sad. Watching folks fall out in the spirit was the only part of church I didn't mind. There was one lady, Ms. Everett-Reed, who would jump up out of her seat, walk into the middle of the aisle, and scream: "Glory! Glory!" Then she'd get to hopping. She always wore a blue hat with a red bird on it, and I couldn't hear the sermon for watching it bounce. Another lady, Ms. Katie May, would wait until the part of the sermon where Reverend Powers left the pulpit. You always knew when she was about to get going, because she'd start fanning herself and breathing real heavy. "Yes! Yes, pastor! Yeah!" she'd stand up and scream. Then she'd bend her knees, give her shoulders a shimmy, go stiff, and, if Reverend Powers was close enough to catch her, fall backward. She wouldn't do it if the assistant pastor preached, though, no matter how good he whooped and hollered. I always thought that was kind of spiteful.

On the day of Grandpa Robert's funeral, I walked through the doors of Mount Carmel with Momma holding one hand and Aunt Mary holding the other. Everyone was on their feet and everyone—even the choir, even Reverend Powers—had their eyes on us. I turned around to see what everybody was staring at, but there wasn't nothing to see except John and Dad. John wiped his eyes with a handkerchief, and Dad, his eyes red, his lips tight, walked with his hands on John's shoulders. Momma and Aunt Mary faced forward, dry-eyed. The only differences between that day and this one are: I'm old enough to wear black, I'm taller than Aunt Mary, and Momma is in the casket instead of holding my hand.

* * *

I hear the song before I see the singer. He's familiar, this man, but I can't square the otherworldly tenor of his voice with anything I've ever known. Hands are in the air, and all of a sudden, I'm a little girl again, making my way to the altar, hoping that by the time I get there I'll feel whatever it is everyone around me does. Only now, instead of a white-robed old man waiting to dunk me into ice-cold river water, there's what's left of my mother. The choir's robes are purple, but the singer wears a black suit, black shirt, black tie, and black hat. He balances himself on an aluminum walker, leans forward to pour all the energy he can muster into the song. I didn't cry when I learned my mother passed away, but when I look down into the casket, down at her, every solid thing in me goes liquid.

After we sit, the music stops, but the man is still singing. Everyone in the church, save the drummer, Aunt Mary, and me, is on their feet, clapping out the singer's rhythm. My father is on one side of us, and John is on the other. I hear screaming, and out of the corner of my eye, I see a woman jumping up and down. It's Ms. Everett-Reed. Sometimes, when she really got to shouting, I wouldn't look at her because I was too afraid that whatever had gotten into her would get into me. But now, as I listen to her shout, "Glory! Glory!," I know it's already in me. That it's always been there, and now it's trying to claw its way out.

I shoot up from the mourner's bench. I throw my head back and cast my eyes to the ceiling. Every part of me goes stiff except my right foot, which I can't keep from stomping. Everyone's eyes are on me. Aunt Mary stands up and hugs me to her. I want to sit down. I want to sit down and get this damn funeral over with so I can go become who I was always meant to be, but my body won't let me. It won't let me, because there's something knotted up inside me.

I open my mouth to let it out, but it won't come. It's in the pit of my stomach. Pressing up against me. I can feel its strength gathering. My father stands up. Grabs me and Aunt Mary both and starts squeezing and rocking. He knows it's in me. He's always known it was there, and now he's trying to help me get it out. But it won't come. The singer starts up again. "There's a lily, in the valley." The organ and the choir are a half measure behind him, but he doesn't slow down for them, because he's singing for me, he's trying to show me how to loose what's choking me. John stands up. He comes from around Dad's other side to grab hold of my head and level my gaze with his. He sees it. He sees it and knows that if I don't find a way to let it out, it will kill me. John leans forward over Aunt Mary. Dad squeezes all of us together. I open my mouth and, finally, it all comes screaming out. I miss my mother. I miss my mother. I miss my mother. God, I miss my mother. For as long as I live, I will miss my mother.

"Church, it's nighttime here in Laurent, Tennessee. The sun may be shining, the birds may be chirping, but it's nighttime. It's nighttime, and the light of a star by the name of Twyla Laurent has gone out of this world. Ain't nothing I can say to make it better. But here's what I will say: 'In my Father's house, there are many mansions. If it were not so, I would have told you.' Right now, Twyla Laurent is hanging her coat up. Yes, church, she's in her Father's house, kicking off her shoes, getting ready to break bread with angels. Because when God looked low, saw Twyla suffering, turned to Gabriel, and said, 'Call me Death,' Twyla Laurent obeyed the Great Maker, laid her weary body down to rest, and heard Jesus say: 'Well done, good and faithful servant; you have been faithful over a few things, I will make you ruler over many things. Enter into the joy of the Lord.'

"Yes, church, it's nighttime in Laurent, Tennessee. But I promise you, James, I promise you, Mary, I promise you, John, I promise you, Lucy, that when the sun rises, Twyla Laurent's light, the Lord's light, will shine again on each and every one of you. So shed your tears now. Go ahead and shed them! But come tomorrow, come morning, I don't want you to shed not one more. Weeping may endure for a nighttime, but joy, real joy, everlasting joy, comes in the morning."

"Yes, Preacher!"

"'In my father's house, there are many mansions. If it were not so, I would have told you.' Twyla Laurent's found her room, church. She's found the place Jesus went ahead to prepare for her. Will you? When Gabriel blows down Creation, where will Glory find you?"

After the service, we follow the casket, held aloft by pallbearers, out into the graveyard for the burial. The ground is damp, and my heels sink into it with each step. I have to hold on to John just to make it to the burial site. There is a final prayer, a final song, the laying down of white roses, and then it's over. She's lowered into the ground.

I stand by her until the gravediggers finish sealing the vault and begin to cover her with dirt. I check the dissipating crowd for John but don't see him anywhere, and so I take off my heels and walk back to the church barefoot. I haven't felt mud between my toes since I was a little girl.

On the walk back, I spot the singer standing on the edge of the pavement. His walker prevented him from following us to the burial site. He waves me over. I go to him.

"Ms. Lucy," he says. "I haven't seen you since you was knee-high."

I nod my head in acknowledgment. He takes it as an invitation to keep talking.

"Twyla was a good woman. Always kind to me. Even when she didn't have to be."

"She was like that sometimes," I allow.

"She sure was," the singer says, turning his attention to the graveyard. "You probably don't remember me, but we some kin. I'm your father's people." I squint into his face. It's the same as my grandfather's.

"Mr. Benny," I say, placing him, finally.

"You can just call me Benny. We eye to eye now and I never been nobody's mister."

I nod because I don't know how not to call a man three, maybe four times my age "mister."

"I hate to trouble you," Mr. Benny says, "but this old walker here weren't meant for mud. Could you see it in your heart to help me out to visit my daughter?"

I look around for John, for Aunt Mary, for Dad, for anybody else but me who might be able to lend Mr. Benny their arm, and find no one.

"I don't get out here too often and haven't looked in on her in a while. I'll only be a minute."

"Of course," I say, placing my heels by the church steps. "Of course I'll take you."

Mr. Benny's steps are labored, and his breathing is heavy. As we walk, I realize two things: One, Mr. Benny getting up into that choir must have taken a tremendous amount of effort, and two, no one has ever really leaned on me. It takes all my strength to keep us from falling.

His daughter's grave is only a few rows over from Momma's mound of newly turned dirt. At the base of her headstone, a bouquet of lilacs is just beginning to wilt. Mr. Benny lets go of my arm. I turn my head to give him a little privacy. Most everyone buried here is related to me on my father's side. From where I stand, I can see Grandpa Robert's gravestone, Great-Grandpa Louis's, Great-Grandma Clementine's, and even Great-Grandpa Louis's father Walter's.

Mr. Benny's lips are moving, but I can't make out what he's saying. He's frail, vulnerable in a way that makes me want to hold him. After he finishes saying his piece, I offer him my arm.

"Has he come to you yet?" Mr. Benny asks once we make it back to his walker.

"Has who come?"

"Himself! Has he come to you?"

"I was baptized a long time ago," I say, knowing he must mean Jesus.

"I was, too," Benny says. "But it didn't stop the Devil from coming.

I seen him at the back of the church earlier. He marched in right behind you. I thought he'd come for me, but his eyes were set on you. You tell him to get back. He'll act like he don't know what you mean, like he's your friend, but if you rebuke him, he's got to listen."

"Did anyone come here with you?" I ask.

"One of them young mens in the choir picked me up," he says, squinting at the parking lot. "I don't know rightly which one. They all run together."

I help Mr. Benny inside and sit him down in the back of the church. After asking around, I find somebody who knows where he lives.

"You mind he don't get you," Mr. Benny whisper-shouts to me from the car. "He can't do nothing to you but what you allow him to."

I wave and tell him I'll do my best.

Inside, the funeral home workers are taking down the flowers and packing up their equipment. Dad and Aunt Mary are on the mourner's bench, but before I can approach them, Aunt Mary mouths for me to find John so we can drive Dad home. He's in a bad way.

I don't see John anywhere. I ask the funeral director. She points me in the direction of the creek. I find him on his knees in the mud where the land gives way to water. I haven't been out to this creek since I was a child. This was where the midnight woman used to drag me. I forgot it was a real place. John's blazer is folded, and on top of it sits one of Mount Carmel's Bibles. He looks like the pastel illustration of the praying man hanging in the church bathroom.

"I thought she'd be here," John says, still staring at the water. "I thought that if I came to the water and looked, I might could see her again. But she's not here. She's gone."

I rub his back the same way Dad used to do with Momma.

"Will you pray with me?" he asks.

"I haven't prayed in a good long while."

"You don't have to do anything," he says. "Just hold my hand while I talk."

While he prays, I look out over the water. It's shallow, but if you follow it around the bend, past the poplar trees, it picks up a current and, eventually, feeds the river.

"I don't know what God wants from me anymore," John says after he opens his eyes. "I don't know why He called me to preach. I can't see any point to it."

"Maybe He doesn't want anything from you. Maybe He just is, and you just being you is all you need to do to please Him."

Across the water, a man leans against the trunk of a sycamore tree. I'd know the wide-brimmed black hat and black boots anywhere because I've drawn them over and over again for as long as I've been able to hold a pencil. I stand up, crane my neck to better see his face. He flicks a cigar butt into the water and walks away. I take off my shoes, lift up the skirt of my dress, step into the water, and wade across the creek.

"Hey!" I yell. "Hey!"

But he doesn't turn around, he just keeps walking. By the time I make it across the water, he's gone.

"Momma?" I said as she tucked me in the night of Grandpa Robert's funeral. Dad had already taken one of his back pills, otherwise he probably would have done it. "Why do you pray with your eyes open?"

"What do you mean?" she asked.

"At the funeral, when Reverend Powers asked us to pray, you and Aunt Mary both left your eyes open."

"How do you know our eyes were open unless yours were, too?"

I had mine open because right before Reverend Powers asked us to pray, I could have sworn Grandpa Robert breathed. He had on a navy-blue tie that matched his suit and it rose up, fell, and then rose up again. Momma wouldn't have liked it if I told her what I saw, though, so I didn't mention it.

"Is Grandpa Robert really somewhere with God in a mansion?"

"What do you think?"

"I don't know. Reverend Powers said he is, and everybody at church agreed, so I guess he must be."

"Then there's your answer."

"But what do you think?"

"I think we make our own heaven or hell right here."

"Are your parents with God in His mansion?"

"No, sweetheart. I don't know where they are, but it's certainly not there."

"If Grandpa Robert's with God in His mansion, why's Daddy so upset?"

"Because it's hard to lose someone you love, even if you believe they're in a better place."

"Do you think Daddy would feel better if God let Grandpa Robert come back and visit?"

Momma took a deep breath and sat down on the bed beside me. "Sweetheart, your grandpa is gone and he's not ever coming back. Do you understand?"

"Yeah," I said. "I understand."

She was about to turn off the light and leave but then she stopped, lay down in bed beside me, and hugged me. I didn't realize I'd been crying until she wiped away my tears.

A few months after the funeral, I began work on a new painting based on a picture Aunt Mary showed me. In it, Momma is wearing rounded red-lensed sunglasses; a burnt-orange, low-cut jumpsuit with no sleeves and bell-bottoms; and a cream waist-length jacket to match her pumps. Her hair was short then. Aunt Mary said it was fashioned after Diahann Carroll's haircut in *Julia*, Momma's favorite show when she was a girl. She's standing next to a baby-blue Cadillac with her arms akimbo. The glint from the chrome fender matches the sunlight reflected in her glasses. She's smiling. I start by underpainting the canvas with burnt sienna to highlight the red undertones of her skin. Then I sketch my mother, starting at her shoes and working my way up. The photograph is grainy, faded, so I find photographs of each article of clothing online, go to see them in person when possible, and settle for high-res images when I can't. The pumps I found and purchased on eBay. A similar cream jacket was featured in the '67 Ebony *Fashion Fair*. The jumpsuit I'm having Aunt Mary re-create. Aunt Mary said it would be a while before she was able to get around to it, but that's fine. I'm in no rush to finish. I'm going to let it take as long as it takes.

I'll Fly Away

TWYLA LAURENT
(Eternity)
Mother of John and Lucy Laurent
Wife of James Laurent
Friend of Mary Laurent

THE DAY I died, I woke to find my body still. I swung my legs over the side of the bed and stood just as I did every morning, the exception being that when I looked down at James, I saw myself lying next to him. My first thought was of all the times I'd dreamed of falling, only to be startled awake by my head jerking away from the pillow. I thought maybe this was the other side of a falling dream, the part your mind doesn't like for you to remember because the thought of seeing yourself from somewhere up high is too much to take.

I walked around to the foot of the bed and tried, repeatedly, to fall backward into myself but kept ending up on the floor. I couldn't align the self I was now with the body I had been, and the more I tried, the more separated from myself I became.

James was sleeping on his side, facing away from the me that was. I hated to think of the things my dying would do to him. I wanted his eyes to stay closed, for him to stay there next to me forever. I mourned his loss before I could think to mourn my own.

"It's gonna be all right, sweetie." I turned and saw a young woman standing in the doorway. Her hair had been combed straight, but you could see the wildness of it crackling up just before the ends split. She was pretty, open in the way only girls can be before they realize what the world can do to them. She reminded me of Lucy. More proof of the strength of James's genes. "He'll be all right with time."

James turned over onto his back. His leg kicked my leg, and my leg did not move. The woman came over to where I was.

"He'll be all right with time," she repeated. "I promise you, he'll be all right."

James yawned, turned toward my body, and began to open his eyes. As soon as he saw my body, he'd know. I'd died with eye crust and drool dried on my face. I turned away and the woman put her hand on my shoulder.

"This the worst of it, sweetie," she said. Her voice was much older than her face. "I promise you, this the worst of it."

The bed creaked. He was getting up.

"Who are you?" I asked the woman.

"Family, sweetie. I'm family."

When I finally looked, James had come over to my side and was standing over the me that was. He bent down to kiss my forehead and I felt it. He took my hand in his and I felt that, too.

"James," I whispered. "James."

He placed my hand back on the bed and knelt down beside me. He put his head in his hands and began to cry.

"James!" I screamed. I put my hand on his head and it was almost like touching him. "I'm not touching you; I'm not touching you." I could hear Lucy, finger an inch away from John's face. I heard it as clearly as if it were happening now.

I'm not touching James. I'm not touching James.

"He can't hear you, sweetie," the woman said. "Tell me what it is you want him to know, and I'll see if I can make him understand."

I wanted to tell him everything.

She said there wasn't enough time for everything, but if I could think of just one thing, she would help me find a way to make him know it. She walked me over to him. She placed her hand on top of mine so that both of us were not touching him.

"Think, sweetie," she said. "Just think on what you want him to know, and it will get through."

We stayed there for either an hour or an instant and then James, bracing himself on the bed, stood, walked over to the phone, and called Mary.

I exhaled and was startled to discover I had no air.

"Took me a minute to get used to, too," a man's voice said. I turned to see a man dressed in white with my husband's face come into the room, the first of a host of familiar strangers.

James's grandfather, Louis, the man I met the morning I died, showed me how sweet and loving my husband was as a boy. He showed me James learning to fish, and it was just the same way James had taught John. I heard Louis tell James the same stories James used to calm our daughter, Lucy. He and the woman showed me not only their lives but the lives of everyone they had known. I came to know my husband in death in ways I had not been able to in life. They showed me how death can be another kind of life and how dying was the last "was" I would ever know.

At my funeral, I watch my daughter cry and hear in its echo her birth, the day she fell off her bike, scraped her knee, and screamed for her father. I see my son watching his wife walk down the aisle in an ivory dress with a bouquet of pink roses, daring not to hope for the child growing strong in her womb, and seeing this brings me back around to the first time Lucy kicked.

"I remember this," the woman tells me as we watch James come in from outside to lay his hand upon my belly. "This was his best day."

I see Lucy walking into life with Garrison, then walking out of it to find herself.

"Love from someone else is never enough to replace the love you don't yet feel for yourself," the woman says.

"Ain't no need to worry over her," Louis tells me as we watch her board plane after plane. "She gonna be all right."

Then I see John working over his sermon notes on Saturday and ignoring them on Sunday. After getting fired from that megachurch in Nashville, Mount Carmel, remembering what all Reverend Walter had meant to the church, makes a place for his great-great-grandson.

"Church," I watch John tell Mount Carmel. "Turn with me if you will to John chapter four, verse twenty-four."

It is not the chapter and verse written down on the legal pad before him, but the choir has sung "I'll Fly Away," and hearing it reminds John of the fiery sermons of his youth. The foot-stomping, tear-jerking, fall-out-in-the-spirit, your-arms-are-too-short-to-box-with-God sermons.

"'God is a spirit,'" the congregation reads, more or less in unison, "'and those who worship Him must worship Him in spirit and in truth.'"

"Now, I want you all to sit with that a minute," John says, hearing his father's voice in his mouth. "Just one minute. The Bible says, 'God is a spirit and those who worship Him *must* worship Him in spirit and in truth.' And as you're sitting, you may be seated, I want you to think on what spirit is. What truth is. Now, the Bible doesn't say *soul* here, the Bible says *spirit*. We know what the spirit is, don't we? The spirit is that bit of you that's just you. The bit of you that makes you you and nobody else. You have your father's face. Your mother's eyes. Your grandfather's build. You and your brothers and sisters might all look

just alike. But if growing up in the house with them taught you anything, it's that you ain't them and they ain't you."

There is a "hmm." He's touched on something for somebody. John
wonders for just a moment what that something is. Was it the way they
and their sister butted heads, or how headbutting taught them to be
patient when patience was called for, and to stand up when standing up
was what was needed? Maybe someone realizes the difference between
trying to be your father's son and trying to be your father.

"And that's by design. Ain't no accidents in God's plan," John says,
taking a sip of tepid water. He'd rather it was cold water, but it is water
all the same.

"Now, God picked Mary to bring His light into the world, not her
mother, not her sister, not her cousin, her. And out of all the other children Mary had, God picked Jesus to be that light. Now, the Scripture
don't say this, but let me tell you what I think the Lord picked those
brothers and sisters out to do. I bet you God put it on them to help
Jesus learn how to care, how to share, how to think of others."

As John says these words, he thinks of Lucy. Who would he have
been without a baby sister to envy and love? How long had it taken
him to realize parental love spreads rather than splits? To understand
that she was not put on this Earth to be bossed around by him?

"Now, I see Brother Johnson cutting his eyes at me 'cause I'm
talking outside the text, but bear with me for just one minute. I'm
not going to keep you long, and I promise to bring it all back around.
That's all right, Brother Johnson, I sure appreciate it. God put it on my
spirit to preach from this pulpit, and He put it on your spirit to make
sure I get it right, and I sure do appreciate it."

Wouldn't it be nice to have someone do that for you at home? I
whisper to John. Life is long and short and beautiful and terrible and
wonderful and torturous, and even though we are born alone and even
though we die alone, we do not, cannot, live alone.

"But let me tell you, I'm not the only one. I'm not the only one who needs to be held to a higher standard to know that a higher standard is possible. Turn with me if you will back to John. This time to chapter two, verses three and four. Some of y'all are not even looking! Some of y'all already know what those verses say, don't you?"

"Jesus turning water into wine," someone shouts.

"That's right, Sister Horton," John shouts back. "There was a wedding in Cana and the host had run out of wine. So Mary turned to her son Jesus, the son whom the angel Gabriel had promised, the son whose conception was immaculate, the son who at the age of twelve knew the Word better than the Pharisees. Mary turned to her son, knowing that the power of the Lord was in him, knowing that through him, all things are possible. And you know what Jesus says to her? Sister Horton, can you read out loud for us what the Christ Lord said to his mother?"

"'Jesus said to her, "Woman, what does your concern have to do with me? My hour has not yet come."'"

"Now, church, I'm not ashamed to tell you that when I read this verse as a boy, I was scared for our Savior. I was, Sister Horton. Because I know what would have happened to me if I'd spoken to my momma like that. And it must have happened between verses four and five. I don't know if it was a look, some choice words, or a smack upside the back of his head, but by verse six, this wine is very much Christ's concern, and by verse eleven, you better believe there's some on the table."

They're with him now, my John.

"But what I want to draw your attention to here is Mary. Mary and her unerring faith in Christ. Jesus himself doesn't think he's ready. He doesn't just say it's not his concern; he says his hour has not come. Now, remember, church, this is the Jesus on whom the spirit of the Lord has already descended, this is the Jesus who has convinced Peter and Andrew to leave their boat behind and become fishers of men. The power was already with him, but he needed Mary. God put it on Mary's spirit to show Jesus his own power."

Who will show you your power, John? I ask. Who will hold you?

John faces the choir. He squints at them because he can't see me.

"Church, I tell you, there's a reason the Devil didn't come tempting Jesus when he was at home with his family. There's a reason the Devil didn't come promising our Savior the world and all his riches while he was preaching to the multitudes on the mountaintop. No, the Devil, like any gambling man, knew his odds. The Devil knew his best chance was to catch Christ alone, just as he knows his best chance at catching you is when you're all by yourself. You can't do it all by yourself. All you can be all by yourself is bad. We know that, don't we, church?"

Amen, I say. John's head swivels. It's almost as if he sees me.

"That lesson's been taught, hasn't it? That's why we have a church. That's why we have brothers and sisters in Christ. What I'm here to tell you this morning is that nowhere in the Bible does it say you've got to live like how everybody else lives. God didn't call Mary to preach to the masses, but you know what He did do? He called her to have faith in Jesus, even when Jesus didn't have faith in himself. God didn't call the twelve disciples to die on the cross for you and me. But do you know what He did do? He called them to be witnesses. He called them to question and record. He called them to write Christ's words and build churches in Christ's name.

"Church, even in the Old Testament, God didn't call Joshua to be Moses. God didn't call David to be Saul, or Solomon to be David. God knows your talents, your strengths, and He put you where you are to be your best you and nobody else."

It is then that John sees Angela. She is in the back row near the window, and when he sees her, the great wave of faith that has carried him this far crests, washes out at her feet. He picks his handkerchief up off the podium, wipes away the sweat that has not bothered him until just now.

"God may not have called you to the pulpit. He may not have called you to the soup kitchen every Saturday. And even though I hate to say it, He might not even have called you to come to church every Sunday. But He called you to do something. He called you to do for somebody. He called you to be a sister or a mother. He called you to be a brother or a father. He called you to be a friend. Church, I don't know what all God put it on your spirit to be. But He put it on your spirit to be a blessing to somebody. I got ideas, but I don't know it to my spirit like how you know it to your spirit. You can't be a Christian like how I'm a Christian. The Bible says, 'Those who worship Him must worship Him in spirit and in truth.' It don't say *can*. It don't say *might*. It says *must*. *Must*. You got to worship God in your spirit, in your truth. Otherwise, there ain't no point in trying to worship at all."

I see Angela find John in his office at the back of the church. John has just begun to take his robe off and imagine what the rest of the day will hold. He isn't expecting anyone and is startled when Angela knocks.

John turns to face her. Time has been kind to Angela. She wears a red blouse with a dark gray knee-length pencil skirt, modest though not altogether chaste. Mount Carmel had gone casual at John's urging. He didn't like making folks who couldn't afford fine clothes feel less than, so, after a bit of back-and-forth with some of the holdout deacons, he had the dress code changed. After all, John reminded them, it was Jesus who said come as you are.

"That was quite the sermon, Reverend," Angela says.

"I try to make it interesting," John says, his back still turned.

"But I like your shows better," she says.

"What do you mean?" John asks, swallowing.

"I mean Cassie. I saw you, her, onstage way back when, and I thought she was gorgeous. I thought you were beautiful. Just like you were when we were little."

Look at her, I tell John, but John is not prepared to see her, has not yet recovered from the shock of her being in his church.

"I've thought about you a lot, you know," Angela says. "Things were bad after I moved in with my dad. No, it's okay, I don't want you to pity me. It's just ... There were a lot of times over the years when I thought there couldn't be any good left in the world, but then I would think of you. If you were alive, there had to be some good out there somewhere. I'm glad to know I wasn't wrong."

"I'm only as good as God allows me to be."

"I don't know if I can believe in God," Angela says. "But I believe in you. I'll always believe in you."

I blink and they're married. I blink again and I see Lucy bouncing their baby girl, April, on her knee, making her laugh and vomit before handing her back to Angela and thinking how nice it is to be auntie and not momma. April sets her eyes on me. I move and they move with me. She turns back to her mother, raising her hand to point at me.

I see John at the river, teaching April to fish. She waves at me. I wave back. When did she get to be so big? She doesn't like fishing, but she does it and keeps doing it to make her father happy. Besides, she likes the quiet of the water and the way her mind clears when she slides the knife under the gills. My granddaughter doesn't mind getting her hands dirty. I see her in school, in college, deciding what she wants to study, and in seeing it, I want to go back to when she was a little girl, and I do. She's sitting in James's lap. He's showing her pictures of me, telling her how sweet a thing love can be if you let it. She looks from the album to me and back.

John and April leave, and I see James in the kitchen, warming the plate of beef roast and sweet potatoes Angela sent. She's at home, pregnant with William, a boy whose fatal flaw is that his capacity for love exceeds his self-interest. I see James eating dinner alone, and it takes me to that day in college.

I come back to our apartment and find James and Mary at the table. I look at Mary, but I won't let myself wonder what that life might have been.

James stands up when I walk in, and I see myself thinking, just for a moment, how nice it would be to marry the kind of man who gets the children ready in the morning and sings them to sleep at night, who, on days when it is too much for you even to leave the bed, sits in bed beside you and rubs your back in silence. Too many of my days are too much for me to leave the bed.

"It's not your fault," the woman tells me.

I turn to her.

"You don't have to go there," she tells me. "There are prettier places to go."

But I am there. I'm there on the day, and the weight of it is too much to bear. I pack a bag and leave while John and James are away. I pack a bag and leave without kissing Lucy goodbye because I want her to hate me before she mourns me, because hate is what I deserve. There is so much I want her to understand, but wanting her understanding is selfish. I want my Lucy to live her whole life never understanding.

I'm in the car on my way to the river. I pass the houses of people who know my husband. I blow the horn and they wave. I think of how after I'm found, the people who waved will tell my husband they saw me. They will make up stories about how I seemed off, how they saw it coming.

I park near the water. I get out of the car. It's a sunny day. Clear. The kind where river and sky seem to be cut from the same cloth. A rock and a rope in the water are kinder than a head in the stove.

"Come back," the woman says, and when she says it, she sounds like a small child.

But there is no back. There is only now. Only me and the rock and the water and the memory of my mother telling me, "Get up! Nothing's wrong with you. Just lazy is all." Lazy like her sister, and she was not going to ruin me with coddling the way her parents ruined her sister. No, she wasn't.

I'm kneeling in dry rice. I don't know how to do what I'm told when I'm told, and this is my punishment. "Don't," I tell James the first time he thinks to raise his hand to John. "Please don't." Even as a girl, I know that the rock and the water is going to happen.

"But it won't," the woman says.

I'm back at the river. I'm standing in the river, and the water has soaked through to my socks. My feet are cold and wet, and I'm looking at myself for the last time.

"I don't like it," I say.

"Nobody likes it," Louis says. "But if you don't look at yourself, you won't know what's worth seeing."

I look into my reflection and see Lucy. I see her grown, and she looks just like me. The thought of her is all that keeps me from doing what I mean to do. I imagine her grown, with her own rock, her own rope, sinking beneath the surface of her own waters, and the weight of that is heavier than what I woke up with. I see her questioning the same parts of herself that made me question me. There is a lake she goes to when she feels herself alone.

"She won't," the woman says.

The lake is deep. If she went in, it would be a long time before anyone found her, before anyone knew.

"She won't. Just like you didn't. She won't."

Lucy takes half a roll out of her purse. She breaks it apart and starts feeding it to the crows.

"She'll be all right," Louis says. "I told you that one will be all right."

A woman sits down next to her.

"You're the artist, right?" she says to Lucy. "I've seen you around here before. And I've always thought that you had the look of somebody I might like to know."

Lucy smiles. I smile.

"Can I buy you a cup of coffee?"

I find myself back in my own moment walking away from the water, squishing my shoes into the grass. I get back in the car, decide to visit Mary, let the water run on without me.

"This the worst of it," the woman says. "I promise you, this the worst of it."

"That's what you said before."

"Yeah, but I didn't mean it then. I mean it now."

After Mary helps me pull myself together, I go home.

I walk in and Lucy is on the couch. She follows me. Watches me unpack my clothes and put the suitcase away. I can see the question framing itself in her eyes. She wants to ask it, but she doesn't know how, so she just watches, that day and the next and the one after, but at least I'm here for her to watch.

"And love," the woman says. "There's love, too."

James comes home, and as soon as he sees me, he knows, and when Lucy's not watching, he tells me he's happy. He's so happy I've chosen life.

"Every day he had with you was his best day," the woman says.

I overhear James telling Lucy a story: "Once upon a time, there was a rich man, and one day, a crow came to this rich man's window and told him the date of his death. So he called his two sons to his side and divided up between them what all on this side of life he had to give. To Jack, his son by way of a good wife and a long marriage, he gave all his money, and to John, his son by way of love, he gave all his power..."

Lucy is asleep now, but that doesn't stop James from finishing his story. At first, James tells our sleeping daughter, people thought the woman got her power from her first husband, the Devil. But when she left the Devil she still had it, and so folks thought she'd borrowed it from her second husband, Jack, whom everybody knew to be lucky. It wasn't until after Jack died in a fight with his brother, John, that people realized her power was all her own. She buried her lover and his brother on a Sunday and then, after the ceremony, she walked down to the water, looked once to her left, once to her right, once to the sky, and flew.

Now James is the one being tucked in. John and Lucy have hired a nurse for him, and the nurse tucks James in so sweetly that I'm envious of the both of them. Both John and Lucy offered their houses for him to come and live in because they don't know how to say bye. He says no. The nurse is a compromise. He's given up kneeling for his nightly prayers because one night he kneels and can't get up, so he whispers them with his eyes facing the ceiling, choosing to believe they'll still be heard, and they are. They are heard by me. There is no tomorrow for him. When he wakes, his body will be still, and that stillness will be a blessing.

He opens his eyes to me.

"Good morning," he says.

"It's good," I say. "But it's not quite morning."

He rises out of bed, surprised at the ease of it, and when he turns, I am there and always will be.

"Is this heaven?" he asks, smiling like back when we first met.

"It can be," I tell him.

IN 1914, THE year the Jehovah's Witnesses in the Watch Tower first predicted the world would end, the Devil waited around, hoping, praying, knowing his brother was coming back for him. But that year, along with 1975, Y2K, and the last day of the Mayan calendar, all passed the Devil by without a peep from Jesus. By the time Twyla Laurent's funeral came along, he'd just about lost faith. Once upon a time, he believed that fomenting slave rebellions, leading midnight revivals, and teaching Black folks conjure moved the needle forward. But then came sharecropping, redlining, the dark alliance between the CIA and the Contras, mass incarceration, police brutality, and this and that and the other. Seemed like as soon as he broke one yoke, here come Buckra with another. Maybe Christ had been teasing him all along, he thought. Maybe Black freedom was an oxymoron.

Usually, the Devil loved him a good homegoing service. There was no better time or place to turn a soul. Where is God now? the bereaved wondered. Why are we even here? What does it all mean? What is it all for? But by then, the Devil's spirits were so low over being forsaken, not even blasphemy could uplift him. It was as he was watching Twyla's casket being carried down to the burial ground that he caught sight of Death leaned up against his scythe, watching the procession.

"Ain't you supposed to have came and went?" the Devil asked Death.

"I do as I'm told. I take what my Father gives so my Father can give more. The taking is the giving and the giving is the taking. My Father writes the Book of Life and I turn its pages, and that page over there is long overdue. He's coming up on that hateful bastard Methuselah's record," Death said, nodding in the direction of Benny, who stood with his walker at the edge of the cemetery. Death was generally peaceable and forgiving, but Methuselah could do no right by him. You didn't even want to get him started on Lazarus. "It's on you to attend to him, seeing as how he's one of yours, but you haven't. Why?"

"I been waiting a long time on him," the Devil said. "He too stubborn to die."

The truth was that the Devil doted on Benny; out of all the woman's descendants, Benny was the Devil's favorite. The one whose plight most reminded him of his own. He'd come close to taking his soul many times over the years but could never bring himself to go through with it.

"Every man born of a woman's got an hour of appointment. God's already made a place for him."

"My Father's made a place for him?" the Devil asked, seeing back across the years all the sin Benny had been a party to and wondering how much Death knew of the Devil's deal with Saint Peter.

"God's hand is on him," Death said.

"You's a lie," the Devil said. "I been on him like white on rice. Damn near raised him. God's hand ain't been nowhere near him."

When the Devil said this, Death reared back the hollow of his hood and laughed.

"What are you," Death said to the Devil, "if not the hand of the Father? You think God doesn't know about you and that woman's children? You think His eyes are not upon you, always? Everything you got in you, God put there. He wouldn't have put you in her path if He didn't want you to save her children."

"Well. He sure got a funny way of showing His gratitude."

After Twyla's funeral, the Devil decided he needed some air, and so he walked the woods behind the church, wondering all the while why the landscape felt so familiar, not realizing that where he now stood was the woman's slave cabin, when he happened upon John and Lucy, her fourth-great-grandchildren, hugging each other. The sight of them there, by the water, comforting one another, was almost enough to make him miss his own brother, almost enough to make him want to forgive his Father. How long had it been since he'd hugged his brother or felt the weight of Father God's hand upon his shoulder?

The Devil took his hat off, wiped the sweat from his brow, and watched the westward wind trouble the water. Seeing the woman's descendants there on the other side—tired and angry and grieving, but still laughing, still loving—was almost enough to make him hope, make him wonder. There was still time. In his Father's house, the days were still young. It'd be a while yet before Gabriel put his lips to that horn.

The Devil put his hat back on, crossed the creek, and made his way back to the road, thinking of which dominoes he'd yet to set up, which ones needed to fall. If he could line them up just right, topple them just the way he wanted, then maybe, just maybe, he could get them the freedom he'd promised their foremother—the freedom he'd promised Jesus—and then maybe, just maybe, the hell he knew to be Earth would freeze over and all he would have to do was walk a little bit farther down this road to find his way home.

ACKNOWLEDGMENTS

This book would not have been possible without a tremendous amount of support.

Thank you, Elizabeth McCracken, for being an advocate for this book from its earliest incarnation, reading more unruly drafts than any professor should reasonably be expected to, and helping me shape the book into something meaningful.

Thank you, Michelle Brower, for seeing something worthwhile in what now looks to me like a pretty terrible first draft, taking the time to work with me to make it better, and generally being a great agent.

Thank you, Carrie R. Moore and Tracey Rose Peyton, for helping me rethink the book at a critical juncture; Adam O. Davis for encouraging me to keep writing; and Michaeljulius Idani, Marcela Fuentes, Melissa Daniels-Rauterkus, and Fernando Villagómez for invaluable advice, encouragement, and friendship.

Thank you, Josh Kendall, Ben George, Maya Guthrie, Betsy Uhrig, Brandy Colbert, and everyone at Little, Brown who helped make this book possible.

Thank you, Lena Little, for being a phenomenal publicist.

Thank you, Michener Center for Writers; the University of Wisconsin at Madison; Northwestern University; the Bishop's School; Claremont McKenna College; the Tin House Workshop, especially

Acknowledgments

Lance Cleland and India Downes-Le Guin; Kimbilio for Black Fiction; Yaddo; Bread Loaf; Willapa Bay AiR; and Community of Writers, for supporting me and helping me to find my voice.

Thank you to Adeena Reitberger, Rebecca Markovits, Amanda Faraone, and everyone at *American Short Fiction;* Adam Ross and Eric Smith at the *Sewanee Review;* Autumn Watts at *Guernica;* and Ashleigh Bryant Phillips at *Joyland.*

I would also like to thank Patrick Smith for showing me how to appreciate good writing; La Vinia Delois Jennings for teaching me what literature can be and do; Alexander Weheliye for awakening my mind to critical inquiry; Betsy Erkkila, Julia Stern, John Alba Cutler, Brian Edwards, Mary Pattillo, Evan Mwangi, Helen Thompson, Nick Davis, Viv Soni, Susan Manning, Chris Abani, Jay Grossman, Susannah Gottlieb, Blair Hurley, Jennifer Lane, Sarah Terez Rosenblum, and Paul Yoon for introducing me to all the various ways a novel might be shaped; Laura van den Berg for reframing the way I think about narrative; R. O. Kwon for notes on an extremely early chapter; Brian Van Reet for his Literature of War class; Dinaw Mengestu for notes on "In the Valley"; Angela Flournoy for encouraging me to lean into the Narcissus myth in "The Wayside"; Edward Carey for reigniting my interest in folklore and helping me to see the narrative possibilities of it; Maya Perez for showing me how to write in different genres; Chris Feliciano Arnold for tips about roving versus omniscient third-person point of view; Bret Anthony Johnston for being a writerly therapist of sorts; Danielle Evans for editing early versions of "Spare the Rod" and "What Fire Won't Burn"; and Natasha Trethewey, Mitchell Jackson, Mary Szybist, and Joanna Klink for attuning my ear to prose rhythms.

I write in the shadow of Zora Neale Hurston, Pauline Hopkins, Ralph Ellison, James Baldwin, Edward P. Jones, and Toni Morrison. The worlds they brought into being inspired me to try my hand at crafting my own.

The folklore in this novel is inspired in part by *Mules and Men*

Acknowledgments

by Zora Neale Hurston and *The People Could Fly* by Virginia Hamilton, and the scene of Lucille's death is a reworking of "Go Down, Death," a sermonic poem from James Weldon Johnson's *God's Trombones*. This book also owes a lot to *African Religions and Philosophy* by John Mbiti, *Working the Spirit* by Joseph M. Murphy, *Slave Religion* by Albert J. Raboteau, *Spirited Things* edited by Paul Christopher Johnson, *In the Break* by Fred Moten, *Scenes of Subjection* by Saidiya Hartman, and *Toni Morrison and the Idea of Africa* by La Vinia Delois Jennings.

I would also like to thank the writers who have been kind and generous enough to workshop various portions of the novel over the years: Molly Williams, Emeline Atwood, Alejandro Puyana, Ellaree Yeagley, Colwill Brown, Zack Schlosberg, Megan Kakimoto, Brynne Jones, Beverly Chukwu, Ryan Johnson, Amanda Bestor-Siegal, Bismarck Martinez, Lauren Green, Willie Fitzgerald, Matthew Manning, Avigayl Sharp, Stephanie Morris, Darby Jardeleza, Rachel Heng, Hedgie Choi, Jackson Holbert, Shaina Frazier, David Grivette, Thea Anderson, Kristin Waites, Anya Lewis-Meeks, N. K. Iguh, Chad Infante, Mohwanah Fetus, Lara Ehrlich, Carrie Bindschadler, Joseph Han, Anna Held, Vonetta Young, Mimi Wong, Pooja Bhatia, Emily Atkinson, Anahvia Taiyib, Charlotte Wyatt, Ismail Muhammad, Jessica Van Devanter, Natalie Serber, Amanda Boldenow, Lindsay Tigue, E.E. Hussey, Stephanie Macias Gibson, Van Thaxton, Sophie Newman, Lily Felsenthal, Vinita Mendiratta, Santiago Heredia, Natasha Ayaz, Ho-Ming So Denduangrudee, Christopher Llego, Yvette Ndlovu, Piali Mukhopadhyay, and Nathan Harris.

Thank you, Miya Williams Fayne, for believing in me, marrying me, and sticking out the ups and downs of writing with me. I could not have hoped for a better or more supportive partner in life.

Thank you to Sam Davis, Antoine Johnson, Stanley McGrady, Dawo Rogers, Mike Russom, and Kenneth Woods for still being my friends after I pretty much disappeared to write this book.

Big thank you to my grandmother, mother, and sister for keeping me alive and inspiring me.

Acknowledgments

Lastly, my name is Rickey Fayne Jr., but my father, Rickey Sr., once joked that I should leave *Jr.* off my degrees so that we could share them. I have purposely left *Jr.* off the cover of this book in order to share with him the book I would not have been able to write without him.

ABOUT THE AUTHOR

Rickey Fayne is a fiction writer from rural West Tennessee whose work has appeared in *American Short Fiction*, *Guernica*, the *Sewanee Review*, and the *Kenyon Review Online*, among other magazines. He holds an MA in English from Northwestern University and an MFA in Fiction from the Michener Center for Writers at the University of Texas at Austin. His writing seeks to honor his ancestors' experiences.